BEDFO
BOOK
THE PERFORMERS

Bedford Row is the fifth novel in Claire
Rayner's sequence *The Performers,* in which
she will follow the fortunes of two families
through succeeding generations from the
beginning of the nineteenth century into the
twentieth. The very different professions of
medicine and the theatre set the background
for this compelling family saga. These are the
paths chosen by Abel Lackland and Lilith
Lucas, the two London waifs who first met
in *Gower Street,* whose fortunes become
inextricably mingled – and whose children
continue the saga through the later volumes.
Readers who meet Abel and Lilith for the
first time will want to share their earlier
experiences in the other books.

Also in Arrow by Claire Rayner

Bedford Row

Book V of

The Performers

Claire Rayner

ARROW BOOKS

Arrow Books Limited
62-65 Chandos Place, London WC2N 4NW

An imprint of Century Hutchinson Ltd

London Melbourne Sydney Auckland
Johannesburg and agencies throughout
the world

First published in Great Britain
by Cassell & Co. Ltd 1977
First paperback edition by Corgi 1978
Reprinted 1980
Weidenfeld & Nicolson edition 1982
Arrow edition 1986

Printed and bound in Great Britain by
Anchor Brendon Limited, Tiptree, Essex

ISBN 0 09 944390 2

ACKNOWLEDGEMENTS

The author is grateful for the assistance given with research by the Library of the Royal Society of Medicine, London; Macarthy's Ltd., Surgical Instrument Manufacturers; The London Library; The London Borough of Camden Libraries; The London Museum; The Victoria and Albert Museum; Westminster City Library; Leichner Stage Make-Up Ltd.; Raymond Mander and Joe Mitchenson, theatrical historians; Miss Geraldine Stephenson, choreographer and dance historian; Miss Micaela Economides, Greek scholar; The Imperial War Museum; and other sources too numerous to mention.

Claire Rayner

FAMILY TREE

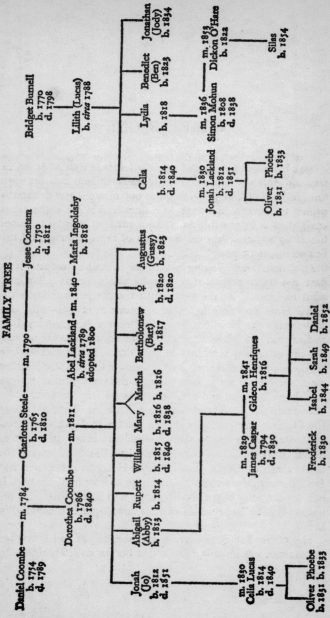

Daniel Coombe b. 1754 d. 1789 ——— m. 1784 ——— Charlotte Steele b. 1765 d. 1810

Jesse Constam b. 1750 d. 1811 ——— m. 1790

Bridget Burnell b. 1770 d. 1798

Lilith (Lucas) b. circa 1788

Abel Lackland b. circa 1789 adopted 1800 — m. 1840 — Maria Ingoldsby b. 1818

Dorothea Coombe b. 1786 d. 1840 ——— m. 1811

Children of Daniel Coombe and Charlotte Steele / Dorothea Coombe line:

Jonah (Jo) b. 1812 d. 1851 — m. 1830 — Celia Lucas b. 1814 d. 1840

Abigail (Abby) b. 1813

Rupert b. 1814 d. 1840

William b. 1815 d. 1838

Mary b. 1816

Martha b. 1816

Bartholomew (Bart) b. 1817

♀ b. 1820 d. 1820

Augustus (Gussy) b. 1823

Jonah × Celia Lucas:
Oliver b. 1851   Phoebe b. 1853

Mary line — m. 1841:
Gideon Henriques b. 1816

James Caspar line — m. 1839:
James Caspar b. 1794 d. 1830

Frederick b. 1830

Isabel b. 1844   Sarah b. 1849   Daniel b. 1852

Constam / Burnell children:

Celia b. 1814 d. 1840 — m. 1830 — Jonah Lackland b. 1812 d. 1851

Lydia b. 1818 — m. 1836 — Simon Mohun b. 1808 d. 1838

Benedict (Ben) b. 1823

Jonathan (Jody) b. 1834

Dickon O'Hare b. 1822 — m. 1843

Celia × Jonah Lackland:
Oliver b. 1851   Phoebe b. 1853

Silas b. 1854

CHAPTER ONE

THE hansom cab wheeled smartly left into Pall Mall, on its way to Trafalgar Square and ultimately home, but not until the Haymarket Theatre was quite out of sight could Martha draw a full breath. Her anger still simmered in her as she sat as upright as it is possible to sit in a rattling hansom cab, her hands tightly clasped over the head of her umbrella, and her lips set in a tight line.

How dare That Woman lecture her in such a manner? How dare she try to point out to Martha where her duty lay, and what she should be thinking about the present political situation? How *dare* she? A flibberty, ignorant, stupid— And unconsciously she lifted the umbrella between her clenched fists and rapped it down again, hard, on the floor of the cab, so that the driver leaned forwards to peer down at her and inquire hoarsely what was amiss? And, coming back to herself with a start, she looked up at him through the murky little window and shook her head and tried to settle back into her seat.

Outside the day was dwindling to its close, the thin blue of the October sky giving way to a thicker twilight, and a few lights were beginning to show themselves behind the porticoes of the heavy handsome houses that edged Pall Mall, and on the upper floors of the St. James's Royal Hotel on the corner, and for a moment she was suddenly aware of how tired she was. It had been a long day since breakfast and *The Times* and the uneasy feeling her reading of that newspaper had aroused in her.

Her father had gone early to the hospital, as usual, and her stepmother was already busy about her housewifely duties by

7

the time Martha had come to read Mr. Russell's dispatches from the battle of the Alma, so she had had no one with whom to discuss them. And even had they been still at the table with her, there would have been little likelihood of there being any fruitful talk, since both Abel and Maria distrusted *The Times* for its radical views and even more radical editor, Delane. So sitting alone over the remains of her breakfast she had read Mr. Russell's descriptions of the dreadful conditions in far away Scutari with a mounting horror that seemed greater since she could not speak to anyone about it.

'It is with feelings of surprise and anger that the public will learn that no sufficient preparations have been made for the care of the wounded,' Russell had written. 'Not only are there not sufficient surgeons – not only are there no dressers and nurses – there is not even linen to make bandages ... the manner in which the sick and wounded are treated is worthy only of savages ... the British Army dies like dogs because the medical staff of the British Army have forgotten that old rags are necessary for the dressing of wounds ...'

No wonder Sir Robert Peel had felt himself called upon to start a fund for supplying the sick and wounded, she had thought, folding the flimsy sheets with her usual tidiness. I must send something this very day. And she had set off about her own morning's activities in a sombre mood, quite unable to shake off the gloom with which the war news had filled her. But she had worked well enough, for Martha always did. No matter what went on in her own life – or did not go on, for in all truth, she led a dull enough existence – she would do the work she had set herself, and do it well.

Today she had planned to spend the morning reorganizing the linen cupboards of the hostel in Bedford Row, where she and Carrie Garling, the resident Lady Steward, together laboured such long hours in caring for the women and children who sought the help of the Committee of the London Ladies' Society for the Rescue of the Profligate Poor, and so she had done just that. And in the afternoon she had planned to seek the support of certain persons in one of her fund-raising sorties (for the money with which her grandmother, Charlotte Con-

8

stam, had endowed the charity had long since been swallowed up, and shortage of money was a constant stumbling block in the Committee's way) and she had done just that too, and with success, for she was experienced in her begging. It had not been until she had arrived at the Haymarket Theatre to talk to the great Lydia Mohun that she had given conscious thought again to her morning's reading; but Lydia's behaviour had forced it upon her.

She had lain stretched out on her chaise longue in her dressing room – a room so bedecked with flowers and frills and gewgaws and so hot and scented that Martha found it positively vulgar – wearing a frilled blue peignoir that displayed more of her body than it seemed to hide, and barely listened to Martha's quiet suggestion that she give a Benefit Night at the Haymarket to this most worthy of Charities and her explanation that the support of the remarkable and famous Lydia Mohun in this most necessary work would help immeasurably in the task of raising the funds so vitally needed.

Instead she had stared at the little woman in the brown merino gown and jacket and plain straw bonnet in an abstracted way, and then sat up and ran her fingers through her curly hair in a way that made it look even more artistically disarranged, and burst out, in ringing tones, 'Oh, stop! For the love of heaven, do stop! How can you talk to me of such things when I am so bouleversée by all I have heard today: Dickon!'

She had turned her head, and the tall man who had been sprawled lazily in the chair before the mirror pleasurably staring at his own reflected countenance turned and looked at her and grinned.

'Dickon, you will agree that I am the most generous creature alive? That I have given and given until my fingers have become positively raw with giving—'

Martha blinked, and tried to visualize this exquisite female doing anything so energetic, and then reddened as the words went rattling on.

'—have I not *myself* gone short for want of ready money which I have thrown to beggars? Have I not suffered dreadfully at the sight of them all clustering about my carriage each

9

evening after the play and seen to it that they are given bread and beer? And now this!'

She turned back to Martha and stared at her with her eyes very bright and hard. 'At a time when we are all in such a dismay at what is happening to our Poor Dear Soldiers and should be concerning ourselves only with matters of war and politics you come to me with your tales of gutter children, and ask me to concern myself with *them*? In normal times they are indeed a worthy object of a woman's concern – especially a woman who is a Mother, as I am blessed to be—' and she slid a sideways look at Martha that took in with one triumphant glance her plainness, her age and above all her spinsterhood and total lack of hope of motherhood, '—but now, when our Dear Boys are dying out there in the Turkish Wilderness, how can you ask it of me?'

'Russian, ma'am, in point of fact,' said Martha quietly, feeling the anger rising in her, and hearing the shake of it in her own voice, and then she clenched her teeth, for Lydia was ranting on as though Martha had not uttered a sound.

'I have been in tears, in tears, I do promise you, all day, about it! I have already this morning been in direct discussion with Dear Sir Robert and have promised him no less than *three* Benefits for his fund, and hard work it will be, since they must be productions in which I am barely off the stage at all, if we are to raise as much money as is possible, for the crowds come but to see me—'

'And me, I suspect, dear heart—' Dickon said sharply, and she threw a quick glance at him over her shoulder and said perfunctorily, 'But of course, dear Dickon, it is *both* of us they adore, as well we know – but either way, it is to be a great battle of effort for me – us. So you really *must* go away, Miss – forgive me, I forget your name—'

'Lackland, ma'am,' Martha said, and once again the tremble of rage was in her voice. 'Martha Lackland. You will recall my niece, and yours, Miss Phoebe Lackland, for I made mention of her when I first wrote to you last month about this afternoon's appointment—'

'Of course, forgive me. But as I said, I am so distressed

about the Soldiers – I really cannot think clearly—' and she burst into most artistic tears, and opened her arms wide to Dickon who, with a barely concealed sigh, got up and went to the chaise longue and allowed her to twine herself about his neck, leaving Martha to take her departure as best she might.

Remembering it yet again as the hansom passed the fountains in front of the National Gallery and then turned south to pass the huge plinth of Nelson's column Martha shook her head as if to shake away her own confusion, for she realized perfectly well why the absurd Lydia had been able to rouse her ire so easily; had she not herself felt that there was a huge irrelevance about her day's activities? As she had folded sheets and counted towels and calico aprons with Carrie, had not her own mind been occupied with the horrors of Scutari conjured up in cold print by Mr. Russell's dispatches? As she had gone the rounds of her Charity's benefactors all afternoon had she not also found it a source of embarrassment to seek – and get – funds at a time when men were dying in a battle field for want of care? It had been the way that hateful woman had held her own uselessness up to her eyes that had made Martha so angry, and being a sensible woman, not much given to deceiving herself, she knew it.

'But I am *not* useless!' She whispered it aloud, then staring unseeingly out at the crowds in the Square, for even though it was close to dusk there were still many abroad. 'Indeed I am not.' Did she not work all the hours God sent for the Charity? She went to no balls, no theatres, no picnics, no dinners, preferring to use her time to better purpose, although her stepmother often told her she should be more out in the social world. But she did not attempt it, having long since resigned herself to spinsterhood, for who would want so plain and dull a creature as Miss Martha Lackland, barely two years short of her fortieth birthday, and by no means the answer to any man's prayer? She had told herself many years ago, even before her beloved twin had died in the cholera epidemic when they were both a sprightly twenty-two, that she had no hope of love and marriage, and been quite glad of it. It had made life so much simpler – and more useful. For if she had been a wife and mother she could not have done as much as she had for others; and she knew perfectly well that she had done much good in her lifetime so far. Many were the women settled in snug homes of their own who had cause to bless her name; many were the children, now grown up, who knew they owed their respectability to her rescue of them from the worst of London's gutters. She had nothing with which to reproach herself. And yet—

The hansom slowed, and then stopped with a rattle of harness and hoofs as the cabby, swearing luxuriously, hauled on the reins and she blinked and leaned forwards over the apron of the cab to look out, and saw blocking their way a small crowd of people standing and staring and pushing a little to get closer to the object of their curiosity, somewhere in the middle of the small crowd.

From her vantage point she could see over their heads between the horse's ears, and as the cabby, still swearing, began to haul on the reins again to pull his animal to the right and so make his way around the edge of the crowd, she tapped on the trap door above her head and called, 'No – wait – I want to see.'

Moving quickly, she unbuttoned the front of the hansom, and stepped down, and leaving her now thoroughly irate driver trying to hold his animal, who was made nervous by the shifting people beneath his nose, she pushed her way through the crowd to the centre.

There were about seven people in the group she had seen from the cab; five men in ragged uniforms, three of them on crutches, and all bedecked with blood-stained bandages and looking most dolorous. One of them was leaning on the shoulder of a woman in a filthy red dress, torn at the hem so that it revealed a pair of slender but very grimy naked ankles over torn shoes, and wearing a heavy paisley shawl over her head and shoulders. There was another woman standing drooping on the other side of her in a dress equally ragged but not as dirty, and holding a bundle which could have been a baby, but which seemed to Martha's practised eyes to be keeping rather too still to be alive.

The woman in the red dress was talking, her voice with its rich heavy sound lifting easily above the rattle of traffic from the far side of the Square and the voices of the more distant crowds.

'—'ell on earth, that's wot it was, 'ell on earth—' she was saying as Martha reached the front of the crowd, dodging under the outstretched arm of one of the men who barred her way. 'My poor dear 'usban' was lost to me for ever at one o' them little battles that no-one never 'ears much of – on account of they don't count as glorious victories but skirmishes, or so the officers say they are, but I lost my man there, and it was as important to 'im as if it *ad* bin a glorious vict'ry – Bulganek, that's where 'e died at the 'ands of the fearful Cossacks in all 'is brave red uniform, and none to care for 'im, nor for me once 'e'd gone, wiv me babe kickin' in me, to be born after its poor dear father'd gone to 'is Maker—'

Here she crossed herself devoutly, and her accent, which had carried only a hint of a brogue beneath the cockney twang became more definitely Irish.

'—n' rest 'is poor dear soul in peace, as befits honest soldiers – and it was my man's comrades in arms, ladies an' gentlemen, as 'elped me and my friend 'ere 'oo'd gorn out there wiv the army on account of our love for our 'usban's an' to look after their washin' an' all like that – they 'elped us to 'ome and comfort after that there battle, for they was wounded, and we 'ad to make our own way back to Scutari, on a stinkin' fishin' boat as belonged to one o' they Turkish infidels, in search of 'elp for our sufferin's. An' when we gets to Scutari, the which they calls a barrack 'ospital – an' there's a laugh, I tells yer, ladies and gentlemen, for it's no more'n a kennel – when we gets there, what do we find? Why, there's nothin' there for none of us, no 'elp, no care, nothin'. There's men with the cholera so bad—' again she crossed herself, '—so bad they are, as they lie there dyin' in their own 'orribleness an' none to care, and me an' my mates, we says as 'ow we got to go 'ome our own ways, for 'oo is there to give a damn for a h'onest British soldier an' 'is wife?— None!'

She jerked her head at one of the men behind her, and he

moved forwards, hopping on his crutches with one bloodily bandaged leg looped up behind him and with his cap held between his teeth. He moved into the crowd, and at once the chink of coins began as pennies started dropping, and he stared mournfully at the givers above the ragged cap and nodded his head in gratitude. And still the rich round voice went on, describing, explaining, whining and yet triumphantly telling a story of a journey through Europe, stealing rides from passing peasants on market carts, and in the open cars of railway trains hauling their sooty way across the heartlands of the continent.

'—an' when we gets as far as Folkestone, ladies and gentlemen, what then? Is there a band awaitin' us wiv all flags flyin' to say welcome 'ome thou good an' faithful servants? No, ladies an' gentlemen, there bloody well ain't, nor no more is there 'elp 'ere for us now we've walked all this way to the Smoke! We've fought fer our Queen and country, Gawd bless 'er 'appy 'ome, and I give my baby fer the cause, for didn't I meet my time in a railway goods yard 'alfway into the middle of them 'eathen parts, and didn't my baby die as soon as 'e breathed Gawd's good air but the once? I've given my share of sufferin' for Queen and country, and my comrades 'ere as suffered wounds and terrible pain, an' not a penny is there for us to 'old body and soul together now we're 'ome – to the joys of English comfort – oh, that's a laugh for poor soldiers an' their wives, I'll tell yer – all you gives us now, ladies and gentlemen, will 'elp to feed not just us but our starvin' children and these noble soldiers' wives an' all—'

Martha stood there watching the expressive face, almost black with dirt beneath the matted hair that showed under the edge of the shawl, and in spite of herself, she smiled. Sal, she thought. Sal, who had first arrived on the doorstep of the Bedford Row hostel twelve years ago, a filthy but bright eyed beggar child of twelve or thirteen, as accomplished a liar as any they had ever dealt with there. They had discovered she was Irish – one of the potato-hungry hordes that had come pouring out of that beleaguered famine-struck island – discovered she was orphaned and did what they could for her. They had cleaned her – much to her shrill rage – and fed her and tried to teach her a decent trade, but she had run off, back to the life of prostitution in the gutters which she enjoyed so much more than cooking and sewing and scrubbing for her betters, only to return as dirty and hungry as ever a year or so later. And then had gone again, and returned again, and gone again; and so it had continued until she had grown up, and finally disappeared eight years ago, and never returned.

And now she stood in Trafalgar Square with a group of beggars she had clearly trained herself, milking the usually cynical London crowd with enormous success – for Martha could see the gleam of silver in the cap now, as well as the dull coppery glow of pennies – in a most modern and well thought out manner. The citizens of the world's greatest and richest metropolis, well used as they were to the hunger and misery and outstretched hands that dogged their steps on each and every day and journey, were no match for this beggar. She had them in the palm of her hand, actually eager to give their money away. The training in reading and writing and Bible study that the London Ladies had given her all those years ago had not come completely amiss, Martha thought wryly, and then moved fowards a little to allow the light from a smoking link held in the hand of one of the band of soldiers to fall on her face.

Sal, still in full flood – she was now describing in lurid detail the sort of injuries she had seen on the men lying in the filthy corridors at Scutari Hospital – turned her own head after a little while, and saw her and her eyes widened, and her flow of speech faltered momentarily, and then started up again, more swiftly now, and her eyes flickered about the crowd, assessing how much more they were worth. Clearly she decided they had been milked to the full, and let her voice drop, and become more of a singsong, and slowly the crowd began to drift away, and the little group of soldiers closed up and at a jerk of Sal's head began to move away.

But Martha was quick, and slid through the few remaining people to reach the woman's side and took her arm, and said with the easy but firm cheerfulness she had learned from years of dealing with applicants for charity, 'Well, Sal? And how much have you obtained today?'

The woman slid her eyes sideways, so that they gleamed in the shadow of her matted hair and shawl, and said in a low whine, ' 'Oo, lady: Don't know no Sal, lady. 'Ow much? Little enough, lady, little enough for the fillin' of so many 'ungry bellies, but we'll live the night out on it, if God is good to us – just a few pennies, lady, is all we got—'

'And what else besides?' Martha said coolly, still holding firmly to the woman's arm, though she tried to pull away. 'I saw the silver passing from hand to cap, for I am not quite blind, I believe! You should be ashamed to make such a play of other's miseries in times of war to line your own pockets—'

'Other's miseries? Wasn't you listenin', lady? It was *our* miseries as I was tellin' of, as well as those of others! We're soldiers and soldiers wives, we are, wiv' children to fend for – and we got to go now. I've a starvin' babe waitin' for me in a garret across in Porridge Island, an'—'

She tried to pull her arm away again, but Martha's grasp was too firm, and now, as most of the crowd had gone, and the darkness was thicker, the men in the little group of beggars closed in a little, and for a moment Martha felt a twinge of fear. But she held on and said very steadily, 'You said your babe died in a railway yard in the middle of heathen parts.'

There was a little silence, in which for a moment the menace in the group seemed to Martha to build up, and then, suddenly, Sal laughed, a heavy raucous laugh, and the men relaxed as though a string had been pulled, and turned and looked at her, and she pushed the shawl back from her face and grinned hugely, revealing big white teeth, and said cheerfully, 'Oh, Miss Martha, wot's the good o' tryin' to tell *you* anythin'? Always knew better than anyone else, you did—'

'Well, I wouldn't say that.' Martha let go her arm now, and tucked her hands into her muff, for the evening was getting rapidly darker and the late autumn chill was digging into her bones. 'But I do tell you that I think it very wrong that you should use the war and what is happening out there as a means of parting people from their money. Beg if you must, if you prefer it to honest work, but there are real funds set up for the soldiers, and it is sinful that you should take any of it for yourselves—'

'Nah, just a minute—' Suddenly Sal's good humour had gone. 'Just you button up for one little minute. 'Oo said as 'ow we wasn't there? We may be beggin', and so do you, as I recall, only o' course it's all right for the likes o' *you*, on account you does it for others, don't yer? It's charity when you got enough to feed yerself, but stinkin' beggin' when it's the only way people like us gets aught to eat at all – but we'll set that aside, Madam 'Igh and Mighty Lackland! We'll set it aside so's we can tell yer as we *was* there. Just like I told it. 'Ow do you think I know what it was like, you stupid cow, if I wasn't there? Some of the fellers 'ere may be deserters, rather than wounded – an' if you'd seen what it was like out there, you'd a' deserted an' all – it's the only thing a feller with any wits about 'im could do , but *we was there*! An' never you say we wasn't!'

Now it was Martha's turn to be silent, and after a long pause during which the two women stared at each other she bit her lip and said, 'I'm sorry, Sal. I was reaching unjustified conclusions. From the past, you know, and what I knew of you then – I beg your pardon.'

At once Sal was all good humour again. 'Well, fair enough! That's as 'andsome a makeup as I've ever 'eard, so we'll say no more about it. We'll be on our way, then, and ta fer yer interest—' and she turned to go.

'No – please, Sal,' Martha said urgently, and again put her hand on the other's arm. 'I want to hear more – please? I've been concerned all day. I read the paper this morning and – well, I want to *know*. And if you were there you can perhaps tell me a little – will you let me take you up in my hansom? It's over there – you can come back to Bedford Row and have some food, if you wish, and then we'll talk – with no strings attached, Sal – no strings attached at all.'

She smiled then, remembering the bitter arguments they had had when Sal had been a child and Martha had traded food for a bath and a new dress for a Bible reading.

'Just the chance to hear what it's all about. Please, will you come with me?'

Sal stared at her, and then squinted up at the now dark sky with heavy clouds scudding over it, for rain was threatening, and she pulled the shawl more closely about her shoulders and stood consideringly for a moment, and then nodded sharply.

'All right then. We didn't get *that* much tonight – one meal less to get aht of it won't be such a bad thing, at that. Go on, you lot – I'll see yer rahnd the Lamb an' Flag tomorrer and we'll work down Westminster way – good pickin's there, I reckon, now the news really is out. Politicians is easier meat than some. Go on, then! I told yer – *I'm* eatin' like a lady tonight!'

And she laughed her raucous laugh again, and cheekily linked her dirty arm into Martha's neat brown one, and went swaggering away towards the hansom Martha had indicated, grinning over her shoulder at her somewhat crestfallen soldiers.

'I'm eatin' like a lady tonight!' she cried again, and followed Martha into the hansom, much to the driver's disgust, who thought his second passenger too dirty to be allowed near his stable, let alone the interior of his cab, and they went rattling away into the noisy traffic-laden streets, leaving the wounded soldiers to make their own way into the alleys and gutters of Seven Dials, away up and beyond St. Martin's Lane.

CHAPTER TWO

THE big kitchen in the basement of 27 Bedford Row was remarkably comfortable and cosy. The huge iron range shone with blacklead, gleamed with satin polished brass and glowed with a vast sea coal fire of truly infernal proportions, while the red repp curtains which shielded the area windows threw back rosy gleams from the oil lamps plentifully scattered about, making the two big rocking-chairs against the brass fender seem even more inviting. A kettle steamed gently to one side of the great fire, while a stockpot bubbled lazily at the back, sending out little puffs of steam scented with marrow bones and onions, and potherbs. To Sal, crouching on the hooked rag rug which covered the floor in front of the hearth and kept the chill off the scrubbed stone flags, it was like heaven, and she wasn't ashamed to say so.

'It's been dunnamany years since I saw so civilized a place as this, Miss Martha, an' so I tells yer! Bin really piggin' it I 'ave, this past few years. Forgot 'ow nice it could be to live like you nobs do.'

Martha, sitting on the far side of the heavy wooden table with the big brown teapot in front of her and a plate of fresh baked muffins beside it, smiled, and filled another cup with the dark brown stewed tea, lacing it heavily with honey and milk, and held it out to the woman by the fire. Who took it, and drank it noisily and with enormous relish, and then took two of the buttered muffins from the plate Martha held out to her and swallowed them almost unchewed.

'I could arrange for you to take dinner with us – Miss Carrie and her brother and myself, you know – if you so wish,'

Martha said after a moment. 'If you would wish, that is, to bath first. No—' she said hastily as Sal looked up and stared at her with a huge hostility in her eyes. 'I pull no strings! I keep my word! I told you you would eat your dinner, and so you shall. The choice is dinner here in the kitchen or above stairs in the dining-room. If you choose to eat with us, I cannot help it, but a bath must come first. Miss Carrie is not so used as I to – to some of the problems you have in—'

'To the way I stink, you mean,' Sal said, and laughed. 'I do an' all, don't I?' And indeed, as she warmed up, sitting ever closer to the fire, the smell of her did become stronger and much more disagreeable.

'Well, I'll tell yer, Miss Martha. I'll *'ave* a bath – but not so's I can eat upstairs all fancy wiv the nobs. I'll eat my vittles dahn 'ere in decent comfort, but I'll 'ave the bath to please myself. It's easy to be clean when you've got 'ot water and bathtubs. And decent clothes to put on again after—' and she half closed her eyes above the rim of her cup, staring at Martha calculatingly. And Martha laughed in her turn and stood up with an air of resignation.

'All right, Sal. A new gown it is. I have a pleasant enough green one above stairs, I believe. And even, perhaps a shift and some shoes and stockings. I'll tell Miss Carrie you are one of us tonight then, but down here, and will bring the gown and the bath things.'

She helped Sal with her bath, scrubbing her back, and washing her hair, and trimming away with the big kitchen scissors those portions of it which were too dirty to be unmatted, combing out the nits and jumping lice with a calmness born of many years of performing such services for others, and they talked desultorily of many things, such as the remarkable changes there had been in London since Sal had gone away – for building was going on apace, with new houses, new shops, even new streets seeming to appear overnight.

And also, although she did not realize how much she was saying, of Martha's own doings. Sal had a sharp mind and a long memory and she had picked up much information about the ladies of the hostel she had used so cheerfully when it had suited her, all those years ago. So, now, with casual questions, she dug out more from Martha, hearing of her father's busy life at St. Eleanor's Hospital, where more wards still had been added, and the old surgeon, though now sixty-five, still ruled with unquestioning and unquestioned authority; of her sister Abby, with her brood of children in elegant Bayswater, still a most successful businesswoman, with her continually growing network of apothecaries' shops, and her chain of manufactories where pills and patent medicines were poured out in their hundreds of thousands; of her nephew Freddy who had become a surgeon himself now, and was working in reasonable amity with his grandfather at St. Eleanor's; of her niece Phoebe, who with her brother Oliver was running with great success their handsome supper rooms in King Street, rebuilt after the dreadful fire in which their father had died three years ago.

A lot of news, and Martha imparted it easily enough, as Sal, under the soothing care of hot water and soap and coconut oil for her hair began to emerge as the handsome young woman she was. And at last stood, dressed and shod and greatly pleased with herself on the damp rag rug before the glowing kitchen fire.

Martha, still on her knees beside the bath tub, drying her hands and rolling down her sleeves to fasten the cuffs, looked up at her, and smiled with real pleasure. Sal stood there, in her dark green dress, her waist neat and elegant beneath her full breasts which strained a little against the buttons of the gown, but not at all unbecomingly, and her broad shoulders rising rosy and capable looking above them. Her jaw was heavy, but with bone not flesh, for there was no spare fat on her, though she was muscular enough; but the years of hunger showed on her, in the fine shadows in her temples and under her green eyes and in the hollows of her cheeks. Her hair, still damp and curling a little as it dried, was a deep brown and her skin was the colour of pale honey. Altogether she looked very well, and Martha told her so.

'Aye, I've no shortage of good looks,' Sal said matter-of-factly, and then grinned widely, her teeth flashing a little in the lamplight. 'There's bin too many fellers as 'ad the joy of me not for me to know what me face is worth. But much good it does yer, in the long run! There's you, plain as a little puddin' – an' you ain't the sort to be upset by what's no more'n the truth – an' what arm 'as it done you? You've never gone 'ungry, 'ave you? No. Nor 'ad to put up wiv some stinkin' feller paddlin' around yer bits and pieces just so's you'll get a dinner inside yer. No, looks don't do you no good. It's wits you wants. An' I've got them an' all!' And she looked hugely complacent and then whirled in her new gown so that the folds twisted seductively around her long muscular thighs.

'Yes, you've plenty of wit,' Martha said equably, and got to her feet. 'Well, come above stairs. I'll send Louisa and Sarah to deal with this lot, and we shall talk. For there is so much I want to hear—'

But despite her new cleanliness, Sal was adamant. She would eat her dinner in the kitchen and nowhere else, so Martha went above stairs to the drawing room, where old Miss Carrie Garling was sitting poring over the Committee's accounts, to beg to be excused from dinner tonight, although she had promised to join her and her brother, Henry – always called by Miss Carrie 'the young one', although he was fully sixty-two – to talk of the Committee's affairs.

'Well, I can do without you tonight, I daresay, dear Martha,' the old lady said, and looked at her sharply through her lorgnette, snapping the lenses open with a rheumatism-gnarled thumb. 'Do you prefer to dine at home?'

'Why, no, Miss Carrie – I would not be so ill-mannered to you!' Martha said, and smiled down at the almost bald old head, hiding its sparse grey locks under a Mechlin lace cap she had inherited from her own mother, who had worn it half a century ago. 'Do you remember Sal? The Irish child who used to come and go so often? She disappeared – oh, it must be eight years ago, now. I remember, I had been away from here for some weeks because of an epidemic of typhus at Queen Eleanor's. I had to help Papa, do you recall the time? And when I returned, she had gone again, and never did return. Well, I found her in Trafalgar Square today – and she has been to the Crimea.'

The old lady looked up and frowned sharply. 'Oh dear, I cannot pretend to recall her, but I imagine from what you say she is a – ahem,' she coughed and shook her head, for even after thirty or more years of working with gutter people for the Charity she could not bring herself to admit that prostitution existed, let alone that one of the people upon whom she spent her Charity's hard-won money was such a one.

But Martha was less squeamish, and nodded cheerfully enough. 'Oh, yes, a camp follower, though she tells the crowds she mulcts that she is a wife! However, that is all one – the thing is, Miss Carrie, I wish greatly to talk to her of conditions out there, for the news is so very dreadful about the War, and it had exercised my mind all day – so will you forgive me if I leave you and Mr. Henry alone this evening? I will arrange with Papa that I will dine away from home again tomorrow, if you will be so kind as to accept me, and I am sure that—'

'Oh, of course, of course—' The old lady sat very still, staring up with her milky old eyes fixed on the younger face above her, and then she said sharply, 'Martha! You know we depend upon you heavily here? I could not manage the daily procession of those seeking outdoor relief if you were not by my side, nor could I imagine dealing with the problems of the women we have here in the hostel. If you were to—'

Martha opened her eyes wide. 'My dear Miss Carrie! Why should you ever think I would let you down? For that is what you mean, is it not? Of course not! But – well, there are many things happening, and many facts I am ignorant about. There are more ways than one to deal with what has to be done, whether it be here or in Scutari – please do not fret yourself! I shall be here as usual in the morning to check the food cupboards and deal with the relief distribution. Goodnight, dear Miss Carrie!' And she kissed the old lady's cheek and went softly away, back to the kitchen and Sal – who was, in some curious way she could not quite understand, making her feel very excited indeed.

Martha ate sparingly, hardly touching the plate of crimped

cod that Louisa, sulking slightly at this invasion of her domain, slapped down in front of her, but Sal more than made up for that. She gobbled the food voraciously, clearing her plate first of the cod, and then of the good boiled beef and pease pudding, and cabbage Louisa gave her, and then a vast portion of boiled suet pudding with raisins in it. Louisa, visibly mollified – for what cook does not find it gratifying to see her efforts so greatly appreciated? – finally gave her a great mug of kitchen tea, laced with rum, and Sal sighed deeply and leaned back in her chair, patting her belly with great satisfaction.

'Oh, a dinner like that every day, an' I wouldn't call the Queen me cousin!' She belched gustily and grinned at Martha. 'I tell yer, Miss Martha, yer a funny lot, you charity ladies, with yer Bibles and yer baths, but yer mean well enough. And I'm grateful for what I've 'ad, an' I'm 'appy to say so.'

'I seek no gratitude, Sal,' Martha said, a little sharply. 'I do what I do because it needs to be done, not because I seek some sort of – of self-aggrandisement.'

'Well, yer different from most on 'em, I'll give yer that,' Sal said, and took another deep draught of her tea. 'Some of 'em make me puke! I useter go rahn' all of 'em – the Mission to the the Poor, the Church Aid lot – all of 'em – an' they all expected yer to bow and scrape an' sell yer bloody soul for a bowl o' lousy gruel! But you lot 'ere – you always was lavish wiv yer givin' an' fair wiv yer preachin'. I useter wonder about you, you know. When I was a nipper I mean, and come 'ere first. Why do you do it? You ain't a Bible-basher by nature, are you? Never used to go on about God an' all that, you didn't. So what are you doin' it for?'

Martha was silent, staring into the flames of the big kitchen fire, and there was a short silence broken only by the sound of a late cab clopping past the area windows, muffled by the thick red curtains. And then she sighed sharply and said in a crisp little voice, 'Because there was nothing else to do. I am not a fool, I believe, and to sit at home doing Berlin wool work or the like was not for me. I would have died of ennui. My stepmother worked in this charity, as my mother did before her,

24

and my grandmother before that. So I thought – well, why not? It keeps me busy.'

'But not 'appy?'

'Oh, what is happy, Sal? I would not know what it was if I had it! I am content enough – as you say yourself, for one that is as plain as a pudding, and has little enough to offer the world, I have been fortunate. I do not go hungry—'

Sal reddened a little, her honey skin flushing very agreeably, and she said roughly, 'Oh, Gawd, Miss Martha, I meant no 'arm by that! I wasn't meanin' to be unkind – but – but—'

'You were not unkind,' Martha said equably. 'Just honest. It is true that I am far from being a woman that will turn any person's head for a second glance. Not like my niece Phoebe, now – she is an enchanting creature—' She smiled then. 'If you seek a decent occupation, instead of street begging, Sal, I daresay I can find you a position with Phoebe. She is sometimes in need of a personable woman to serve at tables in the supper rooms. The food is good, and the customers, I believe, pay well if they take a fancy to those who tend their needs!'

'I don't care if yer niece is the fanciest lookin' piece from 'ere to Land's End – I don't work as a servant for no-one. You thinks it's more respectable than bein' a beggar, but I'll tell you this, Miss Martha Lackland – I'm me own woman, livin' the life I do! If I go 'ungry, it's me own problem – an' if I'm fed – well, I've earned it! Even today and this dinner, I've earned, ain't I? Told the story of what it's like out there in the 'orrors of the land where the wicked Cossacks is, an' that was what you wanted to know – so—'

'Sal – please tell me – *me*, not the crowd of marks out in the Square – the truth of the matter. I have a great wish to know. What *really* happened? Why were you there? And when?'

Sal put her mug down on the table with a little thump and turned her chair so that she could stretch her feet out to the blaze of the fire, and stared at the flames in her turn, and Martha looked at her hopefully. She felt in some curious way that this fortuitous meeting today with Sal was more than it appeared to be; that she held the key in some way to the uneasiness that had lain within her all day. And it took a real effort of will keep her lips closed against the strong words she wanted to use to urge Sal to speak, as she said in as flat a voice as she could, 'You do not have to tell me. I said there were no strings attached to this dinner, and I stand by that. But I would wish to—'

'Eh?' Sal turned her head and stared at her, almost bewildered for a moment, and then shook her head. 'Oh, I'm sorry! I wasn't bein' captious, Miss Martha, I do promise you. I was jus' thinkin'. About some o' me mates and all that—'

She pulled her chair round to the table again, and set her elbows firmly on it, and her chin on her clasped hands, staring at Martha with a sudden intensity. 'I'll tell you – an' so 'elp me it's the total truth. Not a word of a lie, as sure as I sit 'ere bustin' me guts with yer good vittles. It was back in Febr'y last as it all started. I was in Trafalgar Square, see, mindin' me own business and doin' no 'arm to none as'd mind—' She grinned suddenly at that. 'I was dippin' a few pockets, an' that's the truth of it, and I'd picked up a nice fat purse an' was right pleased wi' meself – an' into the Square they comes, the Grenadier Guards. Oh, Miss Martha, if you'd a' seen 'em! *Lovely* they was, all of a jingle and a jangle, and as tall an' as 'andsome as any men you ever saw. The 'orses pullin' the transports, and the music – it fair turned me knees to jelly, it did! I do love a regiment in the full dress, I really do. So, I marches up close, don't I, and start talkin', friendly like, to one or two of the fellers, and friendly right back they are 'an no error, an' they tells me as they're off to Crim Tartary to fight the 'eathen as was killin' Christian monks. Well, a fat lot I cares for monks, though I was reared in the Roman Church when I was a nipper – but these fellers say as it matters, and they reckons the pickins'll be good, so when the officer comes round and says as they'll 'ave the draw for the wives to go, one of the fellers pipes up and says as 'ow I'm 'is wife, fair and square, an' 'e wants me in the draw, an' me, thinkin' it might be a good laugh at that, says all right. And damn my eyes, but I gets drawn to go!'

Her eyes seemed to darken for a moment as she remembered. 'I felt a bit bad, mind you, for a minute or two there, on

26

account o' there was some wives as carried on alarmin' and shrieked and wailed because they wasn't drawn – but I reckon I did 'em a bit o' good, as it turned out, goin' for 'em. I mean of the sixty or thereabouts of us as got drawn to go, there was more'n 'alf of 'em dead before August was out – an' more of the children than that—'

'I don't quite understand,' Martha said softly, unwilling to break into the spell Sal was weaving about herself as she talked, but needing to get it clear in her head. 'What is this draw?'

Sal laughed, a short hard little sound deep in her throat. 'No, I don't suppose you do know! Well, it's like this, Miss Martha, for the ordinary soldier an' 'is woman. Different for officers, o' course. They can pay what they likes, an' get their wives took along wiv their 'orses an' their maids and Gawd knows what else besides. Like that Mrs. Fanny Duberly – you'd a' thought she was goin' on a picnic down to Richmond, the way she set out! But for the ordinary man wot's got a wife as'll starve if 'er feller goes away, an' 'oo can't raise the necessary to take 'er out of 'is own pocket, all 'e can do is put 'is wife in for the draw. They allow just so much space in the troopships for enough women to go to do a bit o' fettlin' for the army – cookin' and a bit o' rough nursin' and all like that – an' for the Grenadier Guards the number they could take was seven to each company – an' there's an 'undred men in a company. So out of a regiment of nigh on nine 'undred men, abouty sixty gets to go. They puts all the wives' names in the drum, an' pulls 'em out, one at a time, an' shouts 'em out, an' they're the ones as gets to go and the others stay be'ind and rot, for all the army officers care! Anyway, along I goes, an' a great time we 'as of it, for a start. The fellers is fun, and the drinks lavish, an' the food's not above 'alf bad, an' some o' the other women turns aht to be real mates. I enjoys it, seein' the world an' that – until we gets to Varna on the Black Sea an' then – oh, it was bad, real bad—'

'Cholera,' Martha said softly.

'Aye, cholera. Lousy stinkin' 'ateful place, it was alive wiv it! The men was fallin' like flies, an' not a soldier as 'ad so much as clapped eyes on the enemy yet! They shoved us all down in the bowels of they troopships, an' the stink of it, and the 'orrors of it – oh, I wouldn't wish it on the worst enemy in the world! It took ten days to embark us all at that place – what was it – Balchik Bay. Ten days o' no water, and smells an' 'orses screamin' and men dyin' – I was wiv the fellers on H.M.S. *Britannia,* an' we 'ad one 'undred and nine dead men to chuck over the side before we gets to the other side to Crim Tartary. An' not a shot fired yet! Oh, it was chronic, chronic it was—'

'And then what happened?'

Sal shrugged. 'It was like I said before. There was a landin' o' sorts over the other side, an' we marches and marches – landed at Eupatoria at Calamita Bay we did, an' set out to march to Sevastopol, an' we 'ad this skirmish at Bulganek – oh, wot's the use o' talkin' more about it? The feller 'as 'ad claimed me as 'is wife – an' right fond of 'im I'd got, I can't deny it – 'e bought it there, an' from then on the army 'ad neither use nor vittles for me. I cut an' run, an' got meself back to Scutari, the 'ospital base, like, the other side o' Constantinople. Thought I'd do all right there. Do a bit o' nursin' and all like that. But there was no 'ope there. There's an 'ospital right enough, but the men was packed in all 'iggledy piggledy, and the women and children too and no-one to give a sod fer any on 'em—'

'Women and children?' Martha said sharply.

Sal sighed with a heavy, almost insulting patience. '*Yes* – women an' children! Can't you take it in? Every regiment gets to take a few women along – an' where's there's women there's babies, ain't there? Soldiers, even sick ones, still wants their oats and makes sure they gets 'em – there was seventeen babies born on the troopships goin' aht, an' Gawd knows 'ow many more's on the way. An' some o' the women took kids along wiv 'em, 'idden in their shawls. There's Gawd knows 'ow many kids out there, down in the cellars at Scutari. Gawd knows 'ow many. An' no rations allowed fer 'em nor nothin'.'

'Who looks after them?' Martha was sitting very upright now, her eyes very bright as she stared at Sal. 'Who feeds them?'

'No-one, God damn it! 'Ow often 'as I got to explain? If their fellers is still alive an' marchin' they gets some of 'is

28

rations, if 'e's willin' to part. But once a bloke's dead then the women and kids as was wiv 'im are reckoned dead an' all as far as the army's officers are concerned. An' most of 'em are, in fact, pretty soon after—'

The room sank again into silence as Martha sat there and stared at Sal's face outlined in the firelight, and Sal herself sat and stared back into her memories of the past year.

A piece of coal settled in the fire with a little rattle and there was a sudden hiss as a tiny gas jet lit among the embers, and that made both of them start.

Sal stood up and stretched, catlike in her sensuousness, and she looked about her, and picked up her heavy paisley shawl from the settle.

'Well, Miss Martha, I've 'ad me vittles an' I've told yer the truth which is that it's a bloody stinkin' 'ell out there, an' I'm bloody glad to be out of it. Ta for me fancy new gown – I'll make the most of it, I promise yer! I'll be on me way now—'

'No!' Martha was on her feet round the table in a flash. 'No – please, Sal, don't go. I want you to – I'm not yet sure what I want, but I want you to stay here. Just a little longer, please! I – there is something I must do. I know that there is something I must do, and tomorrow I shall put it in hand. But I shall need you to help me. Please, Sal. Stay—'

Sal, in the act of wrapping her shawl about her, stared at her, her eyes opaque with suspicion. 'Stay 'ere? Not on yer nelly, ducks, not no'ow! It was all right to be a charity kid when I was a nipper, but not now! I got a good beggin' lay now, an' I'm goin' to use it! I done me bit for me dinner. An' that's all! I'm going'!'

She paused then and stared at Martha, even as she was moving away from her towards the area door. 'What was it made you so excited?' she said after a moment. 'All of a dither, yer in, ain't you? What's it all about, then?'

Martha bit her lip, and then let her shoulders, which had been held rigid as a board, relax a little and she smiled, a small rueful grimace.

'Yes, I am in a dither, I suppose. It's just that – well, I have an idea. There is something I feel I must do – that I am meant

29

to do – but I need your help. That was why I asked you to stay. But of course I cannot force you—'

'Something to do?' Sal's hand was on the latch, but still she lingered, staring back at Martha with a curious frown on her face. And indeed, Martha gave her cause for her puzzlement. She was standing with her head thrown up so that the line of her throat was outlined against the firelight, pencil sharp, and her eyes were so bright under her level brows that they seemed twice their usual size and twice as lustrous. Gawd, thought Sal for a brief moment, she ain't so dumpy after all! There's some fellers as'd really fancy 'er lookin' like that. Got a good bit more fire in 'er belly than she knows of, I reckon.

But all she said was, again, 'Somethin' to do?'

'Something for the women and children,' Martha said. 'I've been looking after poor women and children for years here in Bedford Row. All my life, it seems. Now I want to – oh, I don't know what I want to do! No – that isn't true. I know what I *want* – but I don't know what I can get. That's what I must find out about. I shall need you.'

'Well, I'm goin' 'ome. But if it's that important – well, I'll be at the Lamb and Flag tomorrer. Down by Rose Street, in Covent Garden. If it ain't above you to come there, that's where I'll be, mornin' an' evenin'. If you really wants me—'

And this time she did go, hurrying out into a flurry of October rain, to run with her head down along Bedford Row to Theobald's Road and the twisting turning way back to the slums of Seven Dials, leaving Martha standing in the middle of the big stone-flagged kitchen with her head buzzing with the images of the soldiers and their women and children all those thousands of miles away in Crim Tartary.

CHAPTER THREE

'I HAVE never heard such hare-brained rubbish in all my life!' Abel said loudly, and banged his open hand on the table. 'You hear me? It is nonsense! You shall do nothing of the sort.'

'Papa, you misunderstand me,' Martha said, her voice very level but with her hands trembling in her lap, hidden beneath the breakfast table. 'I do not seek your consent, but your – your – well, I am but *telling* you what I shall do! I would be glad of your blessing in this undertaking, of course, but if I cannot have it, then I must do without it. But I shall go, whether you say me yea or nay!'

Abel thrust his jaw forwards and stared at her, his eyes snapping beneath the heavy grey brows. He looks as handsome and formidable a man as ever he has, Martha thought, allowing memory to seep into her, even though she was so concerned with matters very much of the moment. He used to look like this when he argued with Jonah, all those years ago, when we were children. A little greyer now, but still so very big and strong and so *very* alarming—

'I forbid it!' he roared, and frowned even more ferociously, so much so that he looked for one brief moment quite absurd, and Martha could not help it; her lips quirked and her eyes wrinkled with laughter and she said gently, 'Papa, you cannot! You seem to forget I am eight and thirty! Not by any means a schoolroom chit, you know!'

He blinked and stared back at her, and then stood up and began to prowl about the breakfast room table, his hands clasped behind him beneath his coat tails, and his heavy head bent, and Martha watched him and then turned her head and looked inquiringly at Maria who had been sitting quietly at the foot of the table throughout the discussion, composedly eating her toast and honey, and saying not a word.

Now, she touched her lips lightly with her napkin and folded her hands upon the cloth before her and said in equable tones, 'My dear, I think, you know, that Martha has the right of it. She cannot be forbidden to go, after all! And even if she were still under your jurisdiction in such a way, I believe she would be acting most properly in seeking to do this.'

'Eh?' He turned and glared at her. 'What's that you say? Am I to have both wife and daughter setting their faces against me? It is intolerable! I tell you, it is a hare-brained notion, and not to be borne! That a lady as carefully nurtured as Martha could imagine she can be of any use out in the filth and stench and dangers of a battlefield – anyone with half an eye must see what nonsense it is!'

'There were some that regarded it as nonsense that I should work with you at Queen Eleanor's, in times of epidemic, Papa,' Martha said. 'But I have done that, have I not? As have you, Maria, also. If we carefully nurtured ladies can do such work here I do not see why I should not do it elsewhere.'

'Oh, that is quite different! Here in London, where I am at hand to watch you and to act as your protector – but *there*! In Turkey! It is the edge of the world, you foolish creature! You will die of disease if you are not picked off by a musket ball—'

'While others take that risk on your behalf, Papa, I feel it hardly just to use that as a reason to prevent me from helping. Besides, I do not wish to fight, you know! I have no intention of going any nearer the battlefields than Scutari, which, if you read *The Times*, you will see is many, many miles from the scene of actual shooting—'

Again he glared at her, standing with his head bent and his chin tucked into his collar points so that he stared at her from beneath his brows, and now suddenly he changed his tack. 'Well, what of your duties here? You, who have cared so much for the work you do there at your Bedford Row Hostel for the creatures you rescue from their gutters – what of *that* work, hey? Are their needs to go by the board simply because you have caught war fever from that damned radical newspaper you insist on cluttering the table with? Hey? It is as though I said to the devil with Queen Eleanor's, I shall close the hospital and let the people of Seven Dials die and rot for want of it, while I and my surgeons go racketing off to the excitements of war! Have you any answer to that, hey? No, indeed you have not!'

Martha bit her lip and stared back at him, her resolve seeming to melt and drain away through her fingers' ends. He was right, of course. She suddenly remembered Miss Carrie last night, peering at her through her lorgnette and saying sharply, 'You know we depend upon you heavily here? I could not manage – if you were not by my side—'

It was true, and Abel, as shrewd and sharp as he had always been, had found the weak spot in her argument as surely as he found diseased spots in a patient's body. And he knew he had and looked at her with a mixture of triumph and yet pity on his face. He understood her feelings well, she suddenly realized. He did not seek to prevent her out of any mere pig-headedness. He *did* understand—

'Well, as to that, there is no real problem,' Maria's voice cut in and they both almost started, quietly though she had spoken. 'I believe I can handle Martha's duties in Bedford Row, if she goes away. I have shared her concern, my dear Abel, about the work that needs to be done there in the war, and have exercised my mind a good deal about what *I* could do. I would dearly wish to do as Martha is planning to do, and go there – but I know what cannot be. I am ten years older than you, my dear Martha, and I know all too well the limitations that years set upon even the healthiest of women. But I am, I believe, well fitted to take on your duties here and thus to free you for your good work. I would feel myself much happier if I were to do it. So the matter is settled, is it not?'

She smiled very sweetly at her husband, and walked round the table to stand beside him, looking up at his much greater

33

height in a very appealing way. And he stared down at her, and then again at Martha and shook his head and grimaced and then said gruffly, 'Oh, well, if both of you are set and determined to go against me, what can I do? I dislike it, I dislike it above all things! But you defeat me—'

And Martha suddenly felt tears under her eyelids and had to blink and sniff, and bend her head to fuss with her table napkin, and Abel coughed and moved away from Maria's side to return to the table.

'Well, I will have more coffee, though I make no doubt it is cold by now. What a time to start such hares, Martha! You ruin my digestion, and make me late for the hospital, all because you have taken some notion to go and take care of soldiers—'

Martha jerked her head up at that, and stared at him. 'Oh, not soldiers, Papa!'

'Eh? *Not* soldiers? Then for the love of heaven, what have we been arguing about this past half hour?'

'Perhaps I did not explain myself clearly enough, Papa,' she said carefully. 'I was told last night, by one who knows of the conditions there, of the lamentable state not only of the army but of the army's followers. There are women and children there, Papa, sick and unfed and in a truly dreadful state! The army, I am told, has no responsibility for them, and they suffer quite dreadfully! It is my plan, you see, to seek funds to take with me to look after *them*—'

His cup clattered into its saucer. 'Camp followers? The *women*? Now I know you are clean out of your attic! Where do you imagine you will find funds for *them*? Here's all London run mad with war fever and sending every penny it can lay hands on to Sir Robert Peel for the soldiers' welfare, and you believe you can find the money to take care of *street women*? Oh, come, Martha! Where are your wits?'

'I will find the money somewhere, Papa. I was going to ask you for any guidance you—'

'No, do not look at me!' he said roundly. 'Go if you must – though I now realize how unlikely it is you will get there, for I

34

am convinced you will never raise so much as the price of a ticket to Folkestone – but do not seek any financial aid of *me*! It is all I can do to get the necessary funds to keep Queen Eleanor's alive!'

'Well, now, Martha,' Maria said. 'I think this will not be so difficult as your Papa believes! I daresay Miss Carrie and the rest of the Committee will see that the work you seek to do will be but an extension of the work of the London Ladies, if the truth were known. You will be caring for much the same sort of person as the Committee does here in London! They are but travellers, after all. And, you know, you have in addition your own connections.'

'I have?' Martha said, and turned almost eagerly to her stepmother. So quiet, so mousy and yet so capable a person! 'I must confess, dear Maria, that I have not thought fully of all the problems – any ideas you may have will be gladly welcomed, I do assure you! I am grateful if you will persuade the Committee to offer me some funds, and for any other possibilities that occur to you—'

'Go to Abby, my dear! She and Gideon have considerable influence, you know, among people of substance, and are far from poor! I imagine they will be of aid.'

Martha stood up. 'Indeed, I shall! I shall go this very morning – oh!' She stopped and looked suddenly as crestfallen as a child. 'I cannot. Miss Carrie expects me this morning to check the food cupboards and organize the relief distribution—'

Maria laughed. 'My dear Martha, you should become excited like this more often! It makes you look very handsome, you know! No, there is no problem there. If I am to take over your tasks at Bedford Row then the sooner I start the better, I imagine. Tell me what is to do, and I shall do it. And you go to Bayswater, and then, I suggest, to King Street. No, do not look so surprised! Oliver is a shrewd young man, and may have ideas to help you. And he is very attached to you, you know. Quite his favourite aunt in many ways!'

Impulsively, Martha bent and kissed Maria's cheek, and they both reddened and pulled away, for neither of them were demonstrative women; but they understood each other very well, and the moment of shyness melted away as Martha turned to her father and said gently, 'I do thank you, Papa, for being so – for understanding me so well! I value your concern for my wellbeing most highly, and fully recognize how depressing my plans are for you. Thank you again.'

'Oh, what is the good of words?' Abel said, as irascible as ever. 'I do not like the idea above half, but what can I do? You had best be about your business, as I must be about mine. I have had patients waiting for me this past fifteen minutes. Good day to both of you!'

'You were lucky to find me at home, my dear Martha,' Abby said, bustling agreeably with the Madeira decanter, and pushing the plate of little macaroons nearer to her sister's hand. 'Generally, on a Saturday morning, I am out with the girls, because you know Isabel is of an age now to find shopping the most agreeable occupation in the world and Sarah obliges us by coming along, because we always have a luncheon at Phoebe's and Oliver's afterwards, and she loves that above all things, being a most greedy child! But she is so enchanting, you know, I cannot but forgive it in her! But today we shall not go, because Daniel is recovering from a putrid throat and demands his sisters play with him, and it will not hurt them to put themselves out for once! You have not seen Daniel for a month or more, my love, and he is looking so well, in spite of his illness! Will you come up to the nursery and see him?'

'Later, of course, my dear Abby,' Martha said, and tried not to let her impatience show. Usually she could bear with and even enjoy her sister's motherly chatter, for she was genuinely attached to her small nieces and infant nephew, but today it was difficult to think of anything but her new plan. It was as though she had taken fire, so consumed was she with the importance of it all. It seemed to her that the whole world was concentrated in one small area, all those hundreds of miles away on the shores of the Bosphorus, with everything else lying on the edge, a shadow, an insignificant fringe to reality. It was Scutari and only Scutari she could think of.

Abby looked at her sharply, and then smiled, her face relaxing into its usual happy lines. The years had dealt kindly with Abby; she had been a pleasant enough girl to look at, a handsome enough young woman, but now, at one and forty, she had blossomed into a ripeness that was very appealing. She wore her hair in sleek wings on each side of her rather strong face, softening its squareness, and her complexion, smooth and subtle in its colouring, enhanced the curve of cheek and chin. She had put on a little plumpness with her three pregnancies, but it suited her well, the hint of double chin giving added warmth to her features, and the full curves of her body making her seem positively voluptuous at times, so that she looked, as her husband Gideon had once told her, 'like a Rubens, inadvertently clothed.'

'Well, my dear,' she said comfortably, settling herself on her blue velvet deep buttoned sofa (the house in Stanhope Gate was always furnished in the most modish manner, for Gideon liked to display his good taste as well as his wealth). 'You had better tell me all about it. You are clearly bursting with news!'

She cocked an eyebrow then. 'Have you set eyes upon a gentleman, perhaps who – No? Well no need to look at me so disgusted! I still believe you may marry, you know! It is only because you have always been so determinedly turned in upon yourself that you have remained unclaimed so long!'

'Oh, Abbey, please, let us not talk on *that* score! I believe I made myself clear upon the matter the last time you tried to play the matchmaker! I find it very boring, you know!'

'Well, so be it! This time – but that does not mean I shall not upon another occasion see what we can do to settle you! Am I wrong then? You are not full of news, and this is but a friendly visit?'

Martha shook her head. 'No, you are not wrong – now, Abby, I wish you to hear me out. I need your help, and Gideon's – is he here, by the by?'

Abby shook her head, frowning a little. 'Not on Saturday, my dear. You forget yourself!'

Martha reddened. Indeed she did often forget that her brother-in-law was a Jew, and that on each and every Saturday morning he walked the many miles from Bayswater to the City to worship in his synagogue, and visit his elderly and ailing widowed mother, and she said swiftly, 'Oh, I am sorry! I did not mean to offend! But I am so taken up with it all – now listen, Abby, and you shall tell Gideon later, and then tell me what you can do—'

And she launched herself into an account of all she had heard from Sal, of the positively stunning effect the story of the situation at Scutari had had on her, and of her determination to go out there; and Abby listened to her and watched her and said nothing.

But when, flushed with the earnestness of it all, Martha at last drew a deep breath and stopped, she got to her feet in a rustle of cream silk and moved across the drawing-room to her little escritoire in the corner, and seated herself in front of it and began to write on a sheet of paper she drew from a pigeon hole.

'I shall give you a bill on my personal account at the bank in Lombard Street for one hundred pounds,' she said calmly and signed with a flourish, and then held it out to Martha. 'No, do not look like that! I had intended to send something to the Fund anyway, for who is there who has not been deeply upset by the news? Gideon has his own plans – I believe he sent a large sum yesterday to *The Times* – so you shall accept this from me. And you know, my love, it is just the sort of adventure I would have set out upon myself, had I had the opportunity—'

She sat very still for a moment, staring out of the window at the trees across the road in Hyde Park. 'I used to have so much more courage than I have now, Martha! When I recall – and now here I am with a lapful of children and house and the business – ah well!'

'I do not merely seek adventure, Abby!' Martha said, with a hint of reproof in her voice. 'It is not like that at all – it is more like a – a *call*, I do assure you! I cannot pretend to be one who has much of an evangelical nature, and have always been a little scathing of those who proclaim themselves Called in any way, but for me it feels quite strange, and indeed—'

She reddened then, and smiled. 'But of course, there *is* ad-

38

venture in it, is there not? I who have never been further from London than to Brighton for the sea bathing, to travel so far! I looked on the globe last night and it is a *very* long way to go. I positively shook in my shoes when I realized how far – but I shall go! And I thank you dearly for this money, Abby. I shall account to you for every penny, I do promise you, and—'

'Oh, pooh to that!' Abby said coolly. 'I have no doubt you will use it wisely. You will need food, I imagine, and warm clothes and some medical supplies – ah! – *that* is what we shall do! I shall speak tonight to Freddy and to Gideon, and see if we cannot supply you with medicines and so forth from the manufactory! Freddy, I am sure, will agree – he cares little enough about the business, in all conscience, though he owns a full half share. As to Gideon – well it depends a little, you know, on how much he sent to *The Times*. He is so practical a man when it comes to money—'

'Whatever you decide, you have done handsomely already, Abby.' Martha rose to her feet and kissed her sister warmly. 'And now I must go, for I wish to speak also to Phoebe and Oliver. Maria thinks they may wish to contribute to my plan, and if I do not hurry, they will be so busy with their lunchtime trade that I shall be very unpopular! Thank you again, my dearest, dearest Abby! I will let you know all that is to happen, I promise you – it is my plan, you know, to be gone before the month is out, if I can but arrange it. There is no time to be lost! Goodbye, my love—'

And Abby watched her hurrying down the stairs and then went away up to the nursery to her clamorous children, proud of herself for not being at all hurt because Martha had quite forgotten her promise to come up and see them. Well, perhaps a *little* hurt, she told herself, and then smiled. Perhaps, if the truth were known, she was more jealous than hurt. Happy – indeed, positively lyrical – as she was with her life with her dear husband and her admirable children and her most thriving and enjoyable occupation with the family business she had herself founded, there were times, a very few times, when it all seemed rather too comfortable, rather ordinary, rather, dare she say it, *dull*. To be as Martha was, afire with a plan to cross half the civilized world to perform so huge a task would be very stimulating, she thought, as she pushed open the nursery door. Very stimulating indeed.

CHAPTER FOUR

'WHY, Aunt Martha! How very delightful!' Oliver peered at her over the rims of his round spectacles and shook her hand up and down as vigorously as if it were the old pump handle in Broad Street. 'I cannot recall the last time you came here on a Saturday! Will you take luncheon with us? And see the show? It is a new departure for us, you know, to have a show on Saturday at noon as well as the evening, but we have found there is a demand for it. And we have never a table to spare! But there is our own table, of course, and you shall sit at it – do come along, aunt!'

He led her through the hubbub of the crowded tables, weaving past the outflung legs of the men who sat there smoking and drinking and eating great quantities of broiled mutton chops and Dover soles and beefsteak pies, and settled her at a table close by the side of the little stage that dominated the far end of the rooms.

She could barely remember how the original Celia Supper Rooms had looked, for she had visited them but once when her brother Jonah had been alive, but she knew that this new establishment, built laboriously on the ashes of the original building which had burned down on that dreadful night when Jonah had died, was a faithful copy of it. Oliver, a solemn and rather heavily built young man, had come back to London from York, where he had been working for his Aunt Abby and Uncle Gideon in one of their manufactories, and with all the determination of a man twice his age – for he had been not quite twenty-one years old at the time – had instructed builders and painters, carpenters and upholsterers to re-create it. And had succeeded in his aim, for with its red plush and gilt trimmings, its small but elegant stage and tiny orchestra pit, large enough to hold barely three musicians at a time, it was precisely as it had been when he had been a child.

Now, in his well-cut but rather dull business-like clothes and his incipient paunch he looked every inch the proprietor, as he bustled about settling his aunt at the table, clicking his fingers imperiously at his waiters and setting a glass of champagne before her (for this had always been the favourite drink of the Rooms) and she tried to see in him her brother, his father, and failed completely.

Jonah had been spare and elegant and quite absurdly charming, but she could see no hint of him in this serious young face, with its mutton chop whiskers and somewhat portentous expression. And she pretended to sip her champagne, not wishing to seem to reject her nephew's hospitality but not needing its bubbles to add to the tension within her, and then smiled up at him.

'Oliver, my dear, I know you are busy, but this is a matter of great importance! Can you speak to me for just a little while and—?'

Above her there was a sudden flurry of fabric as the curtains swished and lifted, and the men at every table burst into a great roar of approval, and Martha, startled, looked up and saw the figure of a tall man, dressed somewhat incongruously at this time of day in full evening clothes, sweating heavily under the glare of light that poured on his face from the footlights at his feet, and the floodlights on each side, and mopping his brow with a large white handkerchief.

'Gentlemen, gentlemen!' he roared. 'Gen-tel-men, it is time at last for the real sustenance of the day! Good as are your vittles, fine as is your wine, nothing can be as nourishing to the spirit or the heart or the mind as the fare the Celia Rooms has to offer you now! Gen-tel-men, I bring you, and demand that you should welcome as you should, the one and only, the delectable, the en-tire-ly perfect, Lady of the House – your own, your very own – Miss – Phoebe!'

There was a renewed shout from the audience, and then the

lights changed as waiters darted to the gaslights on the wall, and pulled the little chains to dim them and the Rooms sank into a low buzz as every person there concentrated his attention on the stage, now looking like a little box ablaze with glitter.

The fiddler and the pianist and the flautist in the little pit began a sprightly tune, and on to the middle of the stage stepped Phoebe, and Martha, watching her, marvelled yet again at the look of her. That Oliver, dear, sensible but undeniably stolid and dreary Oliver should have a sister so pretty and delicate and charming with her dark curly hair and her huge grey eyes never ceased to amaze her.

The really surprising thing, of course, she reminded herself, was more Oliver's plainness than Phoebe's charm, for both their parents had been handsome enough, heaven knew. Jonah, with his romantic lock of dark hair flopping over his wide white brow, his green eyes, so like his father's, and his long limbs. And his wife, Celia. Martha had hardly known her, had indeed seen her but twice in all her short life, but she had been a handsome enough creature, she remembered, with her dark coarse curls and her grey eyes, so like her daughter's.

It was the thought of Celia that pulled her back to the present. Celia, whose sister Lydia now queened it at the Haymarket and dared to lecture others on their political and patriotic duty. The memory of Lydia's behaviour yesterday came boiling up in her again, and she shook her head against it, trying to concentrate on Phoebe, who was now singing in a pretty soprano voice an agreeable song about a girl in a garden, much to the delight of the listening men.

It was indeed a charming performance, and although Martha felt privately that Phoebe's voice was far from being as perfect as it might be, she recognized that the combination of its sweetness with the pretty face, the delightful figure and a certain special quality that made it seem that she was singing for every individual in the place, and for him alone, added up to a beguiling whole. She fully earned the great roar of applause that broke out when she reached the end of her song, and the demands for more that followed her attempts to leave the stage.

By the time she had sung three more songs, each as innocuous and pretty as the last – not for Phoebe the sometimes improper and even raucous songs that were so popular in the new music halls, like the Surrey and the Canterbury – Martha was getting restless. There was so much to do, so much to arrange, and to sit here beside Oliver, nodding happily to his sister's rhythm, when she was aching to talk to them of her own plans, was difficult.

But at last the audience let Phoebe go, and the little stage disappeared behind its befringed red velvet curtains, and Phoebe came out, with a neat and sober shawl covering the lemon coloured gown she had worn on the stage, to join her brother and her aunt. And at last Martha could tell them of her errand.

They listened as carefully as Abby had, but without, Martha realized very quickly, her ready sympathy, and when she had finished, Phoebe sat silently staring down at her clasped hands on the table, leaving it to Oliver to do the talking.

'My dear aunt, I cannot think what my grandfather is about to allow such a plan!' he said very seriously after a long pause, pushing his glasses back on his nose, and staring at her most earnestly. 'It will be very dangerous, will it not? And also, not quite, well, you know, not quite the place for a lady like yourself!'

'Oh, Oliver, my dear young man, you really are being very tedious!' Martha was nettled and did not mind showing it. 'I do not believe it is necessary for one so young, however, successful a man he may be at his business, to lecture a relation almost old enough to be his mother! You must understand, my dear boy, that I do not seek any person's consent! I seek funds for my expedition and Maria was of the opinion that you two here are doing so well that you could be prevailed upon to contribute. However—' She began to gather her mittens and her reticule together, her colour rather heightened in her cheeks. '—If you feel unable to share my concern for these poor wretches, there is no more to be said– '

44

'Oh, Aunt Martha, I think it is a most splendid plan!'
Phoebe leaned forwards and set her hands over her aunt's.
'You must take no notice at all of Oliver. He is being tiresome –
yes, you are, Noll, and I will not have it! This is as much my
concern as yours and I believe what Aunt Martha is doing is
perfectly splendid! We shall help! Indeed we shall, and you
shall stop being so—'

'Oh, as to that, you must do as you please, of course!' Oliver
said huffily. 'I sought only to make the points any sensible man
would when faced with so – well, I will say no more! As to
funds – my dear aunt, we *cannot* help. No, Phoebe, we cannot!
We do not have it. It has taken me the best part of three years
to clear the mortgage that we had to carry to rebuild, and we
are now clear of debt – but that does not mean we are entirely
beforehand with the world! I am content that we are as successful as we are, but I tell you frankly it will be two years at
least at the present rate before I have any money to give away
to crackbrained – to charitable schemes such as this. You must
forgive me, Aunt. It cannot be done.'

There was a short silence and then Martha managed a smile
and leaned forwards and patted Oliver's hand. 'And you must
forgive me for being so sharp with you, my dear boy. I am sure
you meant well, and indeed your grandfather spoke just as you
did! Your good sense does you credit. I am sorry to have distressed you with my mendicancy, but it had to be – and do not
fret. I have no doubt I shall manage to find more.'

'Aunt Martha, I have a capital notion!' Phoebe clapped her
hands suddenly. 'If we have not the money, we know many
who have! All the friends of Uncle Gideon, you know, who are
so rich, and many of the City men who come here so regularly – what we need is a Ball! A subscription Ball! I shall plan
it, and they shall all come and pay handsomely for the privilege. Why, if I cannot manage to raise five hundred pounds for
you, my name is not Phoebe Lackland! You see? That is where
the money is, and we shall get it for you! A Ball – oh, I do love
a Ball! Give me a few days, Aunt, just a little time, and you will
see what we can do!'

It had taken all the courage Martha had to go to the Lamb and Flag. It lay deep in the alleyways beyond Seven Dials, tucked away in Rose Street between Long Acre and Floral Street, leaning over filthy gutters and reeking puddles that totally belied the prettiness of the names that were scrawled on the greasy dingy bricks at the entry to each street. She had picked her way there from the Celia Rooms in King Street, a short enough distance in yards, but seeming to go from one world to another. King Street in Covent Garden was far from being a fashionable thoroughfare but it was respectable enough, with its neat houses and shops, and no lady need be ashamed to be seen in it; but Floral Street was quite other, for here the gutter sluts and the drunken costermongers and the beggars and the pickpockets had their homes in greasy cellars and rickety rat-infested attics, and here the decent citizens of London never dreamed to go.

For a few moments Martha had indeed hesitated before plunging into those stinking alleys, but then, with her customary good sense, she had straightened her shoulders, and set her chin firmly and told herself that she was no flibberty miss, likely to be set upon for her good looks, nor was she an obviously rich female likely to be robbed. They would see her for what she was, one of the steadily growing band of charity workers who sought to relieve the miseries of gutter life with a few judicious tracts and occasional gifts of creature comforts. And in she went, and at last stood at the doorway of the old public house, peering into its smoky and dimly lit depths.

It was late now, for the afternoon and evening had dwindled away in Phoebe's eager talk of her ball, as Martha's initial doubts had been swept away in the rush of Phoebe's enthusiasm. It had rankled with Martha at first, this notion of using her plan as an excuse for a party, this idea of tickets being sold and women being decked in frills and flounces to go and dance and drink champagne and eat ices, ostensibly for the welfare of the sick and needy. She had said so, roundly, and told Phoebe she would have no part in such a scheme, but Phoebe had explained and cajoled and finally persuaded her.

'It is all very well to ask people to open their purses, dear

Aunt Martha,' she had said earnestly, with all the wisdom of her twenty-one years, 'just for the good of it. But they will not – because people are greedy and want something for their money. Well, this way they can *have* something for their money, and provide for you as well. We shall ask them two guineas for their tickets – yes, we shall, and they will pay it! You will see – and give them good music and dancing and supper and the company of other rich people, which they will like above all things, and they will be happy to give more when they are there. You will see – I am right, I know I am! I have learned much about people and what they feel about money since I came to work here with Oliver in our Rooms. I am determined upon it, Aunt, indeed I am! I wish myself to give some aid to these poor soldiers – yes, and their wives, of course, I do understand – I wish to give, but if Noll says we have no money to give – then all I can do is this! And I shall do it well, I promise you.'

Despite her ready and most explicit explanations and as-surances, however, it had taken some time to persuade Martha of the rightness of the plan, and even longer, once she had been persuaded, to discuss the finer details, such as where and when and who and how. And now it was past seven in the evening, and dark in the streets and she was very tired as she stood there in the doorway of the 'Lamb and Flag' looking about her for Sal, and feeling very frightened inside.

What am I doing here? she thought suddenly. I ought to be at home taking a bath in my own comfortable room and put-ting on my clean warm nightrobe and eating bread and milk from a tray and going to bed. I am tired and I want to go to bed—

And if you feel like that now, after one short day of effort, here in your own city of London, how will you be in Scutari, you weak-kneed creature? she apostrophized herself sternly, and shook her shoulders slightly, and stepped forwards out of the doorway's shadow and into the crowded room beyond.

It was a dirty place she saw as she looked about her, with streaming greasy walls and a sawdust strewn floor, and the reek of ale lees and heavy gin and cheap shag tobacco was so strong that for a moment her throat tightened and she was afraid she was going to retch. But then gradually she realized that the place did have a certain comfort of its own.

Against one wall an open fire burned brightly, and a dirty boy, dressed in the minimum of rags and with his bare feet curling against the cold stone floor, was crouched beside it roasting chestnuts in the embers. At long wooden tables men were sitting with heavy tankards in front of them, and a few women, very garish in red and yellow and magenta and green frills, sat among them, their shrieking and giggling and chattering making a shrill counterpoint to the bass sounds of the men's voices.

The sound went on undiminished for a moment, and then someone saw her there hesitating in the doorway, and stood up and stared at her and gradually the talk stopped and she felt herself redden as all eyes were turned upon her.

'Well, bugger me, but you're a right one an' all!' Martha peered further into the dimly lit room, seeking the source of the familiar voice, and at last saw Sal and was so grateful to have found her that she moved forwards impulsively, quite unperturbed by the fact that Sal was leaning back against the brawny chest of a heavily bearded man, his arms round her and with one huge hand tucked negligently inside the bodice of her gown.

'I never reckoned you'd 'ave the brass neck to come round 'ere – an' that's a fact!' Sal went on and suddenly roared her great laugh. ' 'ere, this is a right good 'un, fellers – a real mate o' mine, an' no error! Miss Martha Lackland, she is, as give me dinner last night, an' says as 'ow she wanted to talk to me about this an' that, an' I said as I'd be 'ere today an' 'ere she is! You got to give 'er top marks for cheek, ain't you?'

'Not so bloody funny, Sal,' the man holding her said, and his voice was so deep it was like a growl. 'Wot yer thinkin' of, bringin' yer stinkin' nobs dahn 'ere? 'Oo wants the likes o' this in their own 'ome, fer Christ's sake? This is me 'ome, and I don't fancy 'avin' no fancy milk an' water madams comin' 'ere disturbin' o' me peace—'

'Oh, stow it,' Sal said, and sat up, thrusting at his arms with

48

her elbows, but he held on more tightly, and with one swift turn of her head she bit his wrist, so that he swore hugely and snatched his hand out of her bodice, and again she laughed her great laugh.

'Keep yer bloody grousin' to yerself! If this is yer 'ome, then it's mine an' all, an' I asked 'er 'ere, an' if you don' like it, you can do the other thing! She's me mate, an' none of you lays a word nor 'and on 'er, do you 'ear me? None of you—' And she glared round ferociously at the others, sitting sullen and silent around the long tables. 'Do you 'ear me?' she said again, louder now and with a threatening note in her voice, and Martha suddenly realized that Sal was more than half drunk. '*None* of you—'

'Oh, keep yer 'air on,' one of the men said sourly. 'Lookin' at 'er, I'd say only a blind man or a daft one'd even *want* to lay an 'and on 'er, let alone anyfing else—' And now they all laughed, and one of them banged the table and began to sing a song so bawdy and so explicit that Martha felt her face flame. But she suddenly felt safer as she realized that the very real tension her appearance had created in this narrow stinking room had been lifted.

'Well, Miss Martha Lackland, what does yer want wiv me?'

Sal was standing up now, her hands on her hips, and her elbows thrust insolently wide. She held her head well back, and stood with her feet far apart, clearly needing this posture to maintain her balance, but she looked magnificent standing there with her head outlined against the smoky light from the penny dips set on the shelf behind her, and her hair gleaming richly round her flushed face. 'I was glad to make an appointment wiv yer, but me time's precious, an' I can't give yer more'n a few moments.'

Her grandiloquent tones silenced the other occupants of the tables, and then she winked and laughed again, and two or three of them raised their tankards to her, and drank noisily and everyone laughed, and Martha felt the wave of good humour reach out to engulf her too, and relaxed, letting her shoulders sag a little, and leaning against the table beside which she was now standing.

'Then I won't waste any time,' she said crisply, and her voice sounded loud and surprisingly confident in her own ears. 'Is there anywhere we can talk quietly?'

Sal blinked at her, and then grinned and shook her head. 'There's no secrets between me an' me mates,' she said still speaking with great grandeur, and sweeping out one arm in an all-embracing gesture. 'What you got to say to me, you says to them. So out wiv it! Come to offer all of us a fancy dinner, 'ave you? We'll 'ave beef an' oyster pie, then, and a bit o'—'

'No, I have not!' Martha almost had to shout to make herself heard above the laughter. 'Not directly, that is. And not to everyone. Just to you. If you insist on my saying it here in front of all, then I shall. I have come to offer you employment. Regular food and regular money. But a very irregular task—'

At once the room became silent again, as both men and women turned their heads to stare at Sal. Regular food and regular money? For all of them that was something as absurd to contemplate, as ridiculous to hope for, as a regular ride to the moon and back.

Sal was still standing in that defiant pose, still looking magnificent, but now there was some menace in her as she bent her head to tuck her chin into her neck and stare at Martha from beneath frowning brows.

'I told you – I told you las' night! I ain't no servant nor never goin' to be! That'll do for the sort of traitors as likes to turn their backs on their own sort an' go snivellin' to the nobs, just so's they can get their feet under their tables, but it ain't for me. I 'ad my share o' skivvyin' for the likes o' you when I was a nipper – I ad 'em treatin' me like I wasn't a 'uman bein', just because I wasn't one o' their fancy mincing namby-pamby – oh no, Miss Martha Lackland, don't you come 'ere offerin' me the chance to lie down an' be yer bloody doormat an' get trod on and wiped into a rag! I'll beg an' steal me vittles decent, like I was born to do – I wasn't born to be dogsbody to the likes o' you—'

A few people produced a ragged cheer, but it was half-hearted, and as the sound faded away Sal lifted her chin again and turned her head and stared down at the table with a look of total disdain on her face.

'Yes – you lot! You talk fancy enough about revolution, an' 'ow we ought to do 'ere what they once did over in France, but not one of yer's got the guts to do aught about it! Well, if any of you wants 'er stinkin' money and grub in exchange for sellin' yer stinkin' mean little souls, then yer welcome, an' may you rot in 'ell—'

Martha lifted her own chin then. 'I am not seeking to make a servant of you, Sal,' she said evenly. 'Since I now know that you regard that as a somewhat dishonourable station – though for the life of me I cannot see why – then I do not offer you such. What I ask of you is your companionship on a hazardous journey, and your guidance on how to do the task I have set myself. You have knowledge I lack, and I need you. If anything, I will serve *you* – and your friends. I see no shame in service, but – well, there it is. I tell you I *need* you, for I am setting out to go to Scutari to look after the women and children you told me are there, and who have need of care. If you will not serve them, then indeed I have nothing to offer you. But if you will, if you care as much as I believed you cared when you spoke of them to me last night, then you will come with me to Scutari, and help me to set up some kitchens there and feed them, and help me to take medicines there and nurse them. I am hoping to have enough funds to feed and pay you as well. Will you help me? And the women and children you told me of last night?'

There was a long silence and she stood there, never taking her eyes from Sal's face, yet feeling every other person's staring eyes on her. It was as though she were suddenly two people, with one small part of herself standing aside looking at her, looking at Sal, and at all the people looking at both of them, looking at the little boy crouched by the fire, still roasting his chestnuts, but staring at the two women with as fixed a gaze as anyone else there.

And then, suddenly, the spell was broken as the big man

upon whose chest Sal had been lying when Martha came in threw back his head and produced a guffaw of laughter that made Martha almost shrink back, so loud was it.

'Sal? Bleedin' Sal Connors, comin' the charity queen an' goin' back *there*? Oh, that's ripe, that is! That's rich, that is! That's the biggest laugh I've 'ad since the bloody cat died an' its muvver ate it fer 'er dinner. Sal – oh, Gawd –'

'Shut up, you!' Sal whirled and sweeping her arm back hit out with all the power she had in her, and her hand connected with the big man's face so hard that his head snapped back with a sickening jerk, and he sat there dazed and staring at her with the red weals left by her fingers slowly appearing on his cheek.

'What's so funny, eh? What's so bloody funny? I told you lot, I've told you all till I'm bloody blue in the face – I don't go into no rich man's ken except to get what I can, and pick up what's available. I don't work as a skivvy for no one – but that don't mean I don't care for me own people an' – an' wot 'appens to 'em – an' if that's charity, then yes, I'm a bleedin' charity queen!'

She whirled back then and glared at Martha. 'I'll do it. By Christ an' 'is 'oly Mother, I'll do it! There's a lot that's got to be done out there, and no error, an' if you're willin' to take on the job, then you'll need me and that's the truth of it. So I'll do it, if I die o' the stinkin' cholera meself – you 'ear me? I'll bleedin' do it!'

And staring back at her, Martha knew that much of the bravado, much of the passion in her voice, much of the blazing rage that showed in every line of her face was born of drink. She knew that Sal had accepted not because of cool thought but because she had been swept by a mixture of complex emotion she hardly understood herself – pity and anger and hope and fear – and because she wanted to show her friends sitting there around her in their rags and dirt, with only drink to comfort them against the harsh realities of their dreadful lives, that she had strength and ability and a will of her own, even if they did not. She knew as sure as she stood there that next morning Sal would bitterly regret her promise, that she would be sick with sullen anger at herself. But she also knew, just as well as she knew that she herself would be going to Scutari, that Sal would not go back on her word. She would go, no matter what happened. Martha had her ally.

CHAPTER FIVE

FREDDY was standing with his back to the wall, half hidden by the portières and with his face in shadow, watching Phoebe.

Watching Phoebe was still his favourite occupation, as it had been ever since she had first erupted into his life, a thin huge-eyed seven-year-old coming to live with her dear aunt Abby and her funny, kind cousin Frederick at Stanhope Gate all those years ago. She had dazzled and bewildered him then, and she still did, and now as he watched her go skimming about the big ballroom with the many flounces of her crinoline in her favourite shade of yellow dipping and billowing about her slender ankles, he ached a little.

It should not still hurt, he thought, with a moment of asperity. It is three years since it all happened, three years since she became inaccessible to me, three years since I had to face the fact that I am to live and die a sour bachelor; for he knew as sure as he knew he breathed that he would never marry anyone but Phoebe. And Phoebe he could not marry. But even so, the hurt should have abated by now.

And then he smiled wryly into the shadows. It *had* abated, were he to tell the truth. What had been agonizing in 1851 was now, in 1854, an almost agreeable melancholy. They met often either at his mother's house, or at the Supper Rooms where he was a frequent visitor, having struck up a close if apparently incongruous friendship with Oliver, who for all his humour-lessness had an underlying dry good sense which appealed to a similar streak in Freddy's nature. They sat together, he and Phoebe, and talked together and laughed together; but they never spoke together of the dreadful happenings of that

Spring of the year of the Great Exhibition, of what had happened to Phoebe, and how Freddy had helped her. There had been a tacit agreement that all that was secret, never to be revealed to anyone, never under any circumstances to be alluded to in any way. And so it had been. But refusing to talk of it was not the same as refusing to think about it, and Freddy often did.

He would lie in his handsome bedroom in his mother's house, or in the narrow sparsely furnished cell provided for him at the hospital, watching the moonlight trace its journey across the ceiling and asking himself *why*? Why could he not come to terms with what had happened? She had been young, she had known no better, she had been sadly abused by one who was cynical, selfish, and fit only to be horse-whipped. Why should such a thing be allowed to ruin his life? Why could he not still ask her to wed him, and be happy with her, sharing a home in one of London's splendid new squares, setting up their nursery—

At which point he would roll over in bed and bury his head in his pillow, telling himself it was time he sought sleep, for he had work to be done on the morrow. He could never get beyond that point in his thoughts, and in a strange but self-protective way, he did not want to.

Now, standing in this glittering ballroom waiting for other guests to arrive, he watched Phoebe and enjoyed the sight of her and was content. He would not think of anything, past or to come. He would consider only the present, and an agreeable enough present it was. He had enjoyed an interesting day at the hospital, working on as tricky an amputation as any he had ever performed, and seeing many fascinating outpatients with his grandfather, and tomorrow he was to attempt a most delicate blood transfusion, using a calf, in concert with his friend and mentor, John Snow, who despite his fame now he had become a giver of chloroform to the Queen herself, still enjoyed as much as he ever had a new piece of medical work. He shared Freddy's special interest in the possible value of blood when given to an exsanguinated patient, and though they had never yet succeeded in making a successful cross from animal to man, they had high hopes. So tomorrow would be a most interesting day. And tonight – tonight there was a Ball, and the chance to dance with Phoebe. He could ask for little more.

Across the ballroom the orchestra stopped its desultory scraping of fiddles and twiddling of woodwinds and sprang into a sprightly waltz, sending strains of Strauss swaying across the wide polished wooden floor and among the silk hangings and the brilliant gaslight, and Freddy straightened up, and tugged his white silk waistcoat more neatly across his chest, and tweaked his white neckcloth more firmly into position. People were beginning to arrive and if he did not speak now to Phoebe every dance would be booked.

He moved across the ballroom with a smooth even step, his head up and his shoulders squared, and the people who were drifting in looked with approval at his broad back and his well brushed red hair, the mothers of as yet unmarried daughters showing a particular interest. The grandson of the well known Mr. Abel Lackland was not to be sneezed at, especially as he was also the stepson of the rich Mr. Gideon Henriques, and known to be a sizeable shareholder in the family business of Caspar the Apothecary. But he ignored them all and made his way purposefully to Phoebe's side.

She was standing talking earnestly to a servant in the livery that had been fashionable half a century earlier – for it was considered smart this year to be a little antiquated in some of one's modes – and she smiled brilliantly at Freddy as he came up and the footman went importantly away.

'Oh, Freddy, I am so nervous, and yet so pleased with myself! Do you know, it was but last *Saturday* that this Ball was planned? I have arranged tableaux and the like in a couple of weeks, in the past, but I have quite surpassed myself this time! Of course, I cannot deny it was quite easy to gain subscribers – I had but to say we were raising money to send comforts and help out to the Crimea, and people were positively falling over themselves. I was oversubscribed by Monday! Is it not remarkably clever of me?'

'Remarkably,' Freddy said dryly. 'They should run a war regularly for you, my dear, so that people will go on being so eager to come to your Balls!'

She frowned sharply. 'That is unworthy of you, Freddy. You know perfectly well—'

'Oh, I am sorry! I meant it but as a joke, you know! But you are right. It is a far from funny one.' Freddy was all contrition. 'Forgive me! I did but mean to rally you! You have indeed done well, and Aunt Martha, I am sure, will have cause to be grateful to you. As, of course, will the soldiers—'

'The soldiers?' Phoebe said, and then shook her head. 'But did I not tell you? That it is—'

'Phoebe – my dear child, you look ravishing! As always! Give me a kiss, you dear creature, and tell me *all* your news—'

Freddy's brows snapped together, and his face hardened, if so agreeable and sandy-freckled a face could ever be said to be hard. But he did dislike this woman so heartily and even more disliked her companion, now standing there just a pace behind her, with a slightly sneering smile on his too handsome face which made Freddy, usually so peaceable a person, want to hit him.

His clothes, that bit more flamboyant than anyone else's – the silk facings to his evening coat were in dark blue, a positively French sort of style that would make any respectable Englishman's lips curl in disgust – the set of his shapely dark head, the glitter of his absurdly blue eyes, were all repellent in the extreme to Freddy. He did not know for sure, would never know for sure, whether this man had been the cause of Phoebe's troubles that Spring of 1851, and in the absence of any real proof, what could Freddy do? Especially when Phoebe herself treated him as she did. She was closely attached to her Aunt Lydia, enjoying her theatricality and her splendour with an unabashed delight that was very pretty to see, and which greatly endeared her to Lydia herself, who took all the admiration she could get and never tired of it. And, apparently, extended her cordiality to her aunt's husband, although being considerably more reserved with him than she was with her

57

other uncle by marriage – Gideon. But she was courteous to him, and he, it must be admitted, to her, which made it even more difficult for Freddy to judge what might have happened between them three years ago. On their present showing, it was nothing, but all the same, Freddy distrusted the man profoundly, although he had no apparent reason to hate Dickon O'Hare as much as he did. But that made no difference. He loathed the man and always would.

Lydia was still chattering to her niece, fully aware of the stares of the many people now arriving – for the Ball had been promised to start at nine o'clock, and now, at a quarter before ten o'clock, it was fashionably late enough for anyone – but appearing to ignore them. It was a skilful performance, and Freddy, for all his dislike of the performer, had to admit it. He stood there, listening to her prattle on about her new play, and how dreadful the war was, was it not? and the Poor Dear Soldiers, and how Silas, her dear little boy on whom she doted, positively doted, although barely ten months old had fully three teeth and was quite the handsomest child in the world and had Phoebe heard that Dear Sir Robert had already sent a large sum of money out to that dreadful Crimea? and how splendid he was, and how grateful to Lydia for her Benefit night given only last evening for his Fund and how much had been raised and on and on and on and on.

Dickon caught his eye above the two women's heads, and bowed slightly and almost insultingly, and then stepped sideways, and almost as though he could read his mind Freddy knew what he was about to do and was before him. He slid his own hand into Phoebe's elbow and said loudly, 'My dear – my dance, I think—' and before she could answer, had swept her into the galop which the orchestra had just started. And since Phoebe dearly loved a gallop, she let him, throwing a vivid smile over her shoulder at Lydia and Dickon, while Freddy in his turn stared challengingly at the older man, and allowed himself the luxury of a slightly lifted upper lip. Damned mountebank! he thought, and then gave himself up to the pleasures of the dance, for Phoebe was as light on her feet as a child, and as full of rhythm. The present is what matters,

he reminded himself, and I shall enjoy it, no matter what.
Indeed I shall—

Abby, watching them from across the big room, sighed a
little. To see her dear Freddy settled happily in matrimony
would be so agreeable, she thought, and would make all the
family so happy. Not that he wasn't the dearest and most sensible of boys already, but marriage would undoubtedly steady
him even more. There was an occasional hint of recklessness
about him that, while she understood it and even at a deep level
applauded it, did worry her.

He would hurl himself into some activity in a way that was
positively dangerous, limping home from horseback riding in
the Park, or returning bruised and bloody from a furious ses-
sion at one of the boxing parlours that the young men of
Nellie's enjoyed frequenting, and she would shake her head
over him and scold him, as any mother would, and secretly
wish he could find a nice girl who would share with her the
responsibility for his welfare and happiness.

But then she would catch the bleak look in his eye when
Phoebe's name was mentioned, and she knew she hoped use-
lessly. He was quite ensnared by his pretty cousin and what
could even the most loving of mothers do about that? So there
were times, like now, when she looked at her niece with a hint
of anger deep in her eyes, much as she loved the girl – for
hadn't she had the rearing of her from her earliest childhood? –
and much as she knew that mother or no, she had no right to
involve herself with these young people's private feelings. Or
doings. Much had happened to her niece three years ago – and
her eyes slid across the crowds towards Dickon and Lydia
O'Hare – and Freddy had been involved. But it was none of
her affair. She should not even think about it—

Behind her Gideon stirred and sighed sharply. 'How long
need we stay, my dear? I feel, you know, that we have done
more than enough for Phoebe's plans! Half the people here
subscribed because I insisted they should, and I bought and
distributed more tickets than anyone else, I believe! So can we
not perhaps now go home? I am very tired, and there is much to

do tomorrow, you know. These junketings in the middle of the week are far from being wise, I feel—'

'You know perfectly well that time is the problem, Gideon,' Abby said and smiled up at him, patting his hand as it rested on her shoulder. 'Martha wishes to go as soon as it is possible, and money she must have. I think Phoebe has done remarkably well in organizing this so rapidly. All the food came from the Supper Rooms, you know – that is Oliver's contribution – and I do feel we must stay a little longer to encourage them. It would never do to have the evening end too precipitously – and if you depart early, why, many of your City friends are likely to follow suit! Go and dance, my dear. That will entertain you! No, I will not dance this next pair – I find the Viennese waltz rather too exhausting if the truth be known! But you go – look, there is Lydia Mohun – O'Hare I suppose I should say – and I have no doubt *she* will be glad to stand up with you!'

Gideon smiled down at her a little crookedly. 'With the dreadful Lydia? My dear Abby, I recall a time when you were far from content because you thought I had gone walking with Madam Lydia! Yet now you urge me to take her in my arms in a waltz! Are you so careless of my welfare now that you are prepared to throw me to such a she-wolf?'

She reddened and then laughed. 'That is not fair! I was younger then, and foolish – and besides, Sarah was ill at the time and – oh, you are too much of a tease! I care not if you dance or not, to tell the truth! It was you who were complaining of being bored, after all—'

He bent and kissed the top of her head fleetingly. 'Oh, I am not bored, precisely! But perhaps I will be polite and take a turn or two with the lady. Before we go down to supper—' And he straightened his neckcloth and moved across the shining wooden expanse of the ballroom floor towards the little group of which Lydia was the coruscating centre. It was agreeable indeed when one's wife positively advised one to dance with pretty actresses. He would have to be quite foolish not to accept such advice. Quite foolish!

'Really, Miss Lackland, this is a most splendid occasion!

Your niece is to be congratulated on managing to organize it so well, and with such dispatch, and she so young! Today's young people are indeed a remarkable breed, are they not? I hear that many of the young officers on the way to Sevastopol are but children – I am told of boys of barely twenty going out. One's heart bleeds for them, indeed it does!'

The booming voice of the old merchant went on and on, and Martha, who already had a slight headache from the heat, the lights, and the insistent sound and rhythm of the orchestra, did her best to smile and look interested. He was rich, this boring old friend of Gideon's, and not to be offended, but she wished heartily, and not for the first time this week, that in her search for the funds that would enable her to go to Scutari she did not have to waste her time or her strength in talking to such people. But it had to be and she lifted her chin resolutely and tried to smile at the old man, who was now talking about the problems of supplying so large an army.

And caught the eye of a man standing just behind him, a man with so humorous a glint in his eye that involuntarily her own smile widened. He looked so relaxed and friendly, and so aware of her boredom with her companion that just looking at him made her feel better.

As though she had spoken, he moved forwards and slid himself neatly between her and her companion and bowed slightly.

'If I might intrude, ma'am? We have not met, I know, but your father is an old aquaintance I am proud to claim. My name is Laurence, ma'am. Alexander Laurence, at your service.' He turned then to the old man who was still talking, and with some adroitness cut into his monologue with a slight bow, and said smoothly, 'Good evening, Sir James. A splendid Ball, is it not? The organizer is indeed to be congratulated – I have no doubt it will raise a considerable sum for a very good cause—'

Martha studied him from beneath her lids, grateful to him for her rescue, and also very intrigued by him. He looked to be about five and forty, a stocky man, with a lined face that bespoke a spirit much given to laughter, and iron grey hair that clearly was very curly in its natural state, but which he kept cut brutally short; and although the style was far from fashionable it gave him a most interesting look, she felt. His mouth was wide and very mobile and his eyes a nondescript grey, but so full of warmth and humour and general goodwill that he looked almost handsome, even though his individual features were far from classic. Altogether she thought him a most attractive man, and was filled with curiosity about him.

Still adroit, he now led old Sir James to an adjoining group of people, introduced him to one of them, and then slipped back again, and now he stood beside her, smiling down at her, although he was barely two or three inches taller than she, and smiling a crooked smile that made his eyes almost disappear into the lines around them.

'I trust I did not act out of turn, and separate you from a conversation you found interesting, Miss Lackland, but I detected signs of distress, shall we say, and being a medical man, felt you had need of care.'

'Oh, indeed, I am most grateful to you, Dr. Laurence,' she said almost fervently. 'I am sure he is a most worthy gentleman, but to tell the truth he was being very tedious, and I have had so busy a day – well, I am grateful! You know my father, you say?'

'Oh, indeed, yes. I have known him for many years. I was one of his medical students when Queen Eleanor's was newly founded, you know, more years ago than I care to recall. He frightens me a little still, I may tell you, but I have a great regard for him.'

She looked at him curiously. 'So, you are a surgeon, Mr. Laurence? I had assumed, you know, when you said you were a medical man, that you were a physician.'

'Indeed? You surprise me! I imagine physicians always to be sleek well-fed fellows, you know, not rough and ready as I am! Mind you, your revered father looks more like a physican, in those terms, than a surgeon! Perhaps there is a message there for all of us – that we must not judge by appearances!'

Their talk went on, light, rallying and with very little real matter in it, but she was far from bored, as she usually was by such ballroom chatter, and indeed found it exhilarating. There was something about this man that she found very intriguing, and after a little while she managed to steer the conversation into more personal channels, wanting to know more about him. And discovered that he was a widower and had been so for many years – and she was a little startled to discover how that information pleased her – sharing his home with his only son, a schoolboy of fifteen.

The Supper Interval arrived almost to her surprise. She had been so sure that the evening would drag on interminably, for she so hated such entertainments, and to find herself being taken to eat Oliver's hams and vol-au-vents and ice puddings with a sensation of real enjoyment was very remarkable. Walking beside him down the wide stairs to the supper room, she found herself thinking, for the very first time, that there would be aspects of life at home in London that she would perhaps miss, once she had gone away to the war.

'I had heard something of the sort,' Abel said, and pushed his plate away from him with a slightly petulant movement. 'Heavens, how I hate eating such stuff at this hour of the night! As if one needed it after a perfectly good dinner at home! Yes, I had heard. Friend of Herbert's, ain't she?'

'Friend of everyone as far as I can tell! Got more influence among the powerful than any woman's any right to have, in my opinion! But there, you know what women are!' Chadwick gazed gloomily at his old friend. 'Especially charitably minded ones. Try to teach them anything of the Sanitary Idea and they get into a great lather of sensibility! As though talking of a man's bodily functions were something to be ashamed of! Mind you, I hear this woman is more sensible than most. She's a lady, mind you, but she's also a nurse. And—'

'A *lady*? And a nurse?' Abel stared and then laughed hugely. 'My dear Edwin, are you mad? Have you *seen* the nurses we have at Nellie's? And I'll tell you, they are among the best in any hospital in London – and they are all drunkards and dirty sluts, and wicked thieves into the bargain! If it were not for Nancy, who keeps them in close control with a will of iron and a tongue of sulphuric acid I dare not think of what straits we should be in! No *lady* among them, I promise you! Nor would any respectable family allow a lady to do such work—'

He was gloomy suddenly. 'Mind you, Edwin, I am having trouble with Martha on this very score! I cannot make her understand, however hard I try, that this is just not fitting for her, this plan she has! But I get no support, for Maria is in total agreement with her—' He stopped and frowned then. 'And m'grandson and granddaughter as well as Abby. It is too bad of them—'

'Well, I can only tell you she won't be the only lady out there – from all I've heard. This woman who is collecting a party together for Sidney Herbert and the War Office has been running that place in Harley Street – you know the one I mean? A home and hospital for sick governesses and the like. Genteel sort of place. Well, it was run by a committee and they appointed this woman and she turned it upside down in a matter o' weeks! Made it clean and efficient and saved money – oh, the committee were fairly turned on their ears about her! And now they've got to part with her so that she can turn the army in the Crimea on its ears.'

He laughed suddenly. 'Oh, but I'd like to be there when she starts! I hear she's a termagant, and I know these army doctors. They are beyond all – well, not the doctors precisely. but the Purchasers you know, and the Secretaries, the ones who run it. There *are* good doctors in the army – more than a few. But the way they have to work!' He shook his head. 'It would break your heart, Abel, and so I tell you.'

'Retirement is not good for you, Edwin – it makes you prolix. Keep to the point, man – this lady who is to go to the army – you say she is making up a party now?'

'So I'm told. And retired or not, I still have my contacts in the government. I have my contacts—'

Abel smacked his hand on the table sharply. 'By God, you have. And I shall use 'em! Yes, I shall, Edwin, for m'daughter. I'd be twice as happy as I am – indeed much more – if I but knew she was in good hands on this wretched expedition she is so set on. Give me a letter to this woman, for Martha, and we shall see her under her care. Much better than that she should

go alone with just that one servant she has taken on this week –
and she's a strange one, too – but that's another matter. Will
you do that for me?'

'Oh, gladly! I do not know her myself, you understand. She
is a friend of friends of mine, however, and I'll gladly write a
note. But tell your daughter to waste no time. I'm told she
plans to be gone this coming Saturday.'

'I shall tell her. What's the woman's name?'

'Nightingale – and a strange first name, in all conscience.
Airy-fairy sort o' parents she must have had to label her with
geography. She is called Florence. Miss Florence Nightingale.'

CHAPTER SIX

By twelve o'clock, when supper was over, and the dancing had resumed with a noisy Sir Roger de Coverley and gone on to an even livelier set of Lancers, Martha's hint of a headache had developed to a full blown megrim.

It had not perturbed her unduly during supper, while she talked animatedly with Mr. Laurence, but it did make itself felt afterwards, when he told her with what appeared to be a genuine regret that he must leave early, for he had promised his son that he would not be home late '—for I'm all the family the boy has, Miss Lackland, and for all that he is a hearty young man of approaching sixteen years, I cannot hide from you the fact that he is much given to worry if I do not keep my word regarding punctuality. I would not have you think him namby-pamby, you know, but with so many thieves about the streets – and I have a long journey to make, to Camberwell, where I have my house – he fears for my life if I do not appear at the very moment and hour I promised, so I always do. I have perhaps made a rod for my own back.'

She held out her hand to him in farewell. 'I think not, Mr. Laurence. I think you do yourself an injustice. You are a man of concern for the feelings of others, and if this is to make a rod for your own back – well, I believe it to be one a man may bear with the fortitude that comes from knowing he behaves well.'

He reddened slightly and shook her hand with some fervour. 'You are kind to comprehend so well, Miss Lackland. A father of a motherless boy does have problems, but few are the people who recognize them. Goodnight – and I will give myself the pleasure of calling upon you shortly.'

And he was gone, leaving her staring after him, and wondering why she had not told him that unless he called within the next few days, he would not find her. Because, a secret voice whispered deep inside her mind, because you like him, and to make a new friend now would make it too easy to change your mind about leaving London. Would it not?

It was then her headache obtruded itself upon her notice. She went upstairs to the retiring room and took some sal volatile, but with small success, and lay down on the chaise longue for a little while, hearing the distant thrum of the orchestra and the thin shrill voice of the caller crying the steps of a Quadrille, and trying not to think of the way Mr. Laurence's voice had burred so agreeably in its lower registers, and how Mr. Laurence's eyes had crinkled so amusingly, and of Mr. Laurence's attentiveness during supper. It was too stupid, at her age, to be set into such a flutter over a man. Absurd!

Phoebe came bursting into the retiring room in a rush of flounces and a wave of chypre, her ringlets bobbing and her eyes sparkling brilliantly with excitement. 'Oh, Aunt Martha, *there* you are! I have been seeking you everywhere, for we must make the announcement, you know, of the money we have raised and then tell all the people how it will be used, and you must be there for that – please, do come, dear aunt!'

'I?' Martha sat up, aghast. 'My dear child, you cannot possibly expect me to—'

'Of course you must! You cannot think the people who have come to give us all that money will be content without knowing what is to be done with it! Oh, Aunt Martha, come – you have worked with a charity for far too many years not to know that! People wish a return for their outlay, do they not?'

Sitting there looking at the red cheeks and the way the pretty and very rounded shoulders rose so delectably out of her décolletage, Martha felt her heart sink. Phoebe was right, of course. The greater the amount the givers gave, the more they demanded in return. She would indeed have to act the sacrificial lamb tonight, hateful though she found the rôle. She would have to set herself up as some sort of angelic creature, simply to satisfy these rich stay-at-homes— Oh, it was too bad! And she said so, loudly, as Phoebe helped her to replace the dancing pumps she had kicked off, and smoothed her hair for her and tidied her plum silk gown, which had become a little rumpled during her rest.

They went downstairs side by side, the plum skirt and the lemon bouncing gently at each step, and Freddy, waiting at the foot of the stairs and looking up at them thought what a foil for his pretty Phoebe his aunt was, with her neat round head and its rather severe style of dressing, and smiled and held out his arm.

'Freddy, you shall lead Aunt Martha in – and I shall tell the orchestra to play a little fanfare – now, wait for my signal!' And Phoebe went in through the pair of gold-coloured portière curtains, slipping among the dancers like a bird flying through branches.

'This is too bad, you know, Freddy!' Martha said softly into his ear. 'I feel quite stupid! I wish it did not matter – that people would just—'

The music stopped, and after a fraction of a second there was a rather ragged fanfare blown on trumpet and woodwind, and the dancers moved forwards to cluster round Phoebe, who had perched herself on one of the gilt chairs someone had obligingly dragged forwards, and which was now held on each side by a couple of admiring young men. From her place by the doorway Martha could see her clearly, and knew she was having a splendid time indeed.

'Ladies and Gentlemen!' Her voice came fluting, high and very sure of itself, over the heads of the watching dancers. 'Ladies and Gentlemen, we hope that you have enjoyed your dancing and supper, and we think you will like to know now how generous you have all been in your contributions tonight to this Charity Ball. We have been able to count all the money now, and the extra gifts so many of you have so kindly given to me as the evening has progressed, and if you wish to know the grand total – well, shall I tell you?'

She was holding her hands clasped together, as gleeful and as eager to impart the news as a child, and her audience warmed to her and applauded and several voices called out, 'Yes – tell us, tell us!' and one or two of the young men took it up as a chant, until several people were calling, 'Tell us, tell us, tell us!'

And Phoebe clapped her hands delightedly and then held them up for silence.

'Well, I *shall* tell you, and I know you will be as pleased as I am. It is fully seven hundred and twenty-three pounds – there! Is that not splendid?'

A spatter of applause went up, and again Phoebe waved her hands for attention. 'You have all been quite wonderful, and we do thank you for your good hearts, and your compassion and your patriotism – especially those of you who gave more than was asked—' and she bobbed a little curtsey in the direction of Sir James who harrumphed and grinned and blew out his white whiskers with gratification, and again the applause went up and people bowed and smiled at each other, some looking sideways at their neighbours trying to estimate how much they had given when they had dipped *their* hands into their pockets.

'—and now my dear, dear friends,' Phoebe was saying, 'you must hear from the lady who will be taking this money with her to the Crimea. She will tell you how it is to be spent and what she will be doing for all those poor souls. Ladies, and gentlemen, Miss Martha Lackland – come along, Aunt Martha!'

And with her heart in her dancing pumps, Martha came along, clinging to Freddy's arm and wishing to die. Whatever happened in Scutari, it could not be as disagreeable as this, and for one brief moment she thought of Alexander Laurence and wished most heartily that he was there to smile his crooked smile at her and laugh a little with his eyes and make her feel better.

But he wasn't, so as resolutely as she could she allowed herself to be led up to Phoebe's chair, and to be handed up on to it as Phoebe stepped down in a froth of creamy petticoats and a glimpse of long drawers. Standing there, swaying a little and looking at the upturned faces below her, she felt another surge of pain in her head, and wanted nothing more than to jump down and run from this ridiculous scene into which she had been led.

And then, across the room at the fringe of the crowd clustered about her, she saw Lydia Mohun. She was talking behind her fan to the man at her side, who glanced at Martha on her chair and then laughed, and Martha felt a new surge, but this time of anger.

That woman who had dared to lecture her about her patriotic duty, now daring to *laugh* at her? It was the outside of enough, and she drew herself up very straight and spoke very loudly.

'Ladies and gentlemen, I thank you very much indeed for all you have done to help me in my plans for an expedition to the Crimea. Like all of you, I was deeply distressed when I heard of the conditions there. It seemed to me quite shocking – it still does – that our people should suffer so, for want of care and comforts. As one with some experience of seeking funds for charitable purposes, a task which on a few occasions exposes one to the opprobrium and discourtesy of those who should know better—'

She lifted her chin at Lydia at the back of the room, but Lydia was paying no attention to her, still whispering to her companion behind her fan.

'—I realize better than any how hard my niece has worked to bring you all together and encourage you to share the burden of work that must be done. I would like also to tell you of the efforts of other members of my family – my sister and brother-in-law, Mr. and Mrs. Henriques have agreed to provide a large supply of necessary medicines for me to take with me, a most vital service, you will agree—'

A spatter of applause again filled the room, and Abby, standing only a few yards away from Lydia and her companion smiled with a hint of regality, while Gideon, at her side, reddened, which lifted his long sallow face into a greater warmth, and shook his head in disclaimer.

'And of course, the great help given by the Charity with which I have had the good fortune to have been associated for so long.'

She turned her head, looking through the crowd for the familiar faces and then saw them, Miss Garling and her 'young one' sitting tidily side by side at the far end of the ballroom.

'The Committee of the London Ladies' Society for the Rescue of the Profligate Poor, under the direction of Miss Carrie Garling, have agreed to provide me with a large supply of warm petticoats and drawers and shoes and gowns and cloaks, which of course will be much needed in the coming winter months, for the winters there in Turkey I believe can be very bitter—'

'Soldiers in *drawers*?' Old Sir James's voice came booming across the room, and she turned her head to look at him, puzzled.

'I beg your pardon, Sir James? What did you—'

'What's the good o' drawers and petticoats to *soldiers*, ma'am?' the old man said, and blew out his whiskers again and looked at her sternly. 'I'm the first to say m'thanks to what help is offered in charitable matters, but there's no sense in pretendin' that the gift of the Committee is much use, now, is there?'

'But of course it is of use – inestimable use!' Martha said indignantly. 'Those poor women are in the most dire need, in desperate straits—'

'Women?' Someone else spoke now, and the low buzz of chatter which had hitherto made a counterpoint to her speech now died away, as everyone paid very close attention to what was being said. 'I understood I bought my ticket for this Ball, aye, and paid a handsome sum into the Fund besides, for *soldiers'* comforts. What's all this about women?'

Martha frowned sharply, and turned to look down at Phoebe standing at her side, and the girl looked up, her face very red, and shrugged her shoulders slightly.

'I'm sorry, Aunt Martha,' she hissed, and Martha had to bend down to hear her. 'But I – well, I thought it better to let people believe they were buying their tickets in aid of the Army, you know. People can be so – well, they do not always understand—'

Slowly Martha straightened up, and looked about her at the upturned faces, and closed her eyes momentarily against the stab of pain from her headache, now thumping heavily in her temples.

'My niece perhaps did not explain fully,' she said carefully, opening her eyes. 'So I must. I can tell you all that I have discovered that in addition to the army out there in Crim Tartary, there are soldiers' wives and children and—'

'Camp followers!' Sir James bellowed. '*Camp* followers? Soldiers' doxies, by Gad. And I've paid my good money for such a thing? It's disgustin'! It's the soldiers this money is meant for, madam, not these gutter muslins! You have misled us sorely, madam, and—'

It started as a ground swell, moved in erratic waves across the crowd and then burst out into noise, as voices were raised in argument, one agreeing with Sir James, another with Martha, until they were all arguing furiously. And she stood there swaying a little with the stress of it all, and very aware of Phoebe in tears at her side.

'Now stop, do you hear? Stop it, all of you!'

The roar of Freddy's voice made her snap her eyes open, and she saw him come shouldering through the crowd, his face scarlet with rage and his usually neat hair almost standing on end, so rumpled was it. He pushed people out of the way, quite careless of whether it was lady or gentleman, which added to the fury of some of them, until he was at Martha's side. In one comprehensive gesture he held up one hand to help her down from her absurd posture on the chair, and used his other arm to gather in the almost distraught Phoebe and hold her tight.

'Be quiet, all of you!' he roared again, and now he was joined by others, as Gideon and then Oliver came pushing their way to the front of the mob.

Still the din of argument went on, and now people were becoming very heated, some even waving fists at each other, and Martha, raising her head from the protection of her nephew's arm caught a glimpse of Lydia through a gap in the press, and was suddenly hugely angry, for Lydia had her head thrown back and was laughing as though she had never seen anything so funny in her life, while her companion, looking a little sheepish, tried to persuade her to be a little more seemly.

72

It was Gideon who managed to bring them all under control again. He looked round at the red faces of his City acquaintances, all at the stage of the evening when the food and wine they had so enthusiastically absorbed earlier was beginning to sit uneasily in their corpulent stomachs, and knew unerringly how to stop the hubbub. His voice was not particularly loud, but it carried to the far ends of the big ballroom.

'Any person who feels his money has been taken from him for a cause for which he has no sympathy may have it returned. He can regard his evening's entertainment as having been at my expense, for I shall return every penny not given willingly. Please to attend on me at my counting house in Lombard Street in the morning, and all shall be settled. I think there is no more to say—'

The room slithered into a silence, and then Sir James snorted and said loudly, 'Well, do not think you can shame *me* into agreement. I still say it's disgustin' that any decent female should even consider such an action as to take money from respectable citizens for the relief of such trash as camp followers. I shall indeed be at your counting house first thing in the morning, Henriques, and I hope sincerely that many more will do the same!'

And he went stumping away to seize his cloak from a waiting footman — for the servants were gathered agog around the entrance to the ballroom, enjoying every moment of the spectacle of their betters in a brawl — and one or two guests making the same sort of noises of disapproval followed him.

But as Sir James reached the door he turned again, and glared at the little group of people standing there before the silent orchestra, and said loudly, 'As for the idea of a female of any decency actually goin' out there for such a purpose — well, the mind of any proper man must be disgusted! You must be out of your attic, Henriques, to allow such a thing! An unprotected woman, on such a—' Both Freddy and Oliver spoke together but it was Oliver's voice which was drowned out.

'She will not be alone!' Freddy shouted, his face red again. 'Do you think, sir, that my aunt has not members of her family

73

to care for her welfare? We care a great deal, sir, so much so that I shall accompany her on her expedition! I am a surgeon and can add my services to hers for the welfare of these camp followers, as you so sneeringly label 'em. I make no such nice distinctions, sir, as you do. Where there are sick people, suffering people, we in my family believe we have a part to play, and we play it. Whatever *your* part maybe, sir, I beg you to discharge it elsewhere, out of our sight, for we are heartily tired of your company! Good night to you!!'

And he turned his back insultingly, and bent his head over his aunt's, smiling down at her, and she shook her head and said breathlessly, 'No, Freddy You cannot! It is quite unnecessary – I do assure you. I understand your impulse, but really, it cannot be! You are needed at Nellie's, and anyway—'

The crowd was beginning to drift away, uneasily, some of them stopping for a few moments beside the family group to say their farewells and murmur their distress at the débâcle the evening had become, but they were all far too absorbed in their own feelings to pay much attention to anyone else.

And then Abby came pushing through them to stand in front of her son, her face white with anger and fear.

'Freddy! I trust you were speaking in some sort of – some sort of quixotic humour? If your aunt Martha chooses to follow her vocation to Scutari that is her affair, but I am sure she will not feel it necessary for you to do so, when you do not have the same – the same sense of mission, and when – oh, Freddy, do not go! You are too young, and—'

'Freddy!' Phoebe was staring at him now, pulling away from his protecting arm, and rubbing her tear-stained cheeks with one slightly trembling hand. 'Oh, Freddy! Do you mean it?'

Freddy looked round at all of them, his face now rather white as the flush of rage receded, and he smiled a little uncertainly. 'Well, I said so, did I not? And it is true, you know. It has concerned me somewhat ever since I first heard of the plan. Aunt Martha *does* need a protector, and who better than a surgeon who can be of use to her?'

'But, Freddy—' Phoebe began, and then shrank back a little as Abby, who up to now had not taken her eyes from Freddy's face, whirled on her, her eyes glittering. 'Oh, Phoebe, I do beg of you to stop bleating at him in such a missish manner! I daresay it is as much your fault as anyone's that Freddy is seized of this mad notion! If you were not so – so captious and absurd and – and – well, he would not be so bouleversé by such matters as this if you were – oh, Gideon! Take me home! At once!'

And they all stared as Abby, the usually calm and practical and eternally sensible Abby burst into tears and ran blindly to the door, Gideon behind her.

'Wait!' Freddy said breathlessly, and went after her, and they stood there framed in the golden portières, the slightly dumpy shape of Abby, with Gideon tall and spare on one side of her and Freddy firm and square on the other.

Martha stood white-faced and numb, watching them and trying to order her thoughts. Her head was aching so abominably, and she could not fully comprehend all that was happening. She could feel only the wash of emotion, her own as well as other people's swaying her, and she felt suddenly very sick as well as in pain, and had to concentrate very hard and breathe very deeply to prevent herself from casting up her accounts at everyone's feet. And thought, incongruously, of Mr. Laurence and how agreeable it would be to have his arm on which to cling.

At the door Freddy and Gideon turned with an almost comic precision and, with Abby between them rubbing at her reddened nose with her handkerchief and with her eyes rimmed, came back to the little knot of people standing below the orchestra dais.

'I am sorry, Phoebe,' Abby said stiffly, and bent her head to kiss her niece's cheek. 'I meant no harm, and spoke most unjustly. I was distressed you see, at the thought – well, I am sorry. What Freddy does is his own affair, of course, and I am sure he is man enough to make his own decisions for the best.'

She turned her head and looked up at her son beside her. 'I am sure he will think it all through *most* carefully and decide what is best for him and for his family and for his hospital duties as well—' and there was a small note of appeal in her voice and Freddy nodded, acknowledging it.

'What in God's name is going on here?' Abel was standing in the doorway, staring at them all and then came stomping across the floor, his head down so that he looked almost like a bull, and in spite of her distress, Martha smiled fleetingly. So like Papa to look like that, to come at this stage and demand explanations. So like Papa.

'I sit there in the supper room with a friend, minding my own business, and then hear all this fracas up here! What's afoot? Will no-one open his mouth to explain?'

In a few succinct sentences, Gideon told him and Abel stood there glowering at Freddy and then at Martha from beneath lowered brows.

'You see what you've done with all your nonsense about going to that damned place, miss? You see? I told you it was not fitting, but you would not listen! Will you have the wit *now* to say you were wrong, and stay at home and mind your business? Or are you determined to take your nephew to perdition with you?'

Martha glowered back at him, tucking in her own chin until she looked absurdly like him, but no one laughed, although the effect was ludicrous.

'No, I shall not stay at home! Go I must, and go I shall! I do not require Freddy's company, and so I tell him now. You mean well, Freddy, and I thank you for it, but it shall not be. You may not come!'

But Freddy was one of this family too, and could be as stubborn as any of them, and now his head too went into the characteristic bull-like stance and he said flatly, 'You cannot stop me. I shall go because I choose to. It is no affair of anyone's, not Mamma's nor Phoebe's nor Grandpapa's nor yours. Goddamn it, I am a man with a mind of my own! I shall do as I choose!'

And he turned on his heel and went stamping away and Phoebe burst into tears and turned to cling to the silent Oliver, and Abby took Gideon's arm and put out her other hand to touch her father's, now standing staring after his grandson with his eyes bleak and cold.

'Oh dear,' Gideon said softly. 'Oh dear! What a brouhaha. We shall all feel better in the morning, I have no doubt. Much better.'

CHAPTER SEVEN

IT was quite ridiculous how nervous she felt. She stood outside the tall handsome house in Belgrave Square staring up at
its façade as her hansom cab went jingling away, and for one
mad moment considered turning and going home to Gower
Street and telling Papa that she had spoken to the lady and,
finding her much wanting in every respect, had chosen to decline travelling with her.

But then she gave herself a little shake, and moved purposefully up the steps to the massive front door, and rang the
bell. What was there to be afraid of, after all? With the plans
she was making to travel such a distance, there would be far
greater hazards to face than asking a stranger if she could
creep under her wing.

Perhaps, she wondered briefly, I am nervous in case the lady
refuses me her company? Standing there waiting for an answer
to her summons, she pondered that but decided she could
acquit herself of that fear. 'I am going, no matter what,' she
whispered sturdily. 'Whether I have any other company than
Sal's or not—'

And that, of course, was what was worrying her. She
thought about Freddy, about his absurdly impulsive announcement that he would accompany her, and Abby's and her
father's reaction, and felt the tension rising in her again. All of
them all so upset, and all because of her. Why could she not
be like other ladies of uncertain age, and settle quietly at home
to her charitable good deeds and her needlework? Why did she
have this absurd need to travel half across the world to exist in
what was, from every responsible account, a world of mud and

disease and squalor unimaginable to those who lived in snug London? It was none of her business, this war in the Crimea. Why did she have to involve herself?

Because it *is* my business, she thought then, it is, it is. As soon as I heard of what is happening to those women there, I knew it was my affair. They are women like me, my sisters in so many ways. I must go, no matter what happens. Oh, please God, let it be possible for me to travel with this woman, whatever she is like, so that I can do what I must, and Freddy may remain at home and everyone be happy—

The big door opened to reveal a footman of such magnificence that she had to strain her neck to look up at him. His calves were vast, his livery grand to a degree and his expression one of such hauteur that it almost cowed her.

'Ah – Lady Herbert's house?'

The footman inclined his head.

'I understand that I may see Miss Nightingale here. I have a letter for her.'

The footman looked down his nose at the letter in her hand, and held out his salver for it.

'Please to enter, ma'am. Lady Herbert is not at 'ome, but the Ladies of the Selection Committee are awaiting h'applicants in the morning room. Miss Nightingale is with them.'

He stepped back a pace so that she could walk into the high cool hall, resplendent with marble busts on polished stands reflected in the highly buffed black and white marble tiles of the floor.

'Applicants?' she said, as she divested herself of her square cashmere shawl. 'I do not fully understand. I am not applying for anything but a meeting with Miss Nightingale.'

'Miss Nightingale, madam,' the footman said with unutterable scorn, 'is h'interviewing, together with Lady Canning and Lady Cranworth and their friends, women as is considered suitable for the party of nurses as is going h'out to the Crimea with Miss Nightingale. If you wish to speak to 'er, madam, you must wait your turn with the other h'applicants. Them is my h'express orders, madam, and I cannot change them even for a lady such as yourself. I am sorry, madam,' and he went padding away, clearly not the least apologetic, and led her to a small anteroom leading off one side of the hall.

As they reached the door a distant bell tinkled, and the footman moved into the anteroom and said to the invisible occupant, 'Come on then, you. You're next,' and Martha stood back as a woman in a tattered tarlatan crinoline, heavily trimmed with red and green ribbons and looking far from clean, came marching out, her nose in the air, and her mittened hands crossed on her waist against a paisley shawl in very garish colours.

'An' bad piss to you an' all, mate,' she said shrilly as she went past him, smelling powerfully of dirt and patchouli. 'Don't you come the fancy man wiv me, my duck, on account I've et three like you before I've 'ad me dinner, many's the time! I'm goin' aht to be a nurse, I am, wiv all our pore soljers, so you mind yer manners!'

The footman sneered even more, if that were possible, and disdainfully led the woman to the back of the big hall, past the splendid marble staircase, opening a far door and then standing back so that she could sweep in in front of him; and then returned to Martha, to lead her into the anteroom.

It still smelled of its previous occupant, and he stalked to the window to open it with exaggerated distaste in every line of his body.

'You will see, madam, what I mean by the h'applicants. I'm sorry to 'ave to put you in the same station, as it were, but them's me orders. I shall come to take you to the ladies as soon as is necessary.'

And he was gone, leaving her sitting perched on the edge of a small spindly gilt chair and wondering what on earth she was doing here when she ought to be at Bedford Row supervising the packing of the stores the London Ladies were giving, accepting the deliveries of medicines from Caspar's Somers Town manufactory and packing them, and dealing with the thousand and one details that still had to be considered. Not until all that was done could she hope to buy their boat tickets, and time was running on.

It was now Friday, fully a week since she had first caught

fire from Russell's *Times* dispatches, and what had she done? Not enough. Not enough, for she was still here, instead of *there*, doing what had to be done. Time, time – she could not waste it so, sitting waiting to talk to a tiresome woman and ask her protection—

Impulsively she got to her feet, looking about her for a bell to summon the footman. She would demand her shawl and would go back to Bedford Row immediately and if that course of action meant Freddy would still insist on coming with her, well, that was his affair. She could do nothing about it.

But even as she stood up the door opened again and she heard the distant tinkle of the bell and the footman was there, waiting to lead her into the morning room, and she hesitated a moment, almost determined that she was going to leave anyway. But then she shrugged. She was here; the woman was ready; she might as well see her.

They were sitting round a square table, the heavily tasselled cloth in front of them strewn with ledgers and papers, and she stood hesitantly at the door for a moment, looking about her. They were all sitting with their heads bent over one sheet of paper and at her entrance one of them, the slightest of the five, said curtly without looking up, 'Take a seat, if you please.'

'Miss Nightingale?' Martha said, moving further into the room. 'I bring you a letter of introduction from—'

'I will deal with you when I am ready, ma'am. Please to sit and wait,' the slight woman said crisply, and Martha, startled in the extreme by this cavalier approach, sat down with a thump.

'She will not do. Altogether the wrong sort,' the thin woman said very decisively, and the others nodded and murmured, looking at the thin woman with such signs of awe on their faces that suddenly Martha found herself irritated, and luxuriously she allowed her feeling to have free rein.

'I have a great deal to do with my time, ladies,' she said loudly, 'and have no wish to waste it sitting here. I brought a letter of introduction to Miss Nightingale. If one of you is she, I trust you will do me the courtesy of revealing yourself.'

The thin woman looked up, showing a face of remarkable

beauty, with a perfect oval shape, large grey eyes and a delicate mouth, and Martha, suddenly aware of her own somewhat plain and certainly unremarkable face, reddened and lifted her eyebrows at her.

'I am happy to know you, ma'am. I come to you with the recommendations of Mr. Edwin Chadwick, of the Sanitary Commission, and those of my father, Mr. Abel Lackland, the surgeon of Queen Eleanor's Hospital. They sought the good offices of our mutual friend, Mrs. Stanley, to bring us together.'

'Oh, you are a lady, then.' The voice was clear and bell-like and very cold, and the grey eyes surveyed her very coolly, making her redden even more.

'I trust so, ma'am! I would hardly obtrude myself upon your notice if we were not of equal station!'

'I must tell you, Miss – I am sorry, but I seem to have missed your name – ah, thank you, Mrs. Bracebridge—' she took the letter held out to her by one of her companions, who had sought for and found it among the litter of papers before them, 'Miss Lackland – that I refuse flatly to take any *ladies* with me upon this expedition! I need women of good sense and experience who will *work* and not be ashamed to do so, and certainly not ladies who think themselves above handling a bedpan or performing other such necessary menial tasks. I have had my fill of such, I may tell you, and if you will forgive me, I will waste no more of your time or my own in considering the matter. I will not be able to take you with me to the Crimea as one of my nurses, so—'

'I did not ask you to!' Martha said in ringing tones, and stood up. 'I would not so demean myself, Miss Nightingale, as to answer your animadversions upon me, based upon your view of my station in life! The fact that I have nursed the cholera on many occasions in my father's hospital wards, have done every disagreeable task such nursing demands, and made no murmur, is beside the point. So, I imagine, is the fact that I have for many years run the hostel in Bedford Row for women and children rescued from the gutter – but I make no play on any of this, since in *your* eyes the fact that I am of the same station

82

in life as yourself is something of which I should be ashamed! No, ma'am, I make mention of one fact only – that I did not come here for the purpose of seeking to be one of your band of nurses!'

Miss Nightingale leaned back in her chair, and looked up at her, and now there was a glint of humour in her eyes, and Martha felt suddenly for the first time since entering this room that she had in fact made some contact with this cool and alarming woman.

'Then why did you come?' she asked and her voice, though still as firm as ever, had a genuine curiosity in it.

'At my father's request, ma'am, since he is alarmed that I plan to travel to Scutari in a very small party – just myself and my – my guide, a woman of some experience of the situation there. He wished me to ask the boon of your travelling companionship. He felt it would be more seemly and would settle his mind better if I were to travel with a person who enjoys the protection of a large party of fellow travellers. However, Miss Nightingale—'

'*You* are going to Scutari?' Miss Nightingale was now sitting bolt upright, the hint of good humour that had invested her face now quite gone. 'And pray, Miss Lackland, upon whose authority do you go? I may tell you that I have been appointed by the War Office to take on the task of nursing the sick soldiers in the Crimea and have the War Office's solemn assurance that no other nursing party shall go without my knowledge, and that all nurses who do go there will act under my orders and mine solely. So, I ask you again. Upon whose authority do you plan to make your expedition?'

'My own, Miss Nightingale! I need no other!'

'You will find yourself sorely mistaken there, Miss Lackland. The Army hospital and the soldiers in it are under the aegis of the War Office, and as such—'

'Oh, you all make the same assumptions!' Martha said, a wave of boredom suddenly coming up to mix itself disagreeably with her anger. 'I said nothing about nursing *soldiers*, I believe! I am concerned, most deeply concerned, with the

83

welfare of the soldiers' wives and children, who are also suffering untold miseries – and largely at the hands of an uncaring
Army, may I say, which permits the women and children to go,
and then treats them as less than animals!'

'Women and children?' One of the other women spoke now,
staring with a lifted lip at Martha's red face and tousled hair,
for in her excitement she had run her hands over her head and
made herself a sorry sight. 'You mean the—'

'Yes, ma'am. I mean the camp followers, the doxies, the
lights o' love, the muslins – call them what you will! I tell you
they are as worthy of our compassion as any others, and indeed
many of them truly are the wives of the soldiers! The fact that
a man is a common soldier does not always mean he is quite
blind to the dictates of decent living! Many is the man who has
married over the drum! But married or no, these women are
entitled, surely, to some Christian compassion.'

'As to that, Miss Lackland, I am in complete agreement with
you.'

Miss Nightingale stood up, revealing herself to be taller and
even more slender than Martha had at first realized.

'All of God's creatures are worthy of our compassion. However, I am concerned solely with the welfare of the Army and
its soldiers. I cannot concern myself with the problems of their
women. That is a different matter. So I cannot agree to accept
you into my party, nor to offer you the protection of my
company, since your self-appointed task is outside my jurisdiction. I can quite understand your friends' concern on your
behalf – for to tell the truth, Miss Lackland, despite the experience of which you have made such careful mention, you appear
to me to be a lady like many others, full of goodwill but not
very well equipped with the good sense that will enable that
goodwill to be translated into any sort of concrete use. If you
will take my advice, Miss Lackland, you will contain your compassion and use it here at home, in a manner in which you are
clearly competent to do, rather than trust yourself to the
rigours of the journey you are contemplating. Believe me, Miss
Lackland, I have been at some pains to study the situation, by
means of dispatches from the Front – not those of Mr. Russell,

84

you understand, which no doubt fired your enthusiasms, but those from the Staff about Lord Raglan – and the conditions there are truly frightful—'

She had come round the table now, and was standing beside Martha looking down at her, and now that look of good humour was back on her beautiful face, and suddenly she held out her hand.

'My dear Miss Lackland, I am sure you feel I am quite horrid, and have treated you very shabby! Indeed, I meant no ill manners but I have been so set about this week seeking to prepare all and to set all to rights before I leave that I have perhaps become a little sharp with my tongue. We go, you must understand, tomorrow morning very early, and here we are, still with only thirty-eight women who are fit to take as nurses, and I had hoped for forty at least! To be greeted by you at such a stage of my preparations inevitably threw me into some disarray. Accept my word for it, Miss Lackland, your plans, however far advanced, should be abandoned. You have much concern for your fellows I know, and it becomes you, but concern is not enough. You lack, I fear, the other components of a successful expedition – efficiency and dispatch and large sums of money, and above all, knowledge. Stay at home, Miss Lackland. Stay at home.'

Martha looked at her with her face rigid with control. First Lydia and her lectures, and now this. These beautiful women, with their superior wits and superior gifts – they should not treat her so! She would show them, she would show all of them, that she was not to be deflected from her plans by them, or by anyone else. If this woman would not allow her to accompany her party, then by God, she would go alone.

And, she suddenly thought, I *mean* alone. I shall not take Freddy, no matter what anyone says.

'Madam, I thank you for your advice. I do not hesitate to tell you I have not the least intention of accepting it. Good afternoon!'

And she swept out, to seize her shawl from the footman who was standing just outside the door, his sneer even more pronounced, for he had clearly been listening at the keyhole, and so out of the house and into the Square beyond.

It was not until she was sitting in a hansom cab, called up with an imperious wave of her hand across the Square, that her pent-up emotion took hold of her, and she sat there as the horse went wheeling away down Halkin Street towards Grosvenor Place, the Park and ultimately Bedford Row, shaking in every limb.

But however weak she felt in body at that moment, her spirits and her intentions were strong, stronger than they had ever been. It was as though that fifteen minutes spent there in the morning room at Forty-Nine Belgrave Square had been spent in a furnace, a furnace in which every atom of will in her had been forged to a brighter hotter strength. She was going to help those women and children, and no-one, no matter what, would stop her.

And what was more, she was going to do it in her way, and no one else's.

CHAPTER EIGHT

'My dear Lionel, I do not ask you to launch a great government loan, you know!' Gideon said with a touch of asperity. 'I am well aware of the fact that you have much call upon your services at this time! I ask merely—'

'Call upon my services! I tell you, Henriques, I think sometimes the only name any of 'em know in Westminster, when it comes to banks and money, is Rothschild! I have had 'em coming trailing here to New Court in droves, positively in droves! Mind you, I floated a sixteen million pound loan for 'em for the war so it's understandable enough! Even Aberdeen himself was here, you know!'

His large face with its protruding lower lip and rim of white hair lifted momentarily and he got out of his big chair, creaking to his feet and grimacing a little as his arthritic joints cracked. 'But as far as I am concerned, Henriques, I have shot my bolt. No doubt this is a worthy enough scheme your relation has, but I cannot finance it. Nor, I suspect, will any of the other banks. But I wish her well, I wish her well, and you too, in your efforts to maintain a cash life-line for her. It will keep you very busy, I have no doubt—' And he held out his big white hand in farewell, nodding affably but with unmistakable finality.

Outside the deceptively simple office, in the narrow confines of New Court, Gideon sighed and settling his top hat more firmly on his head made his way briskly along St. Swithin's Lane on his way back to Lombard Street and his own more elegant counting house.

He was not as cast down by Lionel Rothschild's inability to

help him as he might have been. Already he had had similar reactions from Barings and from Montefiore, although, again like Rothschild, both had given him a small contribution, despite the fact that they, in common with every other man of substance in the City, were being constantly dunned for money by eager workers for the country's weal. It was all no more than he had expected, and it was becoming ever more clear to him that any support for his sister-in-law's scheme must come primarily from her own family.

His lips were pursed as he hurried along through the Monday morning bustle, thinking hard. Not a mean man, by any yardstick, still he was a careful one and knew better than to recklessly commit himself to the total financial backing Martha would need. Other sources must be found, and found quickly. Already she was chafing at the delay; yesterday had been far from being the usual peaceful Sunday at home he so much enjoyed, what with Martha there as edgy and as restless as though she were on pins, and Abby being so painfully brave in refusing to allow herself to beg her Freddy to change his mind, and Freddy himself, almost as restless as Martha, trying to assess whether or not he had made a good decision, and whether or not he would hold to it. No, not at all a peaceful Sunday. It was quite clear to Gideon that if he was to restore any peace to his home in Stanhope Gate he must see Martha well on her way. And if possible Freddy too.

Not that he held any animus against Freddy. He was a stepson, it was true, the offspring of his wife's first love, and as such would be to many men an incubus. But not to Gideon, for he was genuinely fond of the stocky red-headed young man, genuinely had a care for his welfare, and watched over the business in which he enjoyed a half share as assiduously for Freddy as for himself.

But it was time the boy pulled himself out of the slough of misery and hard work in which he had been sunk this past three years. Gideon was the last person to despise a young man for falling in love and being faithful to that love, whatever happened; had he not himself served many long and lonely years of wanting and waiting for his Abby? It was not because he thought going away would help Freddy forget Phoebe that he felt it a matter of some importance to encourage the boy to stick to his offer; it was because, Gideon told himself with some shrewdness, a physical parting under such romantic conditions as a war – and what, after all could be more romantic than a far distant war? – might have a beneficial effect on both of them.

Whatever it was that had come between them like a wedge three years ago he did not know, though Abby did; but then she was a woman, and the boy's mother, and women and mothers were very good at such matters. It was none of Gideon's affair; but all the same he would like to see the young people as settled and happy as he was himself. His lips curled as he thought of Abby. Indeed he could wish them both no more than he himself enjoyed, for there could be no greater felicity for anyone.

So, what was to be done? And now once more his lips curled reminiscently, but this time with a difference. There was no question but that Benefit Nights at the Haymarket and similar junketings could raise a great deal of money. If he could but persuade the delectable Miss Mohun to offer her services in such a cause, well – Martha would have her money, many people would have an agreeable amount of entertainment and he himself – the smile broadened – he would have the pleasure of the company of a lady of great charm and presence. It was not that he lacked any love for his dear Abby; far from it. It was not that he sought to do as many men of his stamp and wealth did and set himself up with a ladybird; far from that, too. It would not be his style at all. But to count amongst his friends one of the town's most charming, most admired and generally most sought-after personages – now, that was indeed his style and would be more than agreeable.

So, he called into his counting house, left careful instructions about the morning's work, and told them that was he needed he would be found at Rules' chophouse in Maiden Lane in Covent Garden at the luncheon hour. Perhaps with a companion, he added casually, and called a hansom cab and instructed the driver to go – sharpish, mind – to Upper Brook

Street, near Park Lane. Early as it was, he imagined he would find the lovely Lydia available to callers who had important business to discuss with her, and busy though so popular an actress might be, he imagined she would consent to take a luncheon with him. She had seemed to like his company well enough at Phoebe's Ball—

He settled back in the cab, inhaling the agreeable scent of leather and horse and smiled out at the pigeon-swarmed cobbles outside the Royal Exchange. Life in London this autumn of the first year of the war in the Crimea was very agreeable. Very agreeable indeed.

'Are you quite sure as you don't want 'im?' Sal said, peering up at her from the depths of the big box she was packing with the arrowroot and loaf sugar and almond oil and other useful comestibles. 'I tell yer, *I* wouldn't turn 'im away, and that's a fact. It's no pleasure steamer we're goin' on, you know! It's a righty mucky business and '*avin*' a strong man around can't do no 'arm, no 'arm at all.'

'I have no doubt you are right, but – where are those sheets? Ah, yes – I have no doubt he *would* be useful, Sal, but I am heartily sick of all the family talk and troubles it's causing! I spent yesterday at my sister's house, in Stanhope Gate, and I will not hide from you how disagreeable it all was! Abby being so *sensible*, till I could have – well, she was very irritating, although I do indeed sympathize with her, for I am sure were he my son I would do the same. And Freddy being so stubborn – no, I want no more of it. Give me those bolster cases, Sal, and then we can cord this one – splendid! No – I have made up my mind what is to be, and so it will be. Now, are you ready to cord that one too? That should make the last of the food boxes, and Mr. Garling has promised his coachman shall be sent for to bind the edges with tin, to make them safer from damage. How many is it altogether?'

Sal got to her feet and brushed down her green gown – it was a matter of principle with her not to wear an apron, although Martha was swathed in one – and then stretched her back a little wearily.

'Seventeen. An' all of 'em packed betwixt last Friday and now. That's all apart from all the other stuff, o' course, as we done on Saturday – oh, I dunno as we're not wastin' our time, an' that's the truth of it! We've got what looks like a lot, one way an' another, I daresay – but if it's all still like it was when I was out there last, it won't last no more more'n a week! We'll 'ave to get more sent out after us, that's for certain! An' 'ow that'll get done, I've no knowin' – and what if we lose this stuff on the way? They're all thieves and robbers as soon as you gets to the other side o' the Channel, you know, all of 'em! Bleedin' Frenchies – lot of 'ooligans if you ask me – if you'd got 'alf as much sense as 'ope, Miss Martha, you'd take yer young nevvy an' be glad of 'is company—'

'Well, I shan't and that's the end of it. There's that Nightingale woman gone two days now, do you know that? If we wait much longer she'll be on her way back, and all done! I am determined we shall not be far behind her – and if I wait till the family has talked itself dry over Freddy, as well as over me, why, there'll be no hope. So—'

Martha smiled suddenly, looking at Sal with her head cocked birdlike to one side. 'Sal, shall I tell you what we shall do?'

'Try an' stop you,' Sal said sourly, but she grinned back agreeably enough, and took a small snuffbox from a pocket in her petticoats, and inhaled a large pinch with a gusty sniff.

'All this will be sent down to the Folkestone train tonight. There will be instructions to deliver it to the docks to Mr. Buckman the shipping agent. He has instructions to see them carried ahead of us to Marseilles. And you and I, very quietly, shall slip away tomorrow morning by the six o'clock train from London Bridge to Folkestone and take the midday packet that goes to Boulogne. There we shall take the train for Paris, and almost immediately the train for Marseilles. If my reading of the timetables is right, we shall be there by Friday and Mr. Buckman has assured me the heavy luggage will be there by then also. I am told there is a ship going to Constantinople by way of Malta on Friday night, and if we are fortunate we shall be on it! I do hope so, for there is not another for four days, and I should be dreadfully restless in such a place for so long!'

Sal stared at her. ''Ave you bin there before, then?'

'Oh, no, I have not, of course, as well you know! But I have heard it is a very – very—'

'It's a right wicked place,' Sal said with some relish. 'Full o' thieves an' cut-throats. Chop up their grandma to make candles most of 'em would, let alone what they'll do to the likes of you – bein' a lady an' all that—'

'Not you?' Martha said a little sharply, nettled as she always was by Sal's gibes about her superior position in society.

'No, they'd tumble me an' be glad of the chance, that they would! Not that I'd let a bunch of stinkin' frogs anywhere near me – anyway, we won't be there that long, you reckon?'

'Not if all goes as I have now planned it. We will have under half a day in Marseilles where I hope to buy more supplies of food, and then we shall go on the ship. It is a French one, but I have been told I may have a pair of berths for us. So, Sal, make up your mind to it. We go in the morning before anyone else is abroad, and will leave letters to say our farewells. I want no scenes nor tearfulness from – from anyone. So we shall have no farewell parties, you understand me?'

'I understan' you well enough,' Sal said. '*You* don' want no farewells. But as for me – I got a feller I got to talk to, an' that, for a bit. I'll tie this lot up an' see it stowed an' then I'm goin' down the *Lamb and Flag*. No, don't look at me like that! I ain't goin' back on me word! I'll be back 'ere in plenty o' time to get us off. I'll see you in the kitchen in time for a bit o' breakfast before we go. An' I still think we're both clean out of our attics. Me even more'n you, on account you don't know no better. Oh well, if I'm in, I'm in, I s'pose. Where's that bleedin' string, then? Can't tie a box wiv no string, can I?'

'I am glad you could come to see me, Freddy,' Phoebe said, and her voice sounded very prim suddenly, like a child on her best behaviour. 'I know how busy you are, and it was most kind of you to take the time.'

He raised an eyebrow at her, a little amused. 'Dear me! So

formal! You know quite well that all you have ever had to do when you wished to speak to me was crook your little finger. Today you crooked, so today I came!'

'Oh, Freddy, do not be so ridiculous!' She turned away from him, a little petulantly, and peered at herself in her mirror. They were sitting in the tiny dressing-room Oliver had fashioned for her behind the little stage, and with both she and Freddy in it it felt very crowded, for there was room only for her table and mirror and chair, and one other chair, which Freddy seemed to overflow as he sat there four-square and solid.

His closeness made her feel even more uneasy, and she picked up a hare's foot and with exaggerated care began to place more colour on her cheeks which were in truth a little pale.

'I wish you would not do that,' Freddy said, with a sudden edge of sharpness in his voice.

'I know you do. You have always told me. And I have always told you that when one appears on a stage in all the lights, then it is a vital part of one's performance. Let us not, I beg you, start on *that* subject again.'

'There are times when I feel I must,' Freddy said, and now his voice was softer and pitched much lower. 'If you had not been so stubborn about this theatre business three and a half years ago, we could have—'

'Freddy.' She turned, dropping her hare's foot on the floor where it lay between them, unregarded. 'Freddy, it is because of – because of the great – affection you bore me then and – oh, Freddy, you do know what I mean! We have always been close, have we not?'

'Aye, close. But not always in the way I would have wished.'

'Yes – yes, I know that.' She spoke hurriedly. 'And I do not wish to speak of that. All I wish to do now is ask you to remember how we were – *before* – and ask you please to – to do as I ask you, just as you would have done when I was a child. You would, is it not true? Had I asked you to – to climb a mountain you would have done it—

' "Would'st drink up eisel? Eat a crocodile? *I'll* do't" '

93

Freddy said and laughed, a little hard laugh. 'You see, I can quote from the stage as well as anyone! Although I would make a sorry Hamlet, I think! Yes, you are right, I would have done anything—' He grinned then, a little crookedly. 'Well, I did! Stole cakes from the larder for you, and lied to my Mama about your scrapes and—'

She shook her head, and now her face was losing its pallor, as she became more comfortable with him, more aware of the old magic she had been used to be able to work on him.

'I do not mean such little things. I am now asking you – please, Freddy, do not go! Please do not go to that dreadful war! I can understand why you should have offered – and that was all my fault, I suppose, for had I told everyone why Aunt Martha was going, there would not have been that dreadful argument! But there was, and – oh, Freddy, can I persuade you to reconsider? You see, Aunt Abby is so unhappy! And was so angry with me, and I cannot bear it, I really cannot! She has always been so good to me, and I cannot bear it that she should think it all my fault that you are going to risk your life in that dreadful war! Her face that night at my Ball – oh, Freddy, it almost broke my heart! I did not think she could be so distressed as to look at me so! Please, Freddy, will you not go? Will you not change your mind and stay here at home and make Aunt Abby content again? Oh, Freddy, remember how we used to be, and stay for me.'

He sat and stared at her, his face quite wooden, his eyes seeming opaque and expressionless, but behind that façade his thoughts darted about as fast as a moth about a flame, as the words came tumbling out of her.

At first he had responded to her appeal with a lift of his senses that took him soaring away from the dull sick misery that had lain deep in him for all those three and a half years. No matter what had happened, no matter who had been responsible for the dreadful experience they had perforce shared so long ago, he would wed her. They would marry, and yes, they would have children of their own. He could live with that knowledge of the past and and not be sickened by it, could tolerate that old experience of hers as something that was not relevant to him, to her, or to their shared life. As though it were a bad dream that had happened to someone else, long ago, far away and unimportantly. He had looked at her dark ringlets, bouncing against her soft cheeks as she talked with such animation, at her eyes, so bright with appeal, had smelled the warm smell of her and ached to reach out and touch her and hold her and tell her it was all over, the three-year nightmare was past, and he no longer cared—

And then she had said it. 'Aunt Abby is so unhappy!' And it had all gone, his mirror of a gleaming future filled with love and joy and babies shattering into a thousand shards, tinkling and ringing about his feet as she went rattling on and on and on. About his *mother*.

She sat there when she had finished, her hands clasped tightly on her lap, and her lips set in a controlled line that made a dimple appear incongruously at one corner of her mouth, waiting for him to speak, and the silence between them grew and stretched and her lips moved, and shook a little, and she said timidly, 'Freddy?'

He blinked and looked at her with his eyes still blank of any emotion, and stood up, looking about him for his overcoat and then shrugging it on with some difficulty in the crowded little room.

'I would indeed have eaten a crocodile had you asked me to do it for you, Phoebe. I would indeed. But on this—' he shook his head, 'on this matter, I must disappoint you. You must make your peace with my mother as best you might.'

He was standing now with his hand on the knob of the door, staring down at her. 'I may tell you that I go for my own reasons, Phoebe. I did not offer to accompany Aunt Martha simply to get *you* out of trouble, although clearly you believe that to be the case. Well, I am sorry, but I must disabuse you of that notion. Whatever I would have done for you when you were a child – whatever I, in fact, did for you – that is all past. I am a man now, in every way. A man grown. And you, I venture to suggest should regard yourself as a woman grown. You are too old, I think, to look at the world about you with such self-centred eyes, and I may add, too old for those pretty

95

tricks of begging and pleading. They are beguiling in a child —
less so in a woman. Good day to you, Phoebe.

And he was gone, leaving her sitting at her dressing table
behind her little stage with tears compounded of rage and dis-
appointment, and, just a little, of shame, streaking her face.

CHAPTER NINE

MARTHA stood on the top step outside 27 Bedford Row, holding her cloak tightly about her and trying not to shiver in the cold darkness. But it was difficult, for her chin felt as though it belonged to someone else, so determined was it to rattle her teeth together, and her legs were solid and lumpy with the chill. And not just the chill, and well she knew it. She was sick with apprehension, sick with regret, and longing only to run back into the house and throw her arms about Miss Carrie and cry, 'I shall not go – it was all a hum – I shall not go!'

But of course that was all nonsense and she made herself turn away from the front door with determination in her step and marched herself down to the pavement where Sal was standing at the kerb and with the aid of the cursing jarvey was loading the last of their valises. To have found a four-wheeler at just after five o'clock in the morning was no mean feat, but Sal had managed it. Not for the first time Martha congratulated herself on her choice of ally. Sal, for all her crudity, her attacks of bad temper, her jeers and her sneers was a resourceful young woman, and one upon whom anyone could safely lean. There would be no need for any masculine protection with such a one as she to hand, Martha told herself, and pushed away the fleeting thought of how agreeable it would have been to have had Freddy's solid company as well.

The horse stamped softly, its iron-tipped hoof striking a comforting spark on the cobbles and Sal turned and peered into the darkness.

'Where are you, for Gawd's sake? We 'aven't got all day, you

know – oh, there you are! Well, come on then.' And she turned
and with a flick of the skirts of her heavy ulster climbed into
the cab as the jarvey, his heavy breathing pluming the air,
sniffed disgustingly and then spat and hauled himself up on to
his perch.

And Martha put her foot on the little step and reached for
Sal's big hand and set out on her journey to the Crimea.

She was well aware of the significance of this first stage of
her travels as the four-wheeler went clattering along High Holborn, over and on into Little Skinner Street and past St. Sep-
ulchre's church. She peered up at the great spire leaning
bleakly against the only slightly less crepuscular sky and
shivered again in the cold mustiness of the leathery cab, tucking her chin down into the collar of her cloak.

A new feeling was now beginning to invade her; exhilar-
ation. There was no doubt that what she was doing was
crackbrained, foolish, inelegant, all the things everyone had
said it was – but there was also no doubt that it was enormously
exciting. Not all pleasure, after all, she thought with a sudden
flash of superior understanding, needs to be agreeable. It can
be enjoyable in a strange way to be afraid, and to be unsure,
and to be alone. It is all living, it is all feeling, and as such to be
relished. And a snatch of Andrew Marvell came drifting into
her mind; '—the grave's a fine and private place, but none, I
think, do there embrace—' And she thought for a moment how
ridiculously irrelevant it was, and then wasn't so sure that it
was. Being dead would be very final, she thought confusedly.
And there is so much living I have not yet done. And why
should that thought bring a sudden image of Mr. Alexander
Laurence into her mind's eye? She shook herself a little. Last
night's restless sleep was taking its toll; she was having her
night's share of dreams now she was awake.

St. Martin's Le Grand, Cheapside, the elegant curve of King
William the Fourth Street, the reek of Billingsgate, raucous
with curiously hatted men, and then at last the river, with
London Bridge throwing its great spans past the ships and
barges and little rowboats fringing its banks, and she took a

deep breath of the smell of soot and mud and rotting veg-
etation and dirty humanity that came drifting through the
cracks in the old cab's creaking sides and thought, 'This is
London. This is home. And where shall I see tomorrow dawn?'
and liked the poignancy of the thought as she turned her head
and saw the light creeping up over the curve of the river east-
wards. Where indeed would she see tomorrow dawn?

The train journey to Folkestone came as anticlimax, and she
dozed a little, sitting neat and upright in the corner of her first
class carriage, listening to the wheels rattle and the occasional
hoot of the steam whistle as they hurtled through the slowly
greening countryside. And at Folkestone where they ate a frugal
lunch of bread and cheese and tea – to which Sal, as phlegmatic
as though she made journeys like this every day of her life,
added a quart of strong ale – and then the steam packet and the
uneasy swelling roll as it moved southwards towards the
French coast.

Martha stood by the rail, looking forwards, for some reason
not even thinking to look at the receding whiteness of the
cliffs behind her. Her farewells to home had been made in
Bedford Row very early indeed this morning, and to watch the
shores of England dwindle away would have been of little
point.

'They've read my letters by now,' she thought suddenly,
watching the last of the gulls wheel away over the side of the
packet to go soaring back to the coast. 'Freddy first. He is up
and away before Papa and Maria. Then they will have read
theirs, and then Abby and Gideon and by now, even Oliver
and Phoebe. Letters, letters, letters, they'll all be sending messages to each other, the footman from Gower Street running
madly all over town—' and she giggled softly, and Sal at her
side looked round and said curiously, 'What's so bleedin'
funny, then?'

'I'm imagining their faces,' Martha said. 'I left letters of
farewell for all of them, you see. I told you no farewells. Only
to Miss Carrie. I kissed *her* goodbye. But no-one else – and I
was imagining their faces—'

Suddenly it didn't seem so funny any more.

99

Paris was noise and confusion and a struggle to cope with a language to which she had given no thought since she had left the schoolroom more than twenty years ago and the embarrassment of Sal drinking rather more wine than she should and getting quarrelsome with the blue-shirted porters at the Gare du Nord, and feeling her own fatigue beginning to edge her temper with acerbity. But they managed to catch the Marseilles train, and even had time to purchase a hamper of food, for the day was stretching into evening and it had been a long time since that bread and cheese luncheon.

They sat side by side and ate crusty French bread and slices of ham and fruit and, although Martha tried to dissuade Sal from doing so, shared a bottle of wine. But this time Sal seemed no worse for her intake and it certainly helped Martha feel better, for afterwards she slept most of the journey away and woke feeling almost refreshed as the train moved at last into Marseilles station.

And here more confusion, more noise, more arguments and problems about baggage, and more struggles with the language, for the accents were different, but with Sal shrieking louder than any of the fishwives or porters, and swearing horribly in what sounded like an uneasy mixture of German, French and heaven knew what else ('I learned a lot o' new words last time I come travellin'!' she told Martha with great satisfaction), they found their boxes, all seventeen of them, and all five of their valises and finally, and to Martha's huge relief, their ship.

It was a creaking old French vessel that she felt had seen better days, and she stood on the dock below it and peered up at its cracked and blistered sides in the heavy lamplight, and sighed hugely. Her fatigue had come back now, with an overlying ache in her head from the red wine, and she was grateful to Sal for her energy, for she was as she always was, full of noise and laughter and shouts and apparently as fresh as if she had left her bed not two hours before. It was Sal who took over, Sal who supervised the loading of their myriad boxes, Sal who chivvied her along the creaking companionways of the ship to the tiny evil-smelling cabin far below in which they were to spend the next seven days and nights.

'Well, 'ere we are all merry an' bright!' she said cheerfully dropping the valises she was carrying on to her bunk. 'Gawd, a right 'ome from 'ome, ain't it? Bit of all right this is—'

And she looked about her appreciatively at the tiny wash-stand with its cracked bowl and jug, and screwed down table and two straight-backed chairs and the narrow bunks, one above the other and adorned with only the thinnest of blankets and pillows.

'Mayn't be what *you're* used to, Miss Martha, bein' as you've lived soft all yer life, but I'll tell yer, as far as I'm concerned, it's a right little palace! Come on – you'd better get to your bed. You're fair done in, ain't yer? Well, I'm told there's a man I can do a bit o' business with down on the dock and we don't sail till the morning tide, so if you'll give me a bit o' the ready, I'll go an' see what's available.'

Martha stared up at her, blinking owlishly and Sal said impatiently, 'You wanted to buy extra supplies 'ere, didn't you? Well then! I did a bit of askin' around and I'm told there's a man what's got four barrels o' salt pork available for the buyin'!'

She winked hugely. 'So long as no one asks where he got it from, no 'arm done. So I'll do a bit o' business an' we'll have some meat when we get there. You can't feed the sort o' people we'll be goin' to wiv arrowroot and syrup only, you know! They likes a bit of salt pork if they can get it. And a drop o' somethin' else an' all—'

Martha tried to collect her thoughts. This was *her* expedition! She was the one who was in charge, in charge of everything. Stores and travelling and – and then she remembered how Sal had coped with the porters, even when half drunk, how efficiently she had herded her from cab to train to boat and train again, and capitulated.

'I'll be better when we get there,' she whispered, and reached under her skirts, carefully turning her back first, to reach her money belt and give Sal the sovereigns she demanded. 'For they won't take naught but gold, and that's for sure—' Sal said.

And then fell into the narrow hard little bunk, aching in every limb, grateful for even that cold and, she suspected bug infested bed, as Sal went away whistling cheerfully, to do her buying down in the dark and fish-stinking docks.

It was not until they had been at sea for four days that she emerged from that cabin again. They had sailed on the morning tide into a sea far from welcoming, to be greeted by storms of such ferocity and winds of such velocity that the ship creaked and strained and bucketed like a saucer adrift on a whirlpool. Had she been well enough no doubt she would have been afraid, for Martha had never before crossed any sea, and these storms were severe enough to alarm even the seasoned travellers aboard, but she was far too ill to care whether she lived or died.

She had slept uneasily on that first night until the dawn brought the tide and they had slipped out of the harbour, and then the rolling had started almost abruptly, and with equal speed seasickness overtook her. She could only lie there, retching and heaving and hurting abominably from the abortive efforts made by the muscles of her chest and belly, unable to think any coherent thoughts at all.

Sal had been of no help, for she too was prostrated by seasickness, and the two women had lain there in their bunks, with only an occasional visit from a sluttish woman apparently travelling as wife to one of the crew, who came from time to time to give them brackish water to drink and then went away without a word.

It was on the fourth day that Martha's will seemed to come back to her. She woke suddenly in the middle of the morning, having dozed fitfully since midnight, and thought of the sky far above her, and the sea and the wind, and ached for it, feeling she could not bear this fetid cabin a moment longer, and struggled out of the bunk and to the door, opening it to shout feebly for attention.

The slattern came, stared at her, and after shrugging in surly non-comprehension at Martha's attempt to ask for the wherewithal to wash at length understood her gestures and went away and brought a jug of tepid muddy water.

Sal could not be persuaded to budge, wanting only to lie in

her bunk and groan, so Martha washed her, and made her bunk more comfortable, having bullied the slattern for a supply of clean sheets and another blanket, and then at last, having dressed – and been amazed at how her clothes hung on her, for she had clearly become much thinner – made her way through the ship, along swaying corridors and up tortuous companionways until at last she stood on deck, and took a deep and tremulous breath of sheer joy.

Far above her the sky, though still filled with clouds, was vivid with light and scudding and alive and the smell of salt was heady as the wind caught her petticoats and whipped them up – much to the delight of a passing sailor – and she stretched and breathed deep and was, for the first time in days, glad to be alive.

She made her way across the slippery deck towards the rail, aware of how weak she had become, and thinking confusedly of the need to eat. Maybe a little gruel—

And then she just stood there, staring at the sea and breathing deeply, her head back and her eyes half closed, relishing the smell of clean air again, and shrinking at the thought of ever having to return to that near-kennel below decks, where Sal still lay huddled.

She opened her eyes at that thought. Sal. It would be better to force her somehow to make the same effort she, Martha, had made, than to let her lie there like that. If she could be persuaded to drag herself above decks she would feel so much better, Martha told herself, a little solemnly. So much better.

She stood a moment longer staring up at the huge emptiness of the sky above her and then, moving carefully, turned and began to make her way back towards the opening of the companionway up which she had come.

And because she was so concentrating upon her own weak knees and her resolve, and because with the shriek of the wind high above her in the rigging she could hear nothing, she cannoned into a passing sailor, who was bent almost double under a huge coil of rope. As their bodies connected the ship leaned to the starboard in a stately recovery from its rhythmic roll, and this was too much for both of them and they fell headlong.

She lay there on the deck for a moment, stunned and blinking up at the sky dipping and whirling above her, and then her head cleared and steadied, and moving with great care she got to her hands and knees, wanting somehow to become erect again but feeling too weak. And then knelt there, horrified and gaping, for just ahead of her lay the sailor, his coil of rope tangled about his feet and with his head and shoulders lying half over the side under the rail.

Even as she stared the rope shifted as once more the ship listed against the heavy swell, and the man's body slithered further over the side, one arm falling to swing helplessly free. He was clearly unconscious, and she opened her mouth to scream, but the wind mockingly threw the sound back in her teeth, and again the ship reeled and again the rope slipped—

How she did it she was never to know. With every muscle in her body weakened and flaccid from four days of illness she slipped and slid across the deck, and seized the man's ankles, laboriously turning one loop of the tangled rope firmly about one of them, and grimly, she held on. The rope bit her hands, and she clung tighter. There was no possibility that she could pull the man back, but she might, she just might be able to hold on to him until help came.

Somewhere high above her she heard a shout and turned her head to peer upwards, and saw a small black dot of a head appear over the bridge high above, and then there was another shout and the head disappeared and then, after what seemed an eternity, the thrum of running feet and shouts and at last hands coming over her shoulders and seizing the legs of the man now beginning, it seemed, to recover from his unconsciousness, for his limbs were moving as he feebly struggled to regain the deck. And then they were pulling him aboard, and someone was taking the rope from her hands.

She sat and looked at her palms, puzzled and a little remote. They were torn and bleeding, and she stared at them in amazement. To look like that and not to hurt? And then another blast of wind came saltily across the ship, rolling it yet again with its monotonous rhythm and then she felt it, and heard the yelp of her own voice as the salt bit into her torn flesh.

The ship began to rock even more swiftly, and the sky above her dipped and rolled faster still and everything seemed to melt and merge, and she thought, with one corner of her mind being as cool and practical as though she were standing in the hostel at Bedford Row with Miss Carrie beside her discussing the number of sheets the laundress had brought back, 'I believe I am about to swoon.'

She felt someone take hold of her wrists and look at her hands and then she heard voices, seeming to come from a great distance away.

'Elle est blessée, la pauvre – tres blessée – allez! Cherchez le medicin! Vite, vite – le medecin anglais – je crois qu'il parle avec le capitaine – allez *vite*, cretin!'

And then, very gratefully and very quietly she did swoon, or almost. At any rate she let her eyes close and let the distant conversation go on over her, making no attempt to understand or join in, and felt hands about her and felt herself lifted and carried.

The light behind her closed lids darkened and she felt herself being carried downwards, lurching from step to step, and now the arms that were holding her felt constricting and disagreeable, and as the lightness of the sky and the sound and freshness of the wind disappeared, other smells came up and she felt queasy again at the scent of garlic and oil and dirt, and she began to struggle a little, weakly, and tried to open her eyes.

The arms set her down on a yielding surface and for a moment she felt comfortable again, until once more the smells arose, and the sound of the voices became louder and, it seemed, nearer, and again she tried to open her eyes and to sit up.

'No, please to lie still. You have been injured, ma'am, and are in need of – Good God!'

This time she managed to open her eyes and blinked a little against the uprush of light and turned her head and tried to look about her. She was lying in a cabin, not her own but a much more elegant and well furnished one, though still far from as comfortable a bedroom as she was accustomed to, and she managed to smile weakly, and turned her head again to peer up at whoever it was who had spoken.

And frowned and closed her eyes and frowned again and then stared, and finally began to giggle, helplessly, and tears sprang to her eyes and ran down her cheeks and she sniffed and gulped and laughed again, and then he laughed too, and touched her shoulder gently as she tried to sit up, to make her lie down again.

'Miss Lackland,' Alexander Laurence said gently. 'How very kind of you to call upon me, when it was I who had engaged to call upon you! Such an agreeable ball, was it not?'

CHAPTER TEN

'WELL, she has gone, and I would have thought that there was an end of it,' Abby said a little waspishly, and bent her head again over the slippers she was embroidering for Sarah. 'But you know your own business best, of course.'

'Really, Mamma, you make me feel as though you regard me as little more than a mere courier! I did not offer to accompany Aunt Martha simply to *accompany* her, you must understand! It would have been sensible of her to tell me what she was about, and allow me to travel with her – she was impulsive, I think, and meant also to protect you and your feelings in acting as she did – but if she has chosen to go alone, so be it. But she does not have to *remain* alone. Her expedition needs a surgeon, I believe, and I will follow on and be that surgeon. Now, please, let us have no more of it—'

'I can understand your point of view, Frederick, but that does not give you leave to be impertinent to your Mamma, who is naturally perturbed at the whole matter,' Gideon said sharply, and at once Freddy went over to his mother and bent and kissed her cheek.

'Oh, of course, you are all quite right. I am annoyed with Aunt Martha, and in her absence, vent my spleen on you! Unforgivable – but please forgive me all the same.'

Abby smiled thinly and nodded and bent again to her embroidery, but said nothing. She could not, feeling much too near tears to risk any words. Now that the lists of the names of those who had died at the battle of the Alma were filtering through, the risk Freddy was taking in going out there was becoming ever more apparent to her, and the sense of oppression that filled her, the certainty of his early death that made her want to throw her arms about him and physically prevent him from following his mad plan, was becoming more painful to bear every day. But bear it all she would somehow, she told herself grimly, and stabbed the heavy cloth with her needle so sharply that it penetrated her finger and drew blood; and she put the finger in her mouth and sucked it, feeling somehow comforted by this minuscule physical suffering. It was as nothing to what others – and possibly her own Freddy – might suffer, but it was something.

'—The drugs you have packed I have already sent ahead,' Freddy was saying, 'and I thank you for them. Now, I understand from reading *The Times* that dressings and bandages are much in demand. The Bursar at Nellie's tells me that these may be purchased in Paris at advantageous prices, so I will do so there, and also possibly, some instruments. Even Grandpa admits they make some excellent items there. Now, as to further money—'

'I have arranged that you may draw on the Bank of Constantinople. Lionel Rothschild has connections there. It is all settled—' Gideon said, and held out the sheaf of papers he was holding. 'Here is your authority to draw on his cousin's office there, together with various documents you will need to verify your claims on the account—'

Abby looked up, glad to be distracted from her deep anxiety, but also with some real curiosity in her voice. 'All this money, Gideon! Where does it come from? Are you drawing upon your own accounts? It seems to me a great deal is going into this matter—'

Gideon's long white face became a delicate pink and he looked suddenly a little flustered. But he spoke easily enough.

'Oh, it is my Fund, you know! Barings and Montefiore and Rothschild gave me a little, as did Goldsmid, and Mrs. O'Hare, you know, and one or two others.'

She tilted her head, surprised. 'Mrs. O'Hare?'

'The actress, Abby. We saw her last at Phoebe's Ball. You must remember – she was Mrs. Mohun and then married Richard O'Hare, and now has a son. A charming infant, very lively and knowing.'

'Indeed? I knew she was married, of course! I was just surprised that— How is it you know her son so well?'

'She had him with her when I went to see her about a Benefit for Martha's expedition,' Gideon said, and now his voice had a sharp edge to it. 'Really, my dear, such a catechism! Am I to account to you for every moment of my day? You know I am seeking funds for your sister – so I go to many people for aid. Including Mrs. O'Hare. There is no more to it than that, I do assure you.'

'I did not say there was,' Abby said mildly, but there was a little line between her brows as she looked up at him. It was not like Gideon to be so sharp with her on such a matter.

Gideon had turned back to Freddy, his face gradually regaining its usual pallor. 'So, my boy. There you are. I hope you enjoy your days in Paris. It is many years since I was there, but I recall it as a city of great beauty, even in the autumn of the year. Buy sensibly – well, I am sure you will! – and do see to it that you send messages to us about your progress – and your aunt's, of course. There will be much anxiety here, I do assure you, and messages will be awaited with great eagerness. You must write as often as the situation permits once you reach Scutari – I daresay it may be difficult to get letters through, but you must try—'

'Please, do not talk about it any more tonight!' Abby said, and stood up. 'We have but one peaceful evening here at home before you go, Freddy, and I want it to be spent without one word – not one word, you understand – of war, or anything else disagreeable. We shall be happy and comfortable together, and eat a good dinner and prose a little as we always have, and tomorrow – tomorrow I shall be up early to see you on your way. Yes, I shall. It is no use making such fusses, for I am determined. When my son goes to war, it is only right and proper I should see him on his way.'

'You are being positively ridiculous, Dickon, and what is

more, exceedingly boring. You do nothing but rant and prate at me – for heavens' sake, man, find something else to occupy you and leave me alone, if all you can do is to be so stupid and so disagreeable!'

Lydia turned with a little flounce of her favourite blue peignoir and leaned forwards to inspect her face in the mirror, turning her head from side to side and staring with great concentration at the line of her jaw, at the soft flesh beneath her eyes, and at the corners of her mouth. These were the places where age showed first, and she was deeply aware of having passed her thirty-sixth birthday. She was still beautiful, still smooth and soft to look at and to touch, and her colouring was as dramatic as it had been when she was sixteen. But thirty-six – time was passing and had to be carefully watched if its stigmata were to be kept at bay.

Behind her Dickon thrust out his legs and pushed his hands deeper into the pockets of his dressing robe, staring at her from beneath his brows, feeling the familiar sick sensation rising in him.

Damn the woman, damn her, damn her, damn her! To need and desire one female so much – it was a dreadful thing to have happened to such a one as Dickon O'Hare! He who had from the moment he left his boyhood behind in the haybarn in Galway where he had made a man of himself at the age of thirteen with a pretty farmer's daughter from the next village – he who had enjoyed women, used women and laughed at women, to be in such a fix! It was outrageous. The farmer's daughter had taken herself and her swelling belly away to face her father's wrath and gave him as little further trouble as had the countless girls and women who had followed her. Never had he given a second thought to any of them once he was bored with them, and that had always happened very soon. But this one, Lydia Mohun – this one was different.

He had thought he had wed her for his own benefit, for the position she held as undisputed queen of the London theatre, for her money, for her houses and her other nice little parcels of property, and also because she had been besotted with him when he had asked her to marry him.

But that had been *then*; now less than two years later he had to admit that all had changed. Her houses, her money and her nice little parcels of property remained as firmly in her hands as they had ever been. Anything that came to him was clearly seen to be her largess, and she never let him forget it. As for her value to him as queen of the stage – it was clear to him before they'd been married six months that he had trapped himself in her shadow. She manipulated the playwrights, the directors and the theatre management, everyone, to such good effect that although he always worked with her, although he always appeared to have good parts, whatever he did he was diminished by her.

Oh, she behaved prettily enough to him, showing a mock deference when they went together to talk about money to the management, or to talk about the structure of a play with a writer, but it was but mockery and everyone knew it. She was the one who held the purse strings, made the decisions, and ruled the roost. And everyone not only knew it but laughed at him for it.

Staring now at her back and at the way the soft curve of her arm melted so deliciously into the line of her shoulder he felt a sudden wave of frustration and rage. If only he had not become so hopelessly, helplessly besotted with her, it wouldn't matter. It was that that rankled most. Living on a woman's money was no pain to him, nor ever had been, when he had been allowing them to share his body with him. He had felt in an obscure way that he was more than paying his share for what he got out of them – and large amounts it had been – because he had not himself been at all attached to them.

But this time, it was different. He took from her not only money and success, like a bird feeding from her fingers, but he also took his manhood. Since loving her, he had lost his magnetism for other women, and it was a painful loss. They liked him well enough to look at, he knew, as they came flocking after the play to the greenroom, but since he had wed Lydia, not one of them had deliberately ogled him, or offered herself or so much as touched his hand in any meaningful way. And it was not because he was now Lydia Mohun's property, but because he no longer felt the least twinge of desire for anyone but Lydia. She had swallowed him whole, and taken all away from him, and given nothing back. And his jealousy simmered in him, and finally boiled up and over until with one smooth easy movement he left his chair, hurling himself across the room and on to her.

He pulled her robe from her back with such violence that it ripped, and she turned her head and stared at him over her shoulder with her eyes glittering and said softly, 'What's the matter then, my little one? Is he distressed, then? Is he all eaten up with jealousy because Mamma likes to talk to the pretty rich Jew? Ah, poor little, dear little, cock robin, all in a lather of jealousy—'

It was a scene they had both played many times with variations as he poured out his rage, his jealousy, his confusion and above all his own disgust with himself at loving her so much, and they played it again, each enjoying it in their own ways. He pulled her to the ground, so that they were rolling on the carpet, she biting, scratching, trying to gouge his eyes with her sharp fingernails, and kicking furiously, while he pinned her beneath him with the skill born of practice and tore her robe from her strip by strip, just once smacking her face hard when her thrusting knee came too close to his groin. Which made her more furious than ever, and she turned her head and bit his hand until the blood ran, and he swore loudly and with one stone-hard knee thrust upwards against her tight-pressed thighs towards her body until she could not help but give way, and she lay spreadeagled beneath him, as he pinned both her wrists to the ground with his iron grip and slowly, deliberately forced her to allow him entry to her.

Usually when they launched themselves into one of these fights she gave in with some grace at this point, and moved beneath him with pleasure, wriggling and arching her back in a way that excited him enormously, for she was still helpless beneath him, however hard she pretended to struggle.

But this time she did not pretend and actually did fight back, hard, and for a moment he feared he would not be able to complete his attack on her, for in his surprise his need for union with her faltered and weakened. But then, the urgency of her movements increased his rage, and with it his ardour, and he was thrusting at her so furiously that she had to give in.

And at last he won, as she caught her breath in a huge inspiration, and began to moan softly, arching her back until she was only held to the ground by her shoulders and her feet. And then she collapsed softly beneath him and lay there panting a little, her eyes half closed and her lips parted.

'Now who is master here?' he whispered into her ear, his hot damp face sticking to her hair. 'Who is master here, hey? If I tell you you may not talk to that damned Jew, then you may not! I am master here – I will be master here—'

She turned her head a little then so that he had to lift his own, and they stared at each other, their noses almost touching, she challengingly, and he trying to be even more challenging, but succeeding only in looking appealingly at her.

Slowly she smiled, and then rolled away sideways, throwing him off quite easily, and stood up, stretching, and stared down on him, lying sprawled on the floor with his robe rumpled and untidily twisted about him, looking, even in her nakedness, infinitely more in control, more elegant and more coolly comfortable than he ever could.

And smiled and said with great insouciance, 'Oh, as to that, I cannot refuse to see him again! I have promised him a Benefit, you know. Next week! And probably more besides. Do go and bath yourself, Dickon. You're a positive fright!'

'Well, I cannot understand why you should be in such a lather about it now,' Oliver said fretfully, and pulled the little curtain back to peer out at the crowded Rooms. 'Phoebe, do stop that silly weeping, and mop your face! Here we are with as full a house as we've ever had, and they are expecting the performance to begin! And all you can do is weep and wail about something you knew was going to happen anyway!'

'I did not know he would do it so – so hugger-mugger! I went to my aunt this afternoon and she – I did not *know*! He went on Wednesday morning last, she said, very early, going to Paris first and – oh, Oliver! How could he not have said goodbye?' And she was weeping again, the tears running prettily down her face, and this time Oliver lost his patience altogether.

'This is to *stop*, Phoebe! No doubt you are upset, no doubt you wish everyone to know you are upset, but I for one cannot afford to allow you to go on indulging your sensibilities in this absurd fashion! Now, here is a kerchief, and you are to dry your face, for I shall bring up this curtain in two minutes flat, you understand? Ready or not, you will be *on*. If you wish to make a fool of yourself in this way, then it is up to you. But you shall do it in full view of the entire Rooms, and that is all about it!'

And he jerked his head at the wings, and Peter Craig, the comedian who doubled as the Master of Ceremonies, came hesitantly on stage, looking sideways at Phoebe in some embarrassment.

'Craig, you will go on now, and announce the performance. Miss Phoebe will be ready!' And Oliver marched off the little stage, puffing a little and with his high forehead shining damply in the lights, for his irritation had brought him out in a sweat, and Phoebe stared after him with her mouth set in a mulish pout, and her eyes glittering moistly in the vivid gaslight.

But she was enough of a performer to know when the time had come to put her own feelings in the background, and as Peter's voice rose before the curtain with the familiar, 'Gentlemen, gen-tel-men, it is time at last for the real sustenance of the day—' she took a deep breath, and pulled her gown to rights and stepped back into the wings, ready to make her entrance.

She stood there listening and watching as the curtain opened, and the full glitter of the footlights flooded the boards, and as Peter reached his triumphant, 'your own – your very own – Miss – Phoebe!' and the music struck up, she went tripping on as light and as smiling as though the mere possibility of tears had never entered her head.

The performance went well. She could feel the great waves of admiration come pouring over the footlights to wrap her in warmth, and she relaxed under them and opened out even more, until she was singing as she rarely did, with every atom of feeling that was in her. Usually she was able to be a little remote from her own performance, almost standing aside to watch herself, monitoring her technique, her movements, every catch of her voice, every sidelong glance and pretty little intake of breath. She knew herself that her voice, though true and charming enough in tone, was not a great one, but she generally used it well, and with a good deal of skill. But tonight it was different. That sense of objectivity had quite gone; tonight she was just one girl, singing, and singing for herself, and not for the listeners who were sitting in rapt silence staring up at her.

And she was singing for Freddy, too. Freddy who had always been there, always cared about her, and who had never ever abandoned her.

Until now. Even as she made the familiar movements about the stage, strolling from side to side with her parasol set saucily over one shoulder, peeping out from beneath its lacy frills as she warbled the silly words about Miss Mary in her Garden, Yearning for her Lover Dear, she thought of him.

He had never left her so alone before, and now he had gone to dreadful dangers and dreadful loneliness, because of *her*.

The words went on tripping out – 'he loves me true, will always do, my Soldier-boy so Handsome' – but she was not thinking of them. She was seeing again that dreadful fuss at her Ball and hearing Freddy snapping out the words— 'She will not be alone! Do you think my aunt has not members of her family to care for her welfare? – we care a great deal, sir – I shall accompany her—' and her breath caught as she sang the phrases of the chorus of her song again. 'He loves me true, will always do, my Soldier-boy so Handsome—'

And it was at that point that her emotions overcame her again, and she stopped in mid-note and stared at the audience, and shook her head, as the music went on for a few bars and then, as the musicians peered up at her in puzzlement, faltered to a ragged stop, and put her hands up to her face and let the tears come as luxuriously as they wanted to.

She heard the rustle at the back of the Rooms, and guessed that Oliver was there, for he usually watched the performance from the most distant vantage point that he could, in order to be sure that all was easily seen and heard by every one of his customers, and wept even harder. Oliver would be so angry and so justifiably. He would shout at her and be angry and she had no one to blame but herself— She wept even more, her head bent and her shoulders shaking.

There was an arm about her then, and above her head Peter Craig's voice rang out, and she sniffed and listened, her hands still covering her face, but her tears coming less urgently now.

'Gentlemen, gentlemen! You will be distressed as I am to see our Dear Miss Phoebe in such a taking – and I can tell you why, gentlemen, I can tell you why! Our dear little girl here – well, it's no wonder the sentiments in her lovely song what she just sung to you should upset her so, for to tell you the truth, gentlemen, they was making me suffer a moistness of the eyes and I ain't ashamed to admit it, neither – for I know something you don't know gentlemen, which is that our Miss Phoebe's Dear Friend, her cousin the surgeon from Nellie's, Mr. Caspar, has gone off this very week to the wilds o' Crim Tartary to look after those poor soldiers of the Queen, what is suffering there at the hands of the Cossacks. Is it any wonder, gentlemen, that Miss Phoebe should be so overcome by the tragedy of it all—'

And now, she was a performer again. She had indulged herself shockingly in so giving way, and she knew it, and now the chance had been given to her to salvage the situation she took it with both hands. She turned her head for a moment to nestle on the sweating Peter's breast, and then, with a brave little lift of her head turned back to her audience and held up her hands, for there was a great uproar of voices as people talked and exclaimed and sympathized. At once the sounds subsided, and she could see Oliver moving purposefully through the crowd, his face set and red with fury, and she spoke quickly.

'Forgive me, all of you dear people,' she said huskily. 'Please to forgive me. I cannot hide from you the truth that Mr. Craig has told you. I am indeed sad for my dear cousin, but—' and she gave a little sniff and then, bravely, went on, '—but I should not have given in to my distress, and I ask your pardon—'

Someone near the front began to clap and then gradually others joined in until the whole of the rooms were ringing with sound, and she smiled and dimpled and looked sad and happy at the same time, and the applause increased. And then someone in the very front row suddenly stood up and threw a sovereign on to the stage. 'Send it to 'im to get comforts for the soldiers, Miss Phoebe!' he roared. 'They've got great need of it – send it out to your brave boy–'

And like the applause, it spread. Other men stood up, not to be outdone, and threw more money on to the stage and there was more gold than silver, and she stood there as the coins came glittering about her, her hands clasped in front of her and her face aflame with the excitement of it all. She looked more beautiful, more entrancing and more appealing than she ever had and Oliver stopped halfway through the Rooms, staring at her and feeling his anger drain away through his fingers' ends. She had behaved badly, to give way so to her private feelings, but she had more than made up for it, and the roars of the delighted audience around him underlined how much.

She held up her hands again, and said breathlessly, 'You are wonderful – all of you, quite wonderful. And I can tell you that not only will all this money be collected up and sent out to the soldiers, but we here at the Celia Supper Rooms will give the takings of the last performance on one night every week to the same cause – shall we not, Oliver?–' and she shaded her eyes with her hands and peered over the footlights, looking for him and saw him and said again, 'Shall we not, Oliver?' and now there was a hint of appeal in her voice.

He looked back at her, his face a little blank as he did the sums in his head. The amount that would be involved would be considerable but it need not damage the progress of the business too much. And if he refused – he looked round him at the audience and smiled. Not too broad a smile, but a smile all the same, and said as loudly as he could and as heartily as he could make himself sound, 'Indeed, we shall! We shall take just such a collection as this each week, and make it the Celia Rooms Fund for Wounded Soldiers–'

The applause broke out again, and Phoebe stood there and

smiled and dropped into a deep curtsey and a few more coins came spattering on to the stage and everyone felt patriotic and important and good, as well as safe, thinking of the dangers of war, and the suffering of soldiers.

CHAPTER ELEVEN

'I THINK, you know, that you may go without your bandages today, Miss Martha.' He touched her fingers gently, flexing them a little against his own broad hand, and she liked the way his warm dry touch made her feel, and she smiled at him.

'I am delighted to hear it. It has been most disagreeable to walk about in such heavy bulky gloves in this hot weather. The people of Malta thought I was quite mad, you know, when they saw me in the streets of Valetta in such a bundled up state!'

'I daresay the people of Malta think all the English are quite mad – most of the people of these Mediterranean countries consider us to be quite out of our attics, I do assure you – and perhaps they are not so far wrong.'

He let her hand fall and stood up and moved away across the deck to stare out over the sea at the distant line of the horizon. Turkey showed as a pale blue smudge almost too fine to be seen, and she came across the deck, walking easily now that she was accustomed to the roll of the ship, and stood there beside him and looked as well. And then turned her head to study his profile, the hard line of his set mouth, and the jut of his chin under the furrowed brow, and knew as clearly as if he had spoken what he was thinking, and ached for him.

She put out her hand and set it on his sleeve, a little timidly, and said in a low voice, 'Please, try not to think about it, Mr. Laurence.'

He looked down at her, and his face softened a little, although he still looked grim. 'I told you, Miss Martha, that in our present situation, it is quite absurd that we should be so formal with each other! Please to call me Alex. I find the stiffness of my full name much too dispiriting.'

She reddened, and then smiled. 'Very well. Alex. If you will drop that odious *Miss*. But I will repeat it, my dear friend. You must try, if you can, not to think about – about anything. You cannot know until you get there—'

He shook his head, almost impatiently, and turned to look out to sea again. 'How can I not think about it? He is the only person in the world who – who is of such importance to me. Since his mother died when he was a babe, we have been as close as a man and his son may be. And to have him take off like that – it is incomprehensible to me, even in time of war!'

'Oh, but it is not, you know,' she said gently. 'Indeed it is not! He is clearly a young man who – who feels his responsibilities deeply, who cares much for his fellows and is not content to let others carry his burdens. And I feel he is very like his father in that—'

He looked down at her again, and now she became a little flustered at the way his eyes were fixed on hers and she looked away and said hurriedly, 'I know that we are but short acquainted, but in six days in the close confines of a ship I believe one can become as close to a person as one may in three years on dry land. And you have been so kind to me, and nursed me and tended me with such care – indeed, I feel I know you well—'

'Do you like me, Martha?'

He said it abruptly, never taking his gaze from her, and she looked up at him, startled.

'*Like* you? That is an extraordinary question.'

'No, it is not. I would wish to know. Do you really like me, or are you simply grateful that I was here to dress your hands and take care of your injuries and help you? Would we have become friends, I wonder, had we both still been in London, and you had not been bitten by the urge to work in Scutari, and my son had not taken it into this foolish head to run away to be a soldier, constraining me to follow him and see to his welfare – would we, I wonder?'

She stood there with her head to one side, considering, and then looked up at him again, and said seriously, 'I cannot know Mr. – Alex. I really cannot know. As I said, the strange life we have aboard this ship, and the strangeness of the situation in which we find ourselves—' she spread her hands wide and looked down at the reddened palms, 'and of course the gratitude one always feels for one who gives one relief from pain, all these things make it impossible to answer your question with the honesty you would demand and to which you are entitled. As impossible as it would be for you to answer the same one if *I* asked it—'

'Oh, no,' he said swiftly. 'Oh, no, I would have no difficulty at all. I like you a great deal, Martha. I liked you when we met at your niece's Ball. I looked at you standing there trying so manfully to be polite to that dreadful old bore, and I thought what a pleasant face you had, and how full of humour it was, and I wished then to know you better. Talking to you that evening, I found you a most delightful companion, and I went away sure we would become friends in due course. That the 'due course' happened to fall out as it has, we could not foresee, of course. But I was right – we *are* friends and I do like you a great deal. I was – interested to know of your own views on our friendship. I value friendship very highly you see.'

'I too. I believe that our friends are the most important people in our lives. Sometimes even more so than family, although I would not have my relations know I said so! Indeed I value friends too highly to – to offer any facile assurances of my regard. I find I am a person who must think carefully about the degrees of – of feeling I have. Which is why I cannot answer your question, you see, although I would be most distressed to think that you were at all perturbed by such unwillingness! It is not because of lack of regard, but because of – of the high esteem in which I hold you that I find it difficult to – oh dear, we are becoming a little too philosophical, surely! Let us, please talk of other matters. To attempt to measure degrees of feeling is so very wearing!'

He smiled and nodded. 'Of course. Forgive me for setting

you such a conundrum. I will say only this, Martha – I find you a person whose companionship I value, and whose sympathy with my concern for my son I greatly appreciate, and whose welfare will always concern me. I wish you to know that whatever happens I will always be ready to come to your aid in any way you may need. I hope you will not hesitate to accept this interest I have in your wellbeing, at any time. I daresay I will remain in Scutari for a little while – unless my son has gone further afield–' He frowned for a moment, and then went on more strongly, 'And as long as I am there, I am your servant. Please do not forget that.'

And he took her hand and held it gently by the fingertips, and then bent his head and brushed his lips against the back of it, and she looked down at his grizzled hair and wanted suddenly to touch it, to hold his head close to her and rock away his distress about his runaway son against her breast. And blinked and pulled her hand away gently. She might not be able to say yet whether she truly liked this man, but find him attractive she undoubtedly did. And after so many years of being so self-contained about men, so many years of resisting her sister's attempts to find her a match, she did not know quite how to cope with such confusing sensations.

He smiled at her then and held out his arm, and she tucked her hand into the crook of his elbow, and they began to walk slowly about the deck, talking lightly of unimportant matters such as the colour of the waves as they broke on each side of the ship, and the way the froth of the crests made such delightful patterns against the water, and how long it would be before they would dock at Constantinople.

And Sal, sitting high on a hatch cover on the after deck watched them and grinned and said something ribald to the sailor who was sitting close beside her, and though he understood not a word of it, he recognized the mood in it, and seized the not unwilling Sal in a garlic-scented embrace and kissed her heartily. Which, despite the sharp smack she immediately delivered to his grinning face, she clearly enjoyed.

Taking it all round, the two women who had arrived on board the ship so tired and bedraggled ten days ago were finding more satisfaction in their travels to the War than either of them would have expected to be possible.

Constantinople was in an uproar. Standing by the rail, their valises stacked beside them and watching their seventeen boxes of stores being swung ashore, both Martha and Sal were affected by it. The hubbub about the docks, the shrieks of the Greek and Armenian stallholders selling sweetmeats and coffee and little pastries and sweet minted drinks, the swearing of the sailors trying to unload their ship and the surly shouting of the men on the docks below, all added up to an atmosphere which should have been exhilarating but was in fact alarming.

Martha pulled her cloak more closely about her shoulders and shivered a little, for it was late in the day now and the chill of the approaching winter was in the evening air, coming heavily from the low-lying clouds that lay thick and threatening over the grey waters of the Bosphorus. She wondered briefly how much longer Alex would be before he returned to their side, and then gave herself a little mental shake.

He was here about his own business, and she must not become too dependent upon him; that they had spent an agreeable week together on the ship, in spite of the dreadful weather that had made them arrive fully three days later than they should have done, was no reason for her to regard him as a person she had a right to include in her party. They had been almost inseparable all through the long blustery rain-pouring days and the dull frowsty lamplit evenings, in the cabin, but all the same, she was travelling alone, with just Sal to call her companion. She must do without the comfort of his presence from now on.

But all the same, she looked eagerly down at the crowds on the docks, seeking for a glimpse of his familiar plaid ulster and narrow-brimmed bowler and felt downcast when she could not find it and leaned back, sighing a little.

' 'E's gorn to talk to the 'arbour master. Says they might 'a seen 'im come through and be able to tell 'im what 'appened to the boy. Though 'ow 'e thinks anyone'd notice anyone in this

123

bleedin' Paddy's market, I'm sure I don't know,' Sal said sourly, and sniffed hard and spat over the side.

'I beg your pardon?' Martha said icily and Sal looked back at her over her shoulder and grinned cheerfully. 'Oh, come off it! Yer feller! The bloke yer fancies! Old Alex—'

'Sal, you may not speak so of a gentleman and – and my friend. It is outrageous of you to even suggest – really, you go too far.'

'Oh, sorry, sorry! Don't get yer rag up! I meant no 'arm. But you *are* sweet on 'im, as any can see with 'alf an eye, though I suppose you 'igh class ladies don't act the honest, the way the likes of us do. If I'm sweet on a feller I don't care 'oo knows it, includin' 'im, but there, you lot are diff'rent. So don't get yer rag up wiv me, 'an I won't say no more about it.'

'Please, Sal, do not,' Martha said earnestly. 'I will not discuss the matter with you, except to say that – that I hold Mr. Laurence in high esteem, but as no more than a friend, and I will be most distressed if I hear any more such talk from you.'

'I said as I meant no 'arm, didn't I? An' I said as I wouldn't say naught more about it. So I shan't.' Sal spoke almost absently, leaning over the rail and peering down into the shifting noisy scene below.

' 'Ere, Miss Martha – look dahn 'ere. That's no Turk, that ain't, or my name's Sal Swing 'Igh! See? Down there. If she ain't an English woman, then I'll be 'ung for a pickpocket!'

Martha followed her pointing finger and looked, and at first could see only the shifting patterns of heads and parcels and mules and lounging uniformed men, and then, as she concentrated, she saw the woman Sal had pointed out. A little woman, with a tight round bonnet, and a short black frieze coat over a green woollen gown. She was standing near the gangplank, talking most earnestly with the sailors who were guarding it, and as she watched, one of them tried to push her away, as with both hands she gesticulated and pointed, clearly trying to get aboard.

Martha felt her temper rise as she watched, for the sailors were being unnecessarily rough with the woman, whoever she was, and then as she was about to turn and make her way down

the deck to the gangplank to see if she could be of help to the
woman – who was now clearly distressed and weeping bitterly
– she saw Alex's familiar square shape come thrusting out of
the crowd, and towards the group by the gangplank.

He talked for a moment to the sailors, and then to the woman,
and after listening to her carefully for a moment, nodded, and
setting one arm across her shoulders led her aboard the ship,
and the sailors looked sulky for a moment, and then shrugged
and turned away, as he quite obviously passed a coin to the
hand of one of them.

He appeared on the deck where Martha and Sal were standing in a matter of moments, leading the little woman before him,
and it was now quite clear that she was indeed English. She
had the indefinable but unmistakable air of a servant, and was
sniffing dolorously and wiping her eyes as they came along the
deck towards the two women.

'What is amiss?' Martha said, and put her hand out and the
little woman, who appeared to be some fifty or so years old,
looked at her piteously, and said thickly, 'Oh, madam, are you
English? Oh, thank Gawd – if this kind gentleman 'adn't took
my part against them sailors, I'd never 'ave got 'ere. Oh, I am
that grateful—' and she wept again, and Sal took her roughly
but not unkindly by the shoulders and led her away to the rail
to talk to her in a low voice.

Martha turned swiftly to Alex and said eagerly, 'Never mind
about her for the moment – my dear friend, have you any
news?'

He shook his head, soberly, and she peered at him in the
rapidly failing light of early evening but could not see his face,
for he kept his head down and the shadow of his hat was
thrown across it.

'None,' he said gruffly. 'The harbour master's office is in
such a state of chaos as it is impossible to describe, but I managed to discover that in the past weeks young English gentlemen have been pouring through here on their way to the
battlefield. He says it has been worse this past week, with three
ships docking since the *Vectis* – that is the one upon which
your friend Miss Nightingale arrived – and all of them bearing

eager would-be soldiers. He swears they have all gone straight on over the Bosphorus to Scutari. So all we can do is the same and seek there for him – but it will not be easy—'

'Oh, come Alex, there cannot be that many young men who are not directly attached to the army here! I am sure when you speak to the army authorities there they will soon discover all you need to know—'

He shook his head very firmly. 'No, there have been more battles since we last had news—'

'Battles? Oh, tell me, please, tell me! Is the war over then?'

He laughed shortly at that. 'My dear, you are, in matters of fighting, a little naive, I fear! It will take more than that to end this war, I am afraid. As long as Sevastopol stands – no, it is not over. But they were bloody battles and very dreadful in their casualties, I understand. Last week – on Wednesday, as I understand, they fought a dreadful affair at Balaclava. I am told the Light Brigade was cut to ribbons, and there are so many dead – there is some mystery about it all, for the news is very confused. But since then news of another battle fought but yesterday is coming through, and the wounded, they say, are pouring into the hospital ships bound for Scutari. It was at a place called Inkerman. I know no more.'

'We must hurry,' she said, with a sudden abstraction in her voice, and she turned and looked over the Bosphorus to the Asian side, where they could see the great bulk of the Turkish Barracks looming above the muddy shores below. It seemed so near and yet so far away, and she felt the need to move urgently, to rush down to the docks and find a ferry boat to take her there forthwith. There was work to be done, and she was burning to do it.

' 'Ere, Miss Martha – we've got a right one 'ere—'

Martha turned, a little startled, and saw Sal standing with arms akimbo and staring down at the little woman in the round bonnet, now sniffing less miserably but still with a tedious monotony into her handkerchief.

'What is that, Sal? Oh, I had forgotten – what is her trouble? Has she no one to aid her?'

'She told me some tale of her employer,' Alex said, moving

closer and looking down on the little woman. 'Now, my dear, you must stop this weeping and tell us more clearly what the trouble is. Be quick now, for we have much to see to—'

'Please, madam, please—' The little woman seized on Martha's hand and peered up into her face with her eyes very wide and red rimmed. 'As soon as I 'eard as this ship 'ad come and there was an English lady aboard, I come at once. I tried last week, I did, when that there other party of English ladies and nuns an' all come, but they wouldn't 'elp. Said as they was 'ere to look after soldiers and my poor lady would 'ave to manage as best she could. But I'm that frightened, madam, I am! She's took ill before but never like this and I'm that afraid as she's dyin'! Please, madam, please to come to 'er! I can't get no one as cares for 'er, no one at all, and I'm near bereft of my wits, I'm that alarmed for 'er. Please to come.'

'Your employer is an English lady then?' Alex asked.

'Oh, yes, sir, yes! I wouldn't be lady's maid to no 'eathen foreigner! Of course she's English, and a great lady at that! Oh, wait till you see 'er, you'll know 'oo she is right away, I'm sure you will, but please to come. Ever since that 'ateful boy took off we've bin alone, and she took so ill an' I 'ad no way to 'elp 'er, and not an English doctor left in all Constantinople, on account of this evil war business and— Oh, madam, please, you must come now.' The little woman was plucking at her sleeve. 'You must come! She's fit to die and I'm afeared for 'er—'

'I think we must go, Martha! We cannot leave a compatriot alone in such straits in such a place—' Alex looked over his shoulder at the teeming dock below. 'I could not do so. Shall I come with you? I will gladly. I imagine she is some traveller stranded here, and caught by the war.'

Martha turned too, to look once more over her shoulder at the bulk of the Barracks over the straits, where the army hospital lay. 'I should not waste time here—' she said uncertainly.

'My dear, this is hardly wasting time! And anyway, it would be better for you to wait until the morning, when it will be light, to cross. I would not be happy for either of us to arrive there at this hour, with wounded soldiers still being delivered from over the Black Sea. I think, you know, that this lady will not delay us too long. And she has need of us—'

'Yes, you are right,' Martha spoke with decision and bent down to pick up two of the valises. 'Come along then. We shall go at once— Sal, take these down and you shall stay with them and the baggage, if you please, and find some food and ask at the harbour master's office about a place to sleep tonight. I will inquire there for you when I return, for I will go with Mr. Laurence to see this lady – what is your name, my dear?'

She looked at the little woman who sniffed and said, 'Sarah Jenkins, madam, if you please, and I'm that grateful, madam. You really are an angel – come along, madam. I've a mule and cart waiting and a fair penny it cost to get 'im, an' all, and we'll go right there. Oh, my dear lady will be that 'appy to see you—'

And she went hurrying away down the deck, with Martha and Alex following her closely, and Sal bringing up a panting cursing rear with the rest of the luggage.

CHAPTER TWELVE

THE cart rattled and rocked so abominably that she felt quite queasy for a moment, and then realized that it was the smells which assaulted her that made her stomach turn. The streets they were moving through were dark, narrow and disgusting, and yet not in the same way that they were in the black alleys of Seven Dials at home in London. They were indeed revolting, but it was a revulsion she could bear. Here, even though she could not see any of the buildings, could make out no detail of the city through which they were moving, there was an alienness, a fear-creating foreignness that made her shrink closer to Alex by her side. And he moved and set his arm about her shoulders and held her close, so close that she felt the roughness of his plaid against her cheek, and at once the fear receded and with it the queasiness, and she sighed softly and peered ahead into the darkness.

Sarah Jenkins was sitting up at the front of the cart, the reins in one hand, and monotonously whipping the mule with the other; and although normally Martha was outraged by such treatment of dumb beasts, she said nothing. Clearly the animal was used to it, for it went plodding on at its own rate, not so much as flicking its ears as the whip stung its back.

'How much further?' Martha said, gasping a little, for it was difficult to get the words out, so hard was she being thrown about, in spite of Alex's restraining arm.

'Not far now, madam – not far. It was the best place we could get. All the proper establishments was full to bustin', or closed down on account o' the war, an' this was all we could find. I done my best to make it comfortable though – round this next corner, madam, and then on a bit—'

They turned into a much better wider road, and the mule picked up speed as its hooves hit the stones, and now they could see more about them. High buildings, shuttered, unlit, apart from occasional flaming torches set up on corners, and with strangely shaped trees set at the roadside, and Martha blinked and shook her head and murmured, 'Turkey. I am in *Turkey.*'

'I know. It is a strange feeling, is it not? To be away from home in so foreign a place,' Alex said, and she looked up at him, grateful for the familiarity of him, the sound of his voice, the faint scent of tobacco that clung to his ulster, and the shape of his bowler hatted head against the darker sky. And then, suddenly aware of the impropriety of her situation, sitting there being hugged by a man who was, after all, but a very new acquaintance, she reddened in the darkness, and sat up straight, disentangling herself, and putting her hands up to set her bonnet to rights. She felt Alex's amusement as he accepted her move and sat back from her himself, and that made her face flame hotter still.

''ere we are, madam, sir,' Sarah Jenkins said breathlessly, and with a surprising agility scrambled down from the cart and tied the reins to an invisible post. 'Please, this way – mind the gutter, now, that's it – over these steps, and you'll be in the garden – that's it! The 'ouse is over 'ere—'

And then they were inside the building, and she stood blinking in the light that seemed so bright, but was in fact quite dim for there was only a single tallow candle burning on a low table.

She looked about her, as she untied her bonnet strings, and saw a room bare of furniture – there was just the low table upon which the candle stood, and a long couch against one wall – but rich in decoration. The walls were covered in small tiles arranged in patterns of mathematical intricacy and, even in this poor light, rich colours, and the ceiling above their heads was fretted and carved and painted in the same luscious colours and she blinked up at it, and shook her head at the strangeness of it all and followed Sarah Jenkins, who had picked up the candle, to the other side of the big room.

Clearly it served only as entrance hall, for Sarah was standing before a curtained door and as Martha and Alex came up to her, she beckoning them on eagerly, she turned and swept aside the curtain and with exaggerated care to be quiet pushed open the door behind it, as Martha peered over her shoulder.

It was a big room, and full of light. There were candles and oil lamps in profusion and again Martha blinked for it was so startling after the dimness she had experienced in the past hour that it was a while before she could register what she actually saw. And then as she looked around, she shook her head again, but this time in puzzlement.

The room had the same sort of wall decorations as the outer hall, tiles, colours, patterns, all of it, and the ceiling was if anything even more fretted and shaped. There were low tables and long low couches, very like those in the entrance hall, but mixed up among them were other pieces of furniture; high straight-backed chairs and heavy polished tables and horse-hair-stuffed sofas, and a great ornate sideboard covered in ornaments, and with a vast silver epergne in the centre.

'We made it as much like 'ome as we could,' Sarah Jenkins whispered, with a note of great satisfaction in her breathy little voice. 'Madam give me the money an' tol' me to get what I could to make the place comfortable, an' I went to the Embassy an' there was these things they 'ad goin' cheap, what the last Ambassador 'ad brought and didn't want to take back 'ome again. Nice, 'n't it? Just like bein' at 'ome in the dear ol' smoke.'

And Martha, looking round at the extraordinary mixture almost smiled, for it was all so absurd, so mismatched, so pathetic in its attempt to imitate a London drawing-room.

But then her eyes rested on the couch in the centre of the room and the incipient smile faded from her lips.

It was piled high with cushions of multi-patterned silks and with shawls and blankets, and in the centre of it lay a slight hump. At first it seemed as though it was just a disarrangement of the shawls, a mere smudge of dark shadow against the scarlet cushion at the top of the heap, but then she realized some-

131

one was lying there and she moved forwards, tentatively, trying to see more clearly.

And realized that whoever was lying there was veiled, startlingly and incongruously veiled in a heavy dark coloured mesh, so that all that could be seen was a shadow of a face beneath it. The figure lay quite still as Martha stood and looked down on it, with Alex looking over her shoulder, and although there was a faint movement of breathing there was also a stillness that was deeply alarming.

'Oh, thank Gawd, she's asleep,' Sarah said, and now her voice was a little louder as she came to the other side of the couch and twitched one of the shawls a little. Still the figure remained motionless apart from its breathing, and Martha leaned closer and said softly, 'Sleeping? Are you sure that is all? I would have thought—'

'Oh, she's sleeping all right, madam,' Sarah said, and now her voice was at a normal conversational level. 'I told 'er and told 'er as she takes too much o' the stuff, but 'er pains and 'er miseries are that dreadful, well, you can't blame 'er, can you?'

She was taking off her black frieze coat, shaking out the folds neatly, and arranging it over the back of a chair. All the urgency that had been in her seemed suddenly to have evaporated, and she was quiet and calm and indeed quite sprightly.

'Can I get you both a little refreshment, madam, sir?' she said, as she took off her bonnet and smoothed her hair with both hands. 'They drinks a lot o' sweet mint tea in these parts – nasty 'eathen stuff, if you asks me, though Madam quite likes it – but I got a bit o' real tea from 'ome left in me private store, an' I'll gladly make you a cup. Just to keep you comfortable while you waits.'

Martha frowned sharply. 'My dear Jenkins, you must know that we have come here only because you told us it was a matter of great urgency! I have my own affairs to deal with, and cannot stay here indefinitely. If your mistress is ill, then of course I will gladly help in any way I can – but—' she turned and looked down on the shape on the couch, '—she appears to be sleeping sweetly enough. There is none of the restlessness of fever about her, and—'

'My dear,' Alex said gently, and began to take off his own coat. 'My dear, you misunderstand, I think. This lady here is clearly heavily drugged. I imagine it is laudanum?'

He looked up at Sarah Jenkins, who reddened a little and nodded.

'Aye, I thought as much. She breathes so – well, let us examine her. Then we shall see what is amiss, and can decide what must be done when she awakes—' and he reached out his hand towards the veiled face.

'No!' Sarah Jenkins almost leapt forwards, and her hand closed round Alex's wrist, hard, pulling his hand back just as he touched the edge of the veil. 'No, sir, not on your life! She'd go mad if she thought any man saw 'er poor face – no, you mustn't!'

Alex stared at her, frowning, and his voice was sharp and rather loud when he spoke.

'Indeed? Then what can I do? If it is not permitted to uncover her, how can I examine and treat her? You said she was English – but you behave as though she was some veiled Arab queen!'

The figure on the couch stirred a little at the sound, and Martha knelt beside it looking earnestly at the veil, trying to see through its heavy mesh as the voices went on above her.

'I didn't ask *you* to come, sir, if you'll recall!' Sarah Jenkins said shrilly. 'It was madam as I asked to come. As soon as I 'eard there was an English lady on the ship as 'ad just docked, I come after 'er, on account I knew my lady wouldn't let any man near 'er! You come just for advice and company as far as I was concerned, sir – I never thought as you'd want to *examine* 'er! That'd be an awful thing—'

'I never heard such nonsense in my life!' Alex said, his voice exploding with anger. 'If the lady is ill, she needs medical care – and I am a surgeon. You exceed your station, to try to tell me what I should or should not do for an ill person – I am a *surgeon*, woman, and I treat as I see fit, and no one, be it mistress or maid, gives me such orders as you are trying to give me! I have never—'

Martha looked over her shoulder at them and then back at

the figure on the couch, and again she stirred, and then turned her head, and almost without thinking, Martha put out her hand and took the edge of the veil in her fingers and gently drew it back. And the head turned more fully and the eyes opened and stared directly into hers, and Martha, staring down, felt her own lids suddenly prickle with shocked pity.

The eyes were lovely. A deep green in colour, long and narrow and thickly lashed. There were lines in the corners, but they were not ugly ones, although they showed their owner to be well past her middle years, even on the threshold of old age. Above those narrow green eyes, which were dazed a little and blank as they stared up into Martha's now rather moist ones, the brows flared smooth and sleek and the forehead over them was broad and white and very delicate. The nose too was finely chiselled, with a flare at the nostrils which was breathtakingly lovely, and below that a soft mouth, lips slightly parted and dimpled at one corner.

But then the shock. One cheek was smooth, the skin looking a little papery and soft from age, but still with a lovely curve to it and the temple above it softly hollowed and as elegantly modelled as any piece of Dresden china. But – the other side – the other side was an obscenity.

The flesh was red, puckered, twisted, and hideous with the scar of a huge injury which ran from just below the eye down past the point of the soft chin, down the long neck and across on to the shoulder, and looking at it Martha closed her eyes and swallowed.

Above her the voices went on, and she put up one hand in an attempt to halt them, but Sarah Jenkins was launched on her tirade and her voice went on and on, with Alex breaking in with an angry expostulation from time to time, and Martha opened her eyes and looked again at the face on the scarlet cushion, and now the eyes were clearing and a look of puzzlement came creeping in.

'Who – who are you?'

The voice was thick and a little cracked, and the effort of producing it seemed almost too much for her, and she closed her eyes and turned her head again, away from Martha.

'Who are you?' she said it again, a little more strongly, but with an enormous weariness, and Martha said as gently as she could, 'I am Martha Lackland, ma'am – from England. I have come to see if I can help you in your illness.'

The head remained very still, but then slowly the eyes opened and stared blankly ahead. 'What did you say?'

'I am Martha Lackland, ma'am. From England, come to help you, if I can, in your illness.'

It was as though a sudden wind had blown, or a sudden surge of power had come into her, for the eyes cleared, losing the blank dazed stare, and the head snapped round, and the woman stared up into the face so near her own, and her eyes glittered with a sudden ferocity which made Martha sit back on her heels, startled.

'Who did you say? I'm dreaming. I do not believe it! I am dreaming – Sarah! Sarah, Sarah, I'm dreaming again, oh Christ, help me – Sarah, Sarah, Sarah—'

The maid moved with a swiftness remarkable in one of her stocky build, and was beside the couch and on her knees and talking soothingly all in a split moment.

'It's all right, madam, it's all right – you aren't dreaming, it's all right, madam—'

'Sarah, Sarah, Sarah—' the shrieks went on, rising to a crescendo, and the woman on the couch began to rock her head, her eyes screwed up tightly, and her lips pulled back in a huge grimace, and now Martha could see just how frail she was, just how tightly the flesh was stretched over her bones, and just how shaky was her hold on life, for her voice was thin and weakening fast, and the movements, too, were attenuated and fluttery, a pathetically small reaction to what was clearly a vast distress.

'Please, ma'am,' she said gently, and put out both hands to set them each side of the sadly scarred face, holding her as gently as she could. 'Please, do not distress yourself. You are too weak to waste your strength so—'

Gradually the little storm subsided, pitiful in its weakness, and the head lay still again, the eyes still closed but with tears now squeezing themselves out beneath the lashes, and she raised her hands with enormous effort, untangling them from the shawls, and lifted them to her face, and they were so thin and clawlike it was as though a bird's wing had touched Martha's own square hands. 'My veil,' she whispered. 'My veil. Please—'

Gently, Martha pulled the veil forwards and the woman on the couch sighed softly and let her hands fall, and at last a silence filled the room again, broken only by the sound of her breath, which was coming fast now and was thin, almost whistling in her throat.

After a moment Martha said carefully, 'We came, ma'am, to help you. Your servant said you were ill and in need of a compatriot's help. And I can see indeed that you are. You should return to England, ma'am. Shall we arrange a passage for you with the captain of the ship which docked with us today? It returns to Marseilles in two days' time, I believe, and from there I am sure you can be carried safe home to London—'

The woman lay there behind her veil, breathing that thin whistling breath and saying nothing, and Martha tried again.

'Or, if you prefer, ma'am, we will send messages to London, to any person of your choice, asking them to come here to fetch you, if you fear that Jenkins cannot manage alone—'

'I could manage, and no error, madam, and never think I 'aven't told 'er so!' Sarah said loudly. ''Aven't I, madam? 'Aven't I asked you time an' again to let me arrange for us to go 'ome? But she won't,' she looked up at Martha then. 'She won't. Not no 'ow.'

'Who did you say you were?' The voice sounded quite different now, and they all turned and looked at her in some surprise, and Martha could see the eyes gleaming through the veil. 'Who are you?'

Patiently, Martha told her again. That she was Martha Lackland come from London, willing and ready to help her, 'as much as I can,' she temporized then, 'for I am, in fact, on my way to Scutari. The war, you know.'

'Yes, the war.' The voice was thin again, little more than a breath, and again Martha sank to her knees beside the couch, to hear her better. 'The war. So absurd. A war. When there are so many more important things to worry about.'

Martha tried to see the face behind the veil more clearly, and could not. Only the faint gleam of those extraordinary eyes.

'Tell me your name again.'

Puzzled, Martha did so, looking up over her shoulder at Alex as she spoke. Is she wandering in her wits? her eyes asked him. He shook his head imperceptibly, and she looked back at the veiled face.

'Lackland,' the breath came soft and then louder. 'Lackland, oh, my God, Lackland. It cannot be otherwise—' and then the veil lifted and billowed softly but soundlessly and after a startled moment Martha realized that the sick woman on the couch was laughing, laughing hugely but so weakly that nothing could be heard of her strange mirth.

'I am glad you are amused, ma'am,' she said uncertainly. 'Indeed, I am. And now you have the better of me, for I do not know your name.'

The laughter stopped, and the gleam of the eyes again appeared and there was a silence and then the soft voice said, 'You saw my face, did you not? You lifted my veil, and you saw my face?'

'Yes, ma'am. I am sorry. I meant no – no invasion of your privacy, I do assure you. I was but concerned for your health, and felt I could not – could not judge of the situation without looking at you and – I am sorry.'

'And you still need to ask who I am? You do not know?'

Hugely puzzled, Martha shook her head. 'Why no, ma'am. You must forgive me, but no. I have no idea.'

Slowly the birdlike hands moved again, lifting with an enormous effort, until they touched the edge of the veil and with another great effort, lifted it, as Sarah Jenkins leaned forwards, as though to shield her from the view.

'No, Sarah. It doesn't matter any longer. It doesn't matter at all. I have so little time left, that even I cannot care who sees it. I am finished with caring now. Almost finished.'

She turned her head, and lay there looking at them, and

behind Martha Alex took a breath and said gently, 'A burn, ma'am. A shocking burn.'

'Aye, a burn.' The eyes moved and looked at him. 'I am beautiful, am I not? To a man, an object of admiration and awe and desire? Beautiful, am I not?'

There was a long silence and then Alex said very gently, 'Yes, ma'am. You are. I see a face that is very lovely. The shape of it, the colour of it – all very lovely. A sad scar, I also see, but that is all. A lovely face with a sad scar. But it does not change the fact that the face is lovely.'

Her eyes glittered suddenly, and she managed a laugh, a trill that was like the echo of falling water, far away. 'You are a courtier, my dear sir! Had such a one as you come to my greenroom in the days before – before this—' her head lifted in a sketch of gesture towards her face, '—I would, I think, have liked you well. Very well. Dangerously well—'

He went suddenly red, and staring up at him and then at the woman on the couch Martha felt her own embarrassment rise, felt as though she were eavesdropping on the most private of secret conversations, and felt too a sudden lift of most disagreeable sensation, and was puzzled by it. But even as it happened she knew what it was. Jealousy.

This woman sick, even dying, dreadfully mutilated, lying helpless and useless on a sofa in the middle of an alien city was making love to a man patently young enough to be her son, a man with whom Martha herself felt some rapport, and she was jealous. And she looked back at the face on the pillow and was angry, enormously angry with herself for feeling so, and let the anger spill over into her voice.

'This does not reveal the answer to our mystery, to me, at any rate, ma'am,' she said with an edge of acid in her tone. 'If you do not wish to tell us of your identity, that is of course, your privilege. But I hope you will tell us the cause of your illness and allow us to do what we can to aid you.'

The eyes moved again, to rest on her face and she smiled, a curious twisted smile that lifted the scar painfully. 'You still do not know? I am surprised. She was your brother's wife, after all.'

Martha stared at her, dumbfounded. 'I beg your pardon, ma'am. My brother – I really do not understand you! I am trying, but I cannot comprehend—'

'Tush!' The little sound exploded softly into the air. 'Tush! You are, you must be his daughter. There cannot be any other Lacklands in all London! He told me once – that was why they called him that. He came from nowhere, and they had to call him something, did they not? So they called him Lackland—'

The voice dwindled away, and the eyes closed and Martha sat there on her heels and looked at the face on the pillow and tried to understand what it was all about. Somewhere at the back of her mind, she knew she knew. Information was there, information once collected but long since consigned to the lumber room of her memory as irrelevant. What this woman was saying did make a curious sort of sense, and she knew it did, but could not make sense of it. And also, Martha realized, in some other deep recess of her mind she knew who she was, but she could not put a name to her.

The eyes opened again, and the voice, stronger again, came flutingly, as she stared at Martha, and again the smile changed the contours of the face.

'My name, Miss Lackland, is Lilith. Lilith Lucas, of the Haymarket Theatre. Did your father never speak to you of me? Not ever?'

CHAPTER THIRTEEN

MARTHA woke suddenly and sat very still, letting sensation come creeping back, tingling and sharp, into her cramped muscles. On the other side of the room she could see Sarah Jenkins, sprawled in an armchair and with her head fallen back and her mouth in an unlovely gape as she snored, and she blinked and yawned and turned her head to look at the woman beside her.

Martha had fallen asleep with her head on her arms, resting them on the side of the sick Lilith's couch and with her legs tucked under her, and now as she peered at the face on the pillow she was glad to see she slept. But it was an uneasy sleep, and she looked even more gaunt and fragile than ever.

'She cannot last much longer, my dear,' Alex's voice came softly and she looked up and smiled to see him standing there. He had been sitting in an armchair too, on the far side of the room, but had heard her slight movement as she woke, and come to join her.

They both looked at the face on the pillow and then Alex said softly, 'An extraordinary tale.'

'Indeed, it is,' Martha whispered back. 'But, I believe, true in every particular. I have heard of some of it before. I had forgot—'

'Poor creature. From all she said I imagine she has not been always – well, all that a lady might be. But all the same – poor creature—'

Martha looked up at him and felt again that sharp stab of resentment and then hated herself for it. To feel so against a woman as pathetic, as lost, as ailing as this one, was shameful.

'I am not sure what we should do for her,' she said after a moment, and at once felt better, for considering practical matters was her forte and always had been and when she was being practical she could hardly be foolishly emotional. 'I cannot possibly stay here long, and yet how can I leave her? It would be a dreadful thing to do. Will she be fit to travel do you think? Can we get her on to a ship?'

He shook his head. 'I doubt she will live much past morning,' he said simply. 'No, do not look like that. It is so, and it is better always to face facts in such situations.'

She was silent for a moment and then nodded, 'I think you are right. It is better to face facts.' And again she looked at the sick woman, and touched her hand gently, and in her sleep Lilith stirred and her thin fingers curled round Martha's like a child, and for a moment tears pricked her eyelids again as she stared down at her.

They had sat and listened, trying to persuade her to rest, to allow Alex to examine her, to offer her some care, but she had brushed all that aside with great impatience.

'I am dying,' she had said. 'I know I am dying. I have been spitting blood this past six months, and then the fever took me, and though that is gone, it has weakened me. I am dying, and I will not waste what time I have on physic.' She had smiled then, a faint grimace that even so bore a trace of the gaiety and charm that once must have been quite irresistible. 'Even from such a physician. I must tell you – there are things I must tell you—'

She had stopped then, and lain gasping a little on her scarlet cushion, exhausted by her own urgency and Martha had soothed her, and brought her a drink which Sarah Jenkins prepared for her, and after a while she had rallied again, and started to talk. And once she started, could not, would not, stop.

'I must tell you. All of it, I must tell you – he went away. I brought him to Italy for his health, and he ran away. My Jody. He ran away.'

'Who?' Alex had asked, his voice crisply practical, and she had closed her eyes for a moment and then opened them and said very clearly, 'Jonathan. Jonathan Daniel Cecil. He was my youngest son, the youngest of my four children and I loved him very dearly. And he ran away from me, and left me, and—'

Her eyes had filled with tears then, and she had said piteously, 'How could he treat me so? I told him I would give him all he needed, but all he wanted was actual cash – gold. I had to wait for it to get it from the bank, and he took my jewels, so many of them, and went away—' and she had wept again, the tears coursing down her cheeks, leaving tracks behind in the softness of the uninjured skin, and lifting the scarred side to a glistening redness.

' 'E was a right villain,' Sarah Jenkins had said softly, standing behind them both, so that she could speak into their ears. 'A right 'orrible little villain. 'E got 'isself cut about something dreadful in London – some mischief he got into, I never knew the rights of it – and she took 'im away to Italy to get better, and what does 'e do but run off! And then the valet went and there was only me an 'er, and would she go 'ome? Not on yer nelly! Went lookin' for 'im, 'igh and low, she did. We was in Greece, and then we was back in Italy and then in Bulgaria, and then 'ere – always people saying as they'd seen him, and 'er following. Poor lady! She idolized 'im, she did, an' 'e treated 'er so cruel—'

Martha had put her hand out then, not to the sick weeping woman on the couch, but to Alex, thinking of his anguish about his own runaway son, and he looked down at her and smiled and closed his hand warmly over hers.

'No, do not fret, Martha,' he had said softly. 'I am grateful for your concern, but my case is different. My boy did not rob me, nor is he fleeing from me. He is but going *to* something, which is quite different.'

He had turned his head and looked down at Lilith. 'Poor lady. Poor, poor lady.' That time Martha had felt no jealousy, only a shared pity for the lonely seeking Lilith, seeing her travelling relentlessly about Europe, hunting and yearning. Poor, poor lady indeed.

Lilith had opened her eyes then, as though aware of their gaze, and Martha had leaned over and wiped her wet cheeks and Lilith had smiled at her fleetingly, and then started to talk again.

Only now it was as though her mind had slipped its gear, for she spoke not of the recent past and all that had happened to bring her here to this Constantinople room with its strangely patterned walls and coloured shapes, but of herself, of all she had seen and known and felt in all her life, and listening to her, it was as though, Martha suddenly felt, she was there with her in that long ago, living that life with her.

She saw her as a child, a pretty eager dancing child, with ambitions of such size and absurdity, dreams of such scope and vision that they were ridiculous, and so ridiculous they had to be possible.

She saw her dancing through the narrow streets of the London of more than fifty years ago, down the alleyways into the byways, through Old Compton Street and out again, and saw too, the people she danced with.

Two big men, but also a boy. A handsome boy, a tall thin boy with dark curly hair and eyes as green as hers, who followed her and laughed with her and watched her, and even went with her on strange expeditions to graveyards – for quite what purpose Martha could not fathom, but it did not matter, for it was the two children she cared about, and not what they did.

She saw them together, happy and laughing and loving, and then she saw them apart, both so far apart, as Lilith talked of the 'country days' when she went away, of the 'learning days' when she became a lady, and found the name of Lucas, and peacocked about the pretty house in Kent and was happy. And then was bored and yearning to be free, dreaming once more her ridiculous dreams, and plaiting her mad ambitions into reality.

And then the boy again, and London – it was all such a tangle, for her speech rambled and wandered and went round in circles as she lay there staring up at the fretted ceiling above her and talked and talked till her voice grew husky and her face was flushed with the effort. They could not stop her, and after a while they stopped trying.

On and on she had talked, of great days at the Haymarket, and of early days when Sheridan was at Drury Lane, of men whose names tripped from her tongue like confetti, of pretty babies – Celia – Lydia, Benedict – Celia—

And then Martha had remembered, and knew, and thought with a sudden stab of pain of her brother Jonah and his tragedy, and shook her head and pushed away such thoughts, for this was Lilith now. Lilith who was speaking of days long before Jonah and Celia's sad time.

And at last she had fallen asleep, leaving them both exhausted with her efforts, and staring down at her, and Alex had sat down and Martha had rested her weary head on her arms beside the now silent Lilith, and slept.

She yawned now widely and then stretched and Alex said quietly, 'You must sleep again, my dear. You will be quite a rag tomorrow if you do not.'

'What is the time,' she whispered, and he pulled his big round watch from his waistcoat pocket and peered at it, and shook his head.

'Too late perhaps, for more sleep after all! It is almost six in the morning. I think we must decide what to do, my dear. Will you wait here with her, until as long as is necessary? It cannot be much longer—'

'I think—' Martha began, and then as though she knew they were speaking of her, Lilith's eyes suddenly snapped open and she said urgently, 'You must not go!'

At once Martha bent over her, smoothing the rumpled hair back from her brow. 'No, of course not,' she said. 'We will not leave you. Do not be afraid—'

However long it meant she would be delayed, she could not go. At the back of her mind she tried to make a plan, tried to think ahead. I must send Sal on with all there is, get her to find us some sort of place to put all our stores, find us somewhere to lodge—

'There is no time, no time—' Lilith said suddenly, and with an effort that was painful to see, tried to sit up, and at once Martha leaned forwards to help her, until at last she was sitting upright, her back supported by the extra cushions Alex pushed down behind her.

Her parlous state was even more apparent now, for they could see how little flesh remained on her bones, and her breathing moved the cage of her chest so painfully that Martha felt her own muscles ache in sympathy. Her movements had rearranged her shawls and blankets too, and below the scent of chypre that came from her there was now the smell of death, that cloying almost sweet heaviness that presaged decay. Martha had smelled it too often not to know it now, and again she tightened her hand on the clawlike fingers.

Lilith looked up at her and said urgently, 'Paper. Get it now. Paper.'

'Please, do not fret yourself, my dear,' Martha began, but Alex touched her shoulder and at once she stopped.

'Of course, Mrs. Lucas. Of course. Where is it?'

'My bureau. In my bureau. Sarah knows—' she began to cough, and Martha held her shoulders and as the cough became stronger helped her to lean forwards and with the expectation born of experience pulled one of the shawls free and held it to the pale lips; and just in time for a bubble of scarlet froth appeared and then more and more and still she coughed, and Martha thought, 'Oh, God, let her die easy. Please to let her die easy—'

But the time was not yet, for after a while, the coughing stopped, and Lilith leaned back against Martha's restraining arm, gasping a little, her face a ghastly white, and stared up at her with eyes wide and frightened.

'Not yet,' she whispered. 'Please, not yet.'

'No, my dear, of course not – of course not,' Martha soothed, and wiped the lax lips and Lilith's eyes closed and she took a shallow breath, and a little colour came back into her face.

'I have the paper here, and a pen,' Alex said softly. 'If you say it as you wish, I will write it. Is it a letter?'

She opened her eyes then and looked at him, seeming to be puzzled, as her gaze moved from him to Sarah Jenkins peering over his shoulder and then up at Martha. And then her vision cleared and she spoke more strongly.

'No. Not a letter. A will. I must make a will. I never did, and never would, for I was going to live for ever, was I not?' She almost laughed then, a short intake of bubbling breath.

'My dear, you will live for ever as the actress who made people so happy, so often,' he said gently. 'We all live on in one way or another. Through our work – through our children—'

That seemed to rouse her, for she had slipped back again into momentary sleep, but she opened her eyes wide and said loudly, 'It is all to go to Abel. To Abel Lackland. The houses, the money, the jewels, all of it. Not to him, not to Jody. No matter what happens, never to Jody! He ran away—'

Her eyes seemed to cloud over again, and then snapped wide once more as Martha said involuntarily, 'Oh, no – you cannot!'

'I cannot? Who says I cannot? I will do with my money as I choose, and I have a lot of it – so much of it, so very much—' Again the voice dwindled, and Alex said softly, 'Martha, my dear, she is leaving. You must let her do as she thinks best.'

'*He* never ran away from me. Not Abel,' Lilith said suddenly, and smiled, a soft and reminiscent smile. 'Poor dear Abel! He loved me very dearly, you know. I knew he did – loved me dearly! But they told him some lie or other and he could not – but never ran away from me! He never stole from me, nor ran away. I think—'

Alex, who had been writing as fast as he could with his sprawling handwriting moving swiftly across the page, looked up.

'Yes, Mrs. Lucas – you think—'

Again the rictus of a smile. 'I think I stole from him. He never loved anyone else, you know, as he loved me. I would not let him. I never let any man love anyone else as much as me. All of them. Loved me most. Gave me most—'

'Do not exhaust yourself, please do not,' Martha said, feeling the way the strain was telling in her narrow frame, as her breathing grew faster and more erratic. 'Please do not.'

'Have you got it down? My will – all for Abel – all, all for Abel. All that is there in the banks in London—'

She turned her head fretfully against Martha's arm, and looked up at her. 'Will that make it better, do you think? Will he love me still as he did when it started? Will he?'

Martha, now frankly weeping and not caring who saw it, nodded her head, and said nothing. Whatever this woman had been in her past, whatever her doings had been, she was so pitiful now in her attempts to hold on to what little there was to hold on to that Martha's pity was being wrung out of her, and she sniffed and tried to smile and the woman leaning against her arm smiled too, and nodded in a sort of satisfaction.

'It is ready, Mrs. Lucas,' Alex said softly. 'You must sign it if it is to be legal, and we shall witness it – but there is one thing more. Do not be angry – but Sarah here: you cannot leave her unprovided for so far from home. Will you arrange for her?'

Lilith turned her head and smiled, a sweet rather absent smile, and stared about her, looking, and Sarah Jenkins, her face also wet with tears, but all the same with an eagerness about her moved forwards and said, 'Here I am, Madam, if it's me you wants.'

'Who is that? Oh, – it is you. It is you, Hawks, dear old Hawks. You are a wretch, Hawks—'

'Do not fret, Sarah,' Alex said softly. 'Her mind is wandering. Just give her a little time. She has confused you with someone she once knew, I imagine, but she will return, you will see—'

And he was right, for after a moment she opened her eyes and said clearly, 'Sarah. Of course. Sarah. Take the furniture, Sarah. All that is here is yours. And all that is in the cash box in my bureau. It is the London property I leave for Abel—'

' 'Ere, sir!' Sarah said, and her voice was filled with awe. 'There's nigh on seven 'undred gold sovereigns in that there cash box!'

Her face went red, suddenly, a great flaming red, and she said defensively, 'Oh, Gawd, I'd never 'ave touched it, not without 'er say so, but I'm 'uman, an' I wanted to know, so I looked! She can't never mean all that for me!'

'Well, she does, Sarah. You heard what she said,' Alex said, and finished his scribbling and moved softly over to the couch side.

'I have done it for you, Mrs. Lucas,' he said gently. 'If you will sign it, then Martha and I will witness it.'

'Me too, shall I?' Sarah Jenkins said eagerly. 'I've always done everythin' for her, ever since I took my place, and I wouldn't want to leave 'er now, not when she needs me most—'

'No,' Alex said crisply. 'I believe that a legatee may not witness a will, not if it's to be legal. Leave it to us—'

She signed, her hand wandering a little, but her signature, though shaky, was clear and had a remnant of the dash it must have shown once, and solemnly and wordlessly Martha and then Alex set their signatures to the document.

He folded it carefully, and tucked it into his pocket 'When – afterwards,' he said softly, 'I will see to it that this is sent to London. Meanwhile, Sarah, you have my authority, which I take to myself in this difficult situation, to take your legacy, when – when it is proper for you to do so. You understand? I will give you a signed paper to that effect to help you. Later—'

He turned to Martha then. 'My dear, I must go, I think, to seek Sal. We told her we would return last night and she must be perturbed.'

Martha looked up, her face drawn, and nodded gratefully. 'I had forgotten Sal, I am afraid. I would be grateful, Alex – and you must make inquiries for yourself, for a ferry to Scutari. You must seek your son – you must not waste time. Please, do go – I will remain here. It will not be long. But return to me once more before you go, please?'

He nodded, and came and took her hand and squeezed it gently, and then stood for a moment looking down on Lilith.

She lay back on Martha's arm, her head lolling to one side and her eyes half closed, so that just a rim of whiteness showed beneath the lids. 'Poor lady,' he murmured once more and bent and touched her forehead with his lips, and turned and went, leaving the three women alone in the hot room, the lights dimming now as the candles guttered and died and the lamps used up their oil, and still the shutters remained closed against the morning.

They sat there in silence for only a little while. Before the street sounds had built into a morning crescendo, pushing their way through the dark shutters, Lilith Lucas died in Martha's arms, bubbling away her gaiety and her scheming, her beauty and her mutilation, her past and all her future in a tide of red froth.

CHAPTER FOURTEEN

GIDEON was very glad that Abby had the headache. Usually the most concerned of husbands and fathers who fretted a great deal when any of his family, and especially Abby, were unwell, this evening he felt differently. Abby's headache meant she had gone early to bed and did not ask him for the day's news, and therefore he was able to keep the contents of the letter to himself. It was never easy to lie to Abby and he would have been hard put to it to keep his secret.

He was not quite sure, in fact, why he wanted to, and sitting there in the dining-room over his solitary dinner he took the heavy sheets from his pocket and unfolded them and smoothed them out and began for the tenth time that day to read them.

'My dear Gideon,' Martha had written in her strong sloping hand. 'I trust and pray this letter and its enclosure will reach you. I have been much exercised in my mind about what I should do, and how I should best serve the interests of a lady – of whom more shortly – with whom I came into contact, and also my father. I was anxious about the state of the postal arrangements here, and then recalled your kind offices regarding the movement of money and thought how better to safely send so vital a document?

'In short, dear Gideon, I was asked to give succour to an English lady in Constantinople when the ship docked here, and in doing so discovered to my amazement that she was a connection of ours – not a direct one, you must understand, but a connection none the less, being in fact the mother of Celia and therefore the grandmother of dear Phoebe. You may judge of my astonishment at so fortuitous a meeting, although Mr. Laurence, a physician who has travelled with us on the same ship, and who most kindly lent his good offices to this lady also, says it is not so strange once we allow for the strangeness of my being in Constantinople at all! However, be that as it may, the lady died here of the phthisis while I gave her all the help I could, but not before she made a will, which I enclose with this letter, while praying most earnestly that no harm will befall it and it will reach you. You will see from it that all the lady's fortune – I have no idea how sizeable it may be but have a strong impression that it might be considerable – has been bestowed upon my father with whom, as I understand from the lady's dying talk, she was acquainted.

'Will you convey this document to the necessary persons? I do not know whether it should go to my father or to an attorney, but I have great trust in your acumen, my dear Gideon, and am happy to leave all to your discretion.

'I would ask only this – when you tell my Papa of his legacy please to be gentle with him. I suspect, on the basis of the little the lady told us, that he held her in some regard when they were both children. He may be distressed at the news. Perhaps you should tell Maria first. I do not know. As I say I leave this to your discretion.

'For myself, we are leaving this evening by ferry for Scutari. There is much confusion here, as reports come in of a battle fought at Inkerman. No doubt fuller news will reach London in due course. I will write again as soon as I may. Thank you for your help and please give my dearest love to all my friends.

'Your sister, Martha.

'Post Scriptum: I have but now recollected that Lydia Mohun is Phoebe's aunt on her mother's side, is she not? Does this not mean that Mrs. Lucas – the lady who died here – is *her* mother? These family ties are so difficult to unravel! Perhaps you should speak to her too about the lady's death? Although perhaps I am wrong for there is no mention in the lady's will about any other legacy but that to my father and a servant and surely she would at least have *mentioned* a daughter if she had one living in London? I believe she did mention some names in her mumbling as well as Celia, Phoebe's mother, but to tell the truth, Gideon, I was so tired and anxious that I did not comprehend all she did say. I leave it all to you, I am sure you will know best what to do. In haste,

Martha.'

Slowly he folded the sheets and sat and stared unseeingly at the white tablecloth before him, his fingers kneading a little piece of bread into a putty-coloured pill. He remembered Jonah, the brother-in-law who had, in his own way, brought him and his Abby together. If Jonah had not sought Abby's help with the care of his children, she would not have asked his, Gideon's, aid in the way she had, and perhaps they would never have reached the understanding that had led at last to the haven of his happy marriage.

He shook himself a little at the thought. So absurd! Whatever Jonah had done or not done, it would have made no difference. He and Abby had been friends long before Jonah had intruded upon their lives, and the inevitability of their matching would not have been altered. But still, it was sad to recall him, that lonely bleak man who had lived only for his children and for his Supper Rooms. To think that Martha should cross half the world, only to meeet the woman who was grandmother to these children – it was a strange occasion.

He stood up and at once the butler moved forwards to open the dining-room door. 'I shall bring the tea tray to the drawing room as usual, sir? Or would you prefer to have it in Madam's boudoir?'

'Neither, thank you, Ryder,' Gideon said crisply. 'Madam is asleep, I trust, and will not wish to be disturbed, and for myself, I find I must go out on a business matter. I will take my keys, so you need not wait up for me. Lock all else besides the front door and I will deal with that. Goodnight to you.'

He had fully intended to go to Gower Street. Abel would have to be told, for although the will would require considerable legal investigation before Probate could be granted, Abel was surely entitled to know of his good fortune.

But somehow he did not get there. He walked quickly along the Bayswater Road towards Cumberland Gate and the Marble Arch, but recently moved there from Buckingham Palace, his hands thrust deep into his pockets, for the November night was bitingly cold, his head down and the brim of his top hat protecting his eyes from the wind.

He meant to hire a hackney carriage from the rank that stood just outside Cumberland Gate but, sunk in thought, he walked on, wheeling right into Park Lane and then left again into Upper Brook Street. Not until he was virtually outside her house did he lose his abstraction, and look up and realize where he was.

He stood there in the quiet elegant street staring up at the brightly lit windows of the drawing-room on the first floor and wondered. Would she be there at all? After all, an actress – and then he recalled that of course she was not working at the Haymarket every night this week, having given a Benefit for Peel's Fund on Monday and promised one for his own Fund on Friday. Another play was on in the interim. So she might well be up there in that bright drawing room. And she had, after all, a right to know of her mother's death, if in fact the woman who had died in Constantinople *was* her mother. And there was, of course, always the Benefit to be discussed.

He ran up the steps and rang the bell firmly, stamping his feet a little against the cold and not of course, to use up his nervous energy, born of the anticipation of seeing her. Of course not.

She was very, very angry. Lately Dickon had been tiresome enough, heaven knew, picking arguments with her on the most flimsy of pretexts, but this was altogether the outside of enough.

She had been sitting there in the nursery with small Silas on her lap, cooing at him and playing with him – much to the hovering nurse's disapproval – when he had come to her dressed in the most elegant of street wear and with his hat set at a downright insolent angle over his eyes.

'I'm going out, m'dear!' he had said jauntily. 'Don't wait up for me – just wanted to tell you I needed a bit of the ready, and took it from your cash box in your boudoir. Wouldn't want you blaming the servants for robbin' you, when it was the master, would I? That'd never do!' And he had winked hugely at the nurse who, alarmed, had bobbed and reddened and looked sideways at Lydia's face and then looked more alarmed than ever.

She had sat there glowering at him, for once almost lost for words. He knew perfectly well that she had an abhorrence of any discussion other than the purely trivial being carried on before servants. He knew that she regarded it as the sure way to scandal, to allow servants to know that there was any rift between them, and he also knew that it would be strange to the point of amazing if she were to send the nurse away from the nursery. That would cause even more gossip.

All she could do was smile as severely as possible and say, 'Indeed? I trust you have a pleasant evening, my dear! Am I permitted to ask where you are going?'

He grinned at that. 'Aye, you may ask!'

'Well?'

'Ah, but your asking and my answering ain't necessarily the same thing, eh?' And he laughed delightedly. 'No, m'dear, don't get up! You look too beautiful there with your baby in your arms for a mere man to dare to disturb you! I shall see you tomorrow, no doubt! Goodnight'

He had bent and kissed her noisily and with a sort of angry relish and winked again at the nurse and gone clattering away down the stairs, whistling, leaving her able to say nothing and do nothing but thrust her baby back at the nurse and go marching away to her drawing-room in a rage.

And there she had sat for the past hour, drinking champagne and brooding. How dared he – how *dared* he behave so to her? All because she refused to agree to take a cut from the Benefit takings in excess of her usual ten per cent.

He had stormed and shouted and tried his usual technique of attacking her and making violent love to her, but for once she did not succumb, scratching his back so cruelly that he had bled and lost all his interest, for when it came to matters of money, she was undisputed queen of this household, and was determined to remain so. How dared he, she thought again, how dared he behave so?

He had almost spat at her, standing there trying to rub his bleeding back, and staring at it over his shoulder in the mirror. 'It's all that damned Jew! I know! He's your fancy, and so you refuse to take your fair share of the door money from him – d'you seek to buy him, as well? You'd need a damned lot for that, madam, and so I tell you, for he's warm, he's warm! More than you can imagine, I'll be bound. They all are, his ilk!'

'You make me puke!' she had said, her voice ice cold and full of contempt. 'You think only of yourself and of what you want, what you can steal and what you can beg – you cannot imagine any person ever having any altruistic motives! I will not take more than ten per cent because this money is for the War – it is a Benefit, and I refuse to take more than is justified for my expenses! If I chose, I could give it all, every penny, and who would you be to say me nay?'

'If you do, you would have to work the play without me!' he had roared back. 'I do not work for nothing for any damned Jew's Benefit—'

'The Benefit is for the *War*, God damn you,' she had flared at him. 'Are you too stupid to comprehend that? As for you not playing – that would be a benefit in itself! We would be happier with your understudy, I tell you, for you are as inept on stage as any supernumerary and always have been and always will be!'

Which made him lose his temper again, and come lunging at her, and again she had scratched him, on his neck this time, and he, realizing how easily she could mar his face in the same way, swore at her, and gave in – that time.

But he had started it again, not a day later, and again, and again, so that the whole week had been scarred with their wrangles over the Friday night Benefit, and she had become more and more contemptuous of his cupidity, while he had become more and more wildly jealous of her friendship with Gideon.

Which was absurd, she told herself now, sitting there

stretched out on her chaise longue and staring gloomily into her champagne glass. For why should I choose *him* to dally with? He is so boringly uxorious, talking all the time of his tedious wife and even more tedious children. Why in God's name should Dickon or anyone else ever think I would play with such a one? Her sense of aggrievement was aggravated by the fact that in her eighteen months of marriage she had in fact been most chaste. She, who for many years had selected any man upon whom her eye alighted as her fancy and used him as she wanted, had for eighteen months been as chaste and as virtuous as any farmer's wife, and yet Dickon chose to display this lunatic jealousy and to try these silly games to make her suspicious and jealous too! He, who had dallied with others when it suited him, even in the days before their marriage, when he had been playing the loving swain so assiduously, when he had been courting her and sniffing around her, he had still taken himself off and made hay with young Phoebe.

She thought of that now for a little while, brooding over those long ago days; of course she had only Abby's word for it that Dickon had behaved so with Phoebe, and she had shrugged that off as a nonsense when she had first heard it, a mere canard. But now, she wondered, sitting there staring into her wineglass. Had he? Had he give her true cause then for jealousy, as he was trying to do tonight?

She snorted then; angry with herself. As if she cared where he had gone tonight! As if she cared for the few sovereigns he had filched from her cash box! It was all stupid and yet – oh, he was impossible! It was all the outside of enough, she told herself again. The outside of enough, and again she refilled her glass from the almost empty bottle.

The door opened softly and she lifted her head to try to see who it was but the champagne had made her eyes more than a little misty and all she could see was a vague glitter.

'Mr. Henriques, ma'am, asks if you are At Home,' the butler said heavily and she blinked and frowned and then giggled and shook her head and giggled again.

'Mr. Henriques! How very droll! Indeed, I believe I am at home! Please to bring him in at once!' and she sat up more upright and rearranged her gown and sat smiling brilliantly and expectantly at the door.

Gideon stopped as he came in, staring across the big room at her, and feeling his spirits lift as he did so. She looked so altogether delectable, so very charming and welcoming – it was balm to a man's eyes to gaze upon so delightful a sight, and he smiled widely, his long cheeks creasing into parallel lines, and his eyes shining a little, and came across the room to take her hand.

'My dear Mrs. O'Hare! It is good of you to receive me at such a late hour!'

'I am delighted to receive you, my dear Gideon – for so I shall call you, and you shall call me Lydia! I insist! I am delighted to see you, my dear man, because I am, as you see, quite deserted! My husband has gone about his own affairs and left me quite alone and quite desperately lonely. You cannot know how much pleasure it gives me to see you!'

He blinked a little at the warmth of her welcome, but enjoyed it all the same, and made no demur when she took his hand, and moving to one side of her chaise longue drew him down to sit beside her.

'Now, we shall have a lovely cosy prose! I wish to talk only of agreeable things, of happy things and joyous things. Not wars, nor Benefits to make money for those injured in wars, nor disagreeable husbands who leave a wife alone, not the weather – which is hateful cold! – not anything but *lovely* things. Then you will ensure that I remain as happy as I was at the moment when you arrived.'

He looked down at her, smiling a little, but still very serious. 'I am happy always to oblige a lady, ma'am, but it is not always possible. Sometimes, I am afraid, there is a disagreeable matter which must be talked of, and disagreeable news to be imparted and—'

'Oh, no doubt there is – but not for us, and not now! Tell me – ah – tell me about – let me think – there must be something you have done recently that will bear telling me about and that is agreeable! Understand me, nothing of wars or nastiness of any kind – just pleasant things!'

He sat and looked down at her, and tried to think fast. He had come to tell her that a lady who might be her mother — although she has never spoken to him of her family connections — might be dead in Constantinople. However he wrapped that up in fine linen, it could not be regarded as pleasant conversation, and looking down on her lovely eager face, he suddenly could not bear the idea of telling her anything that would take away the glitter from her eyes or the joy from her smile. He could not do it.

'I — I saw squirrels in the Park yesterday,' he blurted out, 'small and russet coloured and very charming. They were running along the branches of the trees in such a beguiling fashion.'

She clapped her hands delightedly. 'There — I knew I could rely upon you! That is altogether the most agreeable thing I have heard, not just today, but all the week! Tell me more about them! About their little eyes, their little ears and pretty bushy tails — every tiny detail. I want to hear it all!' And she tucked one hand into the crook of his elbow and moved closer to him, looking up at him through her eyelashes and laughing quite enchantingly.

So he told her. He talked absurdly of squirrels, and when he had finished with them, of birds and lambs and even of the fish in the Long Water in Kensington Gardens, and she sat close and smiled up at him, and thought *I will show Dickon! I will show him. If he thinks I am partial to this man, then he shall see what will happen! And he is really quite attractive, in his own stiff way, and it would be amusing to push that tedious wife quite out of his mind. It has been a long time since I played with any man but Dickon and he is not here and I am very bored—*

The thoughts went round and round in her head, slipping in among the wildlife of Gideon's conversation much as his own thoughts interleaved their words with those he spoke. *It is quite ridiculous,* he was thinking, *absurd, even mad, to be sitting here talking such nonsense with this woman, and feeling quite so breathless and unsteady at the way the touch of her hand on mine makes me feel, when I should be telling her of her bereavement – if that is what it is – or at least talking about the Benefit on Friday, and anyway, what would Abby say? Abby at home in a darkened boudoir with her head bound in an ice pack and cologne-soaked pads over her eyes, and the children asleep in the nursery above her head, and I sitting here with quite the most delicious pair of eyes to look into, and she does smell remarkably—*

His voice faltered, as he lost the thread of his words, and then tried again, and then floundered dreadfully, and, his face quite pink, came to a stop. But still she sat there and stared up at him and smiled very sweetly and said softly, 'No more pretty little creatures, dear Gideon? No more pretty little creatures?'

And he shook his head, wordlessly, but did not move, so when she put up both her arms and twined them round his neck and very, very gently let her lips touch his, it was undoubtedly with his co-operation.

In the event, it was fully three days before Gideon could bring himself to visit Abel and impart to him the news sent by Martha. He had to go to the hospital to see him at all, for since the war had taken so many surgeons to care for the army, establishments like Nellie's were hard put to it to maintain their services, and the older men, like Abel, were perforce working harder then than they had for many years.

Gideon had stood there in the little cluttered room Abel called his office, and in a few halting sentences had told him the news and then given him the sheet of paper with its scrawl of writing, and stood with his glossy top hat in his hand watching him read it. Abel had taken it and gone over to the lamp to see it more clearly, his head bent above his unfastened neck-cloth, his sleeves rolled up to his elbows and looking very tired indeed, and watching him Gideon had felt a moment of wrenching memory of his own father, who had never been reconciled with his only son, and who had died as intransigent in his rejection of Gideon's marriage as he had lived. He wanted to put out his hand to this tired man with his heavy grey hair, his face cut into crevasses of fatigue, to comfort him and be a son to him, but Abel folded the sheet of paper and thrust it back at him and said harshly, 'I want none of it,' and the moment of tenderness Gideon had felt shivered and disappeared.

'I am sorry to be the bearer of sad tidings, sir,' he said carefully, 'and I offer you my condolences at the loss of your friend. But—'

'I have lost nothing,' Abel said loudly, so loudly that Gideon almost jumped. 'I have no interest in this matter, no interest at all. Do as you wish with your piece of paper. Martha was mistaken in her belief that there was any – that I would be concerned. Do as you wish with it all. I am not interested—' and he turned to go.

'But sir!' Gideon was horrified, as any good man of business would be. 'This is a *legacy*! You cannot be uninterested in a legacy!'

'I want no part of it, you hear me?' Abel said, and now although his voice was no longer so loud it came sharp and decisive and unmistakably determined. 'I am unconcerned. Do as you wish with it. I will take no money from such a – such a source. I am not involved in any way. Good day to you, Gideon, send my greetings to Abby. We will never speak of this matter again, you understand me? Never again.'

So Gideon took the document to his attorneys, and consigned it to their care, and told them of Abel's reaction, and they, sensible men of business and the law, shook their heads over the absurdity of it all, and discussed what to do; and decided that all they could do was file the will with the courts and leave it to others to deal with the matter. And so they did.

As for Lydia – somehow Gideon never did find the right moment to tell her of his sister-in-law's letter. After all, he could not be sure the matter concerned Lydia, and he had no wish to seek her out to discuss it all, no wish at all. If the lady who had died in Constantinople was indeed a connection of hers, well, the truth would come out soon enough. He did not have to play the part of courtier, did he? Of course not, he told himself. Of course not. And went about his daily business trying hard to think of nothing but his business, while Abby watched him and wondered and worried.

CHAPTER FIFTEEN

ALTHOUGH she was tired, she was far from unhappy. Indeed, she thought almost guiltily as she rolled down the sleeves of her gown and looked about her with satisfaction, *I cannot remember the last time I felt quite so content with life.*

Not, she assured herself hurriedly, that she was content to see the horrors of Scutari. That was not to be thought of. She stood still for a moment, trying to recapture the sensation of shock that had filled her when she first set eyes on this place; and found it all too easy.

They had come over on a leaky caïque, one of the painted ferry boats that plied the Bosphorus; just the three of them and their baggage and the boatman, a surly Turk who had said nothing and only spat over the side when one of them ventured to address him. He had taken them to the Scutari shore, drawn his boat up on the muddy strand alongside the rickety jetty and then stood there chewing and staring at them as they hauled their seventeen boxes and their five valises, together with the four barrels of salt pork Sal had bought in Marseilles and sundry other mysterious sacks she had added to their stores during the night and day they had spent in Constantinople, and stacked them on the side.

Alex had tried to bribe the man to help, holding out coins, but he had just stared and again spat insultingly, so, shrugging, Alex had got on with the job. And Martha had been grateful to him for not expostulating with her when she did so too. Glad as she was to have his company, she did not want from him the sort of protection a gentleman usually offered a lady, but much preferred the easy camaraderie that was so steadily growing between them. She had felt he was aware of it too and was grateful to him, and had tugged at the boxes and valises with a will.

They had managed to find a couple of men to help them carry the luggage up the steep slope that stretched up to the looming barracks building above, soldiers recovering from wounds and therefore ambulant, and despite the breathlessness the climb induced in her, Martha had been able to ask a few questions.

Yes, it was bad, as bad as it could be, the soldiers said. Mind you it might be better now, now the lady's come. Not that they expected much of anything, not here.

'Are you coming to be wiv' 'er, lady?' he asked, looking at her from beneath heavy brows.

'Miss Nightingale, you mean?' Martha said, and shook her head and shifted her load from one aching arm to the other. 'No. She came here to nurse soldiers, but I have come for another purpose – to look after the women. I am told there are many women and children here in need of aid, and it is those for whom I have – for whom I have been instructed to care. Can you tell me where I will find them?'

The other man gave a raucous laugh. 'Tha's easy, lady. Under the nearest able bodied soldier, that's where—'

'Mind yer tongue, you bleedin' 'eathen!' Sal had snapped, coming up behind them, and with one well booted foot she had kicked out at the soldier's ankle, and he had sworn and almost dropped his boxes. 'This 'ere's a lady, an' you ain't got no call to talk to 'er in that fashion! I'm the only one as can do that! So answer the bleedin' question yer were asked, and get on with it.'

Red-faced, Martha had struggled on, climbing ever upwards, glad indeed that Alex was so far behind them with his huge load that he had not heard this little exchange, and Sal, seeing her embarrassment, had laughed and said in a low voice, 'You'll 'ave to get used to it, Miss Martha, an' that's a fact, on account of there's no other way soldiers talks. They're a rough lot, all of 'em, but great fellers – great fellers by and large – well, you?'

She had turned her head and was staring ferociously at the soldier she had kicked. 'Miss Martha asked you a question, didn't she? Bleedin' well answer it!'

'The women's mostly dahn in the cellars. It's a bad place to go, I can tell yer. You'd be better orf stickin' wiv Miss Nightingale and 'elpin' 'er. Not that she's got all that much to do, mind you.'

Martha stopped her climb, glad to rest for a moment, and stared at the man who stopped too. 'What do you mean, nothing to do? I understood there was a great need of care for the men here.'

'Oh, there's that all right – men's dying 'orrible everywhere. Me own mate went yesterday. But the army's in charge 'ere, an' no matter 'ow many great ladies comes 'otfootin' out from 'ome, the army's the one what says 'oo does what, and 'ow it gets done. An' accordin' to the talk – an' there's plenty of it – the army ain't 'appy to let Miss Nightingale nor one of 'er women set any 'and on any soldier.'

He sniffed and then hawked and spat with a gloomy relish. 'Three days she's bin 'ere, and there they are stuck in them six rooms and not doin' nothin' in the wards.'

'But I do not understand! How can it be so? Are there not sick men here, in need of nursing?'

'Of course there is – but it's like I told you,' the man seemed disgusted at her inability to comprehend. 'This is the *army*, lady. An' if the orficers don't give no orders then nothin' gets done. An' no-one ain't give no orders for these women to look after any of the men. It's as easy as that. Come on, I ain't standin' 'ere all night arguin'! If we don't get back up to the wards quick, they'll be bringin' the meat, an' our share'll be taken by those thievin' orderlies—' and again he humped his load on to his back and went on climbing.

Her first sight of the actual hospital had left her almost numb with shock. The men had led them into the huge central square, dumped the boxes and left them, Alex's coins jingling in their hands, and they had stood there, the three of them, staring about them in silence.

Mud, everywhere. The whole huge central square, with the

great wings of the old barracks in which the hospital had been formed looming over it, was floored with an ocean of churned reeking grey mud, shining a little, as the failing light caught it, with the sheen of sewage. On all sides were heaps of refuse, piles of rubbish that stank revoltingly, and Martha could see the swollen corpses of a couple of dogs in among it. Her throat constricted with nausea and she stood and stared and thought – I cannot. I cannot set foot into this.

And then Sal's voice, cool and collected as ever had brought her back. 'Well, there's a door over there with a stair goin' down – can you see? That's the way in, as I recall. I reckon as you'd better get over there, the two of yer, an' I'll go an' find me a couple of other fellers as'll bring up the rest afore it gets stolen off the jetty. Go on then! You can't stand 'ere all night, can you?'

Martha had turned her head to look at her, standing there in her neat green gown and shawl, her bonnet tied firmly over her thick brown hair and looking as sprightly and as comfortable as though she were standing in the middle of Trafalgar Square, and opened her mouth to speak and then closed it again, and Sal had said roughly, but with a certain tenderness beneath it; 'Well, I warned you, didn't I? I told you as it'd be disgustin' 'ere, as you'd be sick at the sight of it, but you wouldn't 'ave it otherwise. You was goin' to come, whatever anyone said. All right then! Get on with it, now you're 'ere. It'll get worse yet, I promise you, so the sooner you gets into it, the better. Go *on* then—'

And she turned and went swinging away across the mud, looking as insouciant as ever, and Alex laughed softly and said, 'She is right, you know! That woman is indeed a treasure. Come along, my dear. We may as well see what there is to be seen.'

So they went and saw. The stairway Sal had pointed out indeed led down to the cellars, and as they had picked their way down the slippery steps the stench rose to greet them, the age-old stench of unwashed humanity, rotting food, sewage, and beneath it all, the more sinister sweet smell of death and dying.

They had found themselves in a huge sprawling cellar, ill lit with sour tallow dips set haphazardly on odd shelves and protruding bricks against walls down which water trickled in a never-ending stream. The floor beneath their feet was sticky with mud and ordure, and the sounds that assaulted their ears were almost as offensive; children crying piteously; women's voices, shrill and angry, swearing and bawling; the low moans of the sick, as well as the shouts of agony as someone suffered a twinge of pain she could no longer tolerate. It made Martha's flesh shrink on her bones and she had stood there breathing deeply, making herself be calm.

Her effort of will succeeded and a sort of angry coolness took over, a sense of fury that channelled itself into a great burst of energy. She had pulled off her shawl, rolling it firmly into a ball, and reached out for the first woman she could, and taking her by the arm spoke to her loudly and crisply.

'I am Martha Lackland, come to provide the sick among you with care. You must show me where I may set up a dispensary and where I may find sleeping accommodation for myself and my helper, who is fetching the remainder of our baggage, and then you must tell me more about the situation here!'

The woman she had seized, a big woman with flaming red hair pulled back from her face into a tight knot, and with huge red arms showing beneath the sleeves of a man's shirt which she was wearing, barely fastened, over a sacking skirt, stared at her, her mouth half open, and then had tried to pull away. But Martha had held on to her, firmly, and said loudly, 'You heard what I said. Do as you are told!'

And amazingly, the woman did. Whether it was the controlled rage in Martha's voice, or the sight of her white tight face, or the presence of Alex, quiet but indubitably a strong man, behind her she was never to know. But the woman led her further into the higgledy-piggledy mess of straw and thin tattered palliasses and people, people, people, lying everywhere, to a far corner of the great stinking cellar.

There was a small window set high against the wall, a long narrow one and looking up Martha could see the first of the stars in the twilit sky, and blinked at it. It looked so ridiculously familiar, but she knew it could not be one of the same stars she had so often seen above her head as she left Bedford Row at this hour of the day, at home in London. It had to be as alien a star as this place was alien, and she looked down at the woman who was standing there with her hand on a tattered curtain that was held up by a piece of string tied from one side of the wall to the other and then looked about her. The curtain set aside a small area about twelve feet square in which there were two unspeakably dirty mattresses, a small rickety table, and nothing else at all.

'You can 'ave that if yer likes. The woman as used it died yesterday, and there's none 'ere as'll take it on account of she died o' the fever. We kept away from 'er and 'er kid, and got the corpses shoved out o' that there winder once they'd died, but there's none as fancies usin' it nah. You can 'ave this if yer likes. If you really wants to make a *dispensary*,' and she said the word with a huge scorn, staring at Martha with her chin up, and her eyes filled with dislike.

It was a challenge, and Martha knew it. If she refused this accommodation, on the grounds of the contagion that probably still remained in it, they would reject her, would make it obvious to her that any help she had to offer was not wanted by them. She had to make it clear to them that she was one of them before she could tend them, and as she stood and stared at the challenging look on the face of the woman before her, she felt, almost more than she saw, the watchful faces of the other women ranged behind her, for they had crept closer, curious about this extraordinary new arrival, and were staring and staring as though they had never seen the like before.

Behind her, Alex stood and watched, saying nothing, his jaw set and his eyes bright and watchful. That he wanted to intervene was clear; his back was rigid with his control and his mouth was in a very straight line, but he knew as well as Martha did how crucial this moment was, and how vital it was that he did nothing to interfere in it. So he stood and watched and was silent.

The challenging stare did not falter, and after a long moment Martha took a deep breath and reached up her hands to take off her bonnet.

'Very well,' she said crisply. 'If this is all that is available, this is what we shall take. Sal – my helper – will be here shortly with the luggage. There is more of it outside. Bring it in.' She lifted her eyes again to the red-headed woman. 'You hear me? Bring it in. At once. It contains food among other things—'

There was a sudden movement of the watching women and children towards the door at that, and Martha said very loudly, 'If any is taken without my knowledge and consent I will take all of it away, every crumb. I have food, clothes, comforts of all kinds, but only *I* shall dispense them. If you forget this then you lose all of it. You understand.'

She stared at the red-headed woman, who stared sullenly back and then Martha said, her eyebrows raised slightly, 'I will need some help, of course, in this. I will have to employ that help I imagine. Anyone who volunteers to be my assistant, and who agrees to take responsibility for the safety of my stores, will be paid with extra rations—'

Slowly the red-headed woman's face changed, and she took her hand away from the curtain, which she was still holding up, and then she nodded curtly. 'All right. You got yer assistant. I'll get yer boxes—' and she turned to go.

'Wait!' Martha called, and the woman turned back. 'I shall need, in addition, some water. In a bucket. This place must be scrubbed—'

Again the woman stared at her challengingly and then, slowly, shrugged and turned away. 'I'll get it,' she said.

And get it she had. By the time Sal had returned, panting, with the last of the precious supplies, the water was there and Martha had rolled up her sleeves and was ready to set to work. She had opened the first of the boxes as soon as it was brought to her, carefully taking from its impeccably ordered depths a large piece of coarse yellow soap and a scrubbing brush, and then she had set to work.

She had, first, shaken Alex warmly by the hand and thanked

167

him most fervently for his aid, and bade him set about his own affairs, the searches he had come to make, and felt ashamed at how little thought she had given him in the past few hours.

'Forgive me,' she had said, her face the picture of guilt. 'I have been shocking self-centred, have I not? You are so anxious, and all I could do is burden you with my problems. You cannot know how grateful I am to you, my dear Alex. This past few days would have been a nightmare without you. Bless you for your goodness.'

He had smiled at that, and shook his head. 'My dear woman, you would be quite extraordinary if you had not been so absorbed, when your affairs are so very extraordinary! But you are right – I must be about my searches indeed. I will go to the army people now and see what I can discover about Felix's whereabouts. He must be known here, somewhere—' And he had gone, with one last squeeze of her hand, leaving her to set to work with her bucket of water and her soap.

And work she had until her newly healed hands ached with it, under the eyes of the women and their children, scrubbing every corner of the floor and the walls too, as far as she could reach, though her efforts made little headway there for the stones were thick with the accretion of dirt of many years. But the table responded well to her ministrations, as did the sill of the window and the window itself, and she realized as she worked, the sweat pouring off her face, just how fortunate she had been in getting this corner, for there were only five such slits of window in the entire great cellar, since only on that side of the building did the land permit them.

They threw away the mattresses, for Sal said mysteriously, 'they would have no need of the like of *them*,' and disappeared for an hour, only to return with new clean bags of straw. She refused to say where she got them, or at what cost, only winking cheerfully at Martha and setting them on the floor away from the wall, '—because you'll 'ave bugs and Gawd knows what else besides landin' on you if you gets too close to *them*,' and then made up their beds with blankets and pillows from their stores.

At first Martha had remonstrated with her. 'Those comforts

we brought are for the people here, Sal. We cannot use them for ourselves. It would be very wrong!'

'No, it would not!' Sal said stoutly. 'First of all, what good'll we be to any of 'em if we gets ill? None at all – and if we don't get our bleedin' rest, then ill we'll be! – An' second of all they'll think we're out of our attics if we gives all the good things to them an' doesn't share in 'em ourselves. An' if they thinks that, then they'll 'ave no respect for you, an' without their respect, Miss Martha, take it from me, you won't get nowhere. So take your bed, and shut up.'

So Martha did, and set to work with Sal to unpack, using the boxes they emptied to fashion shelves and cupboards for their stores, until, not long before midnight, she stood and pulled her sleeves down, staring about her and feeling filled with satisfaction, an exhausted but immensely enjoyable satisfaction. This was what she had come for, to help the women and children of Scutari, and at last, after all the planning and hoping and thinking and begging, she was here, and ready.

Tomorrow she would start to look after the sick, to give out her stores and see what more could be done. And she smiled suddenly as she realized how short a time had passed since she had first even imagined being here. Not yet four weeks! She remembered that day when she had read Russell's dispatches in *The Times* over her breakfast at Gower Street not quite four weeks ago, and wanted to laugh.

The cellar settled to an uneasy peace. Sal and she together had given out some food, for there was little enough there for the two hundred women and their children who inhabited this great place, but it was cold food, being but hard biscuits, and as such not very satisfactory for the little children.

'Tomorrow,' she promised as she showed a mother how to crumble the biscuit and moisten it with water for her crying infant. 'Tomorrow, I shall make soup, and gruel. This will help tonight, I hope—'

She had taken off her gown, and on Sal's advice no more, agreeing to sleep in her petticoats but with her stays well loosened, when he came, picking his way over the recumbent bodies and the sleeping children as easily as though he made such traverses every day of his life, and she stood and watched him come, holding her shawl tightly about her, embarrassed to think he should see her in her petticoats, but not nearly as perturbed as she would have been in such an unthinkable situation in London. Indeed, there was a certain excitement in her as she realized how very intimate the situation was; to greet him in her petticoats – how close could friendship possibly become?

But he seemed unaware of that undercurrent of excitement, as he came and stood before her and looked down on her. It was not that he did not see her, for indeed he did, taking in with one comprehensive glance the flush on her cheeks, the softness of her hair, loose about her shoulders, for she had unpinned it ready for sleep, and the way she held her shawl so firmly about her shoulders. But he was too concerned with his own news to say anything more than, 'I have come to say goodbye.'

She blinked up at him, and felt her chest lurch in a most disagreeable manner. She had known from the moment they had met on the ship that his company was an unexpected bonus, a pleasure and a support she could not hope to enjoy for long, but now she knew it was definitely to be withdrawn she felt suddenly so bereft that her eyes pricked and she let go her shawl to rub her hand over her face.

'I – they know where he is?' she said uncertainly.

He nodded. 'He joined the 49th – Princess Charlotte's Regiment. They must have been mad to take him. But they are – were – at this battle at Inkerman, it appears. I must go to see what has happened—'

'How? Have you the army's consent to enter the battlefield?'

He shook his head. 'Damn the army,' he said, and there was so much suppressed violence in his voice that she shrank back. 'No. I have found a supply ship captain who will take me for a consideration. A handsome one, of course. I will be at Balaclava harbour, he promises me, in just seven days. I pray he may be right, and that I find Felix is there, somewhere—'

'I pray you will, also, my dear Alex – but, please—' she stopped and then shook her head, unable to go on.

'You think I am mad to go on such a search? Well, perhaps you are right. But for thirteen years, since the boy was just two years old, we have been all in all to each other. I cannot do otherwise but seek him. I must. I – You, I hope, above all women, will understand this.'

She nodded. 'Yes,' she said huskily. 'Of course. And I do not think you are mad. Just – just very good. Goodbye, my dear, and God speed,' and she held out her hand to him.

He took it, looking down on her with his face very still, and then he bobbed his head awkwardly and kissed her cheek, and she smelled the faint sourness of his breath – for it had been many hours since they had eaten properly – and felt the roughness of his unshaven cheeks and was grateful for the way the sensation lingered on as he turned, and she watched him go picking his way once more across the sleeping bodies that lay between him and the doorway, and the steep slope down to the jetty where his supply ship waited.

CHAPTER SIXTEEN

THE morning passed in a fever of activity that though initiated by Martha infected many of the women in the cellar. It was as though they had been lying there in their squalid misery, unable to pull themselves out of it, but needing just a little tug to improve their situation, a tug which Martha provided.

She started by demanding that the place be swept, and the dreadful mess of soiled straw mattresses and rotting waste be removed, and with Sal at their head, six women set out to do just that, hauling the material in great armfuls up to the courtyard outside. They wanted to leave it there, pointing out that amid all the other rubbish that lay in that sea of mud theirs would hardly be noticed, but Martha would not agree to that, and asked Sal if it would not be possible to burn it. And Sal, complaining as she always did but still as resourceful as ever, led her band of helpers to the rear of the great building and bullied a couple of the soldiers she found on the way to build their bonfire for them.

And because it was a cold morning, with the wet wind whistling down cruelly from the heights beyond the hospital, the bonfire became popular, and more and more of the men who were fit to move about came creeping up to warm their hands at it, and to help add more fuel to the flames. By midday, a great heap of rubbish had been reduced to a powdery ash, and Martha was well contented.

Scrubbing the whole cellar as her own dispensary area had been scrubbed was not so easy. There just was not enough water available for it was rationed to a pint a head, for all purposes, having to be drawn from a fountain in one of the corridors of the hospital. But she managed to clean a sizeable area adjoining her own where several more of Sal's bags of straw were put – and Sal refused to say where she had obtained them, simply winking one eye very mysteriously and going off to get more – so that sick women and children could be kept together under her eye.

On the other side of her corner she cleaned the floor and arranged the three spirit stoves she had brought, together with her precious supply of fuel, and by three in the afternoon had made creditable soup from some of the dried peas she had brought with her, together with pieces of the salt pork Sal had bought in Marseilles, which encouraged the women even more.

Not that all of them were as eager to help as they might be. Many remained lying in their corners, furiously resisting any attempts to clean their surroundings, while others sat and watched and jeered and encouraged those of the children who had the energy to do so to get in the way of those who were working.

But Martha worked diligently on, saying nothing; but when the time came to serve her soup, she was well aware of which of the women had helped in the necessary work, and which had not, and she hardened her heart against those who sought food and had not earned it.

That their conditions were enough to dispirit even an angel, that they had little cause to trust her, less still to do the work she demanded and which was so foreign to their natures, was not, she told herself, important. If these people were to be helped, they must first be willing to do all they could to deserve it. Not for nothing had Martha spent all those years at Bedford Row working in her hostel. She had learned much there about how to manipulate the sort of people with whom she was now living.

She did not only feed her own helpers, but the sick women and children she found about the place, and also, with the last dregs of the soup eked out with hard biscuits, the soldiers Sal had dragooned to help her. They came creeping down into the cellar, suspicious and very watchful, but mellowed under the warmth of Martha's soup, and sat huddled among the women talking in a desultory fashion, even laughing sometimes, but above all reminiscing.

They talked of the hell of last September, of the crossing to Calamita Bay on the Crimea Peninsula itself, of the horrors of the troopships that left Varna, so crammed with men and horses and women too (for hundreds of the wives had made such a wailing and such a commotion when attempts were made to leave them behind, that they had been embarked as well) that conditions were intolerable, of the storm-tossed days in the Black Sea, and above all of the arrival.

'They was dyin' like flies,' one man said, sitting hunched over his cup of soup, his thickly bearded face sombre and heavy. 'The cholera – an' they tied weights to their feet and threw the bodies overboard. But it didn't make no nevermind, because the weights wasn't heavy enough, and up they floated and they was bob-bob-bobbin' about the sides of the ships, head and shoulders out of the water, a sight to make your blood run ice in your veins. It was like those death's heads was watching and laughing and waiting for us, telling us we'd be joinin' 'em soon enough. And enough of us did, God knows, enough did—'

'Oh, stow it!' Sal said shrilly. 'Where's the sense in talkin' about last September? It's now as matters! Will this last battle they fought be the end on it, that's what I want to know – eh? Will we all be goin' 'ome victorious in time for Christmas dinners down the *Lamb and Flag*? Now, there's something *worth* talkin' about!'

'No such luck,' growled the bearded man, and finished his soup and wiped the back of his hand across his mouth. 'Ta for that, lady. You're a right good one, you are. No, we won't end this war this year, matey, and never you think it. There they'll bloody sit, before Sevastopol, waitin' for the spring. There's nothing else they can do. When the weather really starts – oh, we'll know it then! There'll be snow and ice and winds as'd freeze your legs off. I been talking to some of them as knows

174

these parts—' He shook his head, and got to his feet. 'We'll be here a long time.'

'Well, if that's the best you can say, you can stow that an' all,' Sal said, and also stood up, to begin collecting the men's cups and one of them, more lively than the rest, ran one hand up her skirts and she turned and slapped at him but laughed all the same, and another of the men joined in, and the small spurt of laughter and shouting built up as Martha prudently stepped back and pretended not to notice. To try and remonstrate with such behaviour would be of small use, little as she liked such taproom japes, for this was as these people usually behaved, and however much it grated on her views of moral behaviour, it was their affair. And anyway, to try to tell Sal not to behave so – no, it would not do.

She felt the presence of the newcomer even before she saw her, and turned her head away from the stove, which she was carefully extinguishing, to look through the little crowd of still laughing men who now had Sal on the lap of one of them so that the others could tickle her, and saw a small woman in a heavy black gown and white apron standing with her arms tightly entwined in the purple shawl she was wearing over the top, and scowling heavily. She did not look at all like one of the women of the cellar, and Martha frowned a little, and then her face cleared; this must be one of Miss Nightingale's party come to see her and she moved forwards, holding out her hand impulsively.

'My name is Martha Lackland, ma'am,' she said eagerly. 'Are you one of Miss Nightingale's ladies? I had hoped to wait upon you later today, but as you can imagine, there has been much to do! I did not part from Miss Nightingale in London in total amity, I must admit, but all the same I would wish to speak to her, now that I am here—'

The little woman made no move to take Martha's hand, and never removing her eyes from the giggling shouting knot of people clustered round the cooking stoves said abruptly, 'Miss Nightingale asked me to come and see you. She has heard of your arrival, and is most perturbed at certain activities of your party. Please to come and see her, immediately.'

175

'My party?' Martha said, puzzled. 'I have no party here! Just myself and Sal – she is my helper, you know. She was here earlier in the year, and saw much of the horrors of the situation, and it was because of her account of it that I am here at all. She inspired me to offer my aid to her fellow – wives,' she reddened a little at that, and then went on, 'but we are by no means a *party*.'

'Miss Nightingale is waiting for you,' the woman said flatly, and with one last withering look at Sal, who was now sitting upon her tormentor's lap, one arm cheerfully draped about his neck and staring at the two women, she turned and began to make her way back out of the cellar.

' 'Oo's that?' Sal called.

'One of Miss Nightingale's people,' Martha said, buttoning her cuffs slowly. 'She says that Miss Nightingale wishes to see me. She is, it appears, perturbed – I do not know why. Well, she was perturbed in London as well, and she will have to be again, if she is going to try to take the same line here as she did there! I shall soon tell her—'

'An' while you're at it, tell 'er we don't think much of those as call 'emselves nurses an' then don't do no nursing!' One of the men shouted and then laughed. 'Just sittin' about doin' nothing, that's what they are – you tell 'er we don't need that! We need the likes o' you, as *does* somethin'.'

'I might at that!' Martha said grimly and turned and followed the little woman out of the cellar.

She led the way round the edge of the mud expanse, and into a corner of the huge building and then up two flights of hideously dirty stone stairs to a long corridor that made Martha blink at the sight of it; a great vista of emptiness, floored with dirty broken tiles, the walls streaming as wetly as her cellar. It seemed to go on for almost quarter of a mile, for she could hardly see the far end of it. It was an even more depressing sight than her cellar and its squalor.

The little woman was ploughing relentlessly on, and Martha followed her, head held high, along the great echoing expanse, up yet one more flight of stairs, until at last they stopped outside a small door, and the little woman tapped on it.

'Go in when she answers,' she said sourly, and turned and went, clattering noisily down the little staircase, leaving Martha alone among the echoes.

At last the voice came from within the room, a high clear voice. 'Enter!'

And Martha did, pushing open the door with a certain ferocity that was born of her nervousness. Why should she be nervous? She did not know; this woman was after all of no real importance to her. Like Martha herself she had felt some sort of need to come to Scutari to help in any way she could, and this should, if anything, give them a sort of fellow feeling. There was no obvious reason why Martha should defer to her in any way, or have any fear of losing her regard. So why, she asked herself as she stepped into the little room beyond the door, why feel so alarmed, like a naughty child sent for by an angered governess to admit her crimes?

Her tension pushed her into the centre of the room in a little rush and she stood there looking at its occupant with her head up and her eyebrows raised, and Miss Nightingale, sitting at a small rickety desk said coolly, 'There is no need to come in here in quite such a rage, Miss Lackland. I cannot imagine you have any cause to behave so impulsively.'

'I? Behave impulsively? Indeed, I do not!' Martha said hotly. 'I receive a most peremptory message from you, and obey it – if that is being impulsive, then I admit it! I would have thought perhaps that I would be entitled to be greeted with some appreciation of the fact that I obeyed your summons! There is no reason why I should, after all! I am not one of your people.'

'Indeed, you are not. As I made it very plain that I would not have you—'

'I did not seek to be one of your party!' Martha said furiously.

'—and, furthermore,' Miss Nightingale went on as coolly as though Martha had not spoken, 'I advised you, as I recall, to give up your notion of coming here to care for the women.'

'Advice I did not feel it was incumbent upon me to heed in

any way!' Martha said, and looked about her for a chair. 'I trust I may be permitted to take a seat, rather than stand here like some recalcitrant servant being lectured? You made great play of the fact that we were of equal station when last we met, Miss Nightingale. That being the case, I would ask you to offer me the same consideration I would offer you in this situation!'

'Please do sit down,' Miss Nightingale said and stood up, pushing her own chair forward, and Martha sat down, firmly, and Miss Nightingale stood with her hands folded lightly on her apron before her, and looked down at her.

'Now, it is I who stand like a recalcitrant servant,' she said, 'since there is but one chair in this room. No, do not get up—' she smiled very sweetly. 'I am quite comfortable, thank you.'

Mortified, Martha remained seated. She knew this interview, like the last one they had had, had started off on quite the wrong note and regretted it bitterly now that her first surge of irritation had passed; and indeed, looking up at the delicate face with the fine nostrils and calm dark eyes, she felt a sudden pang. It was so lonely here, so far from home; Sal was a great help of course, and a source of much comfort, but could hardly be regarded as the sort of company to which she was accustomed. It would be agreeable to have a friend here, and she felt suddenly that she could have been a close friend of this woman, with her calm exterior and her steel core – for that, Martha was certain, was very much there.

There was a long pause and then Miss Nightingale said crisply, 'There are matters which perturb me, Miss Lackland, and which I must discuss with you. I am told that since you arrived here last night you have been very busy. I saw your bonfire, and was most impressed that you had seen the need to dispose of all the rubbish that litters this dreadful place, although I would have been more impressed had it been sited downwind of the hospital. The smoke caused much added suffering, I suspect, to those poor fellows in the wards which took the brunt of it all – however, the intention was good and I recognize it. I am not so happy, however, to hear of the arrangements you have made to provide mattresses for your dispensary, as I believe it is to be called.'

Martha looked up at her sharply. 'Mattresses? I have no mattresses.'

'Oh, indeed you have, Miss Lackland. Bags stuffed with straw. Eleven of them have found their way into your cellar.'

Martha's brow cleared. 'Oh, *those*! We shall of course be using them as beds, but I did not consider dignifying them with the name of mattresses!'

'Indeed!' Miss Nightingale's voice was very cool indeed. 'My nurses did, when they made them.'

There was a stupefied silence and then Martha said, stammering a little, 'Your – your nurses, Miss Nightingale? I do not understand.'

'Since we arrived here a few days ago, Miss Lackland, we have had many problems. Not least has been to persuade the army that we are here to be used and may safely be used. I do not scruple to tell you that there is some opposition to our presence here by some sections of the army authorities, for they feel we will do little good and may do harm. I am determined, very determined indeed, that we shall start nursing here, but with the full acceptance of the army and its doctors, and only with that full acceptance. While we wait for such acceptance, we waste no time. My nurses have been spending their time making mattresses. Stuffing those bags with straw is hard and tedious work, and not what we came here for, but it has to be done. And when we find, as we did, that several of them have been stolen from the place where we put them for safekeeping, we are naturally perturbed. I trust you share my concern.'

Martha had closed her eyes as the import of the words sank in and now she snapped them open.

'Indeed, I do. I did not know – Sal – she is my helper – obtained them, and I was glad enough to see them I must admit. But I should have checked with her about where she obtained them. I did not and it is much to my regret. They will, of course be returned to you forthwith.'

'Oh you need not,' Miss Nightingale said, and suddenly her voice sounded very weary, and she turned away to look out of the narrow window behind her. Martha could see how much thinner and more frail she looked than she had in London, and felt another stab of concern for her; it would be *so* agreeable to have her as a friend!

'It is kind of you, Miss Nightingale,' she said, and stood up, to move impulsively forward. 'I appreciate your generosity—'

'Oh, generosity! Pooh to that! It's its *practicality* that concerns me! Those mattresses, if they have been used by those women who are disgusting in their state of living will already be infested with diseases and lice, I have no doubt. They are of little use to me now they have left my stores.'

She turned back to stand with her shoulders very straight, staring at Martha. 'I must tell you, Miss Lackland, that your presence here is to me an abomination! There is enough real work to be done without having about the place meddling charity-minded females with no experience, no backing and no common-sense, bumbling about attempting to do good! I cannot insist that you leave this place – if I could, I would have you off the premises within a matter of hours, I assure you – but I *can* bring some pressure to bear upon you, supernumerary to my party though you are. I have talked today with one of the army medical officers about the situation, and although he refuses to accept responsibility for the medical care of these wretched females in the cellar, he was agreed with me that it is not proper that you should be taking their care upon your back alone. I am empowered to tell you, Miss Lackland, that unless you have the authority of a medical man in any care you offer these women, you will be regarded as inimical to the authorities here. They have enough problems in this war-torn place without such as you complicating matters further. Since you have no such medical supervision, then you might as well go home. I cannot force you to do so, but I trust your own vestiges of sense will prevail upon you to pack up, bag and baggage, and depart. If you do not, of your own free will, then I must warn you that the army will take it upon themselves to escort you back to Constantinople forthwith. It was to tell you this that I sent for you, and I hope I have made my message very clear.'

Martha had been standing very straight and in total silence during the whole of this tirade, and now she took a deep breath and her eyes glinted and her words came helter-skelter, so breathlessly angry was she.

'Miss Nightingale, you are impertinent! How dare you set yourself up to tell me what to do? You are no greater a person than I – I am the daughter of a great and experienced surgeon, and have worked in the wards of his hospital on many occasions. Furthermore, I have had experience of caring for sick and distressed females and their children, many years of it, and I feel as well qualified as you to do the work I have come here to prosecute. It may seem well enough to *you* to sit here skulking in your comfortable rooms while men die out there for want of care – aye, *die* of it. Well, I will not let those women die so, whatever you may say! I will not truckle to some narrow, official, bumbling jack-in-office of an army clerk! So they say I must have a medical man to supervise me? Pooh to them! *You* may regard that as the only way you can work, under the instruction of some physician or other – but I can feed and wash and care for people without the permission of anyone. Even you!'

Her voice was withering in its scorn, and Miss Nightingale, for all she had maintained her calm posture, moving not a muscle of her beautiful face, responded to it, for there was a faint flush in her cheeks and her eyes too took on a glitter of their own.

'I have tried to explain to you, Miss Lackland, that it is necessary to be politic in a situation such as this. I am concerned for the welfare of not a couple of hundred women – I too would take on that burden without consulting anyone – but with the welfare of thousands of men. *Thousands*, you understand me? There have been great battles fought in the recent past and soon men in dreadful states of injury and sickness are going to arrive here in a deluge. It is a matter of great importance that before they get here, I have the full co-operation of the army medical staff. I cannot get that by taking it upon myself to do for any man here anything that has not been sanctioned by that staff. I tell you this not so that I may excuse myself in your eyes – I care nothing, madam, for your opinion of me – but so that you may understand, if you are capable of such understanding, why I forbid my nurses to do any work until they are given medical permission. And also to explain to you, if it is possible to explain, why you too must have medical supervision. It is out of my hands, now, and happy I am that it is. I tell you simply, out of concern for your welfare, that you should go of your own free will before the army escorts you away, as they will, if you have no medical aid. And that, I am persuaded, you have not. Good afternoon, Miss Lackland.'

And she moved smoothly to the door of her little room and held it open and Martha, after one last glare at this maddeningly cool, maddeningly *right* woman, fled.

She ran down the stairs, along those great echoing corridors, tripping on the broken tiles, headlong into the muddy square and across it to the doorway to the cellar. All she could think of was that woman's voice ringing in her ears: 'Go of your own free will before the army escorts you away – as they will if you have no medical aid. No medical aid—'

The cellar was dark to her eyes when she reached it, and it was not only because of the dimness, but because of the fact that her own eyes were misted with tears of anger, frustration and regret, and she blinked as she heard Sal's voice come carolling across its expanse.

' 'Ere, Miss Martha – guess what's 'appened since you went a'visitin'! You've 'ad a gentleman caller come! What do you think of that, eh? A gentleman caller!' And she laughed loudly and Martha rubbed her eyes with one shaking hand and peered into the little space of the dispensary.

To see Freddy sitting there on the rickety table, his hat in one hand and his coat slung over the others arm, and his face white with fatigue.

'Hello, Aunt Martha! You might have waited for me, you know! But I am here, at last. So, where do we start?'

She stared at him, and then shook her head and then laughed and then gasped, and held out both hands to him.

'Oh, Freddy – dear Freddy! Medical aid! Medical aid!—' and then she laughed again, harder and harder until she was hiccuping with it, and the tears were streaming her face.

CHAPTER SEVENTEEN

'MY DEAR AUNT MARTHA,

'Your letter came so welcome! I had been in a Fever of anxiety, I do promise you, to know of all that is happening, and I positively *Devoured* the pages when I received them. I have shown them to many of my friends, also of course to Oliver and the people here at the Supper Rooms, for everyone is starving for news from the War. I was especially glad to hear from you that Freddy had arrived safe and sound for I will not hide from you, Dear Aunt Martha, that we did not part as Friendly as I would have wished, and fear there remains some Small Acrimony between us. Not on my part, of course, for I do not hesitate to tell you in strictest Confidence of course, dear aunt Martha, that I am dearly attached to Freddy, and miss him sorely. It is his feelings that concern me, and I would be grateful if when next you write – and make it very soon, my dearest aunt! – you can give me more news of Freddy. Is he well? Does he need anything? I must tell you I will send anything at all that he requires, if you but say the word.

'As to sending things, well, I have news from here as well! As a result of what happened the day Freddy went away – and I will not bore you with the account of it – I started here at the Supper Rooms a set of Concerts to raise money for supplies for Freddy, and for you as well, *of course*! and they have been absurdly Successful! Each night the customers crowd in so, that the tables have to be set closer and closer together and the waiters can hardly get about – which makes Oliver a little Surly, I must confess! But no matter, they drink and eat enough afterwards! I sing some very good Songs of the War, and have devised the most charming costume, which the customers quite dote on – I wear a helmet, like Boadicea, you know, and a great flag is used to drape my figure, and I sit upon a throne and sing of the Queen's Dear Soldiers, and the customers quite Swoon with it! I have had some men actually try to *climb* upon the *stage* during the performance, but Oliver will not permit that, as you may well imagine. Halfway through my singing I bring on some of the waiting women, also wearing my flag and helmet costume, but not so well made, you know, and not quite so becoming for I am after all the *Singer*, and they go among the audience with their baskets and take money from them. It is so wonderful to see and hear all the Clinking of the Coins! I have already made Two Hundred Pounds this way, and have arranged with Dear Uncle Gideon to see to it that supplies of food are sent out to you from Constantinople as soon as may be. He says it is in hand, and you should be receiving the Bills of Lading or whatever they are called from the House of Rothschild there quite Soon.

'Dearest Aunt Martha, keep yourself well, and write again as soon as you may with news of yourself, and of course Freddy. We all miss you a Great Deal, and Pray Nightly for your safe Return.

'Your loving niece, Phoebe.'

'My dear Mamma,
'Now, there is no need to worry any more, for here is my letter! I have indeed written several times since leaving London, but you must understand, my dear one, that postal services here are not good. It is easy for Gideon to get letters to and from Constantinople, and that is a great help, but he could not help when I was at sea, could he? I did indeed entrust letters to the captain of a ship when we docked in Malta, a ship that was returning shortly to Marseilles, but it is possible that the weather has been foul and this is why they are delayed. But here is a letter, and with the aid of Gideon's good friends across the Bosphorus I am confident you will speedily receive it.

'So what is news here? There is so much that I could not

describe it all. Cholera rages in a dreadful way both in the hospital and here. The hospital itself, where lie the men, is quite indescribably dreadful. A day or so after I arrived here, the ships bearing the wounded from the other side of the Black Sea came in, and oh, Mamma, but it was shocking! Thousands upon thousands of men in dreadful disarray, bleeding, screaming, suffering appallingly, were hurled ashore by the most casual of Turkish labour, and dragged somehow to the barracks hospital. There, there was no real provision for them as we had heard at home, but Herculean efforts are being made by Miss Nightingale, the lady who came to provide nursing, you will remember, but even she is limited in what she may do.

'There are men lying everywhere, in corridors, in rows upon the floor, so that one can hardly pick a way between them. I am supposed to be here only to help Aunt Martha and her women – about whom more anon – but I cannot in all conscience spend too much time in the cellar where she is accommodated, while so much suffering for want of medical men goes on across the square.

'So, I go to the wards, and some of the army doctors are very glad of my help. Some, I may tell you are of the worst and stuffiest sort, and require ten pieces of paper written out before they will allow a spoonful of beef tea to be given to a dying man! But those I keep away from – I cannot tangle with them, for if I did I would be sent about my business very sharply.

'They are the sort of officers, these doctors, who care more for protocol and for their rank than they do for the needs of the sick for whom they are supposed to be caring. Miss Nightingale has had many troubles with them, but handles them with great aplomb, and is indeed wreaking some miracles there, as she and her handful of women offer what succour can be offered to men who have lost their limbs, or who have been blinded, or who have musket balls lodged in their bellies. But I must not perturb you with such talk, absorbed in it all as I inevitably am, but will tell you instead of Aunt Martha.

'She is amazing, Mamma! To tell the truth I have never paid much attention to her, in past years, for she was always, you know, a little colourless! I thought of her as my quiet spinster aunt, and met her at my grandfather's house, or ours, and that was all. But she is a firebrand! She fights and argues all the time with Miss Nightingale, for although they are both here to do good work, they have for some strange reason taken a violent antipathy to each other. A pity, for they have much in common.

'But she is more like you, Mamma, than I would have thought possible – Aunt Martha that is. So strong and so practical, when she has to be. There are times when I am amazed at her resourcefulness and also her tolerance. She has here with her a street woman of so tough a tongue and so vulgar an attitude that even I quite blush sometimes, and I am accustomed to such women from the wards at Nellie's and I would have thought Aunt Martha would die rather than talk to such a one, for she has always been very proper, has she not? Not at all like you! Well, this woman and Aunt Martha have become such firm friends, it is quite comical. Let one person say aught about Aunt Martha and this Sal is like a fighting cat. Only last week she met one of Miss Nightingale's nurses upon an expedition to get water, and the nurse made some derogatory remark about Aunt Martha's laxness – she finds it wiser to close her eyes to some of the things that go on in this cellar, the way some of the recovering soldiers come here to visit the women, and I agree with her – and Sal was upon her at once, until the two of them were rolling on the floor kicking and shouting, and the men were taking bets about which would win!

'When Miss Nightingale got to hear of it, she dismissed the nurse instanter, and had her sent over to Constantinople on the next caïque – they're the ferries that ply the Bosphorus, pretty little painted gondolas of a sort – and that of course distressed Aunt Martha. She made Sal come with her to Miss Nightingale and admit her fault, and Miss Nightingale said unless Aunt Martha sent Sal away, and preferably herself as well, the other woman would have to go. Of course Aunt Martha could not agree to that, so they were at stalemate, and had even more cause to dislike each other. Such a pity that, for I have great regard for Miss Nightingale. But I dare not say that to Aunt Martha!

'For the rest she seems well, remarkably so, though she is much thinner than she was. But indeed we all are! Not that you are to worry about that, Mamma – for it is due not to disease but to shortage of food as much as anything. What would I not give for one of Oliver's good beefsteak and oyster pies with green peas and a pint of best porter. Tell him I wish he could send such items out to us! Meanwhile, tell Gideon if you will that we have need of many supplies, for the winter comes on apace, and it is bitterly cold. We use the spirit stoves for heat as well as cooking, and it is not adequate. Can he arrange a supply of good spirit through Rothschilds? Please to ask him, for I am sure it would help a lot. We need also bandages, more of the medicines – those on the third page of the original list are what we need most, the list that starts with syrup of ipecacuanha, you will remember, and bandages. Also send, if you please, warm clothing for babies. I have delivered seven in the past two weeks and they are suffering badly in these temperatures. One already has died, a sickly little thing and well out of life, I fear it is necessary to say. These people here have so little in life that is agreeable that leaving it must be less of a wrench for them than for us better found mortals. You see, I wax philosophical! A sure sign I must stop this scribbling and get some sleep. I will write again as soon as I may, and look forward most eagerly to more of your dear letters.

'Your dutiful and affectionate son,

Frederick Caspar'

'Madam O'Hare,

'I am sorry you found my last letter to you disagreeable, and although I note that you would prefer I call upon you to discuss the matter of the Benefits, I feel that I must, for the reasons given in my last letter to you, decline your request. I would wish to reiterate my apologies for my behaviour, which was inexcusable, and assure you that I meant no disrespect. I will refer no further to this matter, and trust that you will understand and applaud my reticence.

'In the matter of the Benefits you have so kindly agreed to give for my Fund – this offer is much appreciated, but I must insist that I can no longer deal directly with you in this affair, for reasons already stated to you. If, as you suggest, you are unable to give any more such Benefits without my presence, then I must tell you I regret the matter but cannot mend it. I cannot accede to your request.

'I thank you for past help in the matter of my Crimea Fund, once more tender my apologies for any insult I may have offered you, for any reason, and on any occasion, and remain, Madam,

'Your obedient servant,

Gideon D'Spero Ramon Henriques'

'Dearest Lucia,

'Well, here I am again with my regular letter to you – it was quite absurd that we go on writing such long gossipy letters after being parted from each other for so *many* years but I imagine you, like me, have great need of a *confidante*, and cannot trust a soul in Edinburgh any more than I can in London! People are so *jealous* are they not? If I told some of them here the things I tell you, why, they would destroy me, out of sheer *malice*! But it was always so. Well, now, what news you sent me! I was *enchanted* to hear of your new beau – he sounds quite perfect! For myself I have given no more thought to beaus, or hardly any, for I have been a positive angel since marrying Dickon, or had been! But I must tell you that matters in *that* department have changed somewhat. He is being so *disagreeable*! I married him for love, I cannot deny, being quite besotted with him at the time, and I must tell you that he is a most attentive husband, in a way that I find very agreeable, and which makes me behave in a very *voluptuous* way. You will remember, I am sure, how *susceptible* I am in that department, and Dickon has always understood me so well. But he has been so tiresomely jealous lately, and though that can be gratifying, especially when it increases a man's power to love, well, it was becoming tedious. He has of late complained most about a man who is most amusing, a pious Jew! Yes, my dear, would you *believe* it! But he is in sort a connection, being the uncle by marriage of my niece Phoebe – still as charming as ever, of

189

course, although she is not so close to me as once she was, we were such good friends before my marriage, but after that she visited me less often which was a pity. Now I have lost the thread of my letter! Ah, I recall, this uncle of hers. Quite appallingly rich as so often they are, but close with it, and living quietly enough. No great houses such as Mentmore for him! He is no Rothschild, I promise you. But rich, *rich*! Anyway, he has organized a Fund for one of his family who has gone out to this boring war and keeps badgering me for Benefits which I gladly give, for it enhances one's reputation *marvellously*, and ten per cent brings in a tidy sum, for they are well attended, and generally makes himself busy. Well, Dickon grew such a hate of this man, and was sure I was taking him as a *lover* – such nonsense! I was so incensed I toyed with the idea but after a most *boring* evening during which he indulged in a little friendly sparring with me – nothing very *exciting*, I do *assure* you, dearest Lucia, for he was so very proper, you cannot imagine what a bore! And became so overcome with remorse that I near burst into laughter in his face! But I told Dickon about this, I assure you making the most of it, and he came to heel at once, I promise you, for there is nothing *that* one fears more than losing me! I can also assure you, my dearest friend, that I would leave him fast as flying if I chose to; and well Dickon knows it. So, all is now *peace* in our home, and Dickon is a perfect husband and Papa – and oh my dear, you should see the little *darling* my Silas is! You cannot *imagine* what a fond Mamma I have become! – and breathes fire wherever he claps eyes on the poor wretched Jew. Which he seems to know, for he has avoided me most *assiduously* since it all happened! All so funny! I am quite worn out with laughing. Now, I must tell you that I was quite *stunned* with amazement about your news vis á vis Thomas and Sophia...'

'My dear daughter,
 'I am gratified to know you are well, and that the work you are doing is not unduly exhausting you. The news we receive from the battlegrounds is dispiriting, but not I think, without hope. I am glad also to hear from you that Frederick is well,

and is of use to you. I will be happy to hear from him of any matters he wishes to impart, and would strongly advise him to make as many drawings of battle injuries as he may happen upon. My old friend Charles Bell did this on the field of Waterloo, and most valuable these drawings have become for the anatomical knowledge they display. I trust Frederick will make time to do the same, for the time wasted can never be regained.

'I must thank you for your good offices, as described to me by Gideon in the matter of the lady who died in Constantinople and whose will you witnessed. But I must tell you I have no interest in the matter. I will be glad, if, when you return home, you make no discussion of it. It is not a subject I wish ever to hear of again.

'Yr affect: father, Abel Lackland'

'Dear Gideon,

'In haste to tell you that I have received the blankets, the biscuits and the sacks of flour and dried peas. I had to pay heavily for the carriage, and suggest you ask the House of R. to employ less rapacious boatmen if they can. I greatly suspect that I have been mulcted in this matter, but in these difficult times there is little I can do but pay. If you can in the next assignment send some brandy, in some sort of disguised barrel, to avoid theft, it would be of great aid. There is much cholera here and I find small doses of brandy most helpful. Freddy sends his respects and will write in the next bag . . .'

'To: Mr. Daniel McFadyen, Attorney at Law:
'Sir,

'I am in receipt of your letter bearing the post mark of November 20th and addressed to Mr. Alexander Laurence which was given into my hands by the messenger who brought it, since I am a friend of Mr. Laurence, and the only person here who knows him. I have not of course opened the letter, but took your name and address from the superscription upon the envelope. I write now to tell you that shortly after our arrival at this place, some four weeks ago, Mr. Laurence left Scutari to go to the Crimean shore to seek his son, Felix, for whom he was most concerned, since the young man had set out from London to join the army. He has not returned and despite making daily inquiries of any vessel that reaches Scutari from the battlefields, I have to report as yet no news. As soon as Mr. Laurence returns, and I pray he will, his letter will be put safely into his hands.

'In the interim, sir, I will guard it with great care and remain,

'Yours etcetera,

Miss Martha Lackland'

CHAPTER EIGHTEEN

THE days pleated themselves into weeks, the weeks into months, and still the work went relentlessly on. The flood of wounded and ill soldiers which had come pouring into Scutari in the middle of November seemed to run unabated, for in the two and a half weeks between the middle of December and Christmas and the New Year, four thousand sick men arrived and the total of deaths rose and rose implacably.

Which affected Martha in her cellar as much as the nurses in the hospital itself, for on every shipful of sick and wounded men there were some of the women who had managed to come back with them. The same wives who had clamoured to embark last September for the great adventure across the Black Sea had clamoured even more shrilly to come back, and in her own way, Martha suffered the same problems of overcrowding and desperate shortages of stores on her side of the mud ocean that was the barrack square that Miss Nightingale did on hers.

Not that they saw a great deal of each other after the early strife-full days. As Martha had said one day to Sal, the one good thing about the situation was that Miss Nightingale was too busy with her own work and the troubles she was having with her nurses – for there were many quarrels between the Catholics and Protestants among them – to bother herself much with Martha and her doings. Miss Nightingale had clearly shrugged off any interest in the welfare of the women and children, and Martha was glad of it.

It was not, she knew, because the other woman had no compassion for the camp followers; it was simply that she felt powerfully that they should not be there, that they should be shipped home to England forthwith so that all the energies and supplies available could be concentrated on the soldiers.

And in truth, Martha agreed with her. She had realized very early in her time at Scutari that there was little of real or lasting value she could do, even with Freddy's help. Each day they would struggle to eke out the few rations of food they could beg from the army, added to their own hard-won supplies brought in from Constantinople whenever the Rothschilds could get a boat across the Bosphorus (for the weather was so furious that sometimes the crossing was impossible for days at a time) and would feed the hungry mouths that clustered so eagerly about them. Then they would make their way through the cellar, from mattress to mattress, from heap of rags to heap of rags, giving medicine where they could, dressing injuries – and there were many suffering from dreadful frostbite – cajoling those fit enough to do so into making some shift to clean themselves and their children, soothing crying babies, removing dead ones – and it was a strange day when there was not at least one small corpse to be taken from its mother's arms – and coaxing, exhorting, soothing, talking, talking, talking until they were hoarse.

And yet it was all so endless. Martha felt sometimes in her moments of despair. 'We do no more than palliate the evils of this place a little, and it is a smaller degree of palliation each day,' she told Freddy gloomily one night, when they sat in the dispensary huddled over a smoking fire built in an old broken stove Sal had 'borrowed' and arranged with its battered chimney leading up to the precious window.

'Well, that is better than nothing,' Freddy said, and yawned hugely. He had become much more gaunt in his weeks here, for hard as Martha worked he was doing much more. From time to time he would slip away and go over to the hospital where the surgeons were amputating, both to give his aid which was accepted gratefully by some of the army surgeons who recognized the young man's skills – and to learn, for the opportunity was too great to be missed – and then come back to work again with Martha.

She watched him and worried about him, and when she

could, gave him extra food, even when it meant a child would have to go without, for she felt that it was to everyone's benefit to keep Freddy well, for without him, where would any of them be? The threat of expulsion by the army authorities still lay over her, and Freddy was her bulwark against that, as well as being immensely useful in the work that had to be done.

Even when she was at her most depressed, even when she was at the lowest ebb of physical strength, she never lost sight of the importance of it. Complain although she did occasionally about the limited good she did, it never entered her head to throw it all up and go home herself, free though she was to do so at any time she chose. Here she would stay until every last woman and every last baby had gone and then, and only then, would she be free of her burden.

She too looked thinner, and Sal, the only one among them who looked much the same – for she had great skill in coaxing extras for herself out of the many soldiers about the place who admired her, and was not one given to the sort of altruism that would make her share her rich pickings with anyone at all – would scold her and chivvy her and make her curl up on her precious straw mattress and sleep, whenever Martha looked ready to drop. And Martha, grateful to her, would laugh weakly and agree and settle down in her petticoat and loosened stays – now made more than a little ragged by the cruel attentions they suffered at Sal's hands at the washtub. but at least clean – and wrap herself in a rough blanket and go to sleep.

Not that she always slept easily. Often as she lay there staring up at the few stars trapped in her sliver of window she would find her mind slipping back to the days on the ship, when she and Alex had walked about the lurching deck, he with his arm held firmly across her back so that she could not slip, and she with her hands heavily bandaged. And sometimes she would open her palms and look down at them and gaze at the scars that still showed beneath the roughness and rawness imparted to them by the bitter cold and the hard work she was doing, and remember his gentle touch as he had dressed them for her, and the way his face would crease when he smiled that gentle slightly self-mocking smile of his, and her eyes would fill with tears of loneliness and fatigue.

For in spite of Freddy's presence, and in spite of Sal, and in spite of the horde of women and children with whom she was surrounded all day and every day, she felt lonely in a way she had never done in all her life. She needed more than she needed food or warmth or clean clothes – and she ached for those – the companionship she had known in those few sea-tossed days. It had become as vital to her as breath itself, and the knowledge of her need was painful indeed.

Each day she would send one of the more sensible of the children down to the jetty to inquire which ships had come in, and whether Alex was on any of them. Each day she sent messages to the army authorities to see if any news had come of Felix Laurence, but over and over again they were fruitless errands, and she would get on with her work, bending over the frozen cold child she was trying to massage back into some sort of warmth, or the woman whose suppurating frostbitten feet she was dressing, and tell herself optimistically, 'Tomorrow. Tomorrow there will be news. He will come back, with his boy. Tomorrow.'

And eventually, tomorrow came. It was a day in late March, a day when the ice and snow, which had surrounded them for what seemed eternity, for the first time seemed less permanent, actually capable of melting. The sky was a milky blue and the sun struggled to show itself above a skim of white cloud, and the frozen mud in the middle of the square showed small patches of softness amid its rigid furrows and hillocks.

She had woken after a better than average night's sleep, feeling a little more energy than she had for some time; the exhaustion that had rapidly overtaken her after her arrival had begun to lift lately, not because there was less work to do, or more food to eat, but because she was becoming more inured to it all.

She had managed to structure a pattern of work into her day, and this in itself took much of the fatigue from it. It was the unendingness of it all that had most wearied her at first, the sense of an inability to impose any order on the squalor about her; but now she had done so, and had the cellar running to a sort of rough timetable with set times to eat and tend the sick, and set tasks of cleaning shared out among the women, and so it was all a little less onerous.

Waking to a grey dawn that carried a breath of hope about it, as though somewhere in the winds it brought up from the east was the hint of the smell of fruit blossom and sandalwood, she got up, peering down at Sal who was still snoring contentedly at her side, and on the other side of the curtain at Freddy, who slept as always wrapped in his greatcoat, and crept away over the sleeping women and children – and for once not a whimper could be heard from any of them – to make her way outside to the square. She stood there, holding her shawl tightly about her, for it was still cold, and stared up at the sky. She could see the shreds of light thickening, clotting into morning and suddenly she stretched as luxuriously as a cat and rubbed her head with both hands, and feeling how lank and greasy her hair was, decided impulsively to spoil herself.

She hurried away to the little open area on the side of the road leading up to the main building, away from the square, where Sal had rigged up a sort of tent in which there were a couple of buckets and boxes and the makings of a small fire, calling it grandiloquently 'the women's bathhouse' and collecting a bucket of snow from the little that remained unsullied on the far side of the steep road up from the jetty, lit the fire and set about her ablutions.

It was remarkably peaceful everywhere. She could hear a few shouts from far below at the jetty, human voices muffled by the distance, sounding jaunty and as blessedly normal as though it were just an ordinary peaceful day about to start, and as she rubbed her freshly washed hair dry with the scrap of old linen Sal had left there she breathed deeply and thought confusedly, 'It is not so bad, after all. There are some things which are not to do with wars. The sun will shine today—' For already there were thin fingers of sunlight moving across the slope, and the fresh wind coming up lifted the strands of her damp hair from her brow in a very agreeable manner.

She pulled a box out from the tent and set it up so that she faced east and the slowly emerging sun, and sat down with her shawl about her shoulders and the tattered piece of old linen over it so that she could spread her hair and let it dry, and after a moment pulled her skirts up to her knees and thrust her legs out to the sun. Her boots, mudcaked and stout, encased her ankles and half her calves, but to have what little warmth there was on her knees would be pleasant indeed.

And so she sat, her face up to the strengthening sun and her eyes closed, and relaxed. She thought of nothing and worried about nothing, and planned nothing, and that in itself was a great luxury. She simply sat and looked at the light behind her closed lids, amusing herself by trying to focus on a sparkle or on one of the whirling patterns her own eyes conjured up out of the blankness, and let time go by her.

How long she had sat so, she did not know, but it seemed that his voice came from so close that it was inside her own head, and for a moment she sat on, her eyes still closed, thinking confusedly, 'I must be dozing—'

'Martha. I did not hope to find you so easily. My dear, I am so glad to see you—'

But she was not dozing. She opened her eyes, slowly, trying to focus in the glitter and the mistiness and blinked and peered, and then lifted her hands like a child to rub her lids and looked again. But it was true, and he was standing there, as foursquare and solid as he had ever been, his coat collar up above his ears, and his hands thrust deep into his pockets, looking down on her.

'I – Alex! *Alex?* Oh, it is, it is! I thought I had dreamed it—' and she jumped up and held out her arms, kicking the box heedlessly away from beneath her so that it went tumbling helter-skelter down the hill, and threw herself at him, and he pulled his hands from his pockets and held her very close, so that her face was crushed against his coat and she could hardly breathe.

They stood so for a long moment, and then she pulled away, putting up her hands to his face to stare at him, and said wonderingly, 'I – you are different – I cannot tell – it *is* you, is it not?'

He laughed at that. 'Indeed it is. But I have a beard — it is that which is different.'

'Oh yes! So — I had not seen — oh, how absurd! Half your face obscured and I had not *seen* it! It is too funny, indeed it is, so *funny—*'

'My dear Martha, do not weep! Please do not weep! I have visualized this meeting so often, but I never saw you weeping! I did not mean to distress you.'

'I am not weeping — oh, well, perhaps I am, but not precisely weeping, you must understand. It is just that — it is all so sad — so funny — I cannot tell—'

And then she was weeping in full earnest, her face twisted into a grimace that she knew was hideous, but she could not help it. The sight of him, of his face so changed and yet so blessedly, wonderfully, achingly the same, was more than she could bear and she sank her own face into her hands and let the tears come as they would.

He put his arms about her again, and held her very still and quiet and after a little while the storm abated and she could sniff and swallow and look up at him with red-rimmed eyes and scarlet nose and smile a watery smile.

'I am so sorry. But I have missed your sorely, so sorely! I would not have thought it possible to miss a person so much!'

'And I you. I have thought of no one else, in all these weeks. No one else — apart from Felix—'

She was all contrition, at once, 'Oh, my dear — my dear, dear Alex, I am a wretch! I was so overcome at the sight of you, I thought of no one but myself. Please, how is he? Did you — did you find him? Pray God your news is good.'

He smiled, a little crookedly. 'It is not good, but it is not the worst and that is all I ever cared about. I found him in Bala-clava, and he was very ill. He had the cholera, and he had been too ill to get aboard the troop carriers. I managed to find quarters for myself and obtained the army's consent to take him into my care, and have spent all these weeks caring for him. He has been so dreadfully ill, and many were the times when I thought I had lost him — long days when he was so sunk in coma that I thought it not possible that he could survive. But—'

he smiled again, 'I am a determined man, and a good physician, you know, and he had very devoted care! So he recovered, though he is still shockingly weak, and will never, I fear, quite regain his old strength and health. But he *is* alive, God be praised, and I have the army's consent to return him to England as soon as may be. There are problems, of course. They say there is no space on any of the ships to send him back – they are returning only very few, and others have priority over him. However, if I can make my own arrangements, they say–'

He shrugged. 'Well, enough of that now. The important thing is that we are here. I managed to get us this far, and I found quarters of a sort with one of the Armenian dealers who throng the jetty there below. Felix is sleeping now, for the journey was very exhausting for one in so bad a state of health. But, I came as soon as I could. I had to find you – you see, I have missed you sorely–'

She smiled up at him, as tremulous as a baby. 'Oh, Alex, and I too. And – and–' She stopped and reddened and tried again. All her upbringing, all her previous experience, all her awareness of what was right and proper behaviour for a lady of her station in life was warring in her with other awarenesses, of the way his touch on her was making her body feel as tingling and as alive and as buoyant as it had not ever been; the way her emotions were welling up in her, her needs, her desires, a whole part of her screaming as it had never before screamed, 'I want – I want – I want!'

And all that emerged from the tug of war inside her were stilted sentences.

'Alex, I do like you, so very very much. You asked me, did I like you, and I really do–'

But he understood, as she knew he would, and smiled down at her with his eyes narrowed with amusement above the heavy curls of his grizzled beard, and said gently, 'I too, my dearest Martha, like you excessively.'

He bent his head and kissed her lips, softly and then more urgently, and though she had never in all her thirty-eight years ever been so saluted by any man, although she had never before felt quite the sensations that surged through her body, turning her belly to a maelstrom of heat and cold intermingled, it was the most natural and inevitable thing in the world. She simply lifted her face and kissed him too, and then they held each other's hands and looked at each other and laughed.

'I think, you know, that we are becoming a little conspicuous,' he said gently after a moment, and she looked about her and flushed and laughed, and collected up her box and ducked back into the tent again, for there were soldiers lounging about now, and a few Turkish peasants, and all of them were staring and some were even pointing.

'I will be very quick,' she called, her voice coming muffled from inside the tent. 'And then we shall go to the cellar, and we shall find some food. I think we can manage breakfast for you!'

'Please do not concern yourself with me!' he said, and pulled his coat collar down, and shoved his hands back into his pockets, turning his face up to the sun, just as she had done. 'For I have some supplies of my own, down in my quarters. I cannot rob you of your meagre stores.'

'It will not be robbery,' she said emerging from the tent. 'But our gift of gladness at having you back.' She smiled up at him, her face wreathed in happiness, and with her still damp hair pinned on her crown, and a few tendrils escaping at her forehead, she looked very much younger than her years, and impulsively, he kissed her again.

'To perdition with the starers!' he said cheerfully, and put his arm about her shoulders and led her back to the square and the doorway that led down to the cellar.

They breakfasted on oats boiled in water and seasoned with a little of the syrup from Martha's dwindling stores, and Sal was so pleased to see him that she even broached her own private hoard, and made a great pot of hot tea for them, a rare treat indeed. And they all sat in the dispensary, happy and comfortable, Freddy and Sal as well as Martha and Alex, and the women and children seemed to pick up from Martha some of her radiant happiness and the whole place was filled with a bubbling good humour that refreshed them all.

Later in the day, while Martha and Freddy as usual settled to do the day's dressings and then while Freddy was at the hospital helping with an operation and Sal and Martha dispensed stores, Alex went away back to his quarters down by the jetty to see Felix and to make what arrangements he could for the boy to be sent back to England.

And although Martha knew perfectly well that once such arrangements for passages on a ship were arranged, she would have to face the problem of parting with Alex again – for she could not imagine, however much she wanted to be with him, leaving Scutari before her task was completed – she refused to think about the implications of it all, refused to think of anything beyond the fact that Alex was alive and well, that Alex loved her as she loved him, and that despite her years of spinsterhood, her acceptance of a life totally free from any attachments, the future held for her what it held for other women. A man of her own.

CHAPTER NINETEEN

THE eating house was full of people, and Gideon was fortunate to find a table at all, even one in such a far corner of the big room, and he leaned back against the oaken settle and stared gloomily at the crowd of businessmen from Holborn, lawyers from Chancery Lane, hack scribblers from Fleet Street and assorted topers and spongers from half London, and hoped he was not making a fool of himself.

He had felt he could not go again to New Court, cap in hand. In some small way he had to make some effort to show Lionel he was not always a beggar, and perhaps one of Benjamin Rules' more lavish luncheons would be the answer.

There was a little flurry at the door and the big bent figure of Lionel Rothschild appeared there, and Gideon was a little amused to see the way heads bent closer together across the tables, and his name was hissed behind hands and the waiters fell back obsequiously. These people who were so in awe of his wealth, who showed such exaggerated respect for him because of it, would, had he not got that wealth, be the first to sneer at him and reject him and even abuse him if they could, on the grounds of his religion. They would not know of the goodness of him, and the charitableness of him, and even if they did, they would not care. Such was the lot of the Jew in today's society, he thought sadly, and stood up as Rothschild came lumbering over to his table.

'Well, my boy?' he said grunting a little as he lowered his great bulk into the chair the waiter was bending over so humbly that his hands threatened to touch the sawdusted floor. 'What is it you want me to do for you now, hey?'

'Come, Lionel, is it not possible for a man to ask a friend for a meal without there being something wanted in exchange?'

'Not when the friend is Rothschild, Henriques, and well you know it,' and Gideon smiled and bowed his head in mock acknowledgement of the justice of it, and said mildy, 'I do not seek money, Lionel With that you have been most generous, and I have no reason to suppose you would not continue to be so should it be required. No, what I want is your influence. But first, let us order.'

'Hmph,' Lionel said. 'Order away then. I leave it to you – as long as it is permitted food. I keep the old ways, remember.'

Gideon smiled and beckoning the waiter sent for bowls of barley soup and big broiled soles and boiled potatoes and a quart of the best champagne and while they waited for their food, and then later while they ate it, they talked only of generalities, of the affairs of the synagogues in which they both had interests, of the doings of their friends, Montefiores and Samuels and Cohens, and the most riveting of all subjects for two such businessmen, the state of the money market, and what the war was doing to trade.

But when they had finished and pushed aside their plates, Gideon leaned back and took from his pocket a folded sheet.

'Lionel, your Constantinople branch have been most kind to my family – I have a deep gratitude to you for the way they have so carefully maintained the flow of money from London, and bought and shipped urgent supplies there. My sister, who writes regularly, tells me that allowing for the vagaries of weather they are exceedingly dependable and she is also most grateful to you. As indeed are all of us, for it is through Rothschild's that our letters travel so swiftly and safely.'

'You need not praise us for efficiency,' Rothschild said, and belched gently, wiping his lips on his napkin. 'It is what made our money, and never forget it. There are those who will tell you it is the machinations of my brothers and cousins that creates our wealth, but I tell you it is simple efficiency. He who can do the job better and quicker and more thoroughly than the next man will always be beforehand with the world.'

'I know it, but that does not mean it is any the less admirable'

'Well, my boy? What are you leading up to? You said you did not ask me here for more money—'

'Indeed not, Lionel. Listen to this letter, and it will, I think, make all clear.'

He unfolded the sheet of paper in his hand and smoothed it on the table and began to read.

'My dear Gideon,

'Once more I seek your help in a matter in which I trust and pray you will be able to advise. It is not to do with supplies or letters. I am beseeching aid this time for a very good friend. I may tell you that a gentleman I first met at Phoebe's Ball, Dr. Alexander Laurence, is here in Scutari. The circumstances of our meeting again on the ship which brought me from Marseilles I will not enter into now, but I can tell you that he came here to seek his son, a young man of not yet sixteen years who in a fever of war and patriotism ran away from home to join the army. They are very close, Dr. Laurence and his son, and his concern was such that he felt constrained to follow the boy. He found him at last in Balaclava, where he was very ill, and nursed him over many alarming weeks to a semblance of health, but I must tell you, having seen him, and he is indeed a charming young man, and one who would I think interest you, for he has a great deal of good sense about him, that he is very frail still.

'Now I come to the point of this letter. Dr. Laurence has permission from the army to take his son home again, but he is quite in despair for there are no passages to be had at any price on any ship. All are so laden with various persons who have priority that there is nothing he can do to get the boy away. We are both very concerned, fearing that if the boy does not return soon to England he might get ill again. Bad as the winters are here, the better weather too can be treacherous, and fevers abound in the spring He may even die.

'However, Dr. Laurence has discovered that Rothschild's might be able to procure a place on one of their ships, to get them home again. I have asked for this aid, but I was told, although with great courtesy and regret for the representative of the Bank actually came out to Scutari himself to give me this answer to the letter I had written to Constantinople, that the Bank here has no authority to release such places. This has to be provided, he says, by the London House.

'Please, dear Gideon, will you use your influence on these very important men to find a safe passage home for Dr. Laurence and his son? I would not ask this of you but for a most dear pair of friends, I do assure you, and trust in God that your influence with the House of Rothschild is enough to facilitate this matter. I await your reply most eagerly.

'Your affect. sister, Martha Lackland.'

He folded the sheet again very deliberately and looked up at Lionel from beneath his arched brows.

'The question is, my dear Lionel, is my influence with the House of Rothschild sufficient to obtain this boon for my sister-in-law?'

'She and this Dr. Laurence – is there an understanding between 'em?' Lionel looked at Gideon quickly, his head on one side. 'Sounds to me as though there's fire under her coals somewhere! Wouldn't you say?'

'As to that, I have no idea,' Gideon said in some surprise and looked down again at the letter. 'Martha? I have never thought of her in such terms! She is eight and thirty, you know – no giddy girl!'

'Hmph! What a marriageable woman is doing to be allowed to get to such an age unwed is beyond me,' Lionel said, and shook his head disapprovingly. 'Never would allow it in a good Jewish family, my boy. Never would allow it!'

Gideon reddened. 'Come, Lionel,' he said stiffly, 'I am not the first person to marry out of the faith, nor, I think, shall I be the last. You must not dig at me on this matter simply because—'

'No, you are right. You are right! I apologize, m'boy. Meant no insult on your wife's family. Now as to this passage—' He shook his head. 'The demand for space on every ship in those parts is prodigious – quite prodigious. I doubt I can do much, and so I tell you.'

'Now, Lionel, I cannot believe that!' Gideon said strongly. 'I do not doubt your word that the pressure is great. But what I do doubt is any weakness on Lionel Rothschild's part! If anyone can arrange it, you can and well you know it!'

'Aye, well, I cannot say as to that,' Rothschild leaned back in his chair, and began to pick his teeth with a neat gold pick taken from his watch chain. 'Two places, damn it! It's asking a lot in these hard times!'

'I know. But my sister is not a woman to ask idly, I believe. It must be a genuine case, or she would not be importuning me so. Can you do it, Lionel?'

'I'll tell you what, Henriques. I'll do all I can. How's that, eh? I make no promises, but I will talk at New Court and see what can be contrived. Now, this is clearly a matter of some emergency, and the letter bag will be leaving Folkestone to-night, and if authority *is* available, then it must go in that bag.'

'I can come to New Court at any time you choose, Lionel,' Gideon said eagerly, and then his face fell. 'Oh, damn it all to hell and back – oh, I beg your pardon – but I have just recalled that tonight I am firmly tied to my wife and family. My niece – my wife's niece that is, who with her brother owns the Celia Rooms in Covent Garden – gives tonight a Gala Benefit, as she calls it, at the Rooms, to get more money for my Fund. But I daresay I can slip away, once it is all under way—'

'The Celia Rooms, you say?' The old man looked decidedly interested. 'Oh, I have heard of that! I am told it's all the crack – everyone in town goes there to see the show. I am told that there is a delicious singer, a girl of such charm and wit that all who see her are quite dazzled!'

'Phoebe Lackland,' Gideon said a little stiffly, embarrassed as he always was by references to Phoebe and her activities, for they still seemed to him to be unsuitable for a member of his family. 'Aye, that is the one, my wife's niece, you must understand. It is her performance we see tonight.'

'Then we shall meet tonight! The bag must leave for Folke-stone at midnight, to be sure to catch the morning tide, and by nine o'clock I will have talked to the Partners and be able to give you an answer! I will try, I promise you, to persuade 'em of the urgency of it, never fear!' He got creakingly to his feet, and grinned down at Gideon, his pendulous lower lip stretch-ing benevolently. 'And I will enjoy seeing your niece tonight. Great singer, they say, great little singer. See to it I have a good place to sit. I will be there about half an hour after nine, then.'

The place was thick with smoke and Gideon coughed a little, and then sent for candles both to augment the light at their table and also to clear the air a little, and Abby smiled at him reassuringly and opened her fan and moved it rather more vigorously than was her wont, trying to make a draught for him.

She was worried about him and try as she might she could not understand why. He seemed well enough, was as punc-tilious as he ever was, as loving to the children, and as affectionate to herself. Indeed, he was more than his usual self, having displayed in recent weeks a degree of uxoriousness that surprised even her. Always a sensuous woman, who had throughout their marriage found much joy in their connubial state, responding to his embraces with an eagerness and delight which much pleased him, still she had found him a little wear-ing of late. At each and every opportunity there was he touched her, kissed her, held her close, and had begun to spend more time in her boudoir during the day then she felt was seemly or even desirable. It was not something she would gladly admit to him, but his demand for her embraces had become so intense of late that she found it occasionally tedious to submit to them.

Perhaps it was this that worried her, she wondered, and watched him covertly from behind her fan, and he caught her eyes and at once the slightly anxious expression on his face cleared, and he leaned forwards to hold her hand firmly in both of his.

'My dear,' she said gently, 'what is it that is worrying you?'

'It is very hot and crowded here – and dearly as I love Phoebe and greatly though I enjoy her performance I must tell you that tonight I would prefer to be at home with you. Just the two of us—' and his hands tightened on hers, and gently she extricated it.

'I know that a wife should be gratified by her husband's ardour, my love, but lately you have been so filled with it that I must confess you exhaust me! That is, in part, what I meant when I asked what worried you.'

He went very red suddenly and said urgently, 'I am worried about nothing – nothing at all. You must not think it! I am the happiest man alive with you and the dear children and – there is nothing worrying me at all!'

'No need to be so vehement, dear one,' she said gently and smiled reassuringly again. 'I believe you!' But she was still concerned and turned her head away ostensibly to look about her at the crowded Rooms, but with her mind still greatly exercised.

The place indeed was very full, with a most fashionable crowd, and with part of her mind she noted the fact and was gratified. She shared none of Gideon's distaste for Phoebe's activities upon the stage of her Supper Rooms, feeling that whatever it lacked in propriety it more than made up for in benefit to the girl. As a woman who had herself been occupied in business all her adult life, from the days before her very young first marrige to today when she was rich enough to be a lady of complete leisure if she so chose, she had found work a balm and a joy. Having a definite activity that mattered lent flavour to life and meaning and value to daily affairs in a way that even the most caring of housekeeping could not do. Dearly as she loved her home and greatly as she adored her children there was a limit to the amount of time and energy she could expend on them, so excellently was everything run by her servants under the control of the redoubtable Ellie, and her work at counting house and sometimes factory filled in the gap most satisfyingly. And for Phoebe, with neither husband nor children, her occupation was even more essential, Abby felt – and anyway, it would be a pity to waste her undoubted talents, for she was indeed the most charming of performers.

It was delightful to see how many highly placed people were in the Rooms tonight, and she looked about her, noting at least four members of the House of Lords, a number of lesser sprigs of the nobility, and large numbers of very rich businessmen from 'Change and Bank. Phoebe had in recent weeks become somewhat of a figure of fashion among the *ton* as well as among the Cits, and everyone with any pretensions at all to style had flocked here tonight for her special entertainment.

Across the Rooms, near the door, she saw a little flurry as the portières parted and a couple of people came through just as the little orchestra sprang to life with its familiar cheerful tune, and she noted that Lydia Mohun and her husband had arrived, and turned to point them out to Gideon. But he was standing up welcoming Lionel Rothschild to the table, for he too had just arrived and in the flurry of greetings and the ordering of drinks and the continuing scrape and beat of the orchestra the moment passed.

The show began with its usual announcement and the Rooms rang with cheers as the audience greeted Phoebe delightedly, and she came swinging on to the little stage, her face alight with laughter and her eyes glittering so that she looked quite enchanting and Abby smiled up at her with great pleasure. There were times when she had been very angry with Phoebe, for the way she had caused Freddy to be so unhappy, but that was, after all, between the two young people, and taking it by and large she was a fetching child, brimming with talent and charm and difficult to be angry with for very long. There was undoubtedly a certain shallowness about her, a self-awareness that was perhaps inevitable in one who worked as a performer – but take her for all-in-all, Abby told herself again, she was a lovable girl.

Lionel Rothschild applauded as loudly as any of them when Phoebe's first number, a rather saucy little song and dance about a girl taking a holiday by the seaside and walking on the beach in a high wind, involving much display of creamy frilled petticoats and drawers, was finished, and the orchestra swung into another tune while a troupe of tumblers came pelting on to the stage and began to throw themselves and sundry balls and clubs about with great abandon. Gideon leaned forwards and above the noise of the orchestra said, 'Well, Lionel? Have you managed to arrange matters for my sister-in-law?'

Rothschild grinned, and lit a big cigar, after raising his eyebrows at Abby for permission to do so, which she gave with a gracious inclination of her head, and coughed a little.

'Compromise, my boy, compromise! Done the best I can, and found there's one ship leaving Constantinople in two weeks' time which will have room for one extra passenger designated from this end. Only one – can't do better. They can get the boy aboard, in other words, but not the father. If I understand your sister's plea aright, it is the boy they are concerned about, so the father can follow later when there is a space for him. Best I can do, so I hope you're satisfied.'

Abby leaned forwards and put her hand on the old man's sleeve. 'More than satisfied, Mr. Rothschild,' she said firmly. 'Indeed, I am most grateful on my sister's behalf. We do not know this young man, nor his father, but clearly Martha is anxious for them, and I am sure will be very grateful indeed for your good offices.'

'My pleasure, my dear Mrs. Henriques, indeed my pleasure. In these hard times we must do all we can.'

The tumblers finished to a burst of applause, and somewhere across the crowded room someone shouted, 'Miss Phoebe! We want Miss Phoebe!' and someone else took it up and then another and another, until almost everyone was shouting her name, and even Lionel Rothschild, his big white face beaming, was rapping on the table with the heel of his glass.

Abby smiled and gave up attempts to talk, for it was clearly not going to be possible, and settled to watch the rest of the show, and indeed tonight Phoebe was at her sparkling best. She pirouetted, she floated, she beguiled. Her voice bubbled with sauciness and sank into pathos only to lift again into ringing seriousness. She smiled, she pouted, she dimpled, and through it all her audience sat firmly in the palm of her hand, responding to every twitch of her finger, every lift of her chin.

Watching her, Abby thought again of Freddy and sighed softly. No wonder the boy loved her so dearly, for contrived and self-aware as it all was, she displayed a lively temperament and a lovely face and figure which any man must find delightful. But he should not have gone away for her, indeed he should not; and she felt a pang for him that sharpened her eyes into a sparkle of tears, and also made her angry with herself. Most of the time she kept her anxiety and longing for Freddy well under control, but on the few occasions it slipped out it frightened her. She shook her shoulders a little and tried to concentrate on the show again.

But it did not help, for the shadow of Freddy's absence together with her still unresolved anxiety about Gideon hung over her, and it made her head ache a little so that she was glad when the curtain fell for the last time, and the crowd unwillingly stopped applauding and began to order more food and drink.

'I would dearly like to shake hands with that little lady,' Rothschild said, and smiled at Abby. 'Your niece is charming - charming! May I be presented?'

'Of course, Lionel,' Gideon said. 'I am sure she will be happy to meet you. Shall we wait until she comes out, as she often does, or would you prefer to go to her dressing room now? It is a small one, but she will gladly meet us there, I think.'

Rothschild stood up. 'The dressing room, I think m'boy if I am to get the necessary papers into that Folkestone bag tonight. Which way?'

'Abby - will you come too?' Gideon said, and she nodded and rose to her feet and together they began to make their way through the narrow passages left between the crowded tables. Oliver, always the careful business man, realizing how successful a draw his sister had become, had added several more tables to his establishment, and movement was not easy

Across the room Abby saw Dickon O'Hare standing up and waving his arms in a rather abandoned fashion, and Lydia was reaching up to hold on to him, and Abby felt her lip lift in scorn. Such a man to get so inebriated in public, and in his wife's presence too! Her Gideon would never behave so, and glad she was of it.

As they reached the back of the room, and were about to duck under the curtain that led to the little dressing room behind the stage, she saw Dickon ploughing his way past protesting diners, with Lydia hard behind him, and her heart sank for a moment. For all her experience of the world, all her closeness to the realities of ordinary life through her time spent among the workmen in her factories, she was a little frightened of drunken men, and there was no doubt that Dickon was very drunk, also that he was making his way to the same place they were. And she put her hand out to Gideon, wanting to seek his protection, but he was already holding up the curtain for Lionel Rothschild, and she had to follow on, very aware of Dickon and Lydia bearing down on them behind her.

They all arrived together. As the three of them turned into the narrow corridor that led to Phoebe's dressing room, she opened the door of it and stood there framed in the light, holding a shawl close over the yellow costume she had last worn on stage and staring at them in some puzzlement, for behind them was Dickon, shouting and swearing horribly and pushing past Lionel Rothschild and Abby to seize Gideon by the collar.

'I'll show you!' he shouted, and his voice was thick and muffled. 'I'll show you, you stinkin' Jew! I'll show you what happens to the likes of snivellers who go paddlin' round my wife's skirts — I'll show you — jus' you take that — and that—'

And he was hitting out furiously at Gideon's startled face, as Lydia and then Phoebe screamed and both Abby and Lionel rushed forward to pull the now wildly flailing Dickon away. But they were not quite in time, for one of his unco-ordinated fists connected with Gideon's cheek, and with a look of amazement on his white face he slowly buckled at the knees and collapsed awkwardly on to the floor.

CHAPTER TWENTY

It had seemed to Abby that not only all the customers in the Rooms must have heard it all, but the passers-by in King Street as well, but in fact the whole episode caused no more than a minor flurry to which all but a very few people were entirely oblivious. Oliver, appearing almost out of nowhere, hurried the drunken Dickon away with Lydia following, only throwing over her shoulder one look at Gideon and Abby and saying cryptically, 'None of it matters one whit, you know,' before she went, while Peter Craig carried the dazed Gideon into a small dressing room.

Sitting beside him, holding his hand as he lay stretched out on the couch, Abby felt calmer than she would have thought she could, under the circumstances. To see her beloved husband actually struck should have filled her with anger, and she knew that had the attacker been anyone but O'Hare, she would indeed have been simmering with rage. But she also knew very deep down that in some curious way the fracas was rooted in the way Gideon had been behaving lately, was linked with the unease of which she had been aware these past weeks. So she waited until he had recovered sufficiently to open his eyes and look at her, and said nothing, only smiling at him as he stared at her mournfully from above a rapidly purpling bruise on his cheek.

'I am sorry, my dear,' he said, his voice a little thick. 'So sorry you were there—' and he closed his eyes again for a moment and moved the muscles of his face experimentally and then winced.

'Shall you tell me about it?' Abby said. 'I think it will be better if you do.'

He turned his head a little restlessly on the pillow. 'There is nothing to tell, Abby. The man was drunk, disgustingly so, and took some megrim into his head. What more is there to it than that?'

'Had it been any other person, I might have agreed,' she said calmly, 'But in this case, it is, I think, a little different, is it not?'

'I don't know what you mean,' he said fretfully.

'Oh, I think you do, my dear. Would you like some water?'

'No – yes – no, oh, I don't know. I do not feel *well*.'

'I am sure you don't.' Abby got up and went and brought a glass of water from the carafe on the dressing table. 'But I think, my dear, that you are perhaps more injured in your amour propre than in any bodily sense. Your bruise is disagreeable, of course, but no greater than those Isabel and Sarah sustain a dozen times a week, with little ill effect. But bruising of the mind – no, that is something else.'

There was a little silence as Gideon obediently drank from the glass she held to his lips and then he took a deep breath and looked up at her, and smiled a little crookedly.

'I do love you, Abby. I do love you so very much.'

'I know you do, my dearest one. As I love you. Nothing ever changes that, you know.' She smiled down at him very gently and bent and kissed his bruised cheek. 'The children say that makes it better. I don't suppose it does, of course, but the idea is pleasant.'

'Very pleasant,' he murmured, and then, moving in a rather gingerly fashion, sat up, swinging his legs over the side of the small couch, and holding his head very straight in an attempt not to cause his bruise to twinge again But it did, a little, and he grimaced, and she sat down beside him and put her arm across his shoulders and gratefully he leaned against her, and rested his head against her neck.

'Now, we shall send for the carriage, and take you home,' she said after a pause. 'But not until, Gideon, you have told me all that is concerning you in this matter If you do not so tell me, I

215

am sure you will feel the effects of his buffet for some time. But explain it all, and you will feel better.'

'I wish you would not talk to me as though I were one of the children,' he said with a sudden spurt of irritation. 'I am not a child, Abby!'

'Indeed you are not! It is because you are not that I speak to you so! You are a grown man, but you have, I suspect, behaved childishly as regards the O'Hare woman, and that is the cause of this present situation. I love you as well as I know you, so you need have no fear in this matter – but I tell you roundly that if you do not explain all this to me, and explain it *now*, then it may indeed drive a rift between us that would be hard to heal. And I have no intention of allowing such a thing to happen! So speak of it now, before we leave this place, and we will settle it all. But leave here with it all still lying between us and we will be both as unhappy as – as – oh, for heaven's sake!'

And now she stood up and moved away from him, her distress no longer allowing itself to be trammelled by her calm exterior.

'Do *think,* man! That disgusting creature talks to my husband about what happens to men who paddle round his wife's skirts – a most felicitous phrase indeed! – and you try to tell me there is no matter to be discussed? Give me the credit for some wit, please, Gideon! Whatever else I am, I am not a fool!'

'No, you are not a fool,' he said wearily, after a second, 'but I am.' And then he closed his eyes and his face tightened into lines of misery and tears oozed from beneath his long lashes to sit absurdly on his cheeks. But she did not move closer, remaining standing on the other side of the little room, her hands clasped in front of her on her green flounced gown. She wanted to go to him and put her arms about him, just as she did when the children were distressed, and indeed in his misery he looked absurdly and most endearingly like Sarah, but she controlled the impulse. It would not help.

He opened his eyes after a moment and still with great care for his painful face, drew a handkerchief from his pocket and dabbed at the moisture.

'Well,' he said after a pause. 'You are right, of course. There is matter here—'

She said nothing, still standing and looking at him and the silence between them lengthened painfully, until at last it seemed to burst out of him.

'You told me to dance with her! Do you remember? At Phoebe's Ball, you told me to dance with her! And I did! I would not have thought of it had you not said!'

'Oh? So it is to be laid at my door, this attack on you?' Her voice was not at all edged, but merely conversational.

'Oh, of course not! But you did, in a sense, set in motion—' He shook his head. 'No, that is not fair. *She* did. Dammit, that is unjust too – it was as much I, since I did not precisely object, did I?'

'I do not know, my dear. You have not yet told me.'

'Oh, well – I cannot deny that I found the woman beguiling! She is quite absurdly personable – in fact, she is all beauty! But I never found, in all those meetings – and I assure you there were really very few of them – that she was anything else. Can you understand that, Abby? Can you believe it?'

He looked at her with an appealing expression in his eyes that both softened and enraged her. How could he, so very personable a man himself, talk of another woman's beauty to her who had never had any pretensions to more than an agreeable countenance? Her anger began to come bubbling up in her, but she said nothing and he bit his lip and looked down at the floor again, and after a moment went on talking.

'Well, so it is. You are my dearest Abby, and I love you more than I love myself, and have for many years, long before you loved me. I will not remind you now of all I suffered for love of you. I loved you for all of you – your spirit and your mind and your charm and your wisdom, and also for your appearance. But that was the least of it, and I had always thought that – you must know that I have never cared very much for mere beauty! My Mamma used to fill her drawing room with exquisite creatures in the days when she was trying to wed me to a wife of her choosing, but I never felt the least interest in any of them. I did not think appearance mattered a whit! But this was different! It was like – it was fireworks over the Long Water on celebration nights. Glittering and exciting, and so beguiling – but soon forgotten.'

'You are talking a lot, Gideon, but you are saying nothing,' Abby said, for the first time allowing irritation to appear in her voice, and he stared at her, and then nodded heavily.

'Yes, well – I went to see her one evening after dinner. You had the headache, and I was bored and a little restless, perhaps – I do not know. Anyway, I went to see her to talk of the Benefit, you know. That was all I had in mind! And somehow—'

'Well?'

He stared at her again, his long lashed eyes as mournful as a dog's, and this time she wanted to hit him herself, so angry had she become, but she controlled it, merely staring at him with her eyes wide and very fixed on his.

'Well?' she said again.

'She began to kiss me,' he said after a moment.

'She began to – oh, come Gideon! You mean you just sat there and gave her no encouragement?'

'Damn it all, Abby, I tried to explain! She is like fireworks! There is no way in which one can ignore them if they are spluttering and glittering under one's very nose! Your trouble is, I think, that you cannot conceive of a woman who behaves as brazen as this one does! She is all hands and mouth and – and – she waits for no invitation as other women might! She throws herself upon one, quite literally throws herself, I do promise you! And she was wearing no stays, just some frilled piece of nonsense, and she had used a great deal of a very pretty scent – it would take a man of superhuman control or indeed no manhood at all to resist it!'

'And you did not resist it,' she said heavily, and felt suddenly very sick. This man she had loved so dearly for so long, with whom she had shared a passion she had not thought she would ever feel again after her first husband's death, this man whose tenderness and strength and gentleness and concern for her in their embraces was of such huge importance to her, to have behaved so in another woman's arms? It was almost more than

218

she could bear and she closed her own eyes against the picture his words had called up.

'That is what is so absurd!' he said, 'I did, I cannot deny, respond a little. I kissed her too. But—' He shook his head, and now she opened her eyes and looked at him and the expression of bewilderment in his face touched her as nothing else he had so far displayed had done.

'It was so extraordinary, Abby! I do not deny I kissed her, and put my arms about her, but after a few moments she pushed me away and said I was of little use to her, for I lacked any muscle! I asked what she meant, for I was very puzzled, and she laughed at me, and said she liked a man who behaved thusly – and then she hurled herself upon me, and – and – well she began to use her body and her hands in such a way as quite amazed me! If it were possible for a woman to ravish a man, then I would say she was trying to do just that – it was quite dreadful, Abby! All the – the feeling she had called up in me – shallow sensation, you must understand, not real emotion – why, it all melted away. I could not bear it – it was so – so *animal*! And she laughed at me, and told me that I was no man of muscle and should go home to you. And I did.'

She was staring at him, her eyes wide with surprise, and a line between her brows. 'Is that all? Just that? She but – but *kissed* you, and – oh, you are bamming me!'

He shook his head. 'Indeed I am not! I am telling you all there is to tell, and painful enough I find it. There is no matter here of pride for me, Abby! I am telling you all – and wretched I have been about it these past weeks, I do assure you. Wretched! To think that I could ever – that I allowed her to – to – oh, Abby, she is a dreadful woman! She is beautiful and beguiling, and the absurd thing is, I still see the enchantment in her, but it is a *bad* enchantment. No woman of any real heart would ever behave so and to think that I – *I* allowed myself to be—' Again he shook his head, and again the tears appeared on his lashes. 'I have been so unhappy about it all, Abby! So sick with remorse, you can never know how dreadful it has been!'

She nodded her head, slowly, and then smiled, a tremulous but rather wicked little smile. 'And that is why you have been so attentive to me these past weeks, my dear one? Because of a few kisses from a woman who does not value your tenderness and loving ways? To prove to yourself that you are a man of muscle?'

She moved then, in a flurry of green silk and sank to the floor at his feet, her gown ballooning about her, and she set her hands into his on his lap and looked up into his face.

'My dear, dear silly Gigi! You have so much muscle it is *absurd*! And you have more besides that is infinitely more valuable! You are kind and concerned and – oh, that poor woman!'

He opened his eyes wide at that. 'That poor woman? Come, Abby, I am grateful, more than grateful if you can see this dreadful episode as one which you can forgive in me, but to pity *her* – that is to take forbearance too far! She is *dreadful*—'

'Dreadful she may be,' Abby said shrewdly, 'but she also has a husband she has to handle like a team of nervous horses, it is quite clear. If that is all that happened between you, then O'Hare surely had no cause to be so angry! She must have told him there was much more to it, and told him for some reason of her own. To spite him, or to use him in some way – it shows they enjoy little domestic felicity, my love. So – poor woman!'

He grinned a little crookedly. 'Not so much forbearance, perhaps, as pity, my love? A most insulting pity! Put so, I can enter into your feelings—'

'Quite so,' she said and stood up and with a gentle tug on his hands drew him to his feet also. 'Come, Gideon. We shall go home. It is all over, this miserable business, and we shall never speak of it again. I bear no anger, I promise you, as long as you bear no guilt. For neither is needed. We shall go home and be comfortable again—'

She smiled once more, that same wicked little smile, and said, 'And perhaps you will let me sleep more o' nights, now that we both know you are a man of muscle!'

'I doubt it,' he said, and pulled her towards him, and held her very close, and then kissed her, trying to impart to it all the urgency of his feelings, but that made his face hurt again, and he yelped a little, and she laughed, and kissed his forehead and tucked his hand into her elbow, and led him to the door.

Outside they found Phoebe, standing talking in a low voice to Peter Craig, and as they emerged she jumped forwards, and held out both hands to Gideon, her face a picture of anxiety.

'Dear Uncle Gideon, are you all right now? That hateful, *hateful* man! To behave so, and unprovoked – he was completely awash, Oliver said. I feel so bad about it all, dearest Uncle Gideon, for she is my aunt after all, and I feel in some way – oh dear!' And she burst into tears and shook her head. 'It is all so dreadful! That hateful man! I too have cause to loathe him, I do promise you and now I will hate him even more. I used to love Aunt Lydia so dearly, but now I feel I can hardly ever speak to her again, because of him—'

'That is foolish, my love,' Abby said briskly, and took her handkerchief from her reticule and gave it to her. 'It is in no way any reflection upon you, nor indeed any of your affair. O'Hare was, as Oliver said, quite awash, and will no doubt be heartily ashamed in the morning. We intend to forget the whole silly episode and so should you. Now, dry your eyes and tell me – where is Mr. Rothschild?'

'Oh, my God,' Gideon said wearily, and rubbed his sore face again, tenderly. 'I had forgot all about him. What on earth he must be thinking—'

'He thought nothing, Uncle Gideon, I do assure you,' Phoebe said, sniffing a little, but in control of her tears now. 'For I told him that O'Hare was a well-known drunkard and one who often made such unprovoked attacks. So he said to tell you he was sorry indeed, and wished you better, and to call upon him and his lawyers at any time should you see fit to sue him for assault – which perhaps you should do—'

'Certainly not,' said Gideon sharply.

'Well, that is what he said, and he said he could not wait but must hurry away to arrange for the documents to go into the

Folkestone bag, and I was to tell you that and you would understand. And—' she dimpled suddenly, 'we had a most agreeable conversation before he went! He said I was prodigious clever and a charming singer and many such delightful things, and promised me he was my servant to command at any time! There, is that not a splendid conquest to have made? I feel very comfortable about it.'

'No doubt,' Abby said astringently and although she tried not to allow the thought to rise in her she could not help it; Phoebe was, after all, Lydia's niece, and perhaps they were more alike in more ways than any of the other side of her family had ever realized. But that was, she told herself, an unkind and unjust thought, and she made herself smile warmly at her. 'Although I would have thought you would be accustomed to such success by now! Perhaps you will call up our carriage, my dear, and then tell us later of all Mr. Rothschild said about you, for your uncle is fatigued, I think, and needs to return home forthwith—'

'One thing,' Gideon said sleepily, an hour later as he lay back at last on his own pillows in his own comfortable bed with a deep sigh of relief. 'One thing, at least we solved the matter of the ticket for Martha. I now hope we hear no more for some time of her needs, for to tell the truth, I am tired of it all. Wars are important, no doubt, but her involvement with this one is making life here at home more than a little complicated for me, I fear. The sooner Martha returns home and no longer needs funds or aid of any sort, the easier, I feel, matters will be for all of us.'

And Abby, settling herself beside him, smiled up into the darkness. Dear Gideon! He always had to find some other cause, some other agent to blame for anything that went wrong in his life. It was in his character, but one she could not dislike too much. Part of Gideon's charm for her was his sense of duty and reliability and he could not have retained that, she felt, as well as a lively sense of his own shortcomings. Whatever lay behind tonight's episode, whoever was really to blame for it, one thing was sure; it was all over, and she had no further need to worry at all about him. Lydia O'Hare might not realize the fact, but in her casual use of Gideon for her own ends, she had shackled him to his wife more tightly than ever. And she turned over and put her arm across the already sleeping Gideon and sighed deeply and fell asleep with great tranquillity.

CHAPTER TWENTY-ONE

THEY stood side by side, watching the ship steaming fussily into the Sea of Mormora, disappearing towards Gallipoli, and neither of them said a word. There was nothing they could say, and she slid her hand into his, and held on tightly.

Felix, whey-faced and dreadfully thin had tried very hard to be brave when the moment of parting came, but he had not succeeded too well, and had clung to his father very tightly, looking so young and frail that it seemed impossible that he had ever been able to convince anyone he was his true age, let alone that he was eighteen.

'I am sorry, Papa. I meant no harm, indeed I did not,' he had whispered. 'It was just that all the boys at school were on and on about the war and soldiers, and I said to them they were only talking, and that talking was not enough. You have always said that, have you not, Papa? It is not enough to talk – you must *do*. So that was why. But I meant no harm, and oh, I do so wish you could come with me—'

'Well, Felix, I cannot,' Alex had said gruffly, but holding the boy's hands very tightly. 'It was our good fortune that Miss Martha, through her friends, was able to get you home at all. Be glad of that. They will look after you at school, and the Captain has instructions about the arrangements that must be made to get you there – and be sure to give Mrs. Bracebridge that letter, now! – and soon you will be well. And, as soon as conditions permit, why, no doubt I shall be able to get a passage home quite quickly and we will be comfortable again. But until then, you must be sensible and brave, and not fuss, nor repine. There is no sense in either.'

The sight of the boy's white face, peering over the rail, had been affecting in the extreme, and Martha had been hard put to it not to weep. Not so much because she would miss the boy himself – for she had after all only met him but a week or two ago – but because he seemed to symbolize all the lonely, unhappy, tired boys and men with whom Scutari and Constantinople now abounded. And also, of course, because of Alex's distress.

He had said little, had taken the news that only one passage was available with apparent stoicism, but she knew perfectly well how it mattered to him that he and his boy were to be parted again. Yet he had made no complaint, nor shown any hint of his distress, simply setting about making the necessary arrangements to send Felix home to school and the care of the headmaster's wife – for there was no one else in England who would take responsibility for him – with his usual calm dispatch.

And she in her turn had done all she could to help, carefully packing the pitifully few belongings Felix had – for, sensible runaway, he had travelled very light – and feeding him up as best she could from their meagre rations.

And had become, in a way, attached to the boy, even though at bottom she knew she was so jealous of him. This tendency to jealousy she was discovering in herself was perturbing her a good deal; she had felt it first when the dying Mrs. Lucas had flirted with Alex, and now she felt it when she saw the close love that existed between him and his son, and she despised herself for it. To feel so about a sick child, and one who furthermore had the first legitimate claim on this man, was both absurd and wicked, but still she felt it, and it was a strange and disagreeable sensation.

She would sit beside the sick boy, as he drifted into the shallow sleep of convalescence, and think about it, and came to the painful conclusion that to fall in love as she had done, at her stage of life, was far from as agreeable as it might be. After all these years of emotional self-containment it hurt to surrender some part of herself to another, for it made her vulnerable. And she knew her vulnerability was the soil in which the little sprig of jealousy grew and sought ways to root it out and destroy it; and did in part succeed, so that by the time the day came when the ship was to sail, she was able to show genuine regret at Felix's departure and could also hold him close, and promise she would take good care of his Papa for him. Which made the boy smile his brilliant tear-glittering smile, and hug her in return.

Now, standing close beside Alex, and holding his hand tightly, she said abruptly. 'I must tell you that I have been feeling wretched, Alex, this last little while, because of Felix.'

He looked down at her, his face quite serious. 'Oh? Now, why should that be?'

'Because I have been jealous,' she said simply, and could not look at him, keeping her eyes fixed on the dwindling ship, now moving rapidly away from them. 'It is an emotion of which I am ashamed, and I have in part conquered it, but not completely. You will perhaps be angry with me for what I am about to say, but I must say it, all the same. I am glad that Gideon was able to arrange only one ticket. I asked him for two, I promise you, but I am glad you were not able to go.'

She looked up at him, almost defiantly. 'There! Are you now disgusted with me? To think that I could put my own desires for your company above Felix's need for you, and yours for him?'

He was staring after the ship himself now, and as she looked at his unsmiling face her heart sank in her chest. She should not have said it. Honesty was all very well, but sometimes it was more politic, even in matters of the heart, to keep one's tongue between one's teeth—

'I know,' he said at length. 'It has been the only thing that made this parting tolerable for me.' He looked down at her and then smiled that narrow-lipped smile of his that could make her feel almost dizzy with love for him. 'To know that you felt so about me made me feel less – less bereft, less alone. Felix will be lonely on the ship, I know, and it will be worse still when he reaches school, and gets well and has to settle to ordinary life again, but as a boarder instead of having me to come home to. I know that and my heart weeps for him. But not for me, not as it would have done, before you. Because I shall have you, and shall be near you, I am fortunate as he can never be. So, you see, I have my guilt feelings too! We have so much in common, dear Martha, have we not?'

'Yes,' she said softly. 'Oh, I do feel so fortunate!'

'And I, my love, and I!' and he took one last look at the plume of smoke approaching the far horizon and very firmly put his hat back on his head and turned away from the dock, Martha still holding his elbow.

'Come! We must find Sal, and see what purchases she has made, and then we must find us a caïque, and return. Freddy is managing well enough, I daresay, but it concerns me that we should not stay away too long.'

'I too,' she said. 'Although it is so much better than it was that I can hardly believe it is the same place we are in!'

For indeed the changes of the past few weeks had been considerable. The flood of sick and wounded men had faltered, thinned and at last become a mere trickle, and this had affected all of them, throughout the hospital.

Miss Nightingale, so they had been told – and Martha would have died rather than actually go to see for herself, for she and the redoubtable Superintendent of Nurses were still at daggers drawn – had worked wonders. Each man had a clean bed and clean bedding, as well as regular and proper treatment for his ills, and the food was improving beyond belief, especially since Alexis Soyer's arrival.

At first Martha, like many others in Scutari, had been amazed and then scornful when they heard of him; this bounding preening little Frenchman, with his blackamoor assistant grandly called his 'secretary' prancing about a place like Scutari! But Miss Nightingale clearly had chosen shrewdly, for in a very short time he had revolutionized the kitchens and with them the food that the men ate.

And, indirectly, the food the women in the cellar ate, for Sal still regarded it as perfectly reasonable to gain all she could, by any means, to feed and comfort 'her' people, and Martha had long since given up remonstrating with her.

So, from time to time, great buckets of stew and soup would

227

arrive in the cellar, carried by a couple of panting soldiers and with Sal strolling cheerfully along behind them as though she knew nothing about anything or where it came from, and they would all eat with huge relish, for the food was more than merely edible. It was actually flavourful and could be felt to be nutritious in a way Martha's thin soups and concoctions, try as she might, could never be. So, now, when she saw Monsieur Soyer tittuping about, she no longer found him funny, but was glad that he was there.

Other benefits drifted from the hospital to the cellar; as the men in the wards became better cared for, they became more cheerful, and this seemed to spread an aura of better spirits, for the wives and children caught the infection, and became happier and more relaxed, even those whose men were still in the Crimea, and of whom there was no news. The children in particular showed how much happier they were, some of them becoming positively mischievous, running about and squealing and playing, poking and prying into Martha's bags and boxes, meddling with all they could touch, and generally being pests. But though Martha scolded them and chased them away outside to play, she was glad to see them behaving like ordinary children, and was not too hard upon them.

It was as though, in these early weeks of spring of 1855, a new spirit of hope had been born and flourished. The hard bitter winter of sickness and ice and rats and disease could be forgotten. Surely, soon, Sevastopol would fall, and they could all go home; but even though they had to wait for that happy day, they could do so with some equanimity, for when one's belly was full and one's flesh was warmed with the rising sunlight, being alive once more became an agreeable state to be in.

They found Sal on the far side of the waterfront, surrounded by a cluster of Armenian dealers, her face flushed and her bonnet pushed back on to her shoulders as she stood, arms akimbo, shouting and haranguing at the men, and they shouted and harangued back.

'Well, Sal, what's amiss?'

'Amiss?' she said and winked at him. 'Not a bleedin' thing,

Mr. Laurence! It's these fellers as reckons they can welsh on a bargain! Well, they can't! I told 'em what I'll pay an' that's all I will. Now, you lot—'

She turned and stared at the men with huge ferocity. 'Bugger orf, you 'ear me? Or I'll be after you with the 'ole bleedin' British army – an' don't think that lot won't foller me if I tell 'em to, neither!' and she made a threatening step towards them, and this time the men, still angry but knowing they had met their match, went away.

And Sal laughed hugely, and grinned at them both. 'Where'd you be without me?' she crowed. 'Oh, it's a great life 'ere! I tell you what, I'm makin' a nice little penny for meself 'ere, an' no error. I've learned more about dealin' and buyin' and sellin' in these last months than I'd have learned in a lifetime at 'ome, and that's a fact. When all this is over, this war, I might just stay on 'ere and make meself a little nest egg. I reckon after a year or so I could be as rich as Kate Hamilton, and come 'ome a lady!'

'Sal, you could take care of yourself anywhere in the world, I have no doubt,' Alex said good humouredly. 'But we have not time now to discuss your future, I think. We must get back to the barracks as soon as we may. How many boxes have you bought this time, for heavens' sake? Indeed, you have done well – eleven! That is a sizeable haul for the amount of money I saw Miss Martha disburse to you.'

'We'll need three caïques to get this lot back,' Sal said equably, 'an' I've organized 'em properly! There's a right shortage of 'em today – lot o' the men's gone orf to some festival or other, so I'm told. I got the last three as is working, and I'll be keepin' 'em busy for a while an' that's all about it! So you'll both 'ave to wait till they comes back to get there yourself because those Armenians is nasty customers, an' the sooner I gets this stuff away the better. They'll be back, otherwise, an' after me. An' I don't want no trouble. What you in such an 'urry for to go back anyway? There's naught much you've got to do, after all! I made a little arrangement with Monsoor's little blackie, an' the dinner's all organized for the cellar today. You've nothin' to cook, Miss Martha, and I'll be back by then, anyway. You done all the treatments and dressings as was needed this morning between you before you come over, so what's yer 'urry?'

She quirked her head to one side and looked at them from beneath her brows, saucy and knowing.

'You know what you two ought to do? It's none o' my never mind, o' course. Not for me to tell me betters what's good for 'em. But I reckon you two ought to get away on your own for an hour or two. There's a feller over there' – she jerked her head towards the hubbub of people clustering at the other side of the dock – 'as'll hire you a pony an' trap, and take you out through the city to one of them gardens they got 'ere. Bin told, I 'ave – you go far enough, you come to real pretty country, and there's eatin' places and they sells good dinners. You could 'ave a real nice rest. You 'aven't 'ad a single day away from that place since we got 'ere, Miss Martha, an' there ain't no reason why you shouldn't take the chance now. I tell you there's nothing there as young Freddy can't 'andle – beggin' yer pardon, then!' as she caught Martha's admonitory eye. '—Dr Caspar – an' you two won't be missed. It's up to you, o' course.'

And she turned away with studied nonchalance and began to count her boxes, as the three ferrymen came climbing over the edge of the wooden slats towards her, to collect their loads.

Alex looked down at Martha and smiled. 'Shall we?' he said. 'Shall we pretend, just for one afternoon, that we are ordinary people, in an ordinary way of life, and take ourselves for a ride to a garden to eat dinner? It is a most attractive thought, I find.'

'Oh, Alex, I think it would be very wrong!' Martha said, looking up at him doubtfully. 'I would not wish to seem disagreeable, but I feel I must demur to such a suggestion. It would not be right—'

'Why not? As Sal says, there is naught urgent for us to do. Oh, I am sure you could find plenty to occupy yourself with when we get back, be it only scrubbing floors again, but you know Sal is right, and Freddy could manage perfectly well today.'

He lifted his head and looked up at the thin tender blue of

the early April sky with a sort of yearning in his face that she found suddenly very touching, and she said impulsively, 'Very well – yes! Why not indeed! It will do you good, I am sure, for you are very tired—'

He smiled at that. 'Well, if you need to salve your conscience by saying it will do *me* good, then I will gladly play the invalid,' and he let his shoulders sag and his head droop in a mockery of fatigue that was very expressive '—although I think it is you who need it most! Very well then – to the man with the pony and trap – Sal! We shall take your advice forthwith. We shall return tonight, before dark I trust, and leave the cellar to you and Freddy to take care of. Be careful of your stewardship, mind!'

And Sal laughed and swore at the ferryman and said, 'Get on wiv yer then,' all in the same breath, and arm in arm Martha and Alex, feeling rather like school truants, made their way through the docks to the waiting crowd of would-be sellers of transport on the far side.

CHAPTER TWENTY-TWO

NARROW streets gave way to wider boulevards, hovels to the minarets and domes of the Soliman and Akhmet mosques, and then hovels again and more magnificent buildings, especially the breathtaking antiquity of St. Sophia, and then at last they had reached the West Wall, lofty, ominous and crumbling with age.

Sitting there beside him in the swaying trap and staring at the way it snaked away on each side to block off the promontory upon which the city was built Martha shivered a little, and shrank closer to his side, and he smiled down at her and patted her hand.

'Do you find it alarming?'

'Very. It seems to threaten so much – dreadful hordes of barbarians on the other side just waiting to come pouring in – sabres and axes waving—'

He laughed outright at that. 'You have been reading too many novels of Sir Walter Scott! It has been many years since this wall, or any other wall like it for that matter, had any such function. In fact, far from protecting the city from living barbarians, it keeps out its own dead past – as you shall see—'

The driver had touched the back of his pony with the tip of his whip, and the animal speeded its trot, wheeling to the right towards one of the small posterns that led out through the wall.

'Here you will find not fear but melancholy,' he said as the trap went through the little gate, and on to a wooded road that ran twisting and turning through heavy trees. 'For we have reached the dead fringe of the city—'

She peered into the green dimness that edged the road,

trying to see, and then, realizing, laughed. 'That is a dreadful pun, Alex, and it is not nice in you to make such jokes at the expense of the dead!'

'Nor is it nice in you to laugh! And anyway they have been dead for so long that there is no need to feel any sense of loss about them, I think. These cemeteries cluster about the city for many miles, I understand. All we will see for some time now is trees and gravestones and yet more trees—'

And so it was; for mile after mile they passed only the dark green spears of cypresses and the lurching yellow stone turban-topped memorials to the long since perished populations of the ancient city whose minarets and towers and domes were dwindling behind them, and they sat and talked in a desultory way, or sat in companionable silence letting peace move back into their bones.

Martha had not realized until now just how tired she was. In the five or so months she had been in Turkey she had hardly left the confines of Scutari, had indeed hardly been outside her cellar. There had been no remission in the pattern of her days – each one starting at sunrise, or even earlier, and following a relentless round of cooking and cleaning and dressing of injuries, and holding of sick children's hands and more cooking and cajoling the women to clean themselves, and then begging urgent supplies and once more cooking until she would fall on to her pallet at midnight exhausted and sleep-sodden.

The coming of Alex and his son had changed matters a little, of course; there had been visits to the boy's sick bed down in the lodgings by the jetty which Alex had found, but even that had been hard work, for having another patient to care for, someone else to feed and fret over, had inevitably added to her burdens.

Curiously enough, today, with its total and almost bewildering change of pattern, had been even more exhausting than any of the previous ones. From the moment they had risen long before dawn to be ready to get Felix over the Bosphorus in time to catch the early tide which was to carry him home, it had been a buzz of activity both physical and emotional, and now, sitting there in the swaying trap, she gave in to the luxury of her fatigue and leaned back against his shoulder, staring out dreamily at the passing blur of green.

She had not even realized she had fallen asleep until she woke with a jerk, to sit up suddenly and stare about her at the strange surroundings, her heart beating heavily in her chest with a sick frightening insistence that made her begin to shake; He seemed to understand, for he put his arm about her and said firmly, 'Take a deep breath and you will be all right again.' And she did, and her little spurt of agitation died down and she could look about her with interest.

'Where are we?'

'I am not, to tell you the truth, quite certain,' he said, 'for I left it to the driver. I told him I wanted somewhere peaceful and pleasant to take a midday meal and this is where he has brought us.'

He stepped down from the trap and held up his hand to assist her and she lifted her skirts and jumped down beside him, feeling suddenly as excited as a child on a picnic, and looked about her.

They were outside a gate, set in a long wall, and the driver was holding it open invitingly and beckoning them and after one inquiring look at Alex, who nodded, she obeyed him and ducked in through the low portal.

And then stood and almost clapped her hands with delight. They were in a walled garden but the walls could hardly be seen for they were wreathed in vines, and the broad leaves, very young and tender at this season of the year, were moving gently in the soft April breeze. There was a small fountain singing and chuckling into a stone basin and scarlet and blue flowers and a patch of well mown grass, and a few fruit trees with the frost of early blossoms dusting their branches; it was altogether idyllic, and she turned her face up to Alex, smiling brilliantly, and said breathlessly, 'Oh, it is beautiful! I am so glad we are here – so glad!'

'I too,' he said, and touched her cheek with one finger. 'It is indeed beautiful here – and you make it seem even more so—' and she reddened and shook her head and tried to speak and could not, and shook her head again, and he laughed.

'Well, let us see what else the establishment has to offer.' He looked round, but the gate was closed, for the driver of the pony and trap had gone, and there was no one to be seen but themselves, nothing to be heard apart from the departing clop of the pony's hooves but the lazy whistling of a couple of birds. 'There must be something beyond this – we shall look.'

Together they walked further into the garden, and at each turn of the path found more to admire and more to exclaim over. A tangle of early roses falling over a stone wall like a cascade, a little stream meandering surprisingly across a corner, under a small bridge and then disappearing as suddenly as it had appeared, under the wall. A long stone bench so moss-encrusted that it looked like green velvet, and trees hiding patches of shade, and flowers, flowers, flowers.

'It is too absurd,' Martha said. 'Like a child's story book. I cannot believe that it is true, or even that I am not dreaming it all. When I think of the cellar and the hospital, only an hour or two away, and then look at this—' She shook her head. 'It is quite, quite ridiculous.'

'It is not this that is riduculous, my love, but Scutari. It is not peace and birds and water we should marvel at, but the disgusting practices of war, and the death and disease and separation and misery it brings—'

There was no answer to that, so she made none, and they walked on in silence for a moment, until the last turn of the path brought them to a low building, itself, like the walls that enclosed the garden, covered in vines and leaves of all kinds.

A woman sitting on a bench outside the door with a bowl of beans on her lap which she was podding looked up at them, her eyes dark and very expressive over the fold of black fabric that covered her mouth and nose, and after one startled glance she pulled the shawl that was over her head even further forward, so that it covered her face entirely, and went scuttling away through the door, the picture of terror.

'It cannot be easy to be a woman in Turkey,' Martha said. 'It is not particularly easy to be a woman anywhere in a world in which, generally speaking, men have all the advantages, but here—' she grimaced. 'Here is positively barbarian! To wear

235

such a garment as that, and always to cover one's face – it must be like being wrapped in a parcel!'

He smiled. 'Your own gown, although sensible of its kind, of course, is hardly rational, my dear!' he said. 'You are yourself, I am sure, quite trammelled in all that fabric. Now, if you were to do as many Turkish women do, and wear *trousers* – ah, then you would indeed be justified in your animadversions on our veiled lady!'

She laughed aloud at that, and the man who had come out of the door through which the veiled woman had scuttled looked at her with some disdain, and turned his head to look at Alex, bowing politely, and Alex's lip quirked.

'I think he finds you as remarkable as you found his lady!' he said, and then turned to the man. 'This will be difficult, for I speak no Turkish. However – perhaps a little Greek.' He took a deep breath and then said carefully, 'Milate elinika?'

The man's face cleared, for he had been looking very puzzled, and he nodded. 'Ligo – ti thelis?'

'He says he speaks Greek a little, and asks what we want. What do we want?'

She laughed, and the man looked at her again with some suspicion. 'Some luncheon I think, and somewhere peaceful to eat it. Can you manage to ask for that? I am most impressed that you speak Greek, Alex. It seems to me a most difficult language—'

'I learned a little from those long boring lessons of my boyhood! Well, go and sit there on the bench in the sun, and I will see what I can do.'

She left them in laboured colloquy and sat down on the mossy stone bench, turning her face up to the sun as she had that day when he had come back to Scutari and found her with her wet hair over her shoulders, and relaxed. Whatever the past months had been, whatever the future held, today was beautiful, and she was enjoying it. And she would go on enjoying it, whatever it brought.

It brought Alex back to her side in about ten minutes, and he took her hand and led her across the garden to the far side, to a quiet enclosed little spot, bounded on one side by a low bank on which thyme was blowing its lavender-coloured flowers, and on the other side by a broadly spreading dark-leaved tree which made patches of shade beneath its branches.

'I did remarkably well,' he said complacently. 'Inasmuch as I conveyed to him that we required sustenance. I cannot pretend I was able to specify *what* sustenance so it will come as a surprise. But something will undoubtedly arrive. He told me to sit here where it is private, and we cannot be seen. I gained a distinct impression, my love, that he feels you are too appalling a sight, with your uncovered face, to be allowed to be seen by any members of his household. Hence the privacy that is forced upon us.'

She gave a little gurgle of laughter. 'Oh dear. Does he think I am a Babylonian woman? How depressing!'

'Not at all. I think he is merely horrified by foreign women in general! He is, as I understand it, a comfortably found farmer who runs a sort of tavern here, but it is rare indeed that people come at this time of day. So we are fortunate to be able to enjoy our repast, when it comes, in peace. I hope the food is good – I am sure, looking at the general ambience of the place, which is so very charming, it will be good of its kind. But it will undoubtedly be exotic to our tastes—'

It was, but she enjoyed it hugely just the same. It was brought on trays by little boys, who set before them plates of rice which had been cooked in oil and butter and plentifully sprinkled with chopped herbs, and skewers upon which pieces of meat had been threaded before being roasted to a crisp succulence that was very delicious. There were bowls of salad lettuces and cresses strewn with cucumbers and olives and pieces of a salty sour cheese which almost certainly came, Alex informed her solemnly, from goats' milk – a thought which she found a little alarming at first – and a straw-covered bottle of red wine.

They ate slowly, savouring it, and she licked her fingers and wiped her plate with pieces of the flat hot bread the little boys brought straight from the oven. Then she ate more, pulling the shreds of savoury meat from the skewers with an abandon of which she would not have thought herself capable.

And when they had eaten all the meat and rice and salad, the boys came back, this time bearing a large flat tart and a plate heaped high with golden croutons dusted with sugar and cinnamon. The tart was delicious, rich with eggs and cream and strewn with nuts, and the croutons were delectable, melting in her mouth and leaving traces of sugar and spice around her lips. She began to reach in her reticule for a handkerchief with which to remove it, but he leaned over suddenly and kissed her, so that the sweetness transferred itself to his mouth, and then he leaned back again, and very deliberately, with the tip of his tongue, licked away the crystals of sugar that had adhered to his lips and she found her face flaming a fiery red. It was quite the most intimate moment they had ever shared, and it set her heart beating as urgently as it had when she had woken, so startled, from her sleep in the trap on the journey there.

To cover her embarrassment she drank more of her wine, and because the salt cheese had made her thirsty, drank a lot of it, and after a little while it began to affect her, making her lips a little numb and her muscles ache in a gently agreeable way, and she leaned back against the trunk of the tree and sighed softly and closed her eyes.

She heard the soft voices of the boys as they came and took away the empty dishes and Alex's deeper tone as he asked them something and they answered, and heard the chink of coins and then was aware that they had gone and he had come to sit close beside her. But still she sat with her eyes closed.

'There is still some sugar about your mouth,' he said softly. 'Shall I tell you what the boys told me? That those croutons are a great delicacy called Esh es Seraya – Palace Bread. It is a dish they make for the ladies of the Seraglio. I think I can see why the Sultan orders it for them—'

And again he kissed her, but this time with much more passion, his mouth opening on hers with a strength she could not resist, nor indeed did she want to, for she let her own lips relax, as his tongue insisted they should, and let herself melt into him. She, who knew nothing of men and less of love, who in all her thirty-eight years had never once loved any man,

238

knew as though instinctively with every fibre of her body what love was and what it was for.

Almost, she knew too well. It was as though for a long time it was nothing to do with her. She was feeling the sensations, and startling and delightful, they were; she was feeling his hands on her body, and feeling his skin and muscles and tensions under her own fingertips, yet it was not she, not Martha Lackland who had spent her life so quietly and virtuously ministering to the sick and needy and never feeling anything very much at all. That Martha was watching in some amazement, if not disapproval.

But after a while, as his caresses became more urgent and much more explicit and she realized somewhere deep in her mind where this interlude under the tree was inevitably leading, the two parts of her, the observer and the observed, melted together and again became one person. Suddenly the clouds of langour created by the wine and food lifted and dissolved and left her very aware of her dishevelled state, of the hardness of the ground beneath them, of his body pressing so urgently against her and she pulled away from him, turning her head under his kisses and gasped, 'No – No, please – no more. Please stop—'

For a moment she thought he was going to take no notice, that he had changed from the person she had known and trusted and learned to love and had become only a large masculine presence, and a very demanding masculine presence at that, but then after what seemed a long time but was in fact but an infinitesimal pause, he seemed to become aware of the rigidity of her body beneath him, to feel the sudden change of mood in her and he too pulled away, and looked down at her, his face creased a little with questions.

'I'm – I'm sorry – I am sorry, Alex. I cannot – it is too soon. I am sorry. It is not right, and I am frightened—'

'Of me?' he said and put up his hand to smooth his hair, and then, as though suddenly aware of how dishevelled he was, began to straighten his shirt and collar. 'Frightened of me? You cannot be – not if you know how dearly I love you.'

She shook her head and then, as embarrassed as a schoolgirl, began to pull her own clothes to rights, and they were indeed in a sorry tangle. 'Not of you – not of love – of the *mind*. It is all this—'

She swallowed, shook her head and began to brush her gown with some vigour. 'I cannot – please try to understand.'

There was a long pause and then he said carefully, 'My dearest one, I am not attempting to seduce you. I never would. I love you too dearly and too well to – to do anything that would distress you. In normal times, in normal circumstances, to have behaved to you as I have just done would have been the behaviour of a bounder, a man who had not the right to expect to be received in any decent company. But these days are not normal, and these circumstances—'

He stood up and looked down at her sitting there in the grass and still trying to tidy herself. 'Oh, but these circumstances are so very strange!'

She got up to her feet too, and they stood there side by side for a moment and then she said in a low voice, 'I hope – I trust you do not feel – I hope that you have not suffered too much because I bade you to stop. I know little of love or of men but I have heard the women in the hostel talk sometimes, and though there is much I could not comprehend and still do not, I believe that for men matters of – of the body are of much greater import than they are for women, and they may suffer if—'

He turned to her, almost violently, and took her face between his hands and looked down at her with an expression of great seriousness on his face.

'Do not believe it! Never believe it, my dear one. Women are as capable of taking joy in matters of the body, as you put it, as are men. Yes, it is true that men have sometimes a great urgency of need but women may have it too! I would feel myself a great villain indeed if I ever attempted to love any woman who did not share with me, in equal measure, the same need. Do you understand what I am telling you? You are as capable of giving physical love and taking joy in it as am I or any man, and it's a wicked lie that has been put about that says women are above such things. They are not, and you are not! I thought,

240

holding you there and kissing you, that your need was aroused, that you felt as I did—'

'I did,' she said softly, and put her own hand to touch his face. 'I did. That was why I had to stop.'

He shook his head. 'Because you are a lady? And you have the belief that ladies do not experience such things? Oh, my dear one, as you love me, listen to me. It is not so – nor shall it ever be for you, with me. Together, when you are ready, we shall have a joy and a happiness that—well you shall see. It can be so, and it must be. But not until you are really ready. And you will be, when you let yourself be. The time will come—'

'Are you not suffering then, now, because I stopped you?' She said it almost timidly, still remembering the odd phrases the Bedford Row girls had used in her hearing sometimes, beginning to piece together the facts that had lain beneath their ribald banter. 'Are you content to be with me, like this, now?'

'More than content – more than content. And I am grateful indeed for your concern, for it displays your love for me with great eloquence!' He kissed her again, but this time much more gently and she responded freely and easily in the same way and peace came back into the day, and she could breathe again. She felt not so much that she had been saved from some frightening experience, not that she had narrowly missed being seduced, and behaved as no respectable unmarried lady should ever behave, but that she had saved some very precious thing, had reserved for the future a joy that would mean much to her. To both of them. It was a feeling of such comfort and security and plain happiness that it brought tears to her eyes, and he saw them and very carefully blotted them away.

They remained there in silence under their tree, standing side by side, for five long minutes, saying nothing, just looking closely into each other's eyes and exchanging a few delicate and very tender kisses, and then, unwillingly, he turned, tucking her hand into his elbow.

'We must return, I think. It must be close on four in the afternoon and by the time we get back to the city and find a caïque to get us over to the Barracks it will be dark, I think. And I would not willingly have you out so late. It might not be safe for you. Dear Martha, I love you very much.'

'I know,' she said and took a deep breath. 'I know. It is quite the most unbelievable thing that has ever happened to me in all my life, and I am almost stunned by it. To be loved by such a man as you – it is quite–' she shook her head and hugged his arm close to hers and let him lead her out of the shade and into the garden.

They stood there for a moment, and the man came out of the house and padded over the green, throwing his lengthening shadow on to the ground before him, and carrying a tray in his hands. He stopped in front of them and spoke to Alex, the liquid syllables seeming to sound as natural as the song of the birds above their heads.

Alex listened courteously and also spoke a few words and then turned to Martha.

'He says, my love, that he, the owner of the tavern of Kagathane, which is this place, offers us some coffee made in the Turkish manner. He says that this has a meaning – those who share such a drink are forming a bond of friendship that will last for forty years.'

She looked at the man and again he stared back at her with that disdain in his expression, but now there seemed to her to lurk deep in his eyes a compassion that she needed and she bowed to him herself and said softly, 'I will be glad to make such a bond with this place – Kagathane? A pretty name. A pretty place–'

She took a cup from the tray and held it between both hands. It was a small cup, and the coffee it contained was very hot and sweet and thick, and they drank it together, all three of them silent and solemn, as the shadows grew longer on the sunny grass, and the birds began to lift their voices in a late afternoon chorus.

They drank glasses of water after that and the man led them back to the gate in the wall beyond which their pony and trap waited, for he had called it for them, and with some ceremony he held his gate open, still not looking at Martha with anything but cool disapproval, and together they climbed into the trap and settled themselves. The driver with a soft click of his tongue against his teeth roused the pony and it wheeled, taking them back to the dim green path between the turbanned gravestones, leaving the garden of Kagathane dwindling away behind them.

They said nothing as they drove, just sitting side by side and holding each other's hands. There was nothing they had to say.

CHAPTER TWENTY-THREE

'OH, thank God you're back! I thought you would never get here!'

Freddy scrambled to his feet, giving one last glance down at the child on the pallet beside whom he had been sitting, and turned to Alex as he came picking his way over the sprawled bodies on the cellar floor. 'It has been a most difficult business, most difficult – I am so glad to see you at last—'

'Freddy! What on earth is the matter? You look quite dreadful! What has happened?' Martha pushed past Alex to stare at her nephew, her face furrowed with anxiety, for indeed Freddy looked quite ghastly. His face was white and drawn in the flickering lamplight, and his eyes were smudged with purple shadows which looked very sickly against his dusting of sandy freckles. 'Oh, I knew we should not have gone away for the whole day! I knew we should not have done! What has happened?' And in an agony of remorse she put her hand out and almost shook Freddy by the shoulder.

'My dear, you must give him time to answer you!' Alex said gently. 'I am sure he will tell us if we give him the opportunity.'

'It is not because you were away today,' Freddy said wearily, and rubbed his face with one hand, and now Martha could see that his shirt sleeve was heavily bloodstained, and as her eyes moved to take in the rest of him, she could see splatters of blood on his waistcoat and trousers, and anxiety seized her again in its cold grasp. But she said nothing, just untying her bonnet strings so that she could cast it aside together with her shawl and be ready for whatever was needed of her.

'Indeed,' Freddy went on. 'I was delighted when Sal told me

244

she had sent you away for a day's rest, for I know well enough how you need it. I was planning to do the same when I had the chance—' He grimaced a little at that. 'Well, it was all so quiet this morning, and we had all our tasks done so quickly it seemed possible to do other things. I went over to the hospital, in fact, to make some drawings of injuries, as my grandfather bade me do, and left Sal in charge, and it is not her fault either—'

'Please, Freddy, do not tell us all the details! Just why it is you look so agitated!' Martha said imploringly. 'It is taking you far too long to get to the point—'

'My instruments,' Freddy said heavily. 'I left my case of instruments here, on the table in the dispensary. I knew to lock up all the medicines and drugs and food and did so, and with Sal here, I thought there would be no problems – but I had left my case of instruments on the table and the children—' He shook his head. 'One forgets about children. When they are well and lively they are as inquisitive as cats, but these children had been so sick for so long, I had forgotten. I had forgotten that some of them are getting healthier and healthier all the time, as they are better fed. They do not sit about in apathy as they did when I first arrived here. Now, they seek mischief – and I went over to the hospital and left mischief for them to find.'

'Your instruments—' Martha said, and looked down at the child on the pallet at his feet. 'Peter MacConachie?'

Freddy nodded, and rubbed his face with both hands. 'My God, but I am tired! Yes, young MacConachie. He took out one of my bleeding knives and said he was going to do an operation on young Ada Manning, the very little one whose father is in the hospital, you recall? She is perhaps four years old. But she would not let him, it appears – it was the other children who explained what had happened – until he showed her it was safe, so he showed her, setting the knife against his arm, as he had seen me do—'

Freddy shook his head again in a sort of impotent rage. 'Oh, God, if I had but locked them away! Or never let them see what we did in the dispensary – but there it was. He had seen me and was able to open the knife, poor little scrap – by the time anyone had realized what had happened and how badly he was bleeding, and they had found me in the hospital he had become quite shockingly exsanguinated. The child is desperately ill, Alex, and there is little we can do. Well, there is one thing we can do, but I need you to help me. And to tell me if we should—'

He knelt down beside the pallet and Alex and Martha came and knelt there too, he reached forwards and took the flickering candle and brought it closer to the head of the pallet, and now they could all see.

Sitting up with her back to the wall, her hair hanging over her face and her arms held protectively across her child, was Mary, the boy's mother. She was a scrawny girl, little more than a child herself at eighteen, for Peter had been born to her when she was twelve years old, and had been following the drum with her own mother, now dead. But she had been one of the lucky ones, for her soldier had cared for her, and taken a pride and pleasure in the lusty son she had borne him, and they had been together for six years now, but they had no more living children other than Peter. Year after year she had presented him with a baby, but none had lived longer than a few hours after birth, so Peter, as the years had passed, had become more important to both his parents than such gutter children usually were. Many times had Martha watched Mary playing with the child, watching her feed him extra food, although she was herself pregnant again and clearly much in need of extra rations, watched her soothe his tears and hug away his unhappiness. The fact that he was a beloved child, Martha had often felt, accounted for his greater liveliness and strength, for there was no doubt that among the myriad children eking out their existence in the cellar he was the ringleader. His tousled black head and boot-black eyes would appear in the middle of every game that the small community of lackadaisical children developed, every small fracas that flared between the scraps of hungry humanity who were his followers.

But now he looked even more frail and helpless then even the weakest and sickest of them. He was lying against his mother's swelling belly, his head lolling against her arm, and his eyes were only half closed, for a rim of white showed beneath the lids. But beneath that rim of white his face was whiter still. It did not seem possible that any child could be so pallid and yet live, and had it not been for the rapid breathing that lifted his narrow chest with an almost feverish speed and the faint bubbling of spittle that appeared on his lips, Martha would have thought him dead already.

One arm was heavily bandaged, with a patch of ominous crimson scarring it, and held against the child's chest in a sling, and the other hand lay lax with the dirt-nailed fingers curling in a most pathetic stillness against the fine bones of the hand, and Martha, kneeling there, put out one hand and touched the child, and felt the chill of him and felt the same chill filling her own belly. He was dying, quite obviously, and not only did she, Martha, know it. So did Mary MacConachie.

She was sitting there erect and still and yet with a sense of terror, even of panic, about her that seemed to come out of every pore of her body.

She sat and stared at them over Peter's black hair, her eyes watchful and dumb with fear in her pale face, and waited. Martha could not look at her, and turned her head to Freddy and said in a low voice, 'What can we do?'

He shook his head. 'He must have lost an unconscionable quantity of blood. It was like an abattoir here by the time I got back, though Sal had done her best. But she lacked the necessary knowledge. If she had but set a tourniquet! Well, that is all by the by now. I think – well, I will tell you what I think. Alex, come over here – I would speak to you about it all.'

'No!' They all turned their heads at that, for the word had come cracking so sharply that it was like a gunshot, but in fact Mary's voice was low and husky. But it was filled with passion as she said it again.

'No! If you're doing aught to my wean, then I'm to know of it. I'll not have you trying yer wild notions on the lad wi'out I'm part of it. He has a need o' me, and I'll not be parted from him, and don't you forget it.'

The softness of her Scots accent seemed somehow to underline the fury in her voice in a strange counterpoint, and looking at her, at the eyes so full of pain and rage and terror, Martha put out her hand and said impulsively, 'You are right, my dear. Of course you are. Whatever you want to do, Freddy, to help Peter, Mary must know of it from the start. So there is no need to move apart.'

The two doctors looked at her and she moved a little closer to Mary and the child, feeling a curious sort of aloneness, as though she and Mary were outsiders, lacking the real understanding of life, the secrets and the inner mystery that these two men knew, and she shook her head almost irritably and said again, 'It is her affair. You must tell her of all you plan for Peter.'

The moment of separateness went as Alex said heavily, 'Yes. I think you are right in this case, Martha. Well, Freddy?'

Freddy still looked doubtful and glanced at Mary, but then he shrugged slightly.

'Well, so be it – Alex, I have seen my grandfather perform tranfusions of blood. He arranged tubes and hollow needles in such a manner that the blood flowed from one to another. In such a case where there has been too great a loss of the life fluid, I believe it is our only chance, the child's only chance—'

'Transfusion?' Alex stared at him, his brows furrowed. 'But that is a nonsense, my boy, and you know it! It cannot be done! It has been tried many times, with dogs and calves, with all sorts of donors, and never has anyone succeeded in any real way! I can see your desire to set blood back into the boy's veins, but how is it to be done? You are anguished, I am sure, because it was your knife that did the damage, but you must not clutch at straws such as this in consequence!'

Freddy set his mouth stubbornly. 'I am telling you – my grandfather did it at Nellie's. He did it many times. I speak now not of the failures, but of the one time when I saw him achieve a success—' His eyes lit up and his whole body seemed to straighten as his enthusiasm kindled. 'I tell you, Alex, it was remarkable! We had a woman who had bled quite shockingly after parturition. The infant was lusty enough but she – oh, we had packed her with ice and tilted her and stopped the bleeding, but she was like this – almost drained.' He looked down at the boy, still breathing his fluttering greedy little breaths as though he were trying desperately to fill his lungs with air they could not take in. 'Just like this—'

'And you performed a *successful* transfusion? I cannot believe it!'

'I am telling you that we did!' Freddy flared, turning on Alex so furiously that the older man took a step backwards. 'Once only, but we did! I believe the success was due to choice of donor. The girl had a sister, a full sister you understand, not a half, and she was willing to help, and so we used her. We set them on adjoining tables and cut into the femoral vein of the dying woman and into the radial vein of the sister. We used different levels for each of them and we used a fine catheter and a couple of trocars and cannulae to make the venesection. I am telling you, Alex, it *worked*, but I cannot do it alone. I must use your aid. If you will give it.'

Alex looked down at the child at their feet and after a moment, he nodded. As though he had spoken the words aloud, Martha knew his thoughts. The child was doomed to die anyway, and that very shortly. What could be lost by trying, apart from effort?

'Very well, Freddy, we shall. And your donor?'

Freddy's eyes moved sideways, but his head remained still, and he looked at Mary, still sitting very still and watching them, and Alex frowned sharply and said carefully. 'Is this a matter you have discussed with – with the interested party?'

'No, not yet. I saw no point until you arrived. It might have been – there was no sense, I thought, in discussing a matter that could not be carried out post mortem in case that was the case by the time you returned—'

'We should not have stayed away so long—' Martha said almost automatically, and tightened her grasp on Mary's hand, but no one took any notice of her, for Alex and Freddy were staring at each other very seriously.

'You believe it will work?'

'I do not know. But nothing else will. What have we to lose by trying?'

'The donor – let me think how to say this – there is the

matter of impending parturition. The foetus in such a case may come to some damage by being deprived of vital life fluid.'

'Are ye tryin' to bamboozle us wi' yer long words and fancy talk?' Mary said suddenly, and again her husky voice sounded preternaturally loud, and Martha raised her head and looked round the cellar and realized why it was all so quiet. Two hundred or more women and children were lying there and not a sound was to be heard because they were all awake and watching and listening in the darkness.

'Is it bamboozlement ye're tryin'? Because I want to know what ye mean to do to my wean—'

'Mary,' Alex knelt down beside her and took both her grimy hands in his and looked very seriously into her eyes. 'Mary, I will explain. Your boy, your Peter, has lost too much blood.'

'I know that. I saw it,' and it was as though she had shrieked her fear, so full of anguish was her voice.

'Then you must understand that blood is vital to life. Peter needs more blood. His own body will create more in time with God's good grace, but we fear he cannot live long enough to do so. And Dr. Caspar has an idea that may help.'

Her eyes swivelled so that she was staring at Freddy, who looked calmly back at her, but said nothing.

'He thinks that he can transfer blood from another person into Peter's veins, in order to sustain him.'

Her face crumpled suddenly. 'Ye want him to drink *blood*?'

'No, my dear,' Alex's voice was very gentle. 'We wish to put it straight into his veins. Through a needle and a tube—'

She drew back at that, as though she would push her body through the dank cellar wall.

'Like a vampire—' and one hand shifted and pulled away from Alex's grasp and she crossed herself devoutly and muttered a prayer under her breath.

'That is nonsense, Mary! Dr. Caspar speaks as a medical man of great experience. He is the grandson of a great surgeon and has seen him perform this task – safely. He can do it for Peter, he believes, though he cannot promise it will save his life—'

He looked down at the child and touched his waxen cheek. 'He has not much life left, Mary. Not without trying. It may not work – indeed it has but a very small chance of working. But it might – it just might–'

There was a little silence and then Mary took a deep breath and nodded her head, so firmly that the wings of greasy black hair that framed her face swung and covered the child's cheeks for a moment and he moved a little and whimpered in his sleep.

'Aye, then do it. An' do it as fast as maybe, an' God go with it–'

'We need you, Mary,' Freddy's voice cut across her muttered prayer, for again she had begun to cross herself. 'We must have a donor – a giver of the blood–'

Her hand stopped in mid-air, and she stared at him. 'A giver of the blood? *Me?*'

'Who else, Mary?'

Again the long pause and then slowly she completed her sign of the cross. 'Aye,' she said, 'who else?'

CHAPTER TWENTY-FOUR

SAL had come back, bearing a bottle of rum and a bottle of brandy, and she said nothing to Martha and Alex, only staring at them with a truculent expression on her face, and Martha also said nothing; this was no time to remonstrate with her for begging of such supplies. And anyway she was right to have thought as she did, Martha told herself as she watched Sal pour a generous tot of brandy and mix it with water and push the tin mug into Mary's hand. The whole business was becoming nightmarish enough to her; what it must be like for Mary, unable to comprehend the preparations Alex and Freddy were making, she could only imagine.

Freddy was kneeling beside his case of instruments, a narrow wooden box open beside it and was spreading various items on to a towel.

'I have but one usable trocar and cannula, God damn it,' he said. 'I blunted the other one on the child with abdominal ascites – we shall have to use the bleeding box.'

'Will you obtain a brisk enough flow that way?' Alex asked, and picked up a brass syringe from the wooden box. It contained in addition half a dozen glass bells, each with a metal nozzle sunk into the top, and a set of fleams, the tortoiseshell-handled bleeding knives which Peter had found so fascinating, and also one of the fast acting trigger operated knives which inflicted a series of six or seven evenly spaced cuts each of the same depth. Alex removed it, handling it with the respect so potentially lethal an instrument deserved, and set it down on the towel at Freddy's side.

'I hope so. I would wish you to set it at the elbow, in such a way that you may, if we are fortunate, obtain entry to a vein, while protecting the artery. Then I shall use the trocar and cannula for Peter. I shall try to get in, I think, at the ankle, for I may have a better chance of entering a vein there, and we can splint the limb to prevent excessive movement—'

He looked up at the boy's face, whiter than ever, if that were possible, and reached for the wrist to feel the thread of pulse that fluttered there.

'If he is fit to move at all, that is,' he added under his breath, and Alex nodded and again bent his head to the wooden box to select a glass bell for use on Mary.

She was sitting bolt upright still, with her back against the wall, but some of the dumb fear seemed to have left her, for she was staring at them with lacklustre eyes and a blank expression on her face.

Sal began to pour out more brandy for her but Alex said sharply, 'No more! There will be little pain for her, and she needs no such protection – and excessive brandy in her blood may reach the child, and be deleterious in its effects.'

Sal grimaced, and drank the brandy herself, tossing back her head sharply and swallowing it at a gulp, and Martha realized suddenly how very distressed the woman was. In all the months they had been working together, side by side very closely, she had become used to the idea that Sal was hard. Not for her the easy sentiment that sometimes reduced the other women in the cellar to maudlin tears. Not for her the attacks of rage or irritability that in other females masked an underlying unhappiness. Always she had been insouciant, full of flippancy and noisy bawdiness, shrugging off pain and distress as though they were no more than the transient attentions of the horse-flies that buzzed so busily over the middens; but now Martha could see that beneath this adamantine exterior lay a spirit as susceptible as any other woman's to pain and fear and children's misery, for above the tin mug her eyes were filled with an expression of sick anger and Martha held out her hand to her, impulsively.

Sal looked at her, her head up challengingly and after a brief moment handed her the mug and said with a sort of savage mockery, 'Sorry, Miss Martha! Did yer fancy a nip yerself? Wouldn't deprive you for the world, I wouldn't—'

'No, thank you, Sal,' Martha said softly. 'But I thank you for the thought,' and smiled at her as reassuringly as she could, and Sal lifted her eyebrows slightly and then managed to smile back, and went to sit on the other side of Mary, to hold her hand in a rough grasp.

The two doctors were ready by now, and Alex moved to Mary's other side and spoke gently into her ear.

'What we must do now is rearrange you, Mary. We will take you and ask you to lie upon the table which Dr. Caspar is bringing from the dispensary – the light is as good here as anywhere, and it is better not to disturb either of you too much, we think. We will arrange a pallet upon it, and ask you to lie on that. Do you understand? It is best for Peter that you lie higher than he does, you see—'

Mary seemed to have lost all interest in the proceedings. She moved like an automaton when she moved at all, as though she were a puppet, allowing others to pull the strings that made her operate. She allowed Alex to lift Peter gently away from her and set him into Sal's arms, and then allowed both Alex and Martha to lift her to her feet. Freddy came picking his way across the cellar, bearing above his head the rickety table which they used for all purposes, from cooking the meals to serving them to doing the daily dressings of injuries, and he set it down beside the pallet upon which Sal had gently laid the child.

Mary let them help her to sit on the table, and then as Alex lifted her legs let Martha gently push her back so that she was lying down, with Sal's shawl, which she had quickly pulled off her shoulders, bundled into a makeshift pillow under her head. She let Freddy take her arm and stretch it out, and bandage a small wooden splint to the elbow, and still said nothing, just lying staring up at the black and dripping bricks of the roof above their heads.

'I do this only so that you will not inadvertently move and

disarrange the apparatus, Mary. It will not discommode you too much, I do promise you – a mere scratch with the – a mere scratch, and then no more that need concern you—'

Deftly he arranged her arm at her side in such a manner that even if she lifted her head – which she was patently not going to do – she would see nothing, for he had a lively awareness of the effects of fear upon patients, and had always done all he could to protect them from it.

'I wish I could use a little chloroform,' he said in a low voice to Alex, 'but I fear the effects on the child – now, Alex, I will endeavour to enter the vein. Sal, will you hold the light nearer? Yes – just so. And Alex, if you can be ready to set the bleeding glass – the smallest one I think will be the best size – but it is of course for you to judge—'

He moved smoothly, bandaging another wooden splint to Peter's flaccid leg, and then washing away the mud that adhered to his narrow ankle with a swab of charpie, the grey teased threads they used for so many purposes, from cleansing wounds to packing them.

There was a moment of silence as he knelt there staring down at the white patch on that fragile ankle, and the boy's foot twitched slightly, and he turned his head and whimpered again and at once Sal was beside him, kneeling down and whispering into his ear. They could not hear what she said, but it seemed to comfort him, for he was silent after a moment and then Freddy shook his head as though to clear it – and Martha noticed again with a pang how weary he looked, how flushed his cheeks were in the lamplight and how feverish an expression was in his eyes. 'I hope he is not ill himself,' she thought suddenly. 'Please God it is but the excitement of the moment that makes him look so—'

He had picked up the trocar and cannula, a slim brass rod of some three inches in length, and setting his hand firmly on the boy's leg, just above the ankle, he brought the tip of the instrument to touch the skin to one side.

Martha watched, standing there beside Mary and holding her unbound hand firmly in hers, and saw the way that Freddy's tight grasp gradually caused the collapsed veins in the boy's foot to fill, and then bulge, and a faint flush of colour appeared there and showed more vividly than anything else had done just how deathly was the child's pallor. But she had no more time to think of that, for now Freddy had brought the bevelled tip of his instrument close to a vein and was pushing and twisting with it and Peter suddenly wailed with startling loudness and seemed to try to move the splinted leg. But Freddy, held on, still pushing, and after a moment said urgently. 'I believe I am in, Alex. Set to, man, set to—'

Alex had been standing poised, and now moved with a speed that was startling. He set the trigger knife he had been holding in his hand against the crook of Mary's elbow, and with one sharp movement of his forefinger made the little knives flash, and Mary winced slightly but no more; and then he dropped the knife and set the glass bell over the little row of cuts now beginning to well with blood. He turned it slightly so that the flesh beneath the edge twisted and made a seal, and then, with his other hand, he set the syringe in place upon the nozzle, and jerked his head at Martha.

She, who had never seen such a technique before, found she somehow knew what he wanted and reached out and held the glass bell in place, so that Alex's hand was free and at once he began to draw back on the syringe.

The glass bell remained firm in Martha's hand, and slowly, as Alex pulled on the plunger, the flesh trapped within the glass rim began to balloon upwards and the blood began to flow more quickly. Alex disconnected the syringe with another swift flick of his wrist, holding the nozzle closed with the thumb of the other hand, and at once reconnected it and again drew hard, and now the flow became brisk and blood began to rise thickly and smoothly up the bell.

Watching it Martha suddenly felt her gorge rise with it. She who had seen so much disease and injury, who had not flinched at the worst excesses of cholera and typhoid, who had dressed the suppurating stumps of amputation wounds, found the sight of healthy blood rising against the glass dome so sickening that she had to take a deep breath to control the nausea and bite her lip hard so that it hurt abominably, as a sort of self-punishment for her weakness.

The moment passed as Alex reached out and connected the end of a long snake of red rubber tubing to the glass bell, and gave the far end to Freddy, who was reaching up for it. They all watched as Freddy carefully and delicately pulled the trocar, the sharp pointed section of the instrument, out of the cannula which was the hollow tube which made up the outside structure, and connected the rubber end to it. And then Alex was pumping with his syringe again, and the blood, the level of which had begun to fall in the bell, once more rose.

They stood and watched, all of them, as Alex went doggedly on, connecting the syringe, drawing more blood, disconnecting it so that the rubber tube could take its place again and send the crimson flow pulsing along, snaking down from the table to the pallet below. Freddy took hold of the boy's other ankle to check his pulse, and watched his face. And there was nothing to be heard but the soft suck and gurgle of the syringe and the faint breathing of the watchers outside the circle of light that held at its core a dying child and his silent numb mother.

It seemed to Martha that she had spent all her life in the cellar, watching blood rising and falling in a little glass bell, hearing the sighing of the syringe and the soft murmurs as Alex and Freddy compared notes and discussed the state of the boy's pulse. It came almost as a surprise to her when Freddy said, 'I think we should stop, Alex. If he has not had enough to restore him by now, then I fear he cannot be restored. And we must not deprive Mary and her babe of any more—'

'Freddy, I am hopeful,' Alex said suddenly. 'I am more than hopeful. It has been now almost two and a half hours, and there has been no sign of any severe reaction in the boy. He would by now have shown many signs of distress if he were in danger from the procedure, of this I am certain.'

Freddy nodded wearily, rubbing his face with both hands.

'Well, I hope you are right. Certainly in those patients upon whom we have tried the technique and then lost, we saw signs of distress early – fever and rigor and severe pain in the lumbar region. But he seems to be peaceful and comfortable enough, I agree.'

They all looked down at the boy, and Martha realized almost with a shock that daylight was beginning to creep into the cellar, and in the light thrown by the now guttering lamps as well as the stain of the dawn, Peter's face was easy to see. He indeed looked peaceful enough; no longer did that rim of white show beneath his lids, for he seemed to be sleeping normally, and his breathing was far less hurried and greedy than it had been. Instead, he breathed more deeply, if still more rapidly than normal, and as she looked closer Martha realized that above all, his colour had changed. The boy was still very pallid, but the marble whiteness that had been so alarming in him was replaced by a muddiness that while it was far from the healthy glow of active life was much less alarming.

As Alex disconnected the tube from the bell for the last time, and Freddy, after allowing the remainder of the blood in the tube to run in, carefully stopping it before it was quite empty for fear of introducing air into the blood vessel, removed the cannula, Martha looked at Mary.

She too was lying just as she had, still staring at the ceiling, but the expression of fear seemed to have gone from her, to be replaced by a dumb acceptance of whatever was going to happen, be it good or ill. It was as though she had given up any interest, not only in the proceedings but even in herself and Peter. She just lay there, inert and inscrutable.

Alex dressed her elbow with a heavy pad of charpie and bound it firmly after he had removed the splint, while Freddy did the same for young Peter's ankle, and then, suddenly, Sal moved forwards, and stood beside Mary, her fists set on her hips and staring down at her.

'Well?' she said, and her voice was harsh and raucous in the cold light. 'Are you goin' to bleedin' well lie there till the crack o' doom? It's finished, ducks, and you ain't got no call to lie there like a bleedin' Lady Muck another minute, So get goin'! This lad o' yours 'll want some breakfast in a couple of hours, or I miss my mark, an' you'll 'ave to be bustlin'!'

Martha put her hand out to protest, but then as Alex set his hand on her wrist stopped, for Mary had turned her head, almost creakingly and was staring up at Sal.

'What's that?' Her voice was thick and came with a great effort.

'I said move yer stinkin' arse off o' my dispensary table so's I can clean it, and get about yer business, that's what!' Sal said, and put her hand out to pull on Mary's shoulder to make her sit up. But her roughness was only a show, for it was clear that she handled the woman with great care as well as remarkable understanding and obediently Mary sat up, and sat there, leaning against Sal for a moment and staring down at Peter on the floor beside her with a dawning awareness in her face.

'Ain't 'e dead, then?' she said at length, and Sal laughed her huge raucous laugh.

'No, 'e ain't, ducks, an' not for want o' tryin', young limb o' Satan that 'e is! Our Freddy 'ere's only done miracles, that's all. Miracles! An' you're all right, 'an all. Get a drop o' good porter into you an' you'll soon make up the difference. You're a full-blooded one, an' no error, you are! You'll be able to make a nice livin' for years out o' tellin' what 'appened 'ere tonight!' And Sal pushed Mary gently, and made her swing her legs over and down, and then she was on her knees beside the pallet and staring down at Peter.

'Peter, Peter—' She began to croon it, softly and then a little louder. 'Peter, Peter—' and Freddy said, 'Leave him be for a moment yet, Mary. He needs to rest, and so do you—'

But Peter had woken and turned his head and looked at his mother and at the sight of her his face crumpled and he began to cry, and Martha felt a sudden surge of sheer joy and found her hands were shaking with it, for the cry was a real cry, full of childish fear and anger, as unlike the pitiful whimpers he had produced earlier as the boom of a gun was unlike the crack of a trodden twig.

259

'I think perhaps it is a miracle,' she said unsteadily, and Alex, who was soberly cleaning up the equipment ready to put it away, polishing the blood off the glass with another wad of charpie, looked up at her and said soberly, 'Not quite, my love. A piece of good fortune born of some skill, I grant you. We have always known, those of us who think of our skills at all, that were it possible safely to put blood in the veins of those who have inadvertently lost a great deal they would benefit from it with great rapidity. The problem has always been, however, that there is some undiscovered part of blood that seems to be at odds in certain systems. There have been many attempts to perform just this technique, but they have failed abysmally, to the best of my knowledge, with several rigors and fevers and damage to the renal apparatus – the kidneys, you understand – which usually leads to death. Some have been made even more anaemic by such attempts, as though God has turned his face against such impious meddling. But clearly, it can be done, and Freddy deserves much credit for his skill and courage—'

They both turned at that to look for Freddy, and again Martha felt that lurch of anxiety she had felt when they had first returned to the cellar, all those aeons ago, as it now seemed. He was as flushed as Peter had been pallid, and he was sitting on the floor, with his back against the wall and his head thrown back. His eyes were half closed and he was breathing heavily through his open mouth, and Martha hurried to his side and knelt down next to him, and put her hand on his forehead.

'Oh, no,' she whispered and the anxiety thickened and clotted within her. 'He is in a dreadful fever – Alex, please come – he is ill—'

'Just a little fatigued,' Freddy mumbled. 'Just a little fatigued—' He turned his head fretfully against the cold bricks of the wall, and said loudly, 'Grandpapa! It was precisely as you said—' and then he opened his eyes again and stared at Martha as though he were puzzled. 'Aunt Martha? I am a little – I have such a headache! Is the child well? Has he had any reactions? It is of some importance that he has no reactions – if

260

he has been well for long enough after the blood enters him, he will remain well always – do you understand, Aunt Martha? Grandpapa says so—'

'Oh lawks,' Sal said, coming softly up behind them. 'Now what? Oh, Gawd, if this ain't a judgement on all of us, I don't know what is—'

CHAPTER TWENTY-FIVE

PHOEBE, standing outside the shabby building in New Court, wished she was twice her age and half as handsome, for there was no doubt that her presence in the City was causing a considerable stir. She had left her hansom cab in Lombard Street, for the great press of traffic about the 'Change had made it impossible for the driver to go any further, or so he had said, and doing so had not demanded too much of a walk. But in the few yards she had to traverse down St. Swithin's Lane to reach the Rothschilds' hidden corner, she had been ogled and accosted so often that she had become quite angry. Willing though she was to display herself upon the stage, she did not regard herself as anything other than a lady of gentle rearing, and to be treated as casually as some street queen was mortifying in the extreme. Or so she told herself with some indignation although deep within her, had she cared to admit it, she enjoyed the attention paid to her by errand boys and loungers, just as she enjoyed any attention. It was balm to her soul as it always was. Perhaps it was this deep-down awareness that now made her so ruffled, and lifted the colour in her cheeks to a most becoming red, and gave her eyes a glitter and liveliness which much enhanced their beauty.

So much so that when she marched into the outer office of the House of Rothschild and demanded in very lordly tones to be taken at once to see Mr. Lionel, the clerk, instead of seeking to protect his august master from interruptions as he usually did, merely nodded, more than a little bemused by the vision standing before him in a lemon crinoline, mustard silk pelisse and flower-trimmed capote hat.

And Lionel himself, although somewhat put out at being interrupted in the middle of the morning by any person with whom he might agree to spend leisure hours but who did not share his business interests, was equally indulgent when he heard who it was, and, when he saw her standing there looking so beguiling, quite captivated. Thus it was that within fifteen minutes of leaving her hansom cab in Lombard Street, Phoebe was ensconced in the Partners' Room in the richest and busiest business house in the City, and had no notion how fortunate she was to be there. She had set out to see Mr. Lionel Rothschild and it had never entered her head that she would fail in her endeavour.

'Well, Miss Phoebe!' Lionel said, and leaned back in his chair, his considerable paunch swelling handsomely over the edge of his vast satinwood desk. 'And what brings so charming a young lady to the portals of grubby commerce on so pleasant a spring morning? You should be out gambolling in the Park, my child, or practising your pretty little songs, not wasting your loveliness on the dead air of these full climes! Not that I am not delighted to see you—'

'Oh, Mr. Rothschild, as to that—' she waved away his fulsome compliments, 'I have indeed come upon a sort of business matter. Well, not precisely, for you will not regard what I have to ask you with any favour, I daresay, for it is by no means a profit-making affair—'

His brows snapped down at that. 'What makes you think I care only for matters of profit, Miss Phoebe? I trust I have more to my heart than that!'

She smiled up at him quite artlessly. 'Well, I thought you might be like Uncle Gideon. He is the dearest soul alive, and I love him very warmly but when it is working hours he is most put out when people come to him with matters which while they are of great importance are not to do with business. I thought therefore that you too—'

'Hmph. Well, he's not wrong at that,' Lionel said, and looked a little pointedly at his clock, hanging solemn and admonitory upon the wall above Phoebe's head. 'Work goes on, even if people do not. And I have learned to my cost how much can be lost by letting idle moments drift by. So, my child! What is this unprofitable matter you wish to discuss with me? I must ask you to be swift about it, for I have much to do today—'

'You made me a kind promise, Mr. Rothschild,' Phoebe said, and her voice was very clear and firm even though within, were the truth known, she was quaking. 'You will recall, the night we met at our Supper Rooms, when poor Uncle Gideon was set upon—'

She giggled suddenly at that thought, and Rothschild's eyes twinkled in shared appreciation. Indeed Gideon had looked so very undignified that evening.

'Well, that night you were good enough to say to me that had I any needs at any time which you could satisfy I was to come to you. So, I have come!'

He looked alarmed for a moment, and said guardedly, 'I said that? Well, indeed I meant, I am sure, to offer you every service I could, within reason, of course.'

She laughed merrily at that. 'Indeed, within reason! I will tell you what it is – and I am in *such* need of your aid, I do assure you! Please read this, Mr. Rothschild, and you will, I think, understand all.'

He took the letter she held out and smoothed out its folds, reaching in his pocket for his eye glasses, and let his eyes skim the pages with remarkable speed.

'Well, I do not *quite* understand, I am afraid! I gather from this that one Freddy is ill, in the hospital at Scutari, and that one Martha – ah, that must be your aunt, Gideon's sister-in-law – Martha is anxious about him. But he seems to be recovering well enough, from all she says—'

'I do not know how you can say that!' Phoebe said fiercely, and seized the letter back from his hands. 'Here – do you see this piece? About how weak he is, and cannot eat properly and has become shocking thin? How can you say he is getting better?'

'Well, she does say at the end that he seems to be feeling less low than he did,' Lionel said mildly and looked at her over the tops of his spectacles. 'This young man is of some importance in your life, Miss Phoebe?'

'Importance? Well – he is my cousin–'

'Ah, no doubt, no doubt. And family feeling can run deep, and none knows that better than I. My people have always put great store by family connections, and always, I trust, will do so. But there is something in your manner that suggests to me more than a cousinly concern.'

'Well, so, if there is!' Phoebe held her head up high and pushed out her lower lip in a stubborn gesture Freddy would have found very familiar, but which looked to Lionel Rothschild new and very charming, and he smiled gently.

'So. This young man is your lover, is he?'

Her eyes suddenly filled with tears. 'Oh, if only – oh, Mr. Rothschild, I treated him so badly! I will not tell you all of it for it is too dreadful, but let me say just that he loved me very dearly, and I loved him, or so I thought. In fact, I did, but did not know it, for another person came along and – and engaged my attentions – and–'

She shook her head and sat and stared at him, her face woebegone in the extreme, and looking at her Lionel Rothschild suddenly stopped seeing her as merely an enchantingly pretty child, to be treated with the raillery and jollity one used for nestlings fresh out of the nursery, but as a woman. A young and pretty woman, but a real one for all that. There was undoubtedly a vanity about her which showed in her choice of clothes, and a self awareness which was displayed in the set of her head and the glance of her eyes, but beneath all that he could recognize, as he had not done before, a capacity for real passion, a depth of experience and feeling that was almost embarrassing in its intensity, and he coughed and looked down at his desk and shuffled with one or two of his papers.

'Well, that's all by the by now,' she said after a moment, and her voice was normal again and the embarrassment had fled, and he could look at her once more and be comfortable. 'But he *is* ill, and I do love him so very much, and fear for him. He has behaved in a foolish way to me this past two or three years, because of what happened all that time ago, and I allowed it to go on, but it must stop now. It is time for us to settle our differences, which are, in many ways, so unimportant! So unimportant—' She lifted her head then with a curious dignity. 'I did not love this other person, you must understand, whatever occurred between us. So it is quite proper for me to love Freddy now—'

She looked at him with her eyes shadowed with memory for a moment and then seemed to become aware of the slightly puzzled look on his face and laughed.

'Oh dear, I am rattling on like a silly child, am I not? As if you knew of any of this past history of mine, or even cared! But you are so kind, Mr Rothschild, and make me feel as comfortable as if I were talking to my own dear Papa, God rest his dear soul in eternal peace. That is why I spoke so – well, forgive me.'

'Of course, my child.' He smiled at her with great benevolence. To be treated as a father by such a young charmer was agreeable even to one who was used to the flattery of women. 'But you know, you have still not told me of your wishes! Of what it is you wish of me, that is—'

'Oh, I thought it was very clear!' She lifted her eyebrows at him in genuine surprise. 'Why, I wish a passage out to Constantinople of course. To be with Freddy!'

'But what can we do?' Abby said reasonably. 'She is very young, of course, but she is not a fool. And many men younger than she have gone to much greater danger.'

'Indeed, *men*,' Gideon said. 'But she is not a man, but a girl, and has only just reached her majority! How anyone of her age be allowed even to *consider*—'

Abby got to her feet in a rustle of coffee coloured silk and came across the drawing room to sit on the rug at his feet beside the fire which was so much needed on this chilly night, during one of the coldest and frostiest springs that had been known for some time. She put her hands on his lap, and looked up into his face, very earnestly.

'My dear, she is free to do as she wishes, you know! She is one and twenty, and that means she has full control of her own money, and no one in the land can say her nay whatever she chooses to do – within the law of course! If her own brother has thrown up his hands in the face of her obstinacy, and feels he cannot prevent her, then what hope have we of stopping her?'

'We could, I suppose, speak to her grandfather—' Gideon began, and at once Abby stopped him.

'No! I will not hear of it, and nor will Maria! He is a very – unhappy man at present, Gideon, and to add this to his burdens would be unforgiveable. Besides, he was never very close to Phoebe. It is Freddy who holds his heart, of all his grandchildren, and well you know it – but apart from that, he has been much cast down by this matter of the woman who died in Constantinople. Maria has been much exercised in her mind about it all, as I have, for he has been quiet and so – not morose precisely, nor apparently miserable. He is never as jocund as are some men! But he has been distressed, although he will not talk of it, and we are concerned for him. To speak to him of Phoebe's plan would be to make his sadness heavier, I am convinced, and it would make no difference to Phoebe! Her mind is made up, and if you do not know, after all the years she lived under your roof, what that means, then you have not the sense for which I have always given you credit!'

He looked at her dolefully and sighed suddenly. 'Oh, I know you speak truth, my love, but suppose it were Sarah, or Isabel? Would you be so calm about it then? Would you let either of them set out on such a journey, unaccompanied? You could not!'

She sat back on her heels and looked down on her hands, clasping them tightly in her lap, and there was a silence for a little while, and then she looked up at him, her eyes wide and pellucid in their honesty.

'No, Gigi, I would not. I would be very distressed. But, Phoebe is not like them. She is more her mother's daughter than you realize – and her family – well, they are different in their attitudes and they are all so much – stronger—'

The silence again fell and they both sat carefully not looking at each other. The matter of Lydia had never been mentioned between them after that night at the Celia Supper Rooms.

There had been no discussion of it nor ever would there be again; they had reached a tacit agreement to that effect, and neither had any intention of breaking it. That episode was over and would never have any effect on their shared lives no matter what happened.

But even though Lydia's name was not spoken, her personality hung between them like a shadow, and Gideon staring miserably at his hands, knew that what Abby was trying to tell him was right. Phoebe *was* different. There flowed in her veins the blood of adventure, of resourcefulness, of action, in a way that his own family could not comprehend. They could see the effects of such a heritage, deplore them, perhaps even envy them, but they could not comprehend them. That his own daughters, or the nieces or cousins of his own blood could be allowed to set off for the Crimea in the manner in which Phoebe planned to do was unthinkable. But for Phoebe it was very thinkable indeed.

'Anyway,' Abby said then, with cool reasonableness, 'Martha is there, and she arrived with little harm!'

'Martha, my love,' Gideon said rather tartly, 'while a lady of great character and value is, I must point out to you, past the first flush of her youth and unlikely on the grounds of her appearance to offer temptation to passing strangers! It is because of Phoebe's obvious charms that I fear for her. However – as you are so clearly thinking, it is I suppose, no concern of mine. She is, after all, your niece, and not mine. I have no right to be so—'

She leaned forwards and took his hands again. 'Do not speak so!' she said sharply. You have the right of love and concern – and – and no child could have had a dearer or more loving father than you have been to her since poor Jonah died. I will not have you feel I am overriding you on *that* score! It is just that I know when to retire gracefully from any argument with Phoebe, and I tell you flatly, dear, dear Gideon, that she will go, whether we agree or no. So it is better that we agree, for then we can set certain rules of conduct for her that will enable her to travel safely. After all, she is going on one of Lionel's ships, and he will see to it that she is treated like the most precious of cargoes! I cannot imagine any captain in Rothschild's employ who would not regard such a charge most seriously, if Lionel told him to! And if we give consent, to match Oliver's, why, we can insist that she takes some sort of servant with her, to watch over her and take care of her. It will not be so bad, you will see.'

She sat there for a moment longer looking up imploringly into his face and then said in a low voice, 'Besides, there is Freddy.'

He looked down at her then, for he had been staring into the fire and took her hands.

'I am sorry, my dearest one,' he said gently. 'I had spoken so much of Phoebe that I let you think I did not care about Freddy. Of course I am as anxious as you are.'

'I know,' she said. 'And I believe all that Martha says in her letters – that it is but a mild case of Crimean fever and he is likely to recover very well, and I am sure she will nurse him splendidly. But all the same, he loves Phoebe very dearly, you know, and I can think of little that will hasten his recovery more than the sight of her. Perhaps I am being selfish in throwing my weight behind Phoebe's wish to go out, knowing her presence will be of value to my boy – I do not know. All I know is that she *will* go, if she says she will, and that I have hopes she will bring better comfort to my dear Freddy than anyone else could, and – and—'

Suddenly she was crying, her head buried on her hands in his lap, and he was bending over, stroking her hair and murmuring soft reassuring sounds in her ear, promising her that he would argue no more, that he would do all he could to help, that Freddy would be all right, he was sure, and they would soon have them all home safe and sound, no matter what happened with the wretched war.

So it was that Phoebe, on the last day of May in 1855 set out from Folkestone for the first part of her journey to Constantinople accompanied by ten pieces of luggage and a frightened servant girl.

CHAPTER TWENTY-SIX

'THIS is perfectly ridiculous,' Martha said waspishly and rubbed her brow, for her head was aching dreadfully and she was feeling very hot. 'Why did you not bring Isabel and Sarah and Daniel too, while you were about it? We could then have had a family picnic!'

Phoebe stood there, her luggage piled about her feet and her hands tucked into her muff, and tried not to show how close to tears she was. The journey had been unutterably boring, once the excitement of actually being on the move had passed off, and laborious too, for the servant girl had succumbed almost immediately to seasickness, although the Mediterranean had been smooth as the Long Water in Kensington Gardens, and Phoebe had had to shift for herself in all things. In addition, the sort of attention she had received from sailors and, after they had docked at Constantinople, waterfront loungers, had been far from the flattering pleasure it usually was; indeed there had been moments when she had been genuinely frightened of the leers and jeers which greeted her, for they seemed even more ominous when delivered in uncouth foreign tongues.

And now, to arrive at Scutari after so unpleasant a journey, having left the useless servant on the ship to be taken back to England, and to be greeted with such scant courtesy, was too depressing.

She had rehearsed in her mind over and over how her arrival would be; the amazement and delight and gratitude with which Aunt Martha would greet her, the joy that would suffuse poor sick Freddy's ailing cheeks at the sight of her, the way she would

270

sink to her knees beside his sickbed and soothe his fevered brow with one white hand – such visions had made the horrid journey supportable and even agreeable. But what had happened? Martha had not only been unsurprised, because a message had reached her via the new electric telegraph just completed between London and Balaclava, but had been thoroughly displeased to see her, and Freddy – Freddy was not there at all. And she swallowed hard and blinked and said in as strong a voice as she could muster, 'I came because Freddy is ill.'

'Did you think we could not take care of him, Phoebe? You really are quite absurd! As if your presence here would make the slightest difference! If he were so ill that his life was despaired of, then we would need all our energies to take care of him as well as do all our usual work, and you would be an encumbrance, for you have no experience of nursing work. You would be far better occupied as you have been all this time, performing on your stage to make extra money for us for comforts for our women – and since in the event he has recovered quite well from his fever, your presence is even more inappropriate!'

Now Phoebe did cry, tears gathering under her lids and spilling over on to her cheeks and her aunt shook her head, half in irritation and half in affection and said gruffly, 'Oh, my dear child, do not weep! I suppose I have been a little hard on you, but you know, we are so busy here, and I have been feeling so dispirited myself – it seemed so *stupid* of the family to even consider allowing you to come. This is war, my child, not an exciting expedition for young ladies to play at! Even though there were such women about at Balaclava—'

She rubbed her face wearily, and then, blinking, smiled at Phoebe and held out her hands. 'Well, you are here now! And I must tell you it is agreeable to just look at you for you appear so fresh and charming and we here are very bedraggled indeed! Come and give me a kiss and we will discuss how to arrange for you to go home again as soon as possible.'

Wisely biting her tongue on the matter of how soon she would agree to be sent home to England, Phoebe did come, and hugged her aunt warmly and they clung to each other for a highly emotional moment, and then Martha pushed her gently away and looked her up and down. 'Well, as I say, you do look delightful. It is no wonder the children are so taken with you—'

Phoebe, untying her bonnet strings, looked about her properly now and saw the cellar clearly for the first time, and she stood there, her bonnet dangling from its strings between her fingers, and stared in horror.

The rows of pallets, the dinginess, the dank and dripping walls, the lackadaisical women and the silent scrawny staring children sitting in clusters between their shabby pallets on the floor were the most depressing sight she could ever remember seeing and she turned back to her aunt and said impulsively, 'Oh, Aunt Martha, how can you bear it!'

Martha raised her brows. 'Bear it: Bear what? The cellar, you mean? Why, you should have seen it as it was when Sal and I first arrived here! Then it was indeed dispiriting. But now—' She looked about her with some pride '—Now it is quite palatial, is it not?' And one or two of the women nodded and grinned their black-toothed grins and Phoebe, shakily, tried to smile back.

She felt the tears rising in her again and couldn't decide quite why. Anti-climax because of her cold greeting? Freddy's absence – and she still had to discover where he was – or the sight of Aunt Martha, so thin and bedraggled herself? Although her hair was pulled back neatly enough from her forehead, and her face was its usual well scrubbed self, her gown was undoubtedly shabby, and her hands red and rough with hard work; she was so unlike the cool and well turned out lady she had been at home in London that Phoebe was almost embarrassed by her, and she turned away to fuss with one of her trunks to hide it.

'You must not even consider unpacking!' Martha said, her voice sharpening. 'For you cannot stay here – you must see that!'

Phoebe looked back over her shoulder. 'I brought some clothes,' she said uncertainly. 'For the women and children, you know. I thought perhaps they would be useful—'

At once there was a ripple of movement among the watchers,

and several of the children crept nearer, still staring in wonderment at the pretty lady, and Phoebe smiled down at them and began to unbuckle her trunk.

The next half hour was almost bedlam, and Martha very soon gave up any attempt to control the situation for, as Phoebe pulled out gowns and wrappers and pantaloons and handed them out, the women and children became immensely excited. A few noisy arguments broke out as two women seized the same gown, but Martha was too tired, too hot and too head-aching to care. If Phoebe wanted to play the Lady Bountiful for a while, let her. She had to be sent packing home as soon as may be; she might as well enjoy her silly games while she could. And, Martha had to admit, she had brought a sensible supply for the gowns were good stuff ones and not the sort of fripperies Phoebe would have chosen for herself, and she had thought of such items as drawers and chemises, which so often were forgotten.

She leaned back against the table, propping herself up with her feet braced against the floor in the way she usually did when she needed to relax — for there were no chairs on which to sit — and closed her eyes. She was so very tired. The past weeks had been a horror, for Freddy's illness had been but the first little wave in a sea of disease that washed through the cellar. With Sal and Alex she had worked twenty hours in every twenty-four, snatching what little sleep she could when she could; they had nursed Freddy, and the women who had succumbed after him to the illness — which was characterized by roaring high fevers, accompanied by delirium and dreadful hacking coughs — and also the children. They had lost five children from the illness in the first week and the wailing of the bereaved mothers had added greatly to the miseries of those others who were ill; but still they had battled on.

Fortunately, the illness, though fierce, was of a short duration; those who contracted it either died in the first thirty-six hours, or were on the road to recovery after a week, as the fevers dropped leaving the patients weak and languid and still coughing.

Freddy, his essentially powerful constitution standing him in good stead, was up from his mattress and moving, albeit shakily, about the cellar after seven days, and he did all he could, sitting beside the sickest of the children and giving what care was possible. To his intense relief – and indeed it was a feeling they all shared – young Peter did not catch the contagion but he was of course still very ill. His new blood had clearly done him much good – was he not alive? – but he remained weak and pale, and needed much care which Freddy gave him gladly. Which left Sal and Martha and Alex free to look after anyone else.

Sal had herself gone down with the disease three days after Freddy had started to get over it, and she had been quite dreadfully ill. Martha had given up all hope of sleep then, and had sat determinedly beside Sal for full forty-eight hours, bathing her forehead with what cold water she could get, restraining her when she threw herself about in her delirium – not easy, for she was a powerfully built woman, after all – and treating her cracked lips and swollen tongue with sweet almond oil, of which she still had a tiny and precious supply.

Then it had been Alex who had done all the work that needed to be done, and somehow he had managed, moving about the cellar in his usual collected unhurried way, from patient to patient, treating, dressing, cleaning – and he set to work to comfort an incontinent child with the same coolness he displayed when dressing a suppurating injury – and even cooking their scant food.

That had been the hardest problem, once Sal had fallen ill, for she had become, gradually, their quartermaster, begging, stealing or somehow obtaining what rations she could for all of them, and after three days of her illness the occupants of the cellar were becoming very hungry. Until suddenly soldiers started arriving with buckets of stew and soup from Monsieur Soyer's kitchens, only shrugging when they were asked who had sent it and why, and Martha had gratefully accepted this manna from some distant heaven and asked no questions. Clearly some of Sal's soldier friends had heard she was ill, she told herself, and good men that they were, were carrying on her stealing for her. Dear Sal, she had thought and felt her eyes fill with tears of gratitude and fatigue as she bent over her and yet again touched her tongue with a swab soaked in almond oil.

To receive in the middle of all this a message from the Balaclava telegraph, via Constantinople, telling her that her flibberty niece was on her way to Scutari had seemed to Martha the final straw. It had arrived on Saturday morning, a few hours after Freddy had left the cellar and that in itself had been depressing her.

Once he had been up and about again, he had recovered with great rapidity, for he was a wiry young man with a great will to health, and had gone, one afternoon, across to the hospital in the great Barrack building to make inquiries about the disease which had so upset the cellar and its occupants. 'For,' he had said to Martha, 'it may be a new sort of fever with which they too are afflicted and the army doctors may have some treatment that is more effective than we have been using.'

And had come back a few hours later with his face set and an expression of great determination on his face.

'Aunt Martha – Alex—' he had said firmly, 'I am going away.'

'Away?' She had looked up at him in amazement from her place beside Sal where she was feeding her a bowl of broth, for Sal was still too weak to manage to hold the spoon herself. 'Away – what do you mean? Are you returning to England?'

She had stared at him almost alarmed, for she had never thought of Freddy as being one who would willingly turn his back on work that needed to be done, or one who was cowardly. If he was going back then it must mean he felt a great deal more ill than he had told them, and wished to return safely to die there – so did her fevered imagination run away with her as she stared at him and her face was blank with anxiety. 'What ails you, Freddy?'

He shook his head impatiently at that. 'Oh, do not be absurd, aunt! As if I should do that! No – I am going over to the field hospital at Balaclava.'

He had fallen to his knees beside her and spoke very earnestly, looking up now and again at Alex, who had come to join them and stood there looking down on them with his face bearing its usual calm expression over his heavy beard, though his eyes were beginning to show, in the heavy shadows beneath them, the signs of the fatigue that imbued his very bones.

'Listen – all of you – and I know you will agree. This fever – they have labelled it Crimean Fever and it is causing great havoc, spreading so fast that none can contain it. They have a great deal of it at the hospital here, but even more in Balaclava. The doctors – they have lost fully five in the past two weeks, and they are in great need of medical aid. With Alex here to help you, I think I should go to help – it is my obvious duty. I have spoken to the adjutant and he says he will accept me as a civilian surgeon, temporarily attached to the army – it is absurd the way they are – there must be forms and papers and labels and so many ridiculous formalities – but they have need of me, for I am a good surgeon and there is much I could do. You are here Alex, and the fever is near finished with us, I believe. We have had no new cases this past three days, so I feel you and my aunt can manage well enough. It is time I did more, after all—'

Martha had tried to remonstrate, but he had been adamant. He had done all he usefully could for the cellar community, and he must now do as he felt was right elsewhere. Elsewhere being Balaclava, and when Alex after a short silence nodded his head crisply and agreed with Freddy, Martha capitulated. She could do little else.

And so he had gone, on the next ship crossing the Black Sea, and Alex and Martha had grimly struggled on, taking care of Sal and Peter and Mary MacConachie and the remainder of their sick women and children, getting more and more overworked, more and more dogged and more and more exhausted. Was it any wonder that when Phoebe had arrived in her flurry of prettiness and with her cache of laden trunks, Martha

276

should greet her with such shortness? Standing there against the table listening to the hubbub about her she told herself it had been inevitable, but still felt distressed about it. The child had meant well, and clearly loved her cousin Freddy very deeply, to have come so far and to such a place to take care of him. It was a touching thought, and she must tell her how sorry she was to have been so unkind.

She tried to move, to open her eyes so that she could tell Phoebe that it was all right, that Freddy was well, if far away by now, and that she had not meant to hurt her, but somehow it was not possible. She was locked inside her own body in a state of suspended life; she could hear the voices of the people about her, diminishing now as the last of Phoebe's largess was distributed, could hear Phoebe's voice speaking to her, but still could do nothing, even when Phoebe's voice sharpened with anxiety.

'Aunt Martha – can you hear me? I said – oh, Aunt Martha, please to answer me! You do look so very strange!'

Martha heard, then, Alex's deeper voice, coming from a long way away and she realized with some surprise that in fact he was very near. She could feel his hands upon her arm, could feel his body near hers, but he sounded so very remote and his voice seemed so very tiny that it filled her with a huge alarm, and she tried to open her mouth to say so. But she could not, and now the panic rose in her, and she feared suddenly she was dying. All that she had ever heard about death, all the deaths she had witnessed – and in her years of work at Bedford Row and at Queen Eleanor's hospital there had been many – had not prepared for her for this dreadful feeling, this sense of aloneness and deep inside herself she heard the little child she had once been crying fearfully and bitterly for comfort.

And it came. Alex's arms closed about her, tight and warm, and raised her up, and she felt herself being carried gently, warmly and safely away, and sound became normal again and she heard his voice coming from both above her and from within his chest, against which her head was resting.

'She has the fever – she is so hot – quick, girl, pull out that pallet – aye, that one. She needs to be bathed to bring her heat down – there, there, my love – do not weep. Do not weep – we shall soon make you well again—'

And realizing with a huge surprise that she was indeed weeping, Martha let his voice wash over and carry her away to the blessed peace of black oblivion.

CHAPTER TWENTY-SEVEN

It seemed to Martha that the world stood still. Time did not pass, stars did not shine, the sun and moon remained held in their places and there was no movement. Only the moment by moment struggle to breathe which consumed her, the effort to fill her lungs and empty them, to cough when the pain and tightness threatened to snuff her out, and then to breathe again. There was heat, heat and more heat, as her body dripped and ached, but unpleasant though that was it was nothing compared to the sick sense of stillness that seemed to fill her.

She knew of course that around her life did go on. Did she not see Alex and Phoebe and Sal looming out of the darkness beside her bed from time to time? Did she not open her eyes to find Sal bathing her naked body with cold wet cloths to cool her, or find Alex beside her urging a spoon against her teeth until she had to open her mouth and swallow the soup he pushed into her? Did she not feel Phoebe's hand upon her cheek as she soothed her?

And there were other faces too; the women and the children to whom she had given care and tending all these weeks – their faces would hang above her staring down mournfully, and she would see them and hear them and yet be unable to talk to them, for there was always this sense of the world standing in its tracks, while Martha struggled to breathe.

And then one afternoon, late, when the sun was slanting across the floor from the row of little windows she opened her eyes and knew the world was back in its normal pattern of movement again. She could breathe without thinking about it, could lie still and languid herself but feel the pulse of life in the

hard packed earth floor beneath her pallet coming up to en-
compass her too, and knew she was going to live.

She lay and stared at the sun on the floor, creeping slowly
across the foot of the adjoining mattress, and could almost
have laughed. She had nearly died; that she knew – and yet
here she was. It seemed to her to be hugely, ludicrously funny
and she managed to laugh aloud. A small sound, little more
than a hiccup, but it came out of her lips and encouraged her.

And alerted others too. She heard a soft scurry across the
floor but felt too deliciously lazy to want to move her head to
see who it was, and closed her eyes for a moment, and when she
opened them again she saw Sal there beside her, sitting back on
her heels with her fists balled on her heavy thighs and a
look of concern masked by an expression of derision on her face.

'Well, you're a right one, ain't yer?' she said. 'Lyin' there
like the queen of all the fairies and laughin' yer 'ead orf. Not
that you'd call it much of a laugh, mind yer, but I knows yer,
don't I? A fine carry on, I must say – frightenin' all of us that
way!'

Martha smiled and when she spoke her voice sounded
absurdly thin in her own ears. 'Did I frighten you? I'm
sorry—'

'Put the fear o' Gawd into us, an' no error!' Sal said severely.
'If you'd a bin a proper Catholic I'd a' sent fer the priest an' so
I'm tellin' yer! You should o' seen yerself – looking fit to snuff
it sooner'n last night's candles you did! Mind, I told you, over
and over, I told you – if you'd a' dared die, I'd've haunted you
through all eternity afterwards, that I would!''

Behind the raillery Martha could hear genuine concern and
relief and indeed affection in the other woman's voice, and she
found it infinitely touching and felt her eyes fill with tears as
she stared at her, and Sal seemed to under stand for she said
roughly, 'Well, enough o' that! Got to get you fit again, that's
what! Bit o' feedin' up, that's what you wants, my duck, an'
I'm the one to see you gets it.'

And she began to fuss with the covers, twitching the blanket
tidy under Martha's unresisting hands, and hoisting her up on
her pillow to plump it afresh and Martha smiled at her grate-

fully and said a little breathlessly, 'What is new, Sal? Tell me all that has happened – I seem to have been ill so long—'

'So long? – you blubbered a bibful there! Nigh on four weeks you bin lyin' 'ere.'

That roused Martha as nothing else had so far. 'Four weeks?' Her voice almost screeched it. 'But the fever – it lasts but one week at the most—'

'Aye, the *fever* do. But you ain't content just to 'ave fever, are you? No – *you* got to go and get the pneumony an' all, you 'ave – four weeks, as Gawd's me witness—'

'Four weeks,' Martha murmured and closed her eyes to understand it. Sal chattered on cheerfully. 'As for what's bin 'appening – everythin' an' nothin', as you might say. The war's the bleedin' same, that's for sure. There they sit before Sevastopol and bugger all do they do apart from a bit of bombardment a couple o' weeks back. Then there was a bit o' toin' an' froin' with the French Fleet – set out one day they did to go to Kertch, wherever that may be in this 'eathen place – and two hours later they gets a message from the emperor at 'ome in Paris as they've all to come back, an' then three weeks later off they sets again. Well, that ain't no way to run a decent war, is it? But what do you expect o' the French? An' then the Commander – what's 'is name – Lord Raglan – died, 'e did. Not that that makes much difference to what goes on, so far as the likes o' me and me mates can tell—'

Martha opened her eyes again. 'Phoebe?' she managed.

'Oh, Miss Phoebe—' Sal's voice softened. 'That's a right little love, that is! I won't 'ide from yer, Miss Martha, niece o' yours though she may be, that when I first got talkin' to 'er after I got better from the fever myself, I thought 'er a proper little madam. All those airs and graces and tyin' of 'er 'air up in rags every night no matter what – but as time went on, I'll tell yer straight, I really took to her. She's a pretty little dollypiece, I grants yer, but she's got 'er 'ead screwed on as right and tight as ninepence and lots of hard work in 'er. Got a lot o' time for Miss Phoebe I 'ave – she looked after you lovely. I don't know as 'ow we'd a' managed if she 'adn't bin 'ere—'

'I'm so glad,' Martha said, and felt sleep stealing up her and fought it back, opening her eyes again with a great effort. 'Mr. Laurence?' she said, at which Sal grinned and laughed and again twitched the blanket tidy.

'Your nice feller? No, don't you give me none o' yer looks – 'e's yer feller, an' no mistake. 'E's fretted over you and looked after you like a mother with a babe. If ever I saw a man as got 'imself smitten out o' mind by a female, it's your Mr. Laurence, and it ain't me 'e fancies, that's for sure!' She laughed again and then said, ''E's over to the 'ospital lookin' for news o' Freddy. The fever's nearly finished there, over at Balaclava, they says, so 'e said as 'ow 'e'd find out when the lad was like to be coming back. 'E wants to send you 'ome to England, see, an' 'e can't do that if there ain't none 'ere to take care o' things; I've told 'im as I can manage on the nursin' side, but we got to 'ave a doctor. An' if 'e manages to get a passage for the pair of you then young Freddy'll 'ave to be 'ere to 'old on, won't 'e? Anyway, that's where 'e is right at the present, and I daresay 'e'll be back soon enough – 'e never leaves you for more'n a few minutes at a time, that's for sure—'

Martha tried to understand it all. Tried to imagine herself going home, with Alex. Back on the ship, with Alex beside her walking on the tilting decks with the wind shouting furiously in the rigging and the smell of wet spray in their noses; and no more cellar, no more disease, no more weariness.

She did not even know she had fallen asleep.

She woke suddenly, her hand held firmly in his and staring up at him almost in amazement, for she had been dreaming she was at home in Bedford Row counting sheets with Miss Garling. And then she remembered, all in a rush, and said, 'Alex? I am well again.'

He laughed at that. 'Almost my love, almost. At least you are with us. For so many days you were hovering between this world and the next, and I was so very lonely – so lonely not to have you here. I am so glad you are with us again.' And his hand tightened on hers and she smiled up at him, and felt the power coming back into her muscles and stretched luxuriously and yawned and that made him laugh.

'Indeed, you are making strides, my love! Yesterday you could not move a muscle and now look at you! I have already sent a message home that they are to fear no more – you are over the crisis of your pneumonia and will recover. Now I must send another and tell them that you have already!'

'Alex, you went for news of Freddy, Sal said?'

He nodded soberly. 'Yes. And could find none. Things are better there but I understand that the hospitals at Balaclava are a shambles. Miss Nightingale was over there in May, you must understand, and set many reforms in hand, but then fell ill of the same Crimean fever that afflicted us here, and you so particularly, my love, and nothing was done, nothing at all. She is now well again, I hear, and has returned to take up her quarters here again. I know you have had many arguments with her, my love, but I must tell you she is a remarkable lady.'

He chuckled suddenly. 'She has taken on half the army's pomposities and made a pudding of them. So funny, the way she sets about her. And looking as weak and thin as you do yourself, my love, and I cannot tell you how weak that is! You must wait until you are better and shall see a mirror then.'

'The women,' Martha said after a moment. 'If we have no news of Freddy, give me news of our situation here. Is all well?'

He nodded. 'Very. Sal has been magnificent, and has been able to keep matters going well. The children – ah, yes – I have a piece of news there! MacConachie got himself invalided home. We had news he was going back on a troopship as a casualty, and we spoke to this one and that one, and we arranged all. And Mary and her boy went with him. I was happy indeed to see him go, and entrusted to Mary a letter to take the child to your father. He will need much further care, I think, and anyway, Mr. Lackland will be most interested to see him. So, there is one good piece of news, is there not?'

'Very good,' Martha murmured and then slowly turned her head at the sound of a breathless voice behind her.

'Aunt Martha! You are awake! Oh, I am so glad! Sal said you were well again, and I kept coming to see but all the time you were asleep! Dear Aunt Martha—' Phoebe kissed her resoundingly. 'It is so good to see you smiling again!'

It was delightful, that evening. One after another the women came to speak to her, to tell her how glad they were she was feeling better, and Phoebe sat on one side of her and Alex on the other and Sal bustled about as Sal always did and she felt happier and more peaceful than she had for a very long time. The whole evening became encapsulated in her memory, framed in the golden light of the fading summer evening sun across the floor which was replaced by the guttering glow of oil lamps and candles as night fell. The moths fluttered helplessly about the flames and the voices about her talked and laughed, and sometimes she dozed; but always when she was awake they were there. Above all, Alex was there, as solid and as sure as the building which loomed over the great square outside, but infinitely more comforting and warm, and she held his hand and was deeply, peacefully happy.

When she came to the women had gone to sleep for the night. They had crept away to pallets and heaps of straw, and Sal and Phoebe had helped settle the children before bidding Martha goodnight – the one with rough cheerfulness, the other with soft kisses and dimpled smiles – and they had remained there together in the darkness, just she and Alex and the flame of one candle.

They had been talking gently, desultorily, when out of the shadows beyond the foot of her pallet she appeared. A tall figure absurdly slender, so slender indeed that it seemed as though a mere breath would bowl her over, she stood there looking down on Martha, and Martha stared up at her, puzzled.

She looked familiar and yet strange, and then Martha realized with a sudden jolt that it was Miss Nightingale. But a greatly changed Miss Nightingale. Her hair was short and clung to her narrow head like a child's cap, and her face beneath it was white and strained. She stood there for a moment and then said quietly, 'You have been more fortunate than I, Miss Lackland. When I was at the height of my fever they cut off all my hair. Thus you see me. You at least remain still a woman.'

Alex had got to his feet and was pulling the rickety table from the dispensary across the floor so that Miss Nightingale could sit upon it. 'I see no sense in that,' he said gruffly. 'As though the length of a patient's hair made any difference to the progress of a fever! I never allowed them to do it to any patient of mine — it is mere superstition, I am convinced.'

She sat on the table gratefully and smiled at him, and pushed her cloak to one side. 'You are right, I think, Mr. Laurence. But superstition, I am afraid, will always reign supreme over mere commonsense. Those same people who cut off hair with such eagerness also make a dreadful racket about the sick bed of the sort that is most cruelly exhausting to the patient. I deplore it – there are so many things about the care of the sick which I deplore—'

She looked down at Martha and said quietly, 'I trust you are feeling better, Miss Lackland?'

'I thank you, yes. A great deal better. I am sorry to hear that you too have been ill.'

'Yes,' she said almost absently. 'It was very tedious. I abominate illness. It is such a waste of one's time and energies.'

There was a silence and then Alex said quietly, 'I think, my dear, that I shall take a turn about the jetty and the village. I am in need of a little air and exercise and I think Miss Nightingale has matters to talk to you about. She will prefer my absence, I suspect,' and he bent his head towards the thin woman perched on the table and smiled swiftly at Martha and disappeared into the shadows, leaving the two women staring at each other.

There was a long silence and then Miss Nightingale said briskly, 'I am sorry that I came so late at night, when I know full well an invalid should be resting. But I thought, remembering my own illness, that you would be still awake, and also, this was the only time of the day left for me. I have been hard put to it setting matters to rights in the hospital, and tomorrow I must leave for the Crimea itself. The hospitals there are in a shocking state – shocking!'

'The Crimea?' Martha became suddenly almost excited, and tried to lift herself on one elbow, but Miss Nightingale made a disapproving sound at her and she subsided gratefully on her pillows. 'I am most interested to hear you are going,' she went on, 'because my nephew, who, you may recall is my medical aid' – and a fleeting smile crossed her lips at that – 'has gone there as a civilian surgeon attached to the army. They had much need of extra help because of the fever, I believe.'

Miss Nightingale nodded. 'Yes, I knew of that. You wish to send him a message?'

'Please, indeed, I do – I—'

'Then I shall gladly deliver it. But do not give it to me now. There is a matter I wish to talk about to you first!'

She stopped then and pushed back her cloak even further and her hands were so thin they looked almost translucent in the candlelight.

'I have thought much, lying there in my sickbed across the Bosphorus, Miss Lackland, and I have come to tell you the burden of my thoughts. I know now that I misjudged you and treated you ill. I offer you an apology.'

Martha lay and blinked up at her. This imperious, high-handed ill-mannered woman who had made her face sting with rage and embarrassment, apologizing? It seemed amazingly against her character, and her astonishment must have shown in her face, for Miss Nightingale smiled thinly and said, 'You may well look surprised. I have always believed – "qui s'excuse s'accuse" – but you have shown me the error of this in your case.'

'I – well, I thank you,' Martha said weakly.

'You see, Miss Lackland, when first you came to see me in Belgrave Square, I thought you were one of a familiar type. Tract-delivering, cant-preaching, do-nothing, self-important females of uncertain age – you will forgive me the personal point – are a great nuisance in the necessary work of hospitals. They get in the way so, and you looked precisely one of them. You showed more than usual strength of will in reaching this place with so little encouragement, but I put that down to the stubbornness that so often accompanies stupidity. Well, I have heard enough of what is happening here in this cellar, among the women of the army, and I know that you are a woman of my own stamp – one who sees work is to be done, and sets about the doing of it. So – I apologize. That is why I came here so late. And now I will go–'

She slipped to her feet from the table, and stood re-arranging her cloak to cover her shoulders, pulling up a veil to hide her shorn head, and Martha said breathlessly, 'I – there is little I can say. Except I set about to do what I felt was needful – I am happy – it is good that we are no longer – oh dear!' She blinked and turned her head upon her pillow. 'Well, I am glad we are no longer ill sorted. It caused me much – distress – when we disagreed.'

Miss Nightingale's eyes narrowed with amusement. 'Not distress so much as irritation, I think. Which can be a most useful emotion! It often drives me to feats of effort I would not have thought possible! By the by, I hope the food is coming regularly?'

Martha blinked at that, and Miss Nightingale laughed softly.

'My dear lady, did you think I did not know that your servant was obtaining regular supplies from my kitchens? I would be a very poor administrator indeed if I did not know of such regular depredations upon my stores! I decided some weeks ago that the best way to handle the situation was to make it a legitimate outgoing and bade Monsieur Soyer to see to it that your needs were met here each day. I trust all has gone as planned.'

Remembering the arrival of the buckets of soup and stew, Martha smiled. 'I thought Sal had taught her men to steal so well that they went on doing it when she was ill!' she said weakly and laughed, and Miss Nightingale nodded briskly at her.

'Well, of course, I cannot approve of systematic stealing – nor can I wholeheartedly approve of a lady who not only allows such behaviour in a servant but actively encourages it. However – it was theft for a reasonable cause. I would not have your charges starve–'

She lifted her head then and looked about the vast cavern of the dark cellar with its two hundred sleeping women and children and said with a sudden hard intensity, 'It is all wrong! They should not be here, any one of them, be they camp followers or legitimate wives! The War Office must find some way to maintain the wives and families of serving soldiers in times of war, and so I shall tell them. It must be changed – it will be changed! I promise it!'

Martha stared up at her, at the white heat of passion that seemed to be consuming that frail figure, and marvelled at her. She seemed to have a source of strength and will that was denied to other people and Martha thought with a sudden sureness, 'She will do all she says she will – she will never be the one to fail—'

There was a rustle in the darkness and suddenly Phoebe appeared in the circle of candlelight, wrapped in a soft shawl and with her dark curls tumbled on her shoulders. She was barefoot, her toes curling against the earth floor and she was clutching her shawl to her and blinking in the lamplight in such a way that she looked barely twelve years old.

'Aunt Martha,' she said uncertainly. 'I was worried. I heard you speak, and was worried—'

'My niece, Miss Nightingale,' Martha said, and suddenly found herself yawning, and was embarrassed at her display of ill-manners. But she was feeling dreadfully tired.

'Ah, yes – the little singer—' Miss Nightingale said, looking coolly at Phoebe and she blushed and dropped her gaze, and Martha looked at her, puzzled.

'I am surprised you know that, Miss Nightingale,' she said after a moment, 'I had not thought you a lady likely to attend a Supper Rooms—'

Now it was Miss Nightingale's turn to look puzzled. 'I know of no Supper Rooms,' she said. 'But I have heard of your niece's singing here. The soldiers tell me they like it very well.'

Martha turned her head on her pillow to look inquiringly at Phoebe who blushed an even more rosy colour, and said breathlessly, 'Well, it seemed so – there was one who recognized me, you know, and asked me to sing, and many of his friends were there – and, well – I thought it would be agreeable for them – so –it was one evening at the jetty. They carried me back on their shoulders – it was very – it was very nice of them, but of course I will not do it again. I know it to have been most improper—'

'It would be if you were to sing the songs of the gin palaces, Miss Lackland,' Miss Nightingale said. 'Of those I could not approve. But men at war need food for their minds and emotions as well as care for their injuries and meat for their plates. I have a plan, Miss Lackland, to open up a recreation room for the men – not the officers, you understand, but the common men – where there will be no alcoholic drink of course. We shall call it the Inkerman Coffee House, and I think if you wish to offer a little genteel music there on occasional evenings it will be no bad thing. I will tell my assistant Mrs. Drake about it, and while I am away at Balaclava she will set matters in hand. Let her know which songs you will sing, for I am determined they shall be only the most proper, you understand – and I am sure the soldiers will enjoy it.'

'My niece's songs are always of the most proper, Miss Nightingale,' Martha said, and now her voice was much stronger for she was most nettled by the note of condescension she had detected in Miss Nightingale's words.

At once Miss Nightingale smiled and said, 'There – a new apology is demanded! I give it freely. I am sure so well bred a young lady would offer only the most ladylike of entertainment,' and she bowed slightly towards Phoebe, who, ludicrous in her shawl and tumbled curls and bare feet, bowed back, her face serious and set in lines of great propriety.

'You asked me to deliver a message in Balaclava, Miss Lackland,' Miss Nightingale was poised to go. 'I leave tomorrow, so you had best tell me now – I cannot wait, I'm afraid for written missives.'

'Oh, Miss Nightingale—' Phoebe started forwards and held out both hands to the tall thin woman so that her shawl fell to the ground, revealing her pretty shoulders and heaving breasts under a very thin nightgown. 'Please to tell my cousin Freddy – Dr. Caspar, you know – please to tell him I am here! Just say his Phoebe is here in Scutari – I am sure he will be so – so happy to know!'

Miss Nightingale, with her brows slightly raised, looked away from Phoebe a little pointedly, and said to Martha, 'The message, Miss Lackland?'

Martha closed her eyes wearily, as the exhaustion of her illness rose in her. 'That is the message, Miss Nightingale. Just as Phoebe said it. It was what I too would wish to tell him.'

CHAPTER TWENTY-EIGHT

FREDDY came toiling up the hill from the jetty, his feet sliding a little against the dust of the footpath, and his head bent. Above him the deep velvet blue of the September night was thick and beautiful but he paid no attention to it. He was so tired he could hardly move, and yet was on edge, feeling as though he would never rest again.

The crossing from Balaclava had been tolerable enough, the Black Sea being in its most dulcet mood, but the men on the troopship had been restless and fretful, as well they might. The long months of sitting there before Sevastopol while senior officers argued and shilly-shallied and politicians deliberated and wrangled had taken their toll of the morale of all of them, and though everyone knew it must be but a matter of weeks or even days before the citadel should fall – indeed it might already have done so, while they made their laborious crossing – it made no difference to their mood. The soldiers had been there for a year, many of them, had seen their comrades, their officers and their commanders as well as their enemies dying like flies with the cholera, the Crimean fever and a host of other horrors, and were beyond feeling the sort of courage and determination they had shown in the high hopeful months of the autumn of 1854. This was 1855, and it was a whole new world, not just a new year.

He tried to think as he climbed, shifting his loaded bag from one shoulder to another; how long was it he had spent there in that dismal peninsula? It was but two months according to the calendar, but could it in truth be so short a time? It seemed to him that he had been there for years, moving among the tents and the roughly built huts that had been hastily prepared for the care of sick men within sight of Todleben's defences of the fortress city, offering what help he could. It had been little enough in all conscience, for what sufferers from Crimean fever needed was expert nursing in good warm beds, with the right sort of nourishment; all they got from Freddy and the few army surgeons there were who were fit to work was a little laudanum – and not much of that as supplies dwindled– and whatever else could be mixed up from the contents of their medical boxes. They lay there on the ground with only a sheet of canvas between the earth and their wasted bodies – if they were lucky – and a scrap of blanket to cover themselves against the cold that could come down so cruelly at night, even in the summer months, lying in their own ordure and unable to do anything to help themselves.

At first Freddy had been sustained by his anger. To see his countrymen in such straits while their officers seemed to care not at all about their welfare seemed to him a sin of most horrendous proportions and he had protested to officers, to fellow surgeons, to all who would listen. But after a while he too had seen the hopelessness of it all. What could anyone do, after all? The supplies were not there, what nursing was available at the Crimean hospitals was inadequate, despite Miss Nightingale's attempts to organize it as well as it was organized at Scutari, and that was all about it. All anyone could do was plod on and do his best.

So Freddy had plodded. Sometimes before he fell into an exhausted sleep late at night he would think about places beyond the hellhole in which he found himself; he would think of his mother and his stepfather sitting at home in tranquil peace in the comfort of Stanhope Terrace and try to remember what it felt like to come home to so agreeable a place and take a bath and eat a good dinner and climb into a soft bed. Sometimes he would think of his grandfather stumping about the wards of Queen Eleanor's from bed to bed, his students trailing along behind him, and marvel at how he had been used to think that those wards were squalid and disagreeable. Yet compared to his present situation they had been Arcady itself.

But most of all he would think of Phoebe. He would imagine her there at home in Stanhope Terrace, sitting at the breakfast table with both hands cupped round a cup of morning chocolate and smiling at him above the rim; would imagine her flitting about the drawing room performing one of the tableaux she had been so fond of, and then would remember that those days had long since gone; would remind himself now that although she had lived in her aunt's house during all their growing years, now she lived with her brother in King Street, and performed upon the stage of the Supper Rooms each night. So he would imagine her there instead, and lie and watch her in his mind's eye as she sang and danced on the tiny light-encircled stage, sending her saucy glances over her shoulder to make the audience shout and stamp its feet, and laughing that delicious laugh of hers—

He stopped now, and stared up the hill at the bulk of the barrack hospital ahead of him, and tried to think. He had come to a momentous decision on those long uncomfortable nights on the heights above Sevastopol. He had lain and stared at the flapping canvas tent roof over his head and thought very carefully about all that had happened between Phoebe and himself in the past, and knew now what he must do. The question was, would his resolve last long enough? If he could have his way, he would walk in now to Aunt Martha and Alex Laurence and tell them bluntly that he had done enough; that he had spent ten full months out here in this wilderness and that was enough for anyone; that he was going home to England on the first available ship, and would brook no argument; that he had his own plans for his life and that the time had come to prosecute them—

But he would not be able to do that, and he knew it, and once more he shifted his loaded bag to his other aching shoulder and went heavily on. If those wretched camp followers and wives and their children were still in that cellar, that would mean that Martha and probably Alex were there too. And if they were there he would not be able just to follow his own desires. He had come out here in the first place to help Aunt Martha and it had been bad enough he had left her for those two months in the front line of the war. Now he must take up the burden of the cellar and its occupants again, and home and Phoebe and the plans he had made for them both must wait.

His eyes seemed to prickle with tears as he thought it, and he shook his head angrily at himself, and walked on, breasting the rise and coming at last to the flat that led into the huge central square of the barracks.

He stopped again, to catch his breath, and stared across the great square towards the cellar door, and could just see the light coming out and spilling itself on the dust outside, but the shape of the beam was cut in half and, puzzled, he moved closer. And saw that there was a new building in the square, a building that had not been there when he went away, and which was lying between him and the doorway beyond which Martha was waiting.

He shrugged then and once more moved forwards. Whatever the building was, it was none of his affair. He must go and see his aunt, and see if just possibly – and his heart lifted with hope as he thought it – just possibly she would be willing to lay down her self-inflicted burden of care for the women and children, and would agree to come home again with him.

As he passed the low wooden building, obviously built very hastily and of the most ramshackle materials, a door opened and light spilled on the dusty ground as a couple of soldiers came out, their arms about each other's shoulders, and Freddy changed the route of his walk to avoid them. He knew enough about drunken soldiers not to want to tangle with them; but then he realized that the men were not drunk at all, but were both limping, and were holding on to each other for support, as wounded soldiers do, and as they came abreast of him a little surge of sound came out of the door they had left open behind them and looking up and beyond them, Freddy shook his head, thoroughly bewildered.

He had heard music, and though the sound of a mouth organ and a jew's harp accompanying rough male voices was a commonplace of the barracks, this had sounded quite different; so absurdly, incredibly different that he could not believe his own ears.

'What is in there?' he asked roughly, and the men looked up at him as they passed him, and one of them said equably enough, 'No need to shout, squire! It ain't no mystery, you know!'

'I'm sorry. I have been away — at Sevastopol. I have just come over on the Zephyr, and — well, this place was not here when I went, in July. I was surprised.'

''Ere, you just back, you say? What's the news, squire? We've 'eard a rumour as the Russians 'ave just scuttled out o' the place and gone 'ome. Is it true?' The men moved closer, staring eagerly into his face in the darkness, but still Freddy stared over their shoulders at the half open door of the low wooden building, straining his ears.

'What is that place?' he said again, and one of the men said impatiently, 'Inkerman Coffee House, mate. Tell us about Sevastopol, will yer? Once that falls we can go 'ome — and they're sayin' that—'

'Eh?' He focused his eyes on the men then, and shook his head. 'I'm sorry. I do not know. The feeling was when I left on the Zephyr that it would only be a matter of time — they were planning a major bombardment, and indeed when we had been at sea a couple of days, no more, some of the men swore they heard the sound of it. But I cannot be sure. As for its falling — indeed, I do not know. If it is true, I will be thankful as any. Tell me — this Inkerman Coffee House, as you say it is — what sort of place is it?'

'Miss Nightingale sorted it out,' one of the men said, and snorted and spat. 'About a month or two back, it was. Started in a room in the barracks and then they set up one o' those private funds and built this 'eap of old timber.'

'Comforts fer poor soldiers, squire, that's what it is,' the other man said. 'No beer or gin, mind yer, but coffee and cake sometimes if we're lucky, and books and pictures an' all like that—'

'Yerss – 'n one from the Queen 'erself, all showin' the Duke o' Wellington an' the little Prince an' all. Very comfortin' that is!' He laughed sardonically and his companion grinned in the darkness.

'Well, Queens – what do they know about soldiers' comforts? Now, the warbler – that's somethin' different, that is!'

'The warbler?' Freddy said.

The men had begun to move away now, as one of them said to the other, 'There may be more news from the other men comin' off the ship – we'll go down to the jetty and find out—' and he had to call again after them, 'What warbler?'

One of the men looked back at him over his shoulder as he hobbled swiftly away. 'You'd better go an' see fer yerself, squire!' he shouted back and they disappeared into the darkness, leaving Freddy still standing there and trying to believe he had heard what he thought he had heard.

He turned back again to stare at the door of the building, but someone had closed it and now there were only the usual night sounds about him, and he picked up his bag again and turned to go towards the cellar door and Aunt Martha. His ears must have been playing him tricks, and to go and actually see what was on the other side of the door to the Inkerman Coffee House would be to indulge his own fancies. And that he would not do.

But as he reached the edge of the building and was about to walk round the corner and strike across the dusty courtyard to the far side again the door opened, and he heard the rush of sound once more and this time he knew it was not an illusion. Someone was in there singing – someone with a high pure voice. A woman.

Of course, he told himself, standing there straining to see in the darkness, listening to the lilt of the voice, that was not so strange after all. Were there not two hundred or more women in his Aunt Martha's cellar? It could be one of them who was entertaining the men as part of Miss Nightingale's newest experiment in soldiers' welfare. But this voice was not the voice of a gutter woman. No camp follower could produce those pellucid notes.

Or sing that particular song.

It was that which had first seized him with such amazement. It was a song he had heard so often before, had sat at a table with a glass of champagne in his hand and heard more times than he could recall ever counting. A song about a girl in a garden.

He moved back towards the door, hesitantly. He was tired, quite dreadfully tired, and though he was so sure now that he had heard what he had heard, tired men suffered strange experiences. Perhaps he was imagining the whole thing; and if he walked in that door and discovered that he had been making up that sound out of whole cloth, that it was all hallucination, he would be a frightened man indeed. For men who heard things that were not there to be heard just because they so very much wanted to hear them could hardly be regarded as reliable in any way. How could such a man hope to be a successful surgeon, or hope to persuade the woman of his choice that he had been wrongheaded this past three years, and that there was a hope of happiness ahead for them both? It could not be.

When he put his hand on the door of the Inkerman Coffee House on that September night, Freddy did the bravest thing he had ever done. He was sick with fear, not only about what he might or might not see on the other side of it, but fear for his own sanity.

He stood there on the other side of the door, his bag still on his shoulder, staring across the great room, with its rough wooden walls plentifully decorated with pictures – and he recognized at once the one of the Duke of Wellington and the infant Prince of which the soldiers had spoken – and with tables and chairs and benches dotted about it. It was full of people, men in various stages of dilapidation ranging from the most tattered uniforms to the neatest and most spanking of red coats and shakos and they were all looking in the same direction, all away from the door towards the far end of the room.

There, perched on a table, were three men, one with a mouth organ and two with jews harps, industriously twanging away at their little instruments, their legs, swinging merrily as they played, and their eyes bright above their hands clasped so near their faces.

And beside them stood Phoebe, her hands set side by side on the shaft of a lacy parasol which was open above her head, and which she was twirling merrily as she sang. He stood there and stared, and closed his eyes and shook his head and stared again, but she was still there, and still those liquid notes came tripping so easily from her.

Yet still he felt he could not believe it. He was seeing her and hearing her, but how could it be? There was no way in which she could actually be here, in the middle of all the filth and horror which was Scutari, no way in which he could actually be standing here listening to the rapturous applause the men were now giving her as her song came to an end, no way in which he could be awake and in possession of his senses. He must be quite mad, he told himself, quite quite mad.

And then she saw him, and it was at that moment that he knew he was as sane as he had ever been, for her eyes dilated, and she dropped her parasol and jumped down from the little platform upon which she had been standing and went pushing her way through the crowd of men, who reached out to touch her and pat her as she went by.

He watched her come towards him, and suddenly it was more than he could bear and he turned and pushed his way out of the door to stand outside in the heavy darkness staring up at the few stars that were now clearly to be seen, and breathing deeply.

He may have discovered that he wasn't mad, he may have the reassurance of knowing that he was not suffering from hallucinations, but he still felt very strange. So strange that he feared for one dreadful moment that he was going to swoon, and he stood there and breathed deeply and waited for the world, which had been turned so topsy-turvy, to right itself.

She came at last, and slid her hand into the crook of his elbow and looked at him in the dimness and said gently, 'Dear Freddy! I thought you would never come. But I knew you would eventually.'

CHAPTER TWENTY-NINE

THEY sat on the cold grass, beside the path that led down to the jetty, their backs to the low stone wall that edged the rough ground that stretched beyond it, wordless and utterly content.

She had led him towards the cellar at first, but he had shaken his head, almost violently.

'There is much to talk about before we go to Aunt Martha,' he had said, 'She will wish to talk to me, of course, and I do not think I could bear to wait while she did so. I must know why *you* are here. I must know when you came, and how you are, and there is much I must tell you for I have been thinking – oh, I have been thinking so much, Phoebe!'

'I too,' she had said in a low voice, and led him away to the little hollow of grass beside the path, telling him it was one of her secret places. 'For although it is so near the road, one cannot be seen from it, you know, for the ground takes such a dip there, and when the sun is agreeable it can be most pleasant to sit there and rest. We shall be private and peaceful here, my love.'

At first they had talked only of practical matters. She told him of how the news of his illness had come to London, and how she had determined at once to come and see him.

'I knew that many people were coming here, all sorts of people, and I had been fortunate to make acquaintance with Mr. Rothschild, and I thought, why not? I had to come to you, Freddy – I had to come. Are you angry with me for being here?' and she had peeped up at him in quite her old roguish manner, and he had managed a tired smile and said, 'Do not mock me, Phoebe! It has been a long time since you have paid any attention to what I have to say about your actions.'

She had bitten her lip at that, and sat silent and then after a moment said, 'I know. I have been – very difficult. Captious. I am sorry, Freddy. I have been thinking—'

He shook his head. 'No – please. There is much of my thinking too which I must discuss with you but I need time to understand it all. Tell me more. How have matters been here with you?'

So she told him. Of Martha's illness, and the long alarming weeks while she had lain there so sick and frail, and how Alex had laboured so hard to take care of her.

'And I tell you this much, Freddy,' she had added with a glint of mischief in her voice again, 'I believe we shall both have a new uncle soon! He was most devoted to her – quite absurdly so! Poor Aunt Martha, looking so dreadful as she did because she was ill, and being so very old anyway – yet he still clearly cares very much for her. I found it very strange—'

Freddy had smiled in the darkness at that; the unconscious cruelty of the young and beautiful, he thought, to hear her speak so of her aunt. It should have repelled him but he could not find it in him to feel so, for there was no malice in her; just an unawareness which was in its own way very appealing.

'Anyway, be that as it may,' she had gone on. 'Aunt Martha is now much better. Thin you know – shocking thin – but working hard about the cellar and those horrid women these many weeks. They *are* horrid, you know, Freddy. I do not know if they feel any gratitude for all Aunt Martha does for them, but I believe they do not for they show no atom of feeling. They abuse her if all is not precisely as they like, and never say thank you for anything. But when I said as much to Aunt Martha she reproved me and said I was a foolish child who could not see beyond the end of my nose, and that they were indeed grateful, in their own way. Not that it mattered to her, she said, for the work itself was reward enough for her. She has no need for fulsome praise! I felt very stupid when she spoke so—'

She was silent for a moment and then went on painfully,

'But I think she was perhaps right, Freddy. I *have* been very stupid in the past, have I not? I have thought only of myself and my own feelings and been quite heedless of others—'

There was another silence and then she said, almost blurting it out, 'Freddy, when I heard you were ill, I was afraid you were going to die. Quite dreadfully afraid, and because I was afraid I discovered so many things. That I had treated you shocking bad three years ago, when – when I – when it all happened and I had to ask you to help me and—'

'Hush,' he said, and put his hand out to her in the darkness. 'Hush. It is not necessary to speak of it again. It is a secret that only you and I know – there is no need to speak more of it. Even between us.'

'Yes, there is.' Her voice came suddenly stronger and she turned her head to look at him. 'That has been your mistake, Freddy, and mine too, perhaps. You have treated me always as the child I was when first you knew me. And I – I let you. It was agreeable then, and for many years afterwards, to be your protected baby. I must confess I enjoyed it hugely. But it has damaged matters for us.'

'Damaged?' he said and frowned, trying to understand. 'How can it damage matters if I try to protect you? I do not regard you as a baby – I could not do that, for you arouse feelings in me that only a woman could arouse – but protection – how can *that* be damaging? Is it not what any man must do who cares for a woman?'

'Not always,' she said, and suddenly there was a wisdom in her voice that seemed so incongruous that he almost smiled in the darkness. 'Sometimes protecting a person from their own foolishness can prevent them from ever overcoming it. What is more, sometimes in protecting another, you are in truth trying to protect yourself—'

She turned then and took his face between her hands, feeling the roughness of his unshaven cheeks beneath her fingers, and liking it. 'Dear Freddy, in not being willing to talk of all that happened that summer four years ago, you have made it impossible for either of us ever to – to *understand* it all. Can you see that?'

He closed his eyes, revelling in her touch and yet unable to respond to it by taking her in his arms, which was what he wanted to do more than anything else, and tried to think of what she had said.

Had he been protecting himself from pain in refusing ever to think about what had happened? Had not his thinking in the last lonely ugly weeks in the Crimea not been painful enough? Had he not come to the right decision, for the right reasons?

He opened his eyes suddenly and because they had been closed he could now see much more easily in the dim starlight and could see her face so close to his own that he had to pull back a little so that he could bring her into clearer focus.

'I had come to a great decision,' he said slowly. 'I thought it a very great decision because it was in spite of what happened. I mean – I—'

'Let me tell *you*, Freddy,' she said, and again despite the young ring of her voice and the girlishness of her figure outlined against the star-dusted sky, she seemed to be the very epitome of knowledge, of wisdom and compassion. 'Let me tell you, Freddy. Ever since that summer, when I was with child by a man you did not know – no, do not wince so! It must be said. When I was with child, by a man you did not know, and you were so good to me and did what I asked of you even though it went so sorely against your conscience – for you are no abortionist by choice – you have struggled with your feelings. You have loved me very dearly. I have always known it, and known it well. At first I was childish enough to regard your love lightly. I do not shame to admit it – because now I have grown up. Oh, so much, Freddy! I have grown up and I know what a love like yours is worth. It is worth everything, for I love you as dearly and know the value of such feeling. And I also know what you have been suffering. Every time you thought of us together, you saw that man between us, did you not? You could not ever forget that I had shared myself with another. That I had borne within me the seed of another man's knowledge of me, and worse still, if that were possible, had torn it from me with your aid. Whenever you tried to imagine us as wife and husband and as parents, which is what wives and husbands eventually must be, your body revolted against all that you knew of me. And that was the cause of your suffering.'

He tried to find words with which to reach out to her, words which would tell her how right she was, words which would make up for the long years that had passed in silence between them, during which he had refused to speak of or even think of all that had happened, but there were no words, and she smiled at him in the dim light, and leaned forwards and very gently kissed his lips. And he leaned his head back against the rough stone wall and closed his eyes.

There was a long silence between them and then she said softly, 'It is not over, not yet, Freddy,' and he opened his eyes unwillingly and looked at her.

'Yes, it is,' he said with a huge weariness. 'It is all over. All the worrying and the wanting and the – all of it. Now we will be wed. I made the right decision there at Sevastopol, and it is now but a matter of time. The war will be over soon and we shall all return home and we shall be wed.'

She shook her head and he stared at her, amazed, and then sat upright.

'I did not misunderstand you! I could not have done! You love me, you do love me – you said you did! Did you not? Or are you being captious again, and playing with me? You cannot do such a thing—'

'Of course I cannot—' she said vigorously and shook her head angrily at him. 'I am no longer that sort of silly creature, and you are the fool if you cannot tell it!'

'Then why—'

'Because only *I* have spoken of it! Only I have said in words that what happened four years ago was a bad thing, a sad thing, and that it makes you feel unhappy. But *you* have not said it! You are still as silent on the matter as you have ever been!'

He bit his lip and again leaned back against the wall and stared up at the stars above his head, counting them with his eyes, trying to concentrate and yet unable to do so. 'One – two – three – four – five – six and seven—' His eyes counted and his thoughts would not sort themselves into any semblance of

303

order, and still she sat beside him and looked at him and waited.

He started at last, painfully, and then with his words gathering momentum.

'It is true, I suppose. I could not bear it – I still cannot. Whenever I remember that time – and the memory comes back unbidden so often – all I can see is you with your face upside down, for that was how you lay on the couch that day. You lay with Nancy at the foot of the bed, and I behind you at the head, with my chloroform bottle in my hand and I was so frightened, so sick with fright, I could only stand there. There you were looking up at me, and your face was upside down, and indeed so was everything else – and then there was blood and—'

He closed his eyes yet again, for his lids were very heavy, but the vision rose so vividly behind him that he had to snap them open again.

'It was such an *exposure* of you. I loved you so dearly, and there you were, so open and displayed and—' he swallowed. 'It hurt.'

She sat silent for a long moment and then said quietly, 'It was your pride that was hurt, Freddy. I suffered but an – an intrusion, but it did not change me for the worse. Indeed it changed me for the better, I sometimes think. I learned much from that dreadful time, Freddy, but above all I learned that a person is a person for what he or she is, not for what they have done. I mean – I cannot feel myself to be a bad person because of what happened. It was all due to my foolishness and – well, perhaps he was a bit to blame as well – he really is not important any more! – but you must understand, Freddy. It is all *over*. I am still the person I always was. If you could love me before and not care about my scrapes then you can love me now, and not care about this much greater scrape. For there was no real wickedness in it, you see. I knew no better – that was why it happened. If it happened now, then indeed I might be said to be a bad person. But then – no. If you cannot see this, Freddy, then it is hopeless for us. I love you dearly, and wish to wed you, and have your babies, and be happy with you.

But if you wed me out of pity, or out of denial of what happened, or to be kind to me – no. That I could not, would not
do. Better I should spend all my life alone, just me and Oliver
and our Supper Rooms with no-one to love but my audience,
than that we should enter marriage in such a frame of mind.'

Again a silence fell on them, and for a little while he almost
slept, so weary was he, so confused and so anxious, lying there
with his eyes fixed on the wheeling stars above his head and
saying nothing.

But at length he stirred and said softly, 'I felt robbed. I had
loved you for so many years, since you were just a tiny creature
in frills, and I believed you to be my own. It was as though
some stranger had come along and stolen my property from
me. But you are not my possession, are you, Phoebe? You told
me that once before – long ago, although then I did not understand. Now, I think I do. Now, I think you are your own
possession and that is good. I did not know you could be so
wise. I did not know. But now I do, and I tell you, my love, I
think we will be a better pair for all this between us. I think it
will be better that we are two people sharing our lives, than just
me owning you, which is what it would have been, had we wed
then, when I first thought of it.'

He turned to her then in the darkness and held out his arms
and she slid into them, and rested her head against him, and
they lay there side by side, for a very long time. They were
neither happy nor unhappy, neither elated nor downcast. They
were just there, existing.

How long it was they remained so they did not know, but at
length Phoebe stirred and sat up and put her hands to his face
again and said gently, 'It is getting rather cold, Freddy. I think
you need to rest properly. Let us go down to the cellar now,
and settle you to sleep. And Aunt Martha will want to know
you are back, and that all is well with you—'

She got to her feet and holding out both hands helped him to
his, and he moved stiffly and awkwardly, scrambling up until
he stood straight and tall beside her, and she looked up at him
and said softly, 'Good evening, Mr. Caspar,' and he caught the
inflexion in her voice and said with mock solemnity, 'Good

evening, Miss Lackland!' and then, suddenly, bent his stiff knees and went down on one of them to hold her hands in both of his and looked up at her with an expression of mock appeal on his face.

'I did this once before, Phoebe. I went on one knee to you, to give you the sort of proposal I thought a young lady ought to have, and then you refused me. Well, I will try again. What care I that nigh on five years have passed? What is five years to one of my constancy? Pooh to five years! Miss Phoebe, Miss Lackland, queen of my heart, mistress of my soul, delight of my – whatever you like – dear Miss Lackland, wilt thou take me—'

'That is the wedding service, stupid!' She giggled and he made a face.

'So it is – I anticipate. So! We try again! Miss Lackland, will you do me the honour to be my wife?'

'Oh, la, sir – such a surprise!' she said and turned her head and pretended to fan herself in shock, peeping at him over the invisible rim of it and fluttering her eyelashes. 'You will make me swoon, sir, indeed you will—'

And then she dropped her bantering tone, and tensed her muscles and pulled him to his feet. 'Fool,' she whispered, turning her face up to his. 'Fool. As if that is not what I have wanted this past many months! What delayed you so long in the asking?'

And she opened her soft lips and linked her hands behind his head to pull him down until his lips touched hers, and then they were clinging to each other with a sort of desperate eagerness that made his head reel and his aching bones seem to rejuvenate themselves.

When at last they drew apart, for want of breath and nothing else, he grinned down at her and suddenly laughed, lifting his chin and letting the sound of his mirth pour out of him.

'It is absurd, too absurd,' he spluttered at last. 'Here we are, in the middle of the foulest of battlefields – well at least on the *fringe* of the foulest of battlefields – playing the most drawing-room of games! Oh, if only all the family were here! I long to tell them, to tell everybody. Oliver and Uncle Gideon and Mamma, *everybody*, how wonderful it all is! For it will be right, now. I know it, and it is all wonderful!'

'We shall tell Aunt Martha!' Phoebe cried, catching his exuberance and bubbling over with it as swift as a kettle on a roaring fire. 'She is all the family we have to hand, so we shall tell her! Come – we shall wake her up if she is asleep and tell her! We are to be wed, we are to be wed, we are to be wed—!'

And she went running away from him, as light on her feet and untired as though she had just risen from her bed, and he went lumbering cheerfully, wearily after her, to look for Aunt Martha and tell her their splendid news.

CHAPTER THIRTY

To do them both credit they did try not to disturb the others. They came almost bursting into the cellar, giggling breathlessly, for all the world like a pair of children just let out of school, and some of the women whose pallets lay near the door stirred and muttered in their sleep and one of the children, startled into wakefulness, let out a wail of distress and Phoebe, remorseful, hissed a remonstrance at Freddy and sank to her knees beside the crying child to soothe him back to sleep.

Freddy stood there and looked down at her, at the bent head outlined in the smoky light of a candle which was burning on the far side of the cellar, and marvelled at it all. So much seemed to have happened in the short time since he had left the ship down there on the jetty, and the most amazing part of all was to be standing there and looking down on Phoebe rocking a dirty child to sleep in her arms. He laughed softly at the absurdity of it as Phoebe, the child at last snuffling his noises of sleep again, rose to her feet and slid her hand into his.

'If you make such a noise you will wake them all,' she whispered reprovingly. 'And then Aunt Martha will be far from as enchanted by our news as she is entitled to be! Come, we shall creep across to find her. But be silent, wretched boy!'

They picked their way across the pallets, hand in hand, though it would have been much easier to progress alone, but neither was willing to forego the fleeting contact, seeking Aunt Martha.

They found her on the far side of the cellar, sitting on a heap of old pallets, with another beside her upon which lay a humped figure, and Phoebe, looking quickly down, saw the grizzled head and jut of beard and realized it was Alex.

'Aunt Martha,' she hissed, '—please to come – we must talk to you – we must tell you our news! See who is here, Aunt Martha! It is Freddy! Is it not capital? He has just come back on the Zephyr, you know, and heard me singing as he passed the Coffee House and came in and saw me – it was all most romantic, was it not, Freddy?' and she turned her head to smile brilliantly at Freddy over her shoulder.

He stepped forwards then and crouched down beside Martha, and said softly, 'Aunt Martha – it is so good to see you!'

She lifted her head, for she had been sitting with her chin tucked into her neck staring down at her clasped hands on her lap and she looked at him and her eyes were blank and uncomprehending, and then after a moment she said uncertainly, 'Freddy! Is that Freddy?'

'Indeed it is, aunt,' Freddy whispered. 'Oh, I am sorry, my dear – we have alarmed you! Bursting in here like this when all are asleep—' He looked sideways at the curve of Alex's back under the blankets and at the line of his curly head – for his face was turned away and he could not see more – and dropped his whisper even lower, if that were possible. 'Perhaps we should just have slipped in and gone to sleep and told you in the morning, but we are so happy! And we wanted you to know! We are sorry, my dear.'

'Freddy,' she said again, and her voice seemed hardly more than a faint breath, and she tried to smile at him, but somehow her face seemed stiff and he peered at her more closely and said a little anxiously, 'Are you all right, Aunt Martha? You look very – or is it just that we have disturbed you when you were dozing? You should be in your bed my dear, you really should!'

'I – are you well, my dear boy?' she said, and still her voice was faint and somehow remote and now he could see how very changed she had been made by her illness. Her face had become much thinner; the slightly square look which had made her so like her sister, his Mamma, had been whittled away so that her flesh was stretched tautly across her bones and there were shadows in her cheeks and temples that had not been there before. Her eyes, which had always been agreeable enough, now looked huge in her wasted face, and had a very real beauty of their own – or would have, his thoughts amended, when there was more life in them, for at the moment there was an opacity, a curious deadness in their grey depths that gave her almost the air of a Roman sculpture. She must be very tired, he thought, remorse pricking him. I am nigh fit to drop myself, and I am young and much more vigorous and have not been near so ill—

'Come, my dear,' he said gently, and held out his hand. 'Let us see you to your corner and let you sleep. Our news can wait—'

'Oh, it cannot, it cannot!' Phoebe said impulsively, and so urgently that she forgot to whisper and her voice seemed very loud in Freddy's ears, and automatically he glanced down at Alex's shrouded figure beside him. But there was no movement, and so he held out his hand to Phoebe and whispered, 'Hush, my love! Aunt Martha is exhausted – we must save talk until the morning, I think—'

Martha seemed to make an enormous effort and lifted her hand to rub her face, and said softly, 'News? You have news?'

'Indeed, yes, Aunt Martha!' Phoebe said, whispering again, but with an unmistakably joyous note in it and dropped to her knees at her aunt's side. 'And I cannot bear to hold it in another second! My dear, dear aunt, we are to be wed. Freddy and I! After so many foolish years of estrangement, we now know that we love each other very dearly, and as soon as the war is over and we return to England, we shall have a splendid wedding and everyone will dance and sing and be as happy as we are! Tell me you wish us happy, dear aunt! You are the only person we know we can tell, and we are fit to burst with it!'

Martha lifted her head and looked up at Freddy then, and still her eyes had that dull look, but now a certain glint appeared in their depths that puzzled Freddy and he could not understand quite why. She looked the same, and yet there was about her a sudden air of desperation that bewildered him and he said again, anxiously, 'Aunt Martha – are you all right?'

'All right?' She looked sideways then, at the humped shape on the pallet beside her and then looked up at Freddy and at Phoebe and seemed to make a huge effort. 'Of course I am all right. A little – fatigued perhaps, for it is so very late. But well enough. As well as I shall ever be – I wish you both happy, indeed I do, with all my heart. It is splendid news, and the family will be as delighted as I am, I am sure. May your future be as – be all you wish it to be—'

And again with that air of huge effort she held out a hand to each of them, and they bent and kissed her cheeks and Phoebe, still bubbling with the excitement of it all, said eagerly, 'Shall you tell Alex, aunt? Or would it be a very selfish thing to waken him and tell him now?' She dimpled a little then, and said impishly, 'It will be a good thing for him to know that weddings are the fashion in our family at present!'

'No!' Martha almost snapped it, and Phoebe drew back, a little chilled, and then Martha shook her head more gently and said softly, 'I am sorry. I did not mean to sound so – no. Not now. Tomorrow is soon enough to think of telling – anyone. Tomorrow—' She cast one brief look down at Alex's figure and then, almost painfully got to her feet.

'My dears, you must be in need of sleep. I shall not go to bed tonight – no, do not gainsay me – I have – letters to write. Very urgent letters. Please do not argue with me. Tomorrow I – tomorrow we can talk of many things. But not now. Freddy, you shall take my bed there in the dispensary behind the curtain. It will not discommode you, I think, that Sal is there – she snores a little, I am afraid, but you will sleep for all that, no doubt—'

There was a faint bustle for a while as Freddy, after one more remonstrance, gave in to Martha's insistence – for he was very tired and she was very firm – and almost fell on to his couch, and Phoebe, after removing her gown and loosening her stays settled on to her pallet on the other side of the dispensary curtain, to lie there staring up at the shape of the dark sky in the window piercing the even darker cellar wall, until she fell asleep to dream of wedding dresses and Oliver and her dead Papa, in a confusion of excitement; and then Martha, still moving heavily, went back to the little circle of candle-light in which lay Alex on his pallet, bearing her writing case in her hands.

She sat there for a long time beside the still figure, and then, moving slowly, opened the case and drew out a pen and her little bottle of ink and a sheet of paper. And bent her head and began to write, slowly and with many hesitations. But steadily, at last, and her firm sloping script covered the pages as she sat there with her head bent and the candlelight sending dancing shadows over the pages.

'My dear Felix,' she wrote. 'I have to write to you news of such pain, my dear boy, that I shrink from doing so. I had thought, to tell you the truth, of waiting until such time as I could return to England and tell you what must be said face to face. But that is too uncertain for although we have hopes the war will soon end, we cannot know when. And you would fret and wonder at the inevitable silence.

'Dearest boy, I have a tragedy to impart to you. Your dear father is dead. He, the kindest, most caring and most loving of men is no longer with us, and my tears are as bitter as I know will be yours. I must tell you, Felix, that he and I had come to care deeply for each other in these long strange months in this dreadful place, and had made plans for a shared future that would of course have included you. We were to be wed, and I was to try to offer you what you have long since lost, the care of a mother who holds your welfare deep in her heart. We did not write to you of this our plan, for we both felt that it would distress you to have the news in such a fashion. You might not have wanted such as I to intervene in your life, and your dear father was most anxious that whatever we might plan it should all meet with your approval. You must know, and I am happy to tell you this, that dearly as we loved each other – and I know as only a woman can that I was much beloved – your welfare came always first with him. Had you taken me in dislike he would have sacrificed his own happiness and mine also, for you. I tell you this that you may know that when he died he did so thinking of you as well as me. It is a bond that ties us both together in a way that can never be severed. I trust and pray, dear Felix, that you welcome that bond as I do. I wish now only to care for you as your Papa would have done had he lived. I know you are near full grown and will perhaps choose not to accept the care of a woman who is, after all, virtually a stranger to you. But I hope you can feel the love I bear you for your father's sake, and the willingness that is in me to devote such years as remain to me in this vale of tears to your life, your welfare and your happiness. Despite your dear Papa's loss, dear Felix, you are not alone. Indeed you will never be alone in this world while I draw breath.

'You will want to know of the manner of your father's passing. I must tell you that for many months he has been working so hard that I have remonstrated with him on many occasions, fearing for his welfare, but he laughed – you know how he laughed, Felix! – and bade me be silent and get on with my own tasks, and he was right, of course. There is here much disease and misery, and we both felt it our bounden duty, and in a curious way, our joy, to do what we could to ease it.

'Be that as it may – he has for the past two or three days complained of feeling some languor. He suffered attacks of pain in his chest and left shoulder which made him gasp and we tried very hard to treat his ailment, because he knew what it was. He told me that he suffered from angina pectoris; although he had never before in all his life had such symptoms he recognized them well enough from the sufferings of patients he had treated. He also sought the guidance of one of the army surgeons here. Unfortunately they are a sorry lot, or so your Papa said, and he felt had little skill in matters concerning such symptoms.

'So he treated himself, using such drugs as he had to hand in his medical box, and I prayed and hoped and prayed again that we should soon be able to return home and he could have better care. I may tell you, dear Felix, that I begged him to permit me to speak to the army authorities on his behalf, seeking a place for him on a ship going home, but he forbade me, with some force. He said that many men had been ill here and died here who had much greater ills than he, and they had not been able to plead a special need and go home; so he would not. And added with his usual commonsense that if he were to die he would do so either here, or on a hospital ship. And he would prefer to be here with me than at sea with strangers.

'I argued no more and went on hoping and honoured his wish that none should be told of his attacks of pain, and it seemed to me yesterday that they had lessened. On the first day he had suffered four episodes and on the second two, and when on the third day he seemed to be so much better I became so happy.

'But tonight, Felix, as we sat talking – he was lying on his bed, for I was determined to make him rest as much as may be – he was seized by a great paroxysm of pain, and do all I might, I could not relieve it, though I sought to give him laudanum to ease it. He died in my arms, and as I write these words to you, lies beside me on his bed in his final rest.

'I must tell you, dear boy, that just before his last attack he spoke to me of you, in such loving words, about how happy he believed we should all be together when all was settled here and we had returned home.

'I am convinced that he died happy, in the sure knowledge that he was a dearly loved man, as indeed he was. I may tell you that I will love him till the day I too die and seek him in Heaven. He will be with me always in his spirit, and I will remember him always. And while a man is remembered with love he is not dead, nor can be regarded so.

'It has pained me much to have to write this letter to you, but it has comforted me also. I feel as if, in writing to you, I have been talking to him. I pray in time to come that we may talk often about him, for he was a very great man, in his quiet way. You were privileged to know and love him all your life, and I but for a few short months, but those months were precious and will make the rest of my life worth living.

'I shall write again soon, dear boy, with all news I can of his funeral, which perforce must be here, and to know of your wellbeing. Please do not forget, Felix, that you have lost your

Papa, but you have me. For what I am worth, I am yours for as long as you shall want me.

Your friend,
Martha Lackland.'

On April the twenty-seventh, 1856, the Treaty of Paris was finally ratified and the Crimean War was officially over.

The soldiers and their women and children – those who had escaped cholera, Crimean fever, starvation, rats and lice as well as the Russian enemy – came limping home, though Miss Nightingale did not hurry back. She still had work to do and would not return to her native land until July; but on May the eleventh a steamer laden with passengers from Constantinople, travelling via Marseilles, came fussing into Folkestone harbour, dressed overall with gay bunting, to meet crowded docks full of exuberant cheering people.

On the foredeck Phoebe waved furiously, as Freddy held on to her, for so eager was she to be seen by Oliver and Aunt Abby and Gideon and the children down there on the docks that she was in very real danger of falling overboard in ignominy.

A little further along the deck Martha stood, her hair whipped by the wind under the rim of her neat bonnet, her hands tucked into her muff, despite the spring sunshine, and her eyes straining to see who waited there below. She saw Abby and Gideon and smiled; they had changed little in the eighteen months she had been away, however much she might have changed herself, and Sal beside her followed the line of her gaze and snorted softly.

'Hmph!' she said. 'No wonder they was so good at raising the ready for you all these months! A right well 'eeled pair they look an' no error!'

But Martha took no notice, letting her eyes move slowly along the crowded edge of the dock, searching, searching, searching. And then she breathed again, and lifted her chin up to the morning air and smiled. He was there, waiting for her.

Felix.

There was something worth coming home for after all.

THE END

On the following pages are details of Arrow books that will be of interest.

ME

Anonymous

The millions of readers who have eagerly anticipated this new book in the world famous series of raw, candid love stories will not be disappointed. Here is all the honesty of *Her*, the power of *Him* and the natural sensuality of *Them*.

Me – where every expectation of lust and love, of dream and desire, will be met, experienced – and surpassed.

HESTER DARK

Emma Blair

Even to a girl from the slums of Bristol, the streets of Glasgow were inhospitable and grey; the wealth and splendour of its mansions cold and heartless. But for Hester there could be no turning back – she would make this cruel city the home of her dreams.

Everyone said that Hester was lucky. Lucky to have a wealthy uncle in Scotland who was willing to take her in. Lucky to have all the advantages that his money could buy. But Hester's new, bright world held dark secrets, jealousies and fears. And no one had spoken of the woman who would despise her for her beauty and her independence – and the men who would buy her soul and call it love.

BESTSELLING FICTION FROM ARROW

All these books are available from your bookshop or newsagent or you can order them direct. Just tick the titles you want and complete the form below.

☐	THE COMPANY OF SAINTS	Evelyn Anthony	£1.95
☐	HESTER DARK	Emma Blair	£1.95
☐	1985	Anthony Burgess	£1.75
☐	2001: A SPACE ODYSSEY	Arthur C. Clarke	£1.75
☐	NILE	Laurie Devine	£2.75
☐	THE BILLION DOLLAR KILLING	Paul Erdman	£1.75
☐	THE YEAR OF THE FRENCH	Thomas Flanagan	£2.50
☐	LISA LOGAN	Marie Joseph	£1.95
☐	SCORPION	Andrew Kaplan	£2.50
☐	SUCCESS TO THE BRAVE	Alexander Kent	£1.95
☐	STRUMPET CITY	James Plunkett	£2.95
☐	FAMILY CHORUS	Claire Rayner	£2.50
☐	BADGE OF GLORY	Douglas Reeman	£1.95
☐	THE KILLING DOLL	Ruth Rendell	£1.95
☐	SCENT OF FEAR	Margaret Yorke	£1.75

Postage ——————

Total ——————

ARROW BOOKS, BOOKSERVICE BY POST, PO BOX 29, DOUGLAS, ISLE OF MAN, BRITISH ISLES

Please enclose a cheque or postal order made out to Arrow Books Limited for the amount due including 15p per book for postage and packing both for orders within the UK and for overseas orders.

Please print clearly

NAME...

ADDRESS..

....

Whilst every effort is made to keep prices down and to keep popular books in print, Arrow Books cannot guarantee that prices will be the same as those advertised here or that the books will be available.